PRAISE FOR RICHARD S. WHEELER

"All of the details and characters ring true. . . . The pacing of the novel is impeccable. He blends the various white and Indian cultures together into a believable world with never a false beat. *Dark Passage* is well worth reading." —*The Missoulian*

"[A] deftly crafted . . . exciting installment."
—*Publishers Weekly* on *Dark Passage*

"An exciting story of a young man coming of age and growing into a reality greater than his dreams."
—*Roundup* magazine on *Rendezvous*

"[Skye] has enough adventures to satisfy the most discerning Western fan, and they ring surprisingly true."
—*The Lincoln Journal Star* on *Rendezvous*

"Wheeler creates characters who never react or behave like clichés." —*Booklist*

"Wheeler is a genius of structure and form."
—*El Paso Herald-Post*

"Wheeler is among the two or three top living writers of Western historicals—if not the best." —*Kirkus Reviews*

"Wheeler continues to be one of the best of Western novelist/historians." —*Salt Lake City Observer*

By Richard S. Wheeler
from Tom Doherty Associates

SKYE'S WEST

Sun River
Bannack
The Far Tribes
Yellowstone
Bitterroot
Sundance
Wind River
Santa Fe
Rendezvous
Dark Passage
Going Home
Downriver
The Deliverance
The Fire Arrow
The Canyon of Bones

Aftershocks
Badlands
The Buffalo Commons
Cashbox
Eclipse
The Exile
The Fields of Eden
Fool's Coach
Goldfield
Masterson
Montana Hitch
An Obituary for Major Reno
Second Lives
Sierra
Sun Mountain
Where the River Runs

SAM FLINT

Flint's Gift
Flint's Truth
Flint's Honor

DARK PASSAGE

A BARNABY SKYE NOVEL

Richard S. Wheeler

A TOM DOHERTY ASSOCIATES BOOK
NEW YORK

DARK PASSAGE

A Forge Book
Published by Tom Doherty Associates, LLC
175 Fifth Avenue
New York, NY 10010

www.tor-forge.com

Forge® is a registered trademark of Tom Doherty Associates, LLC.

ISBN-13: 978-0-7653-5934-6
ISBN-10: 0-7653-5934-0
Library of Congress Catalog Card Number: 98-23486

First Edition: November 1998
First Mass Market Edition: September 2000
Second Mass Market Edition: August 2007

Printed in the United States of America

0 9 8 7 6 5 4 3 2 1

For Tim and Tammy Gable

Dark Passage

one

It had never occurred to Barnaby Skye that domestic discord could ruin a rendezvous or even threaten his future as a mountaineer. Even less had he imagined that it would transform his life. But his young Crow wife, Victoria, was unhappy and on the brink of leaving him, and that was how the trouble began.

He was summering on the Popo Agie near its confluence with the Wind River that summer of 1830, enjoying the great annual gathering of his trapping friends, the thing they all had ached for during the long bitter year. This was the long-awaited shining time. During all those wintry months he had dreamed of these sweet and carefree days when there was nothing to do but soak up sun, eat good buffler hump, play euchre or monte for wild stakes, tell impossible yarns to greenhorns, buy beads, bells, ribbons, and mirrors for the glowing Indian maids, get the sad news about all the coons who went under or quit the mountains, load up with shining new traps, good center-shooting rifles, thick blankets, calico shirts, keen knives—and a few good jugs of whiskey to lubricate it all.

Paradise, at least at first. Never in Skye's memory had there been such a summer. The playful zephyrs cooled him, while occasional thundershowers kept the grassy river bottoms green. The arid benchlands to the north had browned under the hot sun, and now they shimmered in the rising heat. But beyond, tantalizing like an eager lover, rose the mountains, blue and cool and sweet, where a man could suck air into his lungs and rejoice just to be alive and free, without civilization or law or politics or masters to rein him in.

But Victoria was unhappy.

During each of the previous rendezvous, she had borne his little communions with the whiskey jug without complaint. But not this time. Like most of his trapping brethren, he had stocked up on trade whiskey at the canvas emporium of Smith, Jackson, and Sublette and gone on a bender for several days—three, to be precise. Vile stuff, that trade whiskey—grain alcohol, river water, some pepper and tobacco for taste. Worse than monkey spit. When he finally recovered his wits, he felt nauseous and the sunlight intimidated him.

That's when Victoria squinted at him, pursed her lips, and plunged into a hostile silence. He ignored her. If she wanted him to quit the jug, she might as well forget it. He was himself, and couldn't change.

"I want to go visit my mother and father. I haven't been with the People for four winters," she said, looking up from her cook pot one July morning.

"We could do that. Stay a few days right after this breaks up."

"No, I want to be with the People again. Many moons. Maybe always. I am one of the Kicked-in-the-Bellies. Arapooish is my chief. So I will go back—until the next rendezvous, anyway."

He surveyed her, worry coiling through him. He didn't want her to leave. He was hitched to the fur company for a living, and wherever they sent him, that's where he would go. He'd been a camp tender, and had done so well that they had finally made him second in command, the camp clerk and assistant to the partisan, or bourgeois, as the Creoles called the brigade leaders. That was something, rising like that. His pay had gone from two hundred to three hundred a year, too.

Skye sulked. Women! How could any man get along with one?

He eyed her furtively, admiring her lithe, compact figure and her dusky flesh and her taut, clean-boned face and the jet hair she wore in long braids. She was his miracle, and every trapper in camp envied him. From the moment he had fallen for her, while yet a bumbling British seaman who had just fled the Royal Navy, she had worked magic in him. She had given more than love: fierce loyalty, an education in the ways of the Plains tribes, tenderness, his first experience of a shared life, and more. She had lightened his chores as camp tender, brain-tanned every buffalo and elk and deer and moose hide the meat hunters had brought in, which eventually added a hundred dollars to their annual income when they traded the peltries at rendezvous, and had sewn handsome, comfortable skin clothes and fur-lined moccasins for him, year by year.

But now she was threatening to leave him. Well, not that exactly. She wanted him to live in her village for a time. He couldn't imagine what to do about it or how he'd make a living there. She said they didn't need to make a living if they lived with her people. The Absaroka had more than enough of everything. But he said he needed to buy powder and lead, flannels, good four-point blankets, knives, skillets, tin cups, coffee, beans, sugar, flour, and salt. And besides, he owed the company a hundred and fifty dollars and that sum was expanding by the jugful.

She glared at him as if he were crazy.

He should have been happy. That's what rendezvous were for. Six or seven weeks of pure, unbridled fun with the wildmen of the mountains, along with assorted Indians from all the surrounding areas. All except Blackfeet, the ever-present menace to them all. But here, on the Popo Agie, were Nez Perce, Shoshones, and plenty of Crows, though not most of Victoria's village, which was hunting buffalo after a hard and hungry winter.

He glowered at the world, oblivious of the breezes toying with his long hair, his stocky body alive to the delicious warmth of the early summer, even if he was hungover. The sprawling camp lay quiet in the morning light, smoke drifting lazily from a few cookfires, most of the mountaineers still on their buffalo robes after another night's debauch that usually ended around dawn. Skye saw no guards. Did all these veterans of the mountains trust the world that much? Would no Indian venture to steal a horse or a hundred horses? Did all catastrophe cease when these knights gathered?

Skye eyed a knot of men under a nearby brush arbor, and knew they were deciding his fate and the fate of most of the mountaineers gathered at the rendezvous. There sat the owners of the fur company—William Sublette, Davey Jackson, and that legend, Jedediah Smith, back from his three-year adventure to California and the Oregon country, still alive although almost no one else on that expedition had made it. Skye shuddered. He had desperately wanted to go with Smith, but if he had done so he would be lying in a grave.

With the partisans sat some younger men: Tom Fitzpatrick, Jim Bridger, Milt Sublette, Henry Fraeb, and Jean Baptiste Gervais. Skye had an inkling what that was all about. The partners were selling out, just as Ashley, before them, had sold out, and the younger bunch was buying the company. He'd already heard enough to know that the outfit would be called the Rocky Mountain Fur Company. Just what that boded for him, Skye couldn't imagine, but he knew his future was all tied up with their palaver.

"Well, dammit, Skye, you going to eat or do I throw this to the dogs?" Victoria asked.

Skye ate. She glared at him, registering every bite. He didn't thank her for heating up the buffalo stew. He ate lightly, his stomach roiling from the previous night's excesses.

"Can't eat? You were pretty goddamn drunk," she said maliciously. "Maybe you starve to death."

"What's in your craw?"

"Whiskey."

"I'll drink if I want. This is the only time all year I can."

"Except when you take jugs with you."

Skye ignored her, sipped some scalding coffee—itself a once-a-year luxury—and fled. If she was going to go back to her people, he wished she'd be off. He was tired of the nagging.

He didn't like this rendezvous anymore. The others had been the best moments of his life. He'd come to the mountains a refugee from the long arm of the Royal Navy, a man who'd grown up in a watery prison, but here in the mountains he'd become a new man, learning the craft of survival better than anyone else—because he had to. He had no place to run. This last year had been the best. Smith, back from his terrible trip to the coast, had met Jackson and Sublette in Pierre's Hole in August—they had been looking for him—and then set out on a hunt northward toward the Blackfoot country, up into the lush Judith Basin, south of the Missouri River. And Skye, along with Victoria, had been along, blotting up the art and genius of the one man who seemed immune to all the perils of the wilderness.

Skye knew that for as long as he lived, he would consider Jed Smith the finest mountaineer and explorer of the times. A season in Smith's brigade had taught Skye all the things he needed to know: how to make camp in a defensible place, how to listen to nature, how to find forage where there seemed to be none, how to conjure food from the naked earth, water from a desert, shelter in a barren plain. How to discern the presence of animals, birds, and Indians. All those things were what made the Bible-reading Smith a man apart. And the things that spelled the difference between life and death, comfort and misery, nourishment and starvation for man and beast. And there was Smith yonder, fixing to desert him, quit the mountains. That was the gossip, anyway.

It riled up Skye some. He itched to have a sweat. Victoria had introduced him to the sweat lodge, especially when Skye needed to boil the booze out of his pores and clean his body. Now he wanted one that would clean his spirit, too, of all its dreads and angers. He didn't know how to do that, especially with all those partisans throwing the dice of fate. His fate. Who would he work for and what would the wage be? And who would be his brigade companions? That mattered most of all.

Nothing much happened during the mornings at rendezvous, and this one was no exception. Victoria vanished with the packhorse on her diurnal woodcutting mission, which took her farther from camp each day. From the slope of the hill where Skye stood, he could see several hundred lodges, scores of brush arbors—structures resting on poles and covered with boughs to provide shade—and vast herds of horses dotting the browning grasslands. Every week or so the rendezvous moved a mile or two to provide the ponies with fresh pasture, so it was slowly crawling up the purling Popo Agie and toward the blue crests of the Wind River Mountains, which were not visible from where he stood, blocked from view by layer upon layer of brooding brown foothills that censored beauty as if it were sin. Not even the company store—or American Fur's rival outfit—was doing any trade, and its clerks lazed in the mellow sun of a July day. Skye watched a red-tailed hawk as it hunted along the brow of a hill, and emptied his mind of everything.

But at noon things changed. The partisans emerged from their shaded arena and headed for the stew pots. Sky intuited that the bargaining was over. It surprised him that Milt Sublette and Tom Fitzpatrick headed straight for him. They looked to be all business.

"Mister Skye," said Fitzpatrick, "you're speaking to the new owners of the company. We're calling it the Rocky Mountain Fur Company. It's no longer Smith, Jackson, and Sublette. Bill Sublette, anyway. Milt's joined us."

"Well, that's some doings." Skye lifted his top hat and screwed it down again. Ownership didn't much matter to him, as long as he had a living.

"Milt and Bridger and I are headed north with a strong party. Fraeb and Gervais are taking a brigade south. How'd you like to take out a smaller third brigade? We're making you a partisan, and we're offering five hundred for it."

"Five hundred? A partisan?"

"Mr. Skye, you've proven yourself for four years. You're a veteran. Smith recommended it, says there's no one better qualified or more likely to make a successful hunt. You're a team, you and your Victoria. Jed said he had the best outfit he'd ever had, never lacking for anything, including safety."

"She's sure some," said Milt Sublette. "A she-tiger."

"I, ah, I need to think it over, gents," Skye said. "Victoria—"

"Nothing much to think over, old coon. We'll put you on the roster as brigade leader."

Skye didn't answer. He didn't have an answer.

two

Skye broke the news to Victoria when she returned with her packhorse laden with firewood.

"That's a lot of money, Victoria," he said. "A brigade leader. They like us. They say you're as valuable as I am."

He stood there, top hat in hand, hoping it would be all right. But she glared at him and silently unloaded the wood, dropping it near her cookfire in front of their small, tattered lodge. He had the feeling she was torn asunder.

"We can afford lots of good things," he said. "You want more four-point blankets? One for a capote? You want more cook pots? You want a rifle? We could even buy a horse, maybe."

She kept her silence, glancing at him now and then as she started a fire with a coal borrowed from a neighboring blaze, and then led the runty dun packhorse—a wounded war pony she had nursed into serviceability—back to the herd. Skye stood alone, the wind raking his face, the sun punching needles into him, a man with no refuge except the one walking a horse to pasture.

He didn't know what to do. In her silence lay a message, and he suspected that she would leave him if he stayed with the company. He loved her, but he wanted that job as partisan. He'd come a long way, the youthful fugitive from the Royal

Navy who had survived by sheer luck until he stumbled onto the Americans and succor. If he quit the outfit and went with her to her people, he would feel incomplete. If he stuck with the outfit and he lost her, life would darken. She had made their small lodge a paradise. Within its buffalo-hide walls were food, warmth, thick buffalo robes and blankets, shelter from blizzard and rain and cold—and companionship. Once they had learned each other's tongue, they talked and shared, laughed at fools, admired brave men, dreamed, hugged, and coupled. He was not alone.

No child had issued from their union, at least not yet. He feared he was barren, that those long dark maddened years aboard a royal frigate, the bad food and foul air and sickness, had undermined his youth and health. If Victoria only had a child or two, she wouldn't feel this way; instead, she had little more than drudgery and a life as an alien among strange white men, with only Skye for a friend. She lacked even one woman friend. He understood her agony and knew why she was poised like a doe to flee.

He waited for her to return from the pasture. There were many Crows at this rendezvous, some of them related to her, and she would be with them. She had spent every spare moment with them ever since they set up their lodge on the green flats along the Popo Agie. He had seen her laughing with them—no doubt telling wicked stories about the strange white men—and each day she spent more time among them. Hour by hour, as the rendezvous spent itself, he was losing her.

His own summer celebration went sour. This time, the rude jokes weren't funny. Bridger's wild tales were all familiar. The contests didn't appeal to him. He wasn't much of a shot compared to some of the masters of the long rifle, and although he could throw a 'hawk or a knife with some skill, the veterans of the Rocky Mountain college could whip him easily.

Each year he'd heard the same complaints about piratical prices at the company store, and each year the free trappers had bought new outfits anyway, grumbling all the while they fondled their new Hawkens and blankets and powder horns and flannel shirts. This year they had a choice between the American Fur Company's outfit, run by Henry Vanderburgh and Andrew Drips, or the usual one, but the competition didn't make life any better for the mountaineers. Both outfits charged all they could get.

He yearned for a book or two and a quiet time under a tree, reading. He had heard more than enough tales about grizzlies, Blackfeet, and starving times. No one talked about liberty, or the affairs of nations, or fiction. They didn't even know who their president was, and didn't care. No books came out with the outfit this time, and only one St. Louis newspaper, which most of the mountaineers couldn't read anyway. Skye wandered restlessly among his friends and rivals—some of them antagonistic toward him because he had climbed the company ladder a few rungs—discontented, crabbed, and half annoyed because he wasn't having a good time.

July slid into August. The nights turned cool, and the days were dry. The oppressive night heat lifted, and a man could sleep in fresher air, with fewer mosquitoes and flies to torment him. Fitzpatrick and Milt Sublette began forming up the pack outfit that would haul the plews and skins back to St. Louis. Trappers traded the last of their pelts or went into hock another year to put an outfit together. Skye bought another jug of trade whiskey, running his debt to three hundred something.

One day the Crows left to hunt buffalo around the Yellowstone, and the next day the Shoshones and some Nez Perce pulled out for the Snake country, while a few Sioux and even a few Cheyennes headed south or east. These enemies and rivals of the Crows and Shoshones respected the neutrality of the trade fair—up to a point. They would gladly butcher each other a mile from the Popo Agie. Victoria watched them leave, her face pinched and her thoughts unfathomable. She and Skye had all but ceased talking, and he had long since been feeding himself because she was no longer around to cook for him.

He watched her angrily. She would take off after the Crows, and good riddance. He didn't need her anyway. Bloody woman. He'd get another. Lots of pretty Indian girls just itching to make a lodge with a white trapper. One was as good as another.

But he didn't really believe that. Victoria's glares and silences—and furtive tears—tore Skye to bits. He knew she was staying on until he made a decision one way or another. But the moment he chose to lead a brigade, she'd be off to her people and that would be the last he'd ever see of her.

One evening he climbed a foothill to think. The air was thick with smoke from forest and grass fires somewhere else—the summer had turned into a scorcher—and he stared into a blood-red setting sun that looked angry and ominous. He already knew what he would do, and it desolated him. He hated being put into this dilemma. Hated his easy surrender. But he was sour on the whole mountain fraternity with all its adolescent braggadocio. Maybe they were all brave and daring men, but they were mostly ignorant, narrow, and mean, too, most of them meaner than the limey jack-tars he'd rubbed shoulders with, and they were a mean lot.

He came off the hill bathed in red, the blood of the sun dripping off him, and headed for Tom Fitzpatrick, who was smoking a pipe, his back befriending a shaggy cottonwood.

"Ah, mate, you mind if I sit and talk?"

Broken Hand, as the world knew him, nodded Skye to join him. "It's a fair night," Fitzpatrick said. "One of the last, I imagine. Smith, Jackson, and Sublette are taking one hundred ninety packs of beaver to St. Louis next week. Milt, Bridger, and I'll head north with a strong brigade. Fraeb and Gervais'll head south." He turned. "You've been acting like a bee stung your butt."

"I'm giving up the company."

That did surprise Fitzpatrick. "A man's reasons are his own, I suppose."

"I'll lose Victoria if I lead a brigade."

Fitzpatrick nodded, sucked his briar pipe, and studied the dying sun. "Where'll you go?" he asked at last.

"Her people."

"Well, now, this is luck. We're thinking to send you up the Yellowstone with a brigade. We thought with your connections ye'd do a deal of trading with the Crows. Maybe you'd better think this over."

"I did, sir. I'd bloody well lose her."

"I'll confide something to you. Beaver pelts can earn a fortune, and we're facing tough competition from rich men—Pratte, Berthold, Chouteau—who bought the western division of the American Fur Company from John Jacob Astor. They have a brigade in the field this summer, up north. Led by two experienced men, Henry Vanderburgh and Andrew Drips. They're building a post—Fort Floyd—at the confluence of the Yellowstone and the Missouri—a perfect spot to control the mountain trade. And they're planning another on the Yellowstone and the Big Horn. That'll be for the Crow trade. Just put a canoe into water here and you'd end up there. And that's not all, Skye. Our friend Jim Beckwourth—he's a headman with the Crows now, for American Fur. They're paying him a reg'lar salary to steer the Crow trade to that outfit. We'd hoped your brigade could stem that."

"I've made up my mind."

Fitzpatrick grumbled impatiently. "How much do you owe the company?"

"Over three hundred, sir. But I'm outfitted. I thought I'd pay it off next summer with peltries. Victoria tans a fine robe. I don't much like trapping, but I'd get it paid off."

"Suppose we were to employ you to steer business our way. Keep it away from Beckwourth. Bring the Crows to us next summer—Powder River it'll be, and that's Crow country. Take a small trading outfit with you."

"It won't be easy to match Beckwourth, sir. He's been in the mountains since the Ashley expeditions."

"It's worth a try. AFC's paying Beckwourth—we know that. Probably three hundred to steer the tribe their way. They've also given him a trading outfit. He's picking up pelts. You and your lady'd be worth the same to us."

"You'd trust me?"

"The mountains bring out a man's nature."

"Beckwourth's a chief, I hear."

Fitzpatrick nodded. "That's right. But you're married to a Crow from a prominent family. I'll have to talk this over with the partners. I think it'd be a good move to put you there.

"It wouldn't be easy. American Fur's building posts, and Beckwourth can get trade goods whenever he needs them. We can supply you only once a year. We'd give you a small outfit—mostly shot and powder, arrow points, knives, awls—things you could carry on a single packhorse. But mostly we would want you to become an important man among them, win their loyalties, and bring them to us next summer, laden with beaver and robes for trading. In other words, beat Beckwourth at his own game. Do whatever it takes, compete on any terms."

"Well, there might be something in it. I'll talk to Victoria. Maybe she'll like the idea."

"A word of caution, Skye. American Fur's a rough outfit. They'll do anything to whip you. Maybe even resort to violence. Blame you for whatever goes wrong. Beckwourth's certainly capable of ruining you. You'll be facing a gifted man, a fine warrior, cunning and smart—and a man without scruples."

That troubled Skye. "I have scruples, sir."

"Best forget 'em."

"No, I can't do that. I live by my ideals. I'll not do anything dishonorable."

"No one's askin' you to."

"That's got to be understood. Let me say it plain. My word is my bond. I'll not lie, cheat, slander, steal, or kill. I'm a peaceable man and I hate war. Especially for the sake of commerce. If Beckwourth whips me by resorting to those things, then I'll be whipped. There are deeds I won't do, not for anything. But I think I can whip American Fur. And I think the Crows would like a man who lives by his own standards. If that's not enough—then I'm not your man."

Fitzpatrick stared a long while and then shrugged. "The mountains are a hard place," he said. "Your rules don't apply."

"My rules apply to me."

Fitzpatrick grinned suddenly. "I like that, Mister Skye. I like that indeed. I'll talk to the partners."

Thus, willy-nilly, a deal was forged. Victoria didn't object at all. Now she'd have Skye in her village, among her people, and she'd still be able to get blankets and beads and knives and hatchets.

"Dammit, Skye, this is good," she said, looking cheerful for the first time in months. He knew, and rejoiced privately, that she couldn't bear to leave him, either, just as he couldn't bear to leave her, and this new position was a miracle and a cause for rejoicing.

Then one austere August day, Skye watched the old partners, the masterful Diah Smith, Bill Sublette, and Davey Jackson, start a large pack train eastward. The next day he watched Fraeb and Gervais head toward South Park and the high Rockies. And then Bridger, Fitzpatrick, and Milt Sublette leave for the Blackfoot country with a powerful brigade two hundred strong.

He and Victoria loaded their lodge onto a travois, burdened two packhorses, saddled two riding horses, and headed home, and all the while Victoria laughed and babbled like a merry brook.

three

Victoria, Many Quill Woman, rejoiced. The pony beneath her was taking her home.

Home to her father, Walks Alone.

Home to her little mother, Digs the Roots.

Home to her brother Arrow, and to her sisters, Makes the Robe and Rosebud.

Home to her people, to the land of plenty, where buffalo and elk and deer abounded, where clear cold water dashed from the mountains.

Home to the center of the world, which the Absaroka would possess forever.

Home to her father's brother Arapooish, Rotten Belly, great chief of the People.

Home to her own tongue, which tripped lightly through her soul as she rode.

She could not contain her gaiety, and laughed and mumbled as she and Skye traveled through a cloudless August day. She felt weightless, afloat upon a gauzy cloud, no burden at all upon the ugly little pony. She felt lithe and young, her body perfect, her spirit hovering above her, like her counselor, Magpie, who flew along beside her, an ever-present guide.

Her man seemed more somber. He took them down the Wind River, but well to the west of the river bottoms to avoid dangers along that great artery. Soon they would reach the Owl Mountains, where the river vanished into an impassible red-rock canyon, and there they would detour over the crest of the mountains. When they reached the river again it would have a new name, the Big Horn, and it would be nestled in red and yellow rock.

She glanced boldly at Skye. He rode peaceably, almost carelessly, but she knew it was an illusion. His eyes never ceased their study of distant horizons, the heavens, rocks and barriers and gulches that might conceal danger. He took in all of that, weighing and assessing. In their four years of marriage, he had transformed himself from a man who rode boats upon the big waters to a seasoned and careful warrior. His new Hawken rifle rested in its quilled sheath, always at hand. But that was nothing compared to the terrible bear claw necklace he wore upon his chest, the ensign of his medicine and power.

She examined Skye, finding satisfaction in the sight of him. She especially admired his nose. Was there ever such a heroic nose? He wore his long hair gathered into a ponytail, the way of the warrior, and upon his head was the medicine hat that had become his Sacred Way—a top hat, the pale men called it, black felt, scuffed and battered, with a small brim below it.

He paused on a slope, stopping just under the ridge so he could peer ahead without being seen. This heartened her, this innate caution. He would deliver them safely to the Yellowstone country and the village of her people. This time he lifted a hand, and she stopped her pony at once. Behind her, the packhorses stopped too. He had seen something. She slid off and walked to where he sat his horse, just below ridge level. She peered east and saw what he had seen, the dust of many horses on the river, heading north, their own direction. A large and fast-moving party, without lodges. Warriors or hunters. And they would have vedettes to either side, probably one very close.

Not Crows. She knew where her people were. The Absarokas at the rendezvous had told her. She and Skye could stay put, probably unseen in this dry drainage, but if the vedettes cut their trail, they would not be safe. She looked at Skye anxiously. He watched and waited, squinting into the noonday glare, and eventually he pointed. To the west, a small group of horsemen—mere black dots—rode through the dry sagebrush-shot country. She and her man were between the main body and the sentinels.

"Nothing to do but go powwow with 'em," Skye said. "I'll fetch some tobacco."

She watched Skye ride back to the gray packhorse, dismount, and dig through the panniers. Tobacco came in various forms, the most common being the plug, or twist. He pulled out several.

Moments later they topped the ridge and were instantly spotted. Skye led her directly toward the smaller group of riders, while dread stole through her. These were not pale men, but one or another of the Peoples. If Siksika, or Blackfeet, she and Skye were doomed to a slow death by torture. But they were far from the land of the Siksika, and more likely these were Sioux or Cheyenne, who might or might not torment them.

They met on a windy hilltop. Four warriors, none young; small, wiry, lithe, broad faced, wearing only breechclouts—and war honors, eagle feathers in their jet hair. But they weren't painted for war, not displaying their personal medicine. None had a rifle. The bows of three remained unstrung, but the fourth—the headman, apparently—carried a strung bow with a nocked arrow. He could kill her husband before Skye had his Hawken half out of its sheath.

She didn't know who these people were. Not Sioux or Cheyenne. Maybe Arapaho or Ute, far north of their usual haunts. Maybe going to make war on her Absaroka. She glared at them disdainfully, letting them know what she thought.

But her man made the peace sign and offered a twist of

tobacco—sealing the peace, if accepted—to the leader. The burly warrior studied Skye, glanced briefly at her, and then focused on Skye's magnificent bear claw necklace, given him four winters earlier by Red Turkey Head. The medicine necklace told the world his was the power of the grizzly bear.

The elder took the proffered twist of tobacco. Skye, who had learned something of the finger language, asked them who they were. Victoria watched closely, as puzzled as Skye.

Pawnee. Ancient enemies of the Sioux. Friends of white men. Friends of the Absaroka, sometimes.

"Aiee! Pawnee, Skye," she exclaimed. "Goddamn!"

He didn't know much about them, so she explained that these people lived to the southeast, along the Platte River, and hunted buffalo. Maybe friends—if they didn't steal everything in sight.

"I never met one," Skye replied. He turned to the elder and signed for a smoke. But the elder, his eye upon the distant column, motioned Skye to come. They would join the main body.

Reluctantly, they headed for the distant ribbon of water. They were alive, anyway, and no one had stolen anything—yet.

"I never was much good with the sign language. Maybe they've got someone we can talk to," he said to her. "Tell me about these Pawnees."

She didn't know much, but she did remember one thing: they worshiped the Morning Star, and every year they captured a maiden from another tribe and ritually sacrificed her to Morning Star. She glared at these burly Plains people, suddenly cold within. She'd kill a few before they laid hands on her. She didn't know of any Absaroka girls who had been sacrificed, but that didn't mean there weren't any.

Before Sun had gone much farther through the sky, they reached the main body—perhaps fifty warriors, traveling with many packhorses and travois laden with good robes and peltries.

Their arrival halted the procession, and all the Pawnees crowded around. They were good horsemen and rode spirited animals. None seemed menacing to her; she felt more at home in any Indian camp than among the pale men.

Skye was taken to their chief, a lean, corded giant whose experience of war was etched in the scars on his body—an ugly welt across a forearm, another across his ribs. Then a mixed-blood warrior pushed through. He had brown hair and gray eyes, and a freckled, mottled flesh.

"Le Duc," he said, and began talking in the tongue of the Creoles. Skye shook his head. But Le Duc knew a few of Skye's words, and so they communicated.

"Cut Nose," Le Duc said, pointing to the headman. "Pawnee war chief. Me, Antoine Le Duc, Le Duc fils, engagé."

"Barnaby Skye, Victoria—Many Quill Woman, Absaroka," Skye replied. All the while, Cut Nose listened and waited for translations. In time they got the story. These Pawnees had come to trade robes for rifles, blankets, pots, and knives at the pale men's fair but arrived too late, and now were looking for the pale men. And they had decided to visit the Absaroka as long as they were so far from their villages. And maybe steal some Sioux ponies.

"We are going to the Absaroka. The Kicked-in-the-Bellies. Come with us," Skye signaled.

Cut Nose wanted to know where the traders had gone.

"Back east, with many pelts. Some north to the Missouri—Big River—to trap. Some south, to the Wall of Mountains, to trap."

Le Duc explained all that.

"We will visit Arapooish, Rotten Belly," Cut Nose said. "You are our friends, our brothers. You are welcome in our camp. We will smoke the pipe of friendship tonight. We are friends of the pale men, 'Mericans, traders. Yes, you, us, we are like two stars side by side."

Skye didn't like it. Victoria could tell that. Her man was a lone bear. But there was nothing to do but join these Pawnees on their adventure into distant lands.

She would be the lone woman in camp. She eyed the

Pawnees mistrustfully. Who knew what such strange men would do? Skye would protect her, if he didn't start sipping from his jug.

Pawnees along with the Skyes started north again, finding the trail that would take them over the Owl Mountains. The trail led far west of the place where the river vanished into a sinister gorge, up through arid land dotted with juniper that seemed to grow in rawboned rock. They descended all afternoon through red-rock country, her own Absaroka land, the Big Horn basin, and would camp that evening at a famous hot spring where her people had come for healing and prayers. But she didn't like it. She would have liked to soak in the hot water with Skye, but now with all these Pawnees around they'd just set up a lodge. There wasn't much game around the spring, and she hoped the damned Pawnees had some meat.

They made camp at dusk in a green valley girt with red rock and junipers. She didn't like the look of the thunderclouds building over the mountains, so she set up the lodge while Skye took the horses to the nearest pasture and hobbled them. Grass was thin there. Something crabbed at her; unruly suspicions, dark doubts. She dropped the trading packs just inside the lodge door.

The Pawnees cooked a deer and shared the meat. Some of them slid into the healing hot waters as dark descended. She didn't like any of this, but Skye seemed happy.

Later, long after she and Skye had gone to their robes, she awakened with a start. She'd been hearing something and then nothing. She poked her head out of the lodge. The clouds had dissipated and a quarter moon cast pale light—on nothing. The Pawnees were gone. She stalked the camp, finding not a trace of them, and knew, suddenly, that the Skye horses would be gone, too. Along with their packs—everything, including the trade items entrusted to them by Broken Hand Fitzpatrick.

Angrily she walked through the moonlight, confirming her darkest suspicions. The treacherous Pawnees, well known as the great thieves of the prairies, had stolen all the Skyes possessed—and five hundred dollars of trade goods.

"Goddamn," she said, hating to tell her man they had nothing.

She stormed back to the lodge, finding Skye up, sitting in the deep dark.

"Thieves!" she bawled.

"Everything?"

"Everything. Our horses."

"The trading packs?"

"Gone."

Skye sighed, registering that. "Now I owe them five hundred more. Where'd they go? Could you make it out?"

"Not enough light to see. But not long ago. I can still smell the dust."

Skye stalked the abandoned camp angrily, seeing for himself.

"What are we going to do without ponies?" she asked.

"We'll walk," he said.

four

"We'll carry what we can on our backs," Skye said. "It isn't so far. Ten sleeps to my people."

"That's not where I'm going."

Victoria registered that and looked unhappy. "You will not catch them. They have many horses."

"I'll try."

"You are alone; they are many."

"When I was a boy in the boat on the Big Water, I was alone. They would not even let me have my gruel—my food. So I fought them for it. They beat me, but then they let me eat. Maybe I will lose, but I must try. It's a law of my life that I must try."

She nodded. "Maybe you will get everything back. Maybe you will die."

Skye surveyed the abandoned camp in the light of earliest dawn, before the sun rose. No trail led north. So the Pawnees had slipped away in the night, back from where they had come. South to the plains. Away from the Crows. All the talk about visiting the Crows was smoke.

"Victoria," he said, "I have to go after them, away from your people. You may as well go north. This is your country. You'd be safe enough. We can rig up a pack for you. Maybe I can make some meat for you to take with you. There's berries, chokecherries . . ."

It angered her. "Wherever you go, Skye, that's where I go, dammit."

"You could visit your people. I'll come later when I finish this."

"Maybe I wouldn't see you. You and me, Skye. We will find the Pawnee thieves."

"It could be dangerous."

"You got bear medicine. Big, big medicine. Me, I got some medicine, too." She grinned at him. The idea of a daring raid on their tormentors appealed to her.

"I thought you wanted to get home to your people."

"I do. But goddamn, Skye, we're gonna walk into the village with some war honors, Pawnee scalps. You, you'll be a big man among us."

He shrugged. Being a big man had never appealed to him, nor had he ever sought status. Swiftly they inventoried their few possessions. They had the lodge, which they would have to cache and hope to recover later; two summer robes; the clothing on their backs; his rifle and powder horn and fixings; his sheathed knife; her bow and quiver of arrows; her flint and striker. They had what they needed.

They found no place to hide the lodge, so they left it. But before doing so, Victoria hung a small medicine bundle from the lodgepoles, her amulets, some sage, some sweetgrass. The Peoples would leave it alone. They left the robes within; they were too heavy to carry. Then they headed south, back to the Owl Mountains. She carried only her quiver and bow; he cradled his Hawken in its fringed, quilled leather sheath, her gift to him.

Hunger bit him. His stomach growled and complained, and he kept a sharp eye for anything they might eat. She walked wordlessly beside him, every step taking her away from her village and her dream of reunion.

The day turned hot and they staggered through boiling air, crossed the Owls, and reached their base and the Wind River by nightfall. The trail of many horses led ever south, but they had not seen their quarry all day. The Pawnees could be twenty miles ahead for all Skye knew.

They slaked their thirst, and Victoria managed to find some roots and berries. They had no pot but she roasted the roots—prairie turnips, he thought—over coals. That meager fare would have to suffice.

That night, snugged close for warmth, she ran her small hands over his back. "You some hell of a sonofabitch man," she said. He laughed. One thing a Crow woman loved was a good warrior.

She laughed, too, oddly happy. He had come to understand something: she liked having him to herself and not sharing him with all the trappers and mountaineers. Now at last she had Skye without all the rest of it.

He awoke in the night, responding to the rustling of some creature, but saw nothing. She lay beside him, awake. He judged that it might be two or three in the morning.

"Let's go," he said.

"Damned spirits," she muttered. "Bad place. Someone died here."

Hunger tortured him now; his belly howled. But he pushed that aside. They could gain hours on the Pawnee. If they were like other Plains people, they would be in no hurry to start in the morning. He and Victoria could be seven or eight hours closer by the time the Pawnees saddled up. But they would not be able to see the trail, and would have to trust that the Pawnees were heading toward their own country, having done all the mischief they could.

He splashed icy water on his face, gasped, felt the water trickle through his beard, while she silently prepared herself for the day. Then he hoisted the heavy Hawken—the big mountain rifle had been built to withstand abuse, which is why the trappers loved them—and they started south again, with only the Wind River to guide them.

Fool's errand, that's what it would come to, he thought. But it was something he had to do. Some things were iron rules inside of him, and this was one. Maybe he would fail, but they would not forget Mister Skye.

The trail took them over the foothills of the Wind River Mountains, which lay in their path like giant tree roots. The slopes winded them, but at least they could make a living out of buffalo berries and the bitter chokecherries, though all the berries in the world wouldn't do much for the gnawing in his gut.

He pressed forward relentlessly, sometimes worrying whether his mate could maintain the pace. But she walked grimly beside him, her face a mask, enduring hardship in the way of her people. All that brutal day he pushed along the trail, knowing that they were gaining ground. The Pawnees were in no hurry, and their travel was leisurely. The horse manure was fresher, the evidence of passage—bent grass, sharp prints in sandy soil—more immediate.

At dusk Skye and Victoria climbed an endless slope, topping it in the last light, a streak of blue behind the mountains signaling the death of a day. And below, a mile off, a fire. They stared at it, suddenly aware that decisions had to be made.

"I guess we'll walk in," he said.

"And die."

"Maybe not. I'll keep my sheath on the rifle. You keep your bow on your back."

"Maybe they just kill us."

"Maybe," he said. "But if we go in armed, we'll face thirty or forty nocked arrows."

She muttered something to herself, and they started down the long slope, stumbling in darkness, not trying to conceal their presence. A few hundred yards from the fire, some of the Pawnee materialized, alert and ready to kill.

"Well, we're back, mates," Skye said, forcing himself to sound cheerful. "Thought we'd join our good friends the Pawnees."

They didn't understand a word, but that wouldn't matter. Swiftly the warriors enveloped them, eyed their weapons, peered into the darkness looking for others, for ambush, for trouble. Over the fire, a deer haunch roasted, spitting fat into the flame. That was all Skye thought about. He headed straight for the haunch and sliced slivers of hot, roasting meat from it, wolfing some, handing some to Victoria.

"How come you here?" asked Le Duc, the breed.

Skye ate. Filling his belly was the only business he wished to conduct. So he smiled, sliced more meat, fed Victoria, and continued to satisfy the howl of his stomach. Finally he wiped his mouth, sheathed his knife, and examined the Pawnees. Every horse had vanished. Whatever remained of the stolen packs and pack saddles had vanished.

"Come to fetch our horses and packs," he said to Le Duc. "I guess if you Pawnees are friends, you'll return them, eh?"

"What horses? I see nothing."

Skye lifted his topper and settled it again. "Well, this is some," he said. "Let's go ask the headman there. Go on, ask him."

Reluctantly, Le Duc spoke to the headman, and the headman replied.

"He says we don't have nothing."

Skye grinned. "Tell him he does not speak truly, and if he's a friend of white men, he'd better try again."

Le Duc spoke again, and the headman's response was stony silence. Pawnee warriors glared, and Skye noticed that some had bows in hand.

"Tell him he's no match for bear medicine," Skye said, touching the magnificent bear claw necklace on his chest. "Tell him he can have this necklace if he's telling the truth."

Victoria cussed at him.

Le Duc tried again. "He says he's telling the truth and give him de bear claws."

"Tell him that if he's lying, the bear claws will kill him within one moon because he will not be worthy of such medicine."

"Sonofabitch," Victoria said.

The headman stood, undecided and unhappy, and then walked into the darkness without a word.

Skye guessed he had just won, but wasn't sure. "Le Duc, we're fetching our horses and gear now. If you don't give us our own back, we'll take others. If we don't get our gear back, we'll take more horses."

Sullenly, the breed translated to the warriors, who stood stock-still. No one moved. Skye examined them alertly, knowing the moment of truth had arrived, and if he guessed wrong, he and his beloved might not walk away.

"Take us to the herd," he said.

No one moved.

"All right, we'll find the horses ourselves. But first we'll collect our gear."

He deliberately walked the periphery of the camp, where the firelight faded into night, and saw nothing at all. No one stopped him. He guessed that they were astonished that a lone man and woman would challenge thirty or forty able warriors. Wherever the gear was, he couldn't find it.

"What're we gonna do, Skye?" Victoria asked.

"I don't know from one moment to the next." He hiked back to the fire, which cast wavering orange light upon these powerful soldiers of the Pawnee tribe.

He stood in the midst of them, his voice scornful and withering. "I thought we were friends. You told me you were coming to visit my wife's people. Instead, you're liars and thieves." He spat on the ground. "That's what, two-tongued, miserable, thieving curs. I'll tell the Absarokas about the lying Pawnee. I'll tell the Shoshones and Bannacks and Cheyenne. Let 'em know all about you."

They would translate his tone of voice, at least. But none moved.

"Skye," whispered Victoria. "Watch out."

Skye whirled as an arrow thudded at his feet.

"Get out," said Le Duc. "They say go."

So he had lost after all. He was jeopardizing Victoria as well as himself. Wordlessly, he stalked away, this time with a large escort of Pawnees, determined to see him far from their camp. They halted after ten minutes or so, muttering something at him that he took for a lethal threat.

"Thanks for the meal, mates," Skye said.

He and Victoria hastened through the blackness, veering sharply left to dodge any treacherous arrow. But no one followed. He had failed. They would put up a massive guard this night and in the days to come.

"They gonna talk about this a long time, Skye," she said.

"But we didn't get anything back."

"Big medicine," she said.

But big medicine wouldn't replace their losses.

five

The ignominy Skye knew he would face when he reached Victoria's village didn't make the hard walk any easier. He had dreamed of returning with all the ensigns of success: horses, packs, Victoria handsomely accoutered with every imaginable luxury—four-point blankets, pots, knives, awls, conchos for her belt, looking glasses, beads, and all the marvels that bespoke success and comfort. That and a trading outfit that would make him a treasured guest.

Instead, he would walk into the village as a pauper. He would greet her parents as a pauper. He would try to compete against Beckwourth and the American Fur Company as a mendicant, with nothing to show for his four years in the mountains.

But that was the future. Now, on the trail, survival occupied every moment. Victoria's moccasins were wearing out. His shirt was rotting. They were never far from starvation. They were helpless against enemies, rain, cold, brutal heat. They trudged wearily back to the Popo Agie, the plains desolate now, the grass grazed to the roots from the time a thousand horses sojourned there during rendezvous. They trudged north along the Wind River, retracing their steps, the land dry and game scarce. They survived on a hare one day, a badger another, vile meat that gagged him.

Victoria never complained. She not only radiated cheer—he ascribed that to the imminent visit with her family—but oddly, she seemed to love and admire him all the more, even in his defeat. He couldn't understand it.

They toiled over the arid, scowling Owl Mountains once again, and down to the hot spring nestled in the rough redrock country. Their lodge had not been touched. The sacred bundle still hung from within. Victoria retrieved it, rejoiced in its medicine, and they settled into their home—for the night. She cut moccasin leather from one of the robes they had left there and sewed a new pair, awkwardly using his knife as an awl, cussing all the while. She cut a chunk of the summer robe to take with her, knowing that she would need to repair footgear again before they had walked ten sleeps to the Yellowstone—the Elk River, as her people called it.

They stuck to the bottoms of the Big Horn River, working north through a harsh, naked land, and were rewarded with some game. Skye first surveyed the sage flats, saw nothing menacing, and risked a shot with the Hawken. The boom emptied into silence, and a yearling mule deer crumpled. That midafternoon they filled themselves with the dark, soft meat, which they roasted on green willow sticks, and ate again at dusk, and again in the sharply chill morning. Summer was waning. They would sleep cold before they reached her people.

They traversed a depressing and monotonous basin, eating the venison, and then struck greener country east of the Beartooth Mountains. When they reached Clark's Fork of the Yellowstone, Skye knew they weren't far from Victoria's band. He had been there before with one of the brigades, and knew the country. The closer they walked toward the Yellowstone, the more exuberant Victoria became, sometimes laughing or talking softly to herself in her own tongue—the words sweet and melodious, utterly different from her harsh English. She bloomed, laughed, found prairie turnips and other edible roots Skye couldn't name, all the while helping him hunt and keep an eye out for trouble.

But as her spirits soared, his sank. His leggings were in tatters, begrimed and falling apart, rotting day by day, his fringed coat foul with grease. He would arrive in her village half-naked, filthy, unkempt, and starved to a shadow. He looked at his grimed buckskins, his hands caked with dirt for want of soap other than the thick root of the yucca she dug and pulverized for him, his greasy boots, his worn calico shirt, and he beheld a vagabond who had never escaped his misfortune. He had dreamed of triumph, of walking proudly through the camp behind the town crier, showing them all that their Many Quill Woman had a *man*.

Each day, the snowcapped blue peaks of the Beartooths loomed closer, while the Pryors vaulted smoothly upward in the east, and each night the cold crept deeper into their camp, forcing them to keep a fire going all night because they had nothing else with which to protect themselves. But the storms held off. There were always blessings, and one of them was a dry August and September.

The very hour they struck the stately Yellowstone, its icy waters braided by gravelly islands and its banks thick with cottonwoods, they discovered a distant party and hid on an island, unable to tell friend from foe. But they were not discovered. There would be traffic on that great artery, most of it unfriendly, and they would have to be much more careful.

Here game abounded, and they shot what they needed, while Skye worried about his declining supply of powder and ball. His pig of lead, bullet mold, and spare powder had all fallen into the hands of the Pawnees. He might have to buy powder from Beckwourth and watch the man laugh at him.

Still, it did no good to worry about the future. They were traversing grand country, the valley of the Yellowstone running here between tan sandstone cliffs, the bottoms green, the foothill slopes dotted with jackpine, the distant blue peaks noble and exhilarating. Already snow had crowned them, yet it was still summer in the river bottom.

This was Absaroka, land of the Crows, and this would be his

home, his refuge, for at least this winter, and maybe much longer. He realized that now Victoria was usually in front, ten or twenty paces ahead, whirling forward with a girlish joy at returning to her people. He rejoiced in her happiness, and yet it seemed to be saying that he wasn't enough; life with him didn't fulfill her. She needed her people even more. A worm of bitterness slid through him, but he dismissed it. He would not let some petty jealousy erode the bond that had transformed his life.

The Crows, this season, were at the great bend of the Yellowstone, the very spot where, in early 1827, he had found Sublette and the trapping brigade that saved his life. The place was a favorite resort of the Crows, abounding in game and good grass, as well as a safe and defensible site. Then, one glowing September day, they forded the Shields River flowing in from the north, hiked west a few more miles, and spotted the drifting smoke of cookfires.

Victoria was home. She laughed and cried, and urged Skye to hurry, hurry, that last mile along the river flats, across grassland and around mottes of cottonwood, past a multicolored herd of Crow ponies, until at last a village guard, a young member of one of the warrior societies, halted them, his gaze first on Skye and then on her.

"I am Many Quill Woman," she cried. "And you were just a boy when I went away."

Skye was able to follow that with his rude knowledge of her tongue.

"Yes, Grandmother, I am the younger son of Beaver Tail, and my mother is Iron Awl. And this is the man you went away with." His gaze, which raked Skye's bedraggled attire, said all too much.

"We have been insulted and robbed by the lying Pawnee," she retorted acidly. "Come, and I will tell the story to the elders and our great chief, Rotten Belly."

The youth nodded, turned his spotted pony, and accompanied the two visitors through the village, past smoke-stained lodges, tripods bearing medicine bundles, strips of buffalo and other meat drying upon racks, women fleshing buffalo hides staked to the earth, old men sunning, groups of younger men watching the hawks and passing a lit clay pipe from one to another, and women grinding up berries to put into pemmican, the trail food and winter emergency ration.

And with every step a crowd gathered behind them, some examining Skye's tattered buckskins with ill-concealed malice or horror. Was this the fate of the proud daughter of Walks Alone? The one who married the *mah-ish-ta-schee-da,* the yellow eyes, as these people called white men? Skye could do nothing to change their impression of him, so he ignored them all, anger brimming in him at his fate, and proceeded toward his ritual welcome into the village. His feelings were not far, just then, from the hard, isolated, savage feelings that had filled him during his endless captivity in the Royal Navy. He wouldn't let them bother him. He would live and fight and pay no attention to the contempt swirling around him.

Victoria's family engulfed her. Walks Alone, Digs the Roots, Arrow, Makes the Robe. She jabbered with them, their words tumbling so fast Skye couldn't make them out. But except for an occasional glance in his direction, they ignored him.

"Ah, Mister Skye, you fixing to pay your respects to Arapooish?"

Skye turned and found himself facing Jim Beckwourth, who smiled easily at him from coal oil eyes. The veteran mountaineer, known to these people as Antelope, certainly looked as though he owned the place, the ease and grace and status apparent in his finely wrought buckskins, which he wore with a certain flair, and his elaborate manners. Beckwourth had become a war leader, perhaps even a chief.

"I do know the tongue," Beckwourth said. "And even a smattering of your limey one. I'm delighted to see you here in this corner of paradise."

Skye followed Beckwourth toward the great lodge of the chief, located closer to the riverbank and surrounded by a half-moon of lodges that formed a park, or public square, around Arapooish's majestic twenty-one-pole lodge. Antelope walked with an easy grace, wearing his soft-tanned buckskins and Indian ornaments, including war honors, as if he had been born to these people.

Skye was tempted to explain his desperate circumstances to the mulatto—if that's what he was, which Skye doubted because the man showed no sign of mixed blood other than a somewhat swarthy complexion—but decided to narrate the story to the chief, if the chief wanted it. One thing Skye didn't want was sympathy, and neither did he want to make excuses. He had been outwitted by the Pawnees, was paying for his stupidity, and that was all there was to it.

"Well, Mister Skye, you've come a piece, I gather," Beckwourth said, probing.

"A piece."

"One's fortune reverses in the mountains. One moment, one is an emperor of the wilds, the next, one is a pauper. I have a certain small influence here, and perhaps I can be at your service."

"Perhaps you can, mate. We had a bit of misfortune."

Skye liked the Missourian, whose grace and choice of words bespoke education and breeding. Among the mountaineers, Beckwourth had won a reputation for courage, loyalty, and mountain skills. They said around the campfires that he was the son of a Virginia aristocrat, although he had grown up in frontier Missouri, where his father had brought the family.

"Pawnee lifted everything I possessed, except for my rifle, which was at hand."

"I thought it was something like that. Well, that's not unusual here. You have friends among the Crows, and I can no doubt supply you with some necessaries, including some DuPont and galena. I trade it, you know. I have some connections."

They found the Crow chief standing before his lodge

wrapped in a red blanket. Once again Skye marveled at the headman, who was huge, lean, rawboned, formidable, and whose gaze took in everything, not missing Sky's tatters. Around the chief the elders gathered, gray-haired men, patient, curious, and in no hurry.

The chief raised a palm in welcome, while Beckwourth translated. Skye wondered if the wily Missourian could be trusted not to embroider the story. Or invent one altogether. Beckwourth was a famous embroiderer, but no more so than half the men in the mountains. In the end, Skye decided he did trust the man. Antelope Jim actually was well known for fair dealing and honesty, and his wild yarns were well understood to be a form of entertainment not intended to be taken seriously.

"It is the husband of my brother's daughter, returning to us. You are welcome here. Come, you will tell us your story," Arapooish said. "But first, we will smoke."

It took the better part of an hour. They listened to Skye recount his story, his decision to come live with Victoria's people, the encounter with the Pawnees. In simple terms, he described his and Victoria's determined pursuit of the Pawnees, entering their camp, his effort to shame them into surrendering their booty—and his failure. Skye noticed that Victoria and her family had come and were among the auditors. That was good, he thought; it would keep Beckwourth's translation from meandering.

He glanced at the passive Crow faces around him, unable to fathom whether he was in disgrace or merely contemptible in their eyes. Every face was a mask, not least the chief's.

Then, the story done, Skye sought to retire from this august company. But the chief stayed him with a wave of the hand. Quietness settled over the throng. Children, grandmothers, sharp-eyed youths, old men, and impassive warriors stared at him.

"Now hear me," Arapooish said. "Mister Skye, you have

done a brave thing. The People will gladly help you. I will give you a new name. You will be known by it among us. You are now Man Not Afraid of the Pawnees."

Skye saw Victoria clap a hand to her mouth, and it dawned on him that the name was an honor. He might be dressed in tatters, but his name was gold.

six

James Beckwourth—also known as Medicine Calf, Antelope, Bull's Robe, Enemy of Horses, Red Fish, and Bobtail Horse—contemplated the fate of his old friend Skye and decided to help. The presence of Mister Skye in Rotten Belly's village would be a joy; a pair of white men whiling away the winter, lavishly entertained by adoring Crows.

Whatever the world said about Beckwourth's blood, he knew himself as a white. His father, Jennings Beckwith, came from Virginia aristocracy, while his mother was a quadroon, one-quarter black, and the intimate companion of his father for many years. It had been a marriage, though not one ever recorded or solemnized. Beckwith had raised his son as a white, teaching him his letters and making the youth a full member of the large family living on the harsh and dangerous Missouri frontier. Technically, even that bit of black blood made the boy a slave, but his father had, on three occasions, filed manumissions, making sure that Jim would be a free man.

Jim had come up the Missouri River and into the Rocky Mountains with the second of General William Ashley's fur-trapping expeditions, in the fall of 1824, served with Ashley and his successors, was a courageous and imposing trapper, fighter, and enterpreneur, well admired by all his mountain friends. He had come to the Rockies two years ahead of Skye but had made more of his sojourn, becoming by degrees one of the elite of the mountains, with all the prowess of Bridger, Fitzpatrick, Black Harris, or any of the other veterans of the wild whose very names struck awe in the greenhorns who occasionally drifted west.

Beckwourth had been familiar with the Crows from the beginning of his mountain life, and in 1828 he joined them. They thought of him as one of their own, having heard a wild tale from the veteran Caleb Greenwood that Beckwourth was a lost Crow child, found and raised by whites. His swart appearance did nothing to discredit the whimsical story that had started as a joke, and when Beckwourth did arrive in Arapooish's village he was greeted by his supposed father, Big Bowl, as a long-lost son and showered with robes, buckskins, furs—and women.

Since then, life had been a lark. Black Lodge, one of the most honored warriors in the village, gave his daughter Stillwater to Beckwourth for wife, but the Crows being Crows, Beckwourth soon acquired six or seven other women including his remarkable friend Pine Leaf, a lithe woman warrior. How could any mortal be so fortunate?

He, in turn, swiftly gathered that the way to progress from nonentity to honored member of the tribe was through war honors. So he organized raids against Crow enemies, especially the Blackfeet, stole horses, killed an occasional enemy warrior, counted coup, and performed deeds of derring-do that would be told and retold around tribal campfires and during councils. That was how he acquired all those names—honors, really, bestowed by a grateful chief upon an unusually gifted warrior who had come to live with the People. Beckwourth's leadership had enhanced the security and prowess of the Absarokas and made them a terror to their enemies.

From this pinnacle of success, Beckwourth eyed the newcomer, seeing a friend—and potential ally. Beckwourth had drifted far from his old friends who had come west with General Ashley to gather beaver pelts. He had joined the rival outfit, finding lucrative work with the Upper Missouri Outfit, that portion of the American Fur Company that had been purchased from John Jacob Astor by powerful entrepreneurs including the St. Louis Chouteaus and their French relations. They were mounting a ruthless assault on the Rocky Mountain Fur Company by building trading posts along the Missouri River and using them to penetrate the mountains and monopolize the lucrative beaver trade, which could yield a fortune to anyone with the nerve to take the terrible risk.

And they were paying Beckwourth handsome wages to steer Crows to American Fur's trading posts. His four hundred a year bought him every imaginable luxury among the supplies brought upriver by keelboat, including quantities of various fine liquors, all illegal in the Indian territories but a staple of American Fur Company's provisioning.

Beckwourth knew his man; Skye's affection for a jug of corn whiskey had become a byword of the rendezvous. And now a little of that elixir would, he figured, purchase a valuable ally. Thus did Skye appear one evening shortly after arriving in the village at Beckwourth's lodge, where Stillwater greeted him with a shy smile and then vanished.

"Ah, Mister Skye, I see your fortunes have improved. Here you are in fresh buckskins, with some meat on your ribs, and the world looking rather more amiable," Beckwourth said.

"It's that, mate," Skye agreed. "And thanks to some powder and lead from you, I've been able to help provision Victoria's family."

"But you're far from where you were."

"I'm a poor man, Jim. But I've been a poor man before."

"You lack a horse."

"I lack everything. I'm dependent on Victoria's people."

"That might be remedied."

"I intend to remedy it. I'll not be a beggar. I'm in debt to the new outfit, and I'll pay them."

"A worthy sentiment. We'll drink to it." Beckwourth rummaged among his possessions and extracted a jug. Smiling, he uncorked it and handed it to Skye. "Elixir, Mister Skye. A rare thing in the mountains except at rendezvous. I've been saving it for a special occasion, which is now."

Skye eyed the jug eagerly, and then guzzled and coughed.

"Bloody stuff," he muttered, wheezing. "It seems, ah, rather young."

"Very young. In fact, concocted this afternoon of grain spirits, a plug of tobacco, and assorted flavors."

"Trade whiskey."

"It brings in the beaver."

Skye wheezed. His eyes leaked. Beckwourth sipped lightly and returned the jug to Skye's eager grasp. Skye sucked hard, gasped, roared, wept, and coughed. "It'll be smooth sailing soon," he said. "But it takes a bit to put wind in the sails."

Beckwourth got down to business. "Mister Skye, what brought you to our fair metropolis?"

"Victoria. She was plumb lonesome for her people."

"Your loyalty's admirable. You gave up life with your friends, your boon companions, from the moment you walked into that rendezvous of eighteen and twenty-six. That's a moment I won't forget, you and the Shoshones. You excited some curiosity, my friend."

Skye took a swizzle, coughed, blinked, and smiled. "That juice is panther piss. Grizzly sow juice. It's a limey's paradise."

"Actually, it's castorum."

Skye coughed and laughed. Castorum was what mountaineers used to bait the beaver traps. "Mr. Beckwourth, what are we negotiating here?"

The man was not a lummox, Beckwourth thought.

"Perhaps a partnership."

"I'm partnered with Rocky Mountain Fur."

"I thought so. Are we rivals?"

"It looks that way."

"You were outfitted by Fitzpatrick, and in return you'll steer Crow trade toward RMFC. How much do you owe them?"

"Three hundred. Plus the trade goods I lost."

"And you've nothing for it, thanks to the Pawnees. A bit of a mess. Maybe something can be arranged."

"I'm already into you for powder and lead, Jim. There's a robe or two right there. No, nothing can be arranged."

"Why not? American Fur'll pay off your debt and outfit you; it'll be entirely honorable. You will meet your every obligation. And we'll simply steer peltries and trade to Fort Floyd. Kenneth McKenzie's going to be well stocked when he's done outfitting the post."

"Every obligation but one, mate. My word. Bridger, Fitzpatrick, Milt Sublette, Gervais, and Fraeb have my word."

Beckwourth smiled lightly. Skye was not a man who would tamper with his word. It was an asset in the man, and had been noticed in the mountains. "Then we'll be rivals. But I doubt that you'll deliver one pelt to your colleagues."

Skye shrugged, remained silent, and swallowed one last gulp. Then Beckwourth corked the jug and slipped it into a parfleche.

"Mr. Beckwourth, you set a fine table."

They laughed.

"My friend Barnaby, how are you going to deliver? You've an obligation you can't possibly meet. You've not a trap or a horse. You have no influence. You've no reputation among these warriors. You walked off with one of the prettiest girls in the village and made enemies. But now you're going to persuade the whole Crow nation to trade with your fur company, which doesn't even have a trading post."

"I fled the Royal Navy with much less than I have now."

"I'll give you some advice. The way a young man advances among the Absaroka is by war honors, counting coup, proving himself an effective warrior and defender of the People. Now, rivals we may be, but I'm always looking for good fighting men to go with me on raids. Maybe you'll make some progress. I'm a war leader. I'll invite you next time I go out. You want horses? The Blackfeet and Sioux have a-plenty. Yours for the stealing—if you don't get killed. You want influence? Count coup, take a few scalps, beat an enemy. You want power? Shoot buffalo and give the meat away. You want plenty of women—the women here'll throw themselves at you, the fairest maidens, all yours—"

"I have Victoria, mate."

"But surely—Skye, there's not a virtuous woman in the Crow nation. They don't believe in it. They expect you to dally with them. Pretty soon Victoria'll find her pleasures, and you'll find yours."

Skye stood suddenly, his face dark with something, and he plunged into the twilight.

Beckwourth smiled. There were white men like that. A few months in Absaroka, and they were all transformed. The Crows played an amusing mating game, serial adventures, one after another. What else was there to do all winter? By his own reckoning, Beckwourth had shared his robes with seven such beauteous and available ladies—and could have enjoyed a dozen more were it not for his fascination with that lithe cat of a woman, Pine Leaf. She was the storied woman warrior of the Crows, the slim terror at his side in battle who had twice saved his life. And the only Absaroka woman who held herself aloof from his formidable charms. At least, so far.

Well, Skye would soon learn how life was lived among the Crows. And then he would forget about steering beaver to the opposition. War and women; Beckwourth had plenty of both and intended to have even more.

seven

Skye felt the rough bark of the cottonwood against his back and the sharp September air eddy around his beard as he watched twilight thicken over the Crow village just below. This brow of a hill had become a favorite resort of his, a place to think and plan and hope. Sometimes Victoria joined him there, but not often. He saw little of her; it was as if she had returned to her life as a Crow maiden, almost as if he didn't exist.

Perhaps he didn't. He wondered whether their union had been a mistake. Things had been difficult ever since he and she arrived in Rotten Belly's village with little more than the clothes on their backs. Her parents had provided them with a home, but even that was awkward. According to custom, he could not address his mother-in-law, and his marriage was suffering. He could not bring himself to make love to Victoria while her parents and a sister slept a few feet away, not even though that was perfectly acceptable and expected among them.

He had learned the Crow tongue to some degree, but that didn't make him a friend of other young men his age, who preferred to socialize with their own kind. He talked with Beckwourth now and then, which helped mitigate the loneliness he felt. He knew now how Victoria had felt during their years with the trapping brigades. She had been desolately alone among white men. Now it was his turn.

The oncoming cold worried him. Even now, in the twilight, he felt its bite. The peaks had already been dusted with white. He had only an old summer robe for warmth, which he wrapped about him as he contemplated his fate. Below, the cookfires glowed and blue smoke eddied over the camp. The village of the Kicked-in-the-Bellies was a happy place, strong, secure, and comfortable there on the big bend of the Yellowstone. The beauty of it struck him; there, in a corner of the mountains, layer upon layer of blue and black vaulted upward, while at his feet lay an orderly collection of tawny lodges, their tops blackened by smoke. The Yellowstone glinted in the last light, while the reflections of the first stars danced on its swift dark water.

He had spent his days hunting on foot because he lacked a horse, and he had occasionally made meat for Victoria's family. In those cases he usually borrowed a packhorse, one that would tolerate the smell of blood and death, and if he was lucky—mostly he wasn't—he brought back his quarry, usually a mule deer. These additions to the larder were welcomed, and the hides, which Victoria tanned, kept him in powder and lead and moccasins. Beckwourth bought any dressed skin that Skye could provide.

But it wasn't much of a life, and with winter racing toward him, he ached for a lodge, some horses, a pile of blankets, some thick buffalo robes—and privacy. He hardly knew where to turn.

He watched a lean figure toil up the slope toward him, and recognized Beckwourth. The man who had adopted these people as his own dressed like them. His long hair had been coiled into a knot at the nape of his neck, and from it poked two eagle feathers, his war honors. He had wrapped himself in a red Hudson's Bay blanket with black stripes.

"Knew you'd be here, Mister Skye," he said.

Skye nodded and motioned Beckwourth to sit.

"I'm taking a little party out in the morning, and thought to invite you. I'll lend you a horse and saddle, and I expect before we're through you'll have several more. We're heading north, toward the Musselshell or the Judith country, and our plan is to reduce the horse herds of the Blackfeet, count some coup, and make all the mischief we can. It's a grand opportunity for a man to win some prestige and maybe walk off with all the booty he can handle. You might even get a lodge out of it. Should be a lark, Barnaby. I'm taking twenty men, the best in the village, including Rotten Belly's sons. You be ready at dawn. Should be out four or five days. I'll bring a good robe for you. You'll have a chance to use that mighty Hawken if all goes well."

"And if it doesn't?"

Beckwourth smiled. "You'll have even more chance to use the Hawken."

"I don't look for chances to use my Hawken on two-legged game."

"Well, it isn't likely."

"Let me think on it. I'll let you know directly."

Beckwourth nodded and retreated down the slope.

A bold band of blue behind the western ridges was all that remained of this day. Skye knew that before that sliver of light disappeared, he would have to make a fateful decision.

He watched Beckwourth stroll down the slope and felt that he was being pushed into a corner. He had known this decision would come sooner or later, but he was still unprepared for the moment.

He sat in the gathering chill, his eyes on the winking cookfires but his mind elsewhere. He remembered the Kaffir wars, fought in the name of empire, planned and executed by the lords of the Horse Guards. The sailors and marines had traveled upriver, pursuing the bloody natives until the Kaffirs turned the tables on them and nearly enveloped the whole force. A hail of spears had decimated the marines; the fierce natives had then attacked with machetelike weapons that could slice off an arm or cut a head in two. Many a jack-tar and red-coat had died in those weeks, all for empire.

He had fought Burmese river pirates from 'tween decks, watching shot pour through the gun ports, rake his shipmates, blind Will Fellowes, pulp the face of Higgins, blow off Billy Burns's right hand. All for the Crown. He had watched maimed men, the detritus of war, receive their discharges and begin a life as mendicants, wearing their medals on their shabby coats. No hope. He had seen tears, heard howls of pain, listened to the onslaught of death as it captured a man. He had held a dying seaman named Harry Combs in his lap while the man sobbed out the Lord's Prayer and bled out his life.

No, he didn't like war. But that didn't mean he wouldn't fight. It only meant that there had to be grave reasons, larger than commerce or personal honors. That was a distinction the Crows didn't understand. For them, waging war, stealing horses, trapping enemy hunters, all had a preemptive quality: do that to the Siksika or Lakota, and the Absarokas would be all the safer.

But which side had started it? And was a horse raid offense or defense? A new provocation or a retaliation for old troubles? The tribes didn't lack scores to settle. He had always believed he would fight ferociously in defense of those he loved, but he would never start a war. But that didn't make sense out here, when strife among the tribes was ongoing, unending, deadly, and involved the very survival of each tribe. His old, European notions of just war didn't work very well here in a wild land where a tribe warred or died away.

There might be good in it, as Beckwourth predicted. He might return in a few days with horses, a captured lodge, scalps, prestige, power, wealth, medicine, and a say in village councils. He might yet be able to serve Rocky Mountain Fur, repay the lost trade goods, win the respect and allegiance of the war chiefs, Rotten Belly, the headmen and shamans, and bring them all to rendezvous next year with loads of pelts to trade. That would be a grand thing, leading the Crow nation to the rendezvous and the trading tent. If he could do that, the Rocky Mountain Fur Company would forgive him what he had lost.

The night had lowered. He stood, stretched the stiffness from him, wrapped his summer robe about him, and descended into the village, enjoying the savory tang of the woodsmoke in the still air. He paused at Beckwourth's lodge to tell him that he would be ready at dawn, and went to his people. He found Victoria in her parents' lodge and decided to bare the issue at once.

"Beckwourth invited me to go on a horse raid at dawn—and I will go."

She stared at him, the firelight glinting in her black eyes.

"I'm not one for picking fights. But this will help your nation. There are a lot more Lakota and Siksika than there are Absaroka. Maybe I can help even things up." He smiled tentatively.

She beamed, delight swimming in her face.

"I'll need to borrow some things. A horse, for one. A robe."

"I will ask."

"I might not come back."

"You have bear medicine, Skye."

He needed more than bear medicine. The Blackfeet fielded some of the best mounted warriors in the world, and the seaman Skye knew he was no match with lance, club, arrow, or sheer horsemanship. He wished he had her easy confidence, but he didn't.

Victoria's mother ignored him, as she was required to do, but Victoria's father eyed him amiably from his place of honor at the rear of the lodge. With a glance at Victoria, Skye explained his intent to her father and asked for those things he might need in war: a fast horse, a war club, a robe to cover him at night.

"And what does your medicine say, Man Not Afraid of the Pawnee?"

"Grandfather, I have not examined my medicine."

"Your ways are strange to us. When you know, come to me."

Skye understood. He would seek help. He pulled aside the lodge flap and walked into a chill night. He needed to find a small gift, anything, and remembered what had been warmly appreciated before. He hiked into the murky cottonwoods, waited for his eyes to adjust, and then hacked at dead limbs with his hatchet until he had an armload.

These he carried to the small, isolated lodge that was the sole worldly possession of the seer, Red Turkey Head. He scratched gently on the lodge, the polite way of announcing himself, and eventually heard the old man's voice inviting him in.

He ducked inside and found the frail old man sitting in a cold lodge, entirely without light.

"It is the husband of Many Quill Woman, Grandfather," he said. "I have brought you some wood."

"Build a fire so I can see you. Then we will smoke."

Skye did, patiently striking sparks into tinder, until finally a tiny pinch of it glowed, driving the darkness back. He blew on it until it burst into a tiny flame, and swiftly added twigs. It took a long time to build a lodge fire for the old man, and even then the icy lodge didn't warm much.

In time, the fire burned merrily in its pit, but the old man didn't seem to notice. Skye realized Red Turkey Head was not far from blindness.

They smoked, and then the shaman waited.

"I will go with Antelope on a horse raid, Grandfather," he began. "They ask me what my medicine tells me."

"Grizzly bear medicine."

"I don't follow you, Grandfather."

"Yours is the way of the bear."

Skye touched his bear claw necklace, symbol of honor and power among these people. "Sometimes I am a bear, Grandfather, and sometimes I am not."

"No, Man Not Afraid of the Pawnees, you have the bear spirit. That is your path. I will tell the war leaders that you follow the way of the bear."

That puzzled Skye. "What is the way of the bear?"

The old man coughed. "The bear fattens in the fall, before he goes to sleep."

Skye waited, quietly.

"It is right for you to go with Antelope. You saw truly that this is so. Follow your path, Man Not Afraid of the Pawnees. You will become a blessing for the People. Go now, and tell Walks Alone I wish to talk with him. I will tell Walks Alone that his daughter's man follows the way of the bear, and it is a good way, and he will be proud of his daughter's man."

eight

Skye marveled at Beckwourth. The war leader had an unerring instinct about where to find their quarry. For three days, Beckwourth had taken them north, arriving one noon in a mountain-girt basin he called the Judith country. The whole grassy plain was dotted with buffalo as far as the eye could see.

"Where there's meat, there's Blackfeet," he told Skye. He led them west, staying low and out of sight, every warrior alert. By dusk they had reached a rough water-chiseled land under a brooding butte, a place somehow melancholic and foreboding. That was when Bad Heart, one of the Absaroka warriors, paused, sniffed, and announced that smoke was on the breeze, which was eddying in from the northwest.

"We are close," Beckwourth said. "And now, Barnaby, you will see a horse raid. Somewhere nearby, probably in a river valley we'll reach shortly, we'll find a hunting party hunkered down for the night out of sight of the buffalo so as not to alarm the herd. They'll have their best runners with them. A good buffalo runner knows how to gallop close to a running buffalo so the rider can sink an arrow into the sweet spot. They're fast, and they're valuable—and they'll be ours!"

Skye nodded. Night settled while Beckwourth held his warriors in a small hollow, well hidden. Then, in full dark, he led them north again, through a chill night when the stars glimmered in moving air. He left the group and went ahead on foot, returning a half hour later.

"Just as I figured," he said to Skye. Then in the Absaroka tongue, which Skye could at least follow, he explained. The Blackfeet were camped in a creek bottom hemmed between steep bluffs, out of sight of the buffalo. Their horses were being kept in a natural canyon with night herders penning them in. Two prized horses were in the camp itself, saddled and ready for emergencies. There looked to be about fifteen Blackfoot hunters at the fire, plus two herders keeping an eye on the horses, which weren't picketed because they were in a natural pen. But he found a rough passage to the top of the bluffs; the horses could be stampeded up and out. He and several Crows would descend on foot, surprise the herders, and drive the horses over the top. Others, on top, would steer the stolen horses south.

"And you, Barnaby, will settle on the edge of the bluff where you can see the camp and keep 'em pinned down with that big Hawken of yours. Shoot anyone who tries to follow."

Skye nodded.

After that, the long wait began. Beckwourth didn't want to start the affray until the Siksika were asleep and the night was well along. Skye sat quietly, his back to a tree, wondering whether he could shoot a buffalo-hunting Blackfoot who was simply gathering meat for his people. He had shot at Indians many times, and yet this was different. Always, in the past, he had shot to defend himself and whoever he was with. But not this time.

His bones ached from the cold, and time dragged. But finally Beckwourth nodded. His party left their horses with young horse-holders and crept into place. Skye settled on the bluff, trying to locate the camp in the deep mysterious dark, wondering whether the Blackfeet had more sentries out and whether he would find out too late—when a knife or arrow pierced him. Some embers glowed; a sliver of moon gave just enough light to see the vague shape of things.

He waited tensely, hearing soft disturbances in the dark, then the movement of many horses, and suddenly, the victorious howls of the Crows. Everything happened at once. The Blackfoot herd stampeded up the bluff, Crow horsemen on top steered it south, the sleeping camp erupted, and Skye saw faint, blurred movement below. A Blackfoot untied his pony and swung onto it to give pursuit. Skye shot, dropping the horse and throwing the rider. The boom of the Hawken changed the complexion of the night. Swiftly he moved to a new locale, knowing his muzzle flash had revealed his position, reloaded, and fired at another mounted rider giving chase. He missed. He reloaded again, and shot a third time, right into the embers, which shot sparks and light into the dusky camp. Other Blackfeet were running, gathering quivers and bows and lances, hunting for horses, swarming toward their herders, who lay in the grass, either dead or dying.

He'd seen enough. The Crows and Beckwourth were already half a mile away, and Skye knew he would have to get out fast. He reloaded, trotted back from the rim, mounted his borrowed horse, and rode south, steering his horse toward the howling of the Crows and the thunder of the stolen herd. A while later he caught up and rode down the long dark night to the music of the hooves.

Thus they traveled until exhaustion overtook them and Beckwourth decided they were out of danger. They rested until dawn and then examined their booty. Forty-one horses, some of them magnificent. One scalp, too. And several coups. No losses, no wounds. A great victory! Beckwourth had proven his medicine prowess once again.

"That big mountain rifle of yours kept 'em at bay, Barnaby," Beckwourth said. "You did just fine. You've won some war honors now."

"I think we were lucky," Skye said.

Beckwourth laughed. "Look at those ponies," he said. "There's some buffalo runners in there. That's more horses than we've gotten out of a raid in a long time."

The multicolored horses did look magnificent. Some of them bore the medicine markings of their owners; a white handprint on the chest, or yellow stripes painted on the side, or amulets plaited into their tails. One magnificent black caught Skye's eye. He would give anything to own that one.

The solemn Crow warriors kept a sharp lookout for pursuit, but no one came, and late one October afternoon they returned to the Kicked-in-the-Belly village. Beckwourth was ebullient. As far as Skye could fathom, the rest took war too seriously to exult, but he did catch the flash of joy and pride in their eyes. The Siksika had lost a lot of horses and one herder. The other herder, it turned out, had warded off his assailant and fled into the darkness. A victory, yes. But there would be revenge, somehow, someplace, and the tables would be turned.

They paused just outside their village. Skye watched the warriors paint up, using the small kits of paint they had taken with them. They would enter the village in triumph this time, wearing their medicine insignia, wearing their war honors. They didn't neglect their horses either. They groomed the ponies and painted them. This would be a great day for these people. Skye watched, sensing how important this ritual was to these fellow warriors, sensing the pride, status, power, and honor attached to this ritual. But Beckwourth outdid them all, garbing himself like an oriental potentate.

When at last they were ready, Skye marveled. These warriors reminded him of a hundred bagpipers in their plaid kilts, their pipes howling defiance and death. What was grander than a victorious army dressed for a parade?

Villagers swarmed to meet the victorious warriors, crowding the lane leading to Chief Rotten Belly's lodge, where they would each, under the seal of absolute truth, tell their tales to the elders, the chiefs, the shamans, and the delirious crowd who had come to celebrate. At first the village women looked sharply for signs of tragedy, the empty saddle, the horse carrying a burden, a wounded man, death painted upon the faces and chests of these greathearted men. But they found none. This party had gone out into the dangerous world and returned in glory, driving forty-one horses before it. Nineteen men, forty-one warhorses that had once belonged to the despised and dangerous Siksika. Forty-one duns, browns, chestnuts, appaloosas, paints, and the proud black, as dark as coal, that walked with an easy gait and a calm that wasn't evident in some of the other nervous animals. That one fired Skye's imagination, and he felt a pang. There was a horse.

Leading this marvelous assemblage was Beckwourth himself, grinning, wearing the softest white buckskins, a bone necklace over his chest, his hair tucked into a knot that bore two downturned eagle feathers, white and black. A scarlet sash completed his ensemble. He was thoroughly enjoying himself and absorbing the waves of acclaim that washed over him as he passed women and children, old men, yearning boys, and even the blind, who had been led to the parade so they, too, might experience this splendid event.

Skye rode through the village, marveling at the uproar. Horses neighed and whickered, boys yelled, women howled, the town crier, leading this assemblage, bellowed his news and repeated it. Across the way, Skye spotted Victoria, her face flushed with joy, eyes shining, her gaze rapt as she absorbed this great moment of triumph. Her eyes were on the gaudy Beckwourth, but then she spotted Skye and smiled. He nodded to her, enjoying her delight. She was with several other young matrons, a flock of them, crooning their joy.

Beckwourth smiled at many women, and Skye knew that every smile was an invitation and that the Crows sometimes could not count the presence of one virtuous woman in a village. It galled him suddenly. Where was faithfulness and loyalty among these wanton people? He eyed her darkly, hoping that four good years had forged a bond.

At the lodge of Arapooish the crowd collected to hear the

whole story. The chief wore a single braid this day, which fell loosely over his brown chest. He wore only his breechclout and leggings, though the air nipped at him. One thing about old Rotten Belly, Skye thought: the man had a certain presence. He looked like a chief, acted like a chief, inspired confidence and awe, as a great chief should.

In a leisurely way, playing to the eager crowd, Beckwourth described the foray. Three suns to the north, in the rough country near Square Butte, they had spied a herd of buffalo one evening, and also a hunting party camped on a creek. They were Piegans planning a good hunt at dawn when they would have light enough to make meat. Some Piegan boys guarded the herd, which had been nicely pinned into a creek bottom by bluffs that were almost impossible to scale. . . .

This was a great victory, better than any so far this season, and Arapooish commended each of them and gave Beckwourth a new name, Night Man.

Beckwourth, still astride his prancing brown, raised a hand. "To each of my brave warriors, I give two ponies. To my friend Mister Skye, husband of Many Quill Woman, I give two horses. The black horse to ride, and another to pack. Two horses do I give the young man who has come to live among the Absaroka."

The people relished that. Any grand act appealed to them. They exclaimed. Victoria sighed, her eyes more on Beckwourth than upon Skye.

"Take the black and pick a horse, Mister Skye," Beckwourth said in the Crow tongue.

Skye did, easing into the herd, finding a braided halter on the calm black. The horse led easily. He chose an ordinary dun for the second horse, not wanting to deprive any of these worthy fighters of a coveted animal.

"Mr. Beckwourth," he said. "I thank you. You do yourself honor. With these I will hunt the buffalo and bring meat to this village. You have made me a wealthy man."

"It is well said," Arapooish added. "We will dance this night."

The crowd returned to the cook pots and lodges while Skye gently worked his hands over the powerful black, admiring the strength of the stallion, its graceful stance.

"Sonofabitch," said Victoria. "Some damn horse."

"Tomorrow I'll put it and the packhorse to good use."

"Antelope looked so proud. Was ever there such a warrior? I saw the sun pouring from his eyes."

She was paying too much attention to Beckwourth. Or was he paying too much attention to her? The prettiest, most desired maiden in the village not long before? She was even more the beauty after a few years with Skye. Something dark stabbed at him, and he pushed it aside as unworthy jealousy.

She smiled, winked, patted him on the arm, and drifted off. She had been like that lately, not unhappy with him but distant, absorbed in the thousand strands of life that occupied her village.

That evening he borrowed a pad saddle and braided hackamore and tried out his new horse. It glided easily, turned obediently, stopped with the slightest tug of the rein. He urged it into a trot, then a fine, powerful gallop, and knew he had a fleet horse, probably a buffalo runner, and that he could trust it. He wasn't much of a horseman, having spent most of his years imprisoned on a sailing ship, but ever since joining the trapping brigades he had made a point of learning what he could, mastering horses, grasping their nature, riding, packing, picketing, grooming, caring for their feet. He was a passable horseman, but less a hand with a horse than any of these warriors, who had made horses an extension of themselves, so that warrior and pony became a single entity.

He examined the packhorse, too, satisfied that it would carry whatever burdens he placed upon it. Then he took the horses out to pasture in the hills north of the river, intending to leave them with the horse herd guards, doubled this night because of the possibility of retaliation. On second thought, he decided to tie them at the lodge. Early, before the village stirred, he would be off on a hunt. With each buffalo or elk or deer, he added to the security of these people.

In the darkness he summed up his perceptions. He had done well this trip, won war honors, obtained two fine horses, and gained some status in the village. But Beckwourth had gained much more by leading a spectacular raid without any loss, by bringing back many horses, and by giving Skye the black, the best horse of all. The Crows loved a magnanimous giver.

Skye wondered if he could ever overtake his rival.

nine

The next dawn Skye saddled the sleek black, haltered the dun, and rode into the sunrise. Victoria's family still slumbered in their lodge. Not a soul stirred. Smoke drifted from the blackened tips of a few lodges. When he reached the periphery of the silent village a subtle change came over him. He was abandoning its safety and plunging into an uncertain and dangerous wilderness. Frost rimed the brown grasses. It would be a fine day to hunt.

This day he would try to find game and contribute to the well-being of the Kicked-in-the-Bellies. That would not be easy. The band had been at the great bend of the Yellowstone for some while, and the country had been hunted out. Soon they would make their winter camp in the Big Horn basin, but for the moment they would remain in their favorite grounds.

He enjoyed the powerful walk of his black horse. The animal seemed as eager for adventure as he. This was as much a journey to improve his condition as it was an effort to make meat. The Crows honored a good hunter, though perhaps not as much as a successful warrior. Skye had no great hunting skills because he had spent so much of his life as a sailor, but he had determination and that would suffice. The nippy air exhilarated him, and the bountiful and everlasting land, layered in blues and purples and browns, evoked within him a feeling so rare that he reined the horse briefly just to treasure the moment. Here he was, a free man, living entirely by his wits, rejoicing to be alive.

He began to study the ground, looking for the signs of passage: the delicate hoofprint of a mule deer in the frost; the nobler prints of an elk; the surprisingly delicate prints of a massive buffalo. He found nothing, but didn't really expect to. Part of the joy of the hunt was the search, he against nature under the bowl of a bright autumn sky. What more could a man ask?

Still, as he worked eastward along the Yellowstone, he found no sign of game. He paused at a spot where the river glittered over some shallows, and decided to ford it and work his way up into the foothills, far from the great artery of the river.

The well-trained black took to the ford without balking, but Skye had to tug the lead rope of the dun. They crossed without getting into deep water because the river was at its seasonal low, and he rode up a creek valley. He had learned much in his four years on the wild continent; everything meant something. The sudden bolt of a bird, silence, the circling of hawks, the skimming of hills by a hunting eagle, all signaled things that could scarcely be translated to words. By noon he still had found no game. He paused under a barren cottonwood to let the horse graze and to let the faint warmth of the mild sun permeate his soft buckskins.

He rode through an afternoon without luck. Once he saw some tan-and-white antelope on a distant slope, but they edged away as he drew close. Then he saw a pair of gray mule deer at the edge of an aspen grove. But they vanished.

He walked his horse across drainage, topping ridges, looking for some shaggier, as the mountaineers called buffalo, but this was not his day. When the sun began to drop to the western mountains, he hastened back to the village, his Hawken unfired. It had, actually, been a splendid day, one he cherished. But he would enter the village once again with nothing to show for his effort.

He placed his gear in the lodge of his in-laws, hung his sheathed Hawken from the lodgepoles, and slipped on his camp moccasins while carefully avoiding his mother-in-law. They saw he had nothing to show for the day's hunt, but said nothing. Walks Alone gestured toward the iron kettle that contained a supper, but Skye declined. Victoria wasn't present. He retreated into the sharp air, took his horses to pasture—a mile from the village now because every patch of grass had been grazed into the dirt—and entrusted them to the herders, doubled now because these people feared Blackfoot retaliation.

Skye walked back to the village in gathering darkness, straight to the small lodge of Beckwourth, certain she would be there. He scratched on the lodge flap politely, listening to the muffled chatter within. One thing about Beckwourth: he was a spellbinder in several tongues.

"Come in, Skye," he said, and Skye wondered how Beckwourth knew who was there. A tiny fire, no larger than a teacup, illuminated the lodge. And there was Beckwourth, Stillwater, Pine Leaf, Walks Into Wind—and Victoria.

"Home is the hunter. Loaded down with meat," Beckwourth said, swiftly surveying Skye.

"Not this time." Skye turned to Victoria. "Your family has meat in the pot."

She shook her head. "I have eaten, Mister Skye. Antelope has given us buffalo tongue."

Skye bit back the anger in him. He nodded curtly.

"Have some, *amigo,*" Beckwourth said.

Skye teetered on the brink of stalking out, but finally surrendered to his complaining belly and fished some slabs of fine, juicy tongue out of the blackened iron kettle.

"Antelope has told us of the great whiskered fish in the land where he was a boy," Victoria said, making peace. "It is all lies. There are no such fish."

Beckwourth smiled, his coal eyes glowing. "I'll take you there and show you, my beautiful friend."

Skye bridled. The man was flirting with his wife right in

front of his face. Was this how it would be in this village? He chewed on the meat, anger percolating through him. Beckwourth would drive him to a showdown some time soon. All this was deliberate. Beckwourth was making a show of his position and power and gallantry.

Nothing in Skye's life had prepared him for this sort of threat. His years as a pressed seaman had plunged him into an all-male world. Women were mysteries. Victoria was the only one he had ever been close to, and she was a Crow, whose ways he barely understood. During his years with the trapping brigades, none of the trappers had ever crossed a certain line; he and Victoria had been serene in their marriage and companionship, and the mountaineers honored their union. But here was Antelope Jim, enjoying Victoria, winning her smiles, and probably enjoying Skye's discomfort.

Skye choked back his anger and anxiety, and tried to make himself at home around that tiny fire, which Beckwourth occasionally replenished from a small pile of kindling.

"Victoria is the most beautiful thing that ever happened to me," Skye said quietly. "I met her at that first rendezvous and loved her from the moment I saw her." He gazed quietly at his wife. "And I think she felt the same way about me. We couldn't even talk with each other, and yet we communicated. These have been the best years of my life."

Victoria rewarded him with a smile, and for a moment he thought everything was fine.

"I envy you," Beckwourth said. "So fair a woman, the dream of every fine young man in the village. Truly, Victoria, you had your choice of anyone here. And you chose my most estimable British friend. Let me get out the jug, and we will toast Victoria."

"No," said Skye. "We will not toast Victoria now."

Victoria glanced back and forth, not quite sure of what was happening here, spoken in the English she little understood.

"She chose me, mate," Skye said, an edge in his voice.

"Ah, Skye," she said. "I remember."

"Let's go, Victoria."

"But, Skye, we haven't even started telling stories yet."

Skye knew that storytelling was one of the great entertainments of these people—and that no one told a better, funnier, wilder story than his rival across the little fire.

"I thought we'd take a walk. And then go to the robes. I'll be hunting again in the morning."

"Ah, the robes!" she said, and everyone laughed. "You go sleep, Skye. I will listen to stories."

"Victoria. We'll go now."

She smiled at him across the tiny fire and didn't stir.

"Have a good hunt, old friend," Beckwourth said, something calculating in his face.

Skye was suddenly aware that he wasn't really wanted there—and that the moment he departed they would be talking in the Absaroka tongue again, and that later in the night the stories would become bawdier, which was how the Crows amused themselves. He had heard these stories, some of them wildly inventive, some thinly disguised gossip, all of them told in mixed company, which embarrassed him acutely. And where did they lead? In the end, to liaisons, the participants eyeing each other contemplatively through the storytelling, their bodies howling to them.

And there he was. He had just dealt himself out. The dreaded possibility that Victoria would succumb, or abandon him, or return to her people's ways, ate at him like acid as he nodded curtly and retreated into the night. He had rarely felt so stupid or jealous.

The night sky was clean and black, with hard white stars stabbing light from the dome of heaven. He stumbled through a hushed blackness with nothing to light the way. Most lodge fires were out, and no moon guided him. The night was as desolate as his soul.

Still, he had acquitted himself well. He had told Beckwourth, with all the dignity he could muster and all the earnestness in his soul, that he loved Victoria and prized her above everything else in his life. Surely his friend—if Beckwourth could be called that—would respect that. Surely Victoria would, too. . . .

He stumbled across the rim of a lodge and veered into the night, hoping his eyes would adjust. So black was this cold night that he feared he would wander into the wrong lodge. They looked alike in the darkness, vague cones with a forest of poles on top. He paused, trying to orient himself. He was lost in his own village. More by instinct than by sorting things out, he veered leftward, somehow made out Walks Alone's lodge, and crawled through the flap into the utter darkness, enjoying the sudden warmth that persisted even though the fire had long since died. No one stirred. He crawled to his robes—borrowed robes, actually, provided by his wife's parents—and dug into them. But he could not sleep. He tried hard to banish the terrible fantasies crawling across his mind: Victoria and Beckwourth, Victoria and Beckwourth, his friend and his wife . . .

She did not come home, and he did not sleep.

ten

Skye awakened with the first hint of light up in the smoke hole. Victoria lay beside him. He wondered when she had come home and why he hadn't noticed. The evening's dreads eddied through him. Had that damned Beckwourth seduced her? Did she still love him?

He swung out of his robes, pulled on his worn moccasins, and crawled outside into a predawn half-light. The camp stank in the still air. Why hadn't Rotten Belly moved it? Skye walked down to the river and relieved himself, feeling his joints ache from the chill. He would hunt again this day.

He stood there in that terrible quiet, wanting succor. Where was God? In that faint band of blue light to the southeast? Skye prayed briefly, hardly knowing what to say to a deity who could give him anything he asked for—but didn't. "Send me a buffalo, so that I may win the esteem of my hosts. I don't know these people; guide me through the eye of the needle."

He sensed the presence of someone beside him and discovered Victoria's father, Walks Alone. "I will hunt with you today," he said.

"I would like that."

"I will show you things. We will talk."

Skye sensed that all this was good. Maybe the shaman, Red Turkey Head, had said something. Maybe Walks Alone had simply taken things into his own hands. They would talk. Skye could grasp the Absaroka tongue after four years with Victoria, but his father-in-law knew no English. They would get along, and there were the hand signs to fall back on.

They walked together out to the herd and nodded to the sole night herder. Skye found and caught his black easily, but couldn't locate the dun in the half-light. Walks Alone caught his best horse, a buffalo runner, and a packhorse as well. In a while, when the sun rested coyly beneath the horizon, they rode north up the Shields River valley, staying close to the western foothills.

Walks Alone carried a full quiver on his back and his bow in hand. Skye carried his Hawken in his fringed and quilled sheath, hung from the saddle and tucked under his leg. They didn't speak, content with the companionable silence, their senses alert for game. But there would be nothing so close. A hundred hunters a day had streamed out of the village for months, many in this direction.

When the sun finally broke over the eastern mountains, tinting the sky blue and the vast countryside brown and black, the mood changed. A day had begun.

"Among the People," Walks Alone said, "a man with a disobedient wife is without face. The village makes jokes about such a one, and the jokes are cruel. Many Quill Woman does not obey you."

Skye felt a certain helplessness. "And how do I make her obey?"

"You must punish her."

"Is that how the People do it?"

"Yes, it is the custom to beat a woman who does not obey."

"We are talking about my wife?"

"You must beat her. Then she will respect you."

"Then she might run away to someone else."

"That would be good; you would no longer suffer such shame."

Skye digested all that, his instincts rebelling against it.

"Among yellow eyes, it is rarely done, Grandfather." He used the term of utmost respect, "grandfather," which designated his father-in-law as a teacher, a wisdom giver.

"How do your women respect you, then? And why do we never see a pale woman? Yellow eyes hide them from us, and we think maybe you have none and want our women."

"There are many pale women. The man is the head of the marriage but the woman is not a slave, and she may do what she will. A husband and wife become companions and make decisions together."

"Among the People it is done differently. A man must protect his family, and they must be obedient for their own safety."

"Grandfather, is it not the right of each of the People to follow his own path? I follow my path—that which has been given to me by my own people."

Walks Alone nodded. "That is your right. But it won't protect you from gossip or malice among the Absaroka. There is much gossip about you and Many Quill Woman. It brings unhappiness to my lodge."

Skye scarcely knew how to respond to that. It had not been easy to live with these Absarokas. A lodge offered no privacy. People lived in unusual intimacy. Skye had not enjoyed Victoria's embrace since they had moved into her parents' eighteen-pole lodge. Two sisters, a grandfather, her parents, and assorted visitors conspired to ruin his lovemaking. Once, when he and Victoria had ridden through the narrows where the Yellowstone burst out of the mountains, they had come to a sunny meadow, got off their ponies, and joined together with all the old fire and joy.

But the family had not shared Skye's compunctions. Often, at night, he could hear Walks Alone and Digs the Roots coupling just a few feet from him, sometimes screened by a hide barrier strung up in the evening, sometimes not. The women went about their toilet nonchalantly, as if Skye weren't there. The daily cycle of life within the lodge hinged on the master's whim. When Walks Alone felt like sleeping, he put no more wood in the fire and drew his robes around him. The rest did, too. When Walks Alone felt like staying up, the rest stayed up. When any had to get up in the night, the fact was known to all. Walks Alone's elderly father, Standing Weasel, wandered in and out all night. All that had been hard enough, but the custom prohibiting Skye from addressing his mother-in-law, or even gazing directly at her, complicated matters all the more.

He was mad with need for privacy, wild to possess a lodge of his own, a sanctuary for Victoria and himself. He had been catapulted from years on board a royal warship with no family to life with too much family, and it took a strange toll on him.

And now Walks Alone was telling him plainly that they were not pleased with him. Well, he thought bitterly, he was not pleased with them; he was coming to regret this whole lash-up. He wasn't an Indian; he didn't really want to live in this sort of intimacy, without space or privacy, where everything about him was known and he knew more than he wanted about the rest. How could he be himself in such a circumstance?

Nor was that all. The lack of privacy assailed him from unexpected quarters. Sometimes one or another of Victoria's sisters vanished for a time, sometimes overnight, sometimes to the menstrual hut. And sometimes unexplained people stayed in the lodge; a boy, probably some kin, occasionally made himself at home. Yet no one told him who the child was or why he was there. Probably he was an adopted son; the children of the village were constantly being adopted by other families, and children were constantly acquiring new parents. Yet no one explained any of that to Skye.

In the midst of all this enforced society, Skye felt a deepening loneliness. He had only the dubious friendship of Beckwourth. All this was a lesson. He knew now how Victoria must have felt all the years in the white men's fur brigades. And how courageously she had adapted herself to a way of life so strange. No wonder she rejoiced just to talk with someone who spoke her language. It had been years since he escaped the Royal Navy, but now his thoughts turned to civilization. Maybe it was time to head for St. Louis and whatever the future might bring. There he would pay off his debts and make something of his life. And he would forget Victoria.

But to think it was to know that he would not forget her. She had come miraculously into his life during a time of change. The thought of her wry good humor restored his determination to make something of himself among these strange people. His mind teemed again with questions. He would ask his father-in-law how a young man made his way among the Absarokas. There would have to be some way.

But before he could form a question, Walks Alone reined his pony and signaled to Skye to stop. They had been traversing undulating barrens not far from the foothills of the western mountains. Walks Alone had seen something. He signaled Skye to wait and then steered his pony up a long grassy draw with a halfhearted rill running along its bottom. Skye saw nothing.

The Crow dropped off his pony, tied it to a juniper bush, and glided up the side of the draw. Then at last Skye saw the quarry, a cow elk standing on the ridge with only her head showing. She was watching Walks Alone, but didn't move. Walks Alone didn't approach directly, but angled in a way that gave the impression he was ignoring her, all the while drawing closer, until he was within bow range.

Skye marveled. He had not seen the elk, but now was receiving a valuable lesson. Walks Alone continued to veer toward the ridge, apparently paying no attention to the elk, which was growing restless. Then, swiftly, he drew his bow and loosed an arrow. It struck the elk's midsection. She staggered but did not fall, and headed upslope toward the foothills, gouting blood. Skye rode up while Walks Alone returned to his pony and mounted. Then, silently, they followed the trail of blood, which crimsoned the grass ahead of them with bright red drops. The elk had vanished ahead but left a clear trail. It would not be a clean kill, and she would suffer.

For a mile, two miles, more, they rode their ponies into the foothills, past the first pines and past some slender aspens that had lost their leaves. Sometimes they found no blood and could only guess where the elk went; other times the elk's flight was clear. Walks Alone ignored Skye, focusing entirely on the chase until at last they found her, still standing, her head lowered, her belly red. Walks Alone drew his bow and loosed another arrow, this one piercing the elk, which shuddered and folded to the earth.

Skye and Walks Alone rode the rest of the way and studied the lifeless elk, a fine cow, heavy with fall fat. Walks Alone slid off his horse and circled the elk. Then he lifted his arms and sang something. Skye knew the Crow was apologizing to the spirit of the elk for taking its life. He thought maybe that was how it should be, and a better way of viewing hunting than the ways of the whites.

Walks alone neither gutted nor butchered the elk. He retrieved one arrow, which slid out easily amidst a bloody flux, but couldn't free the other. He headed for a nearby aspen grove and cut two saplings with his hatchet, and then trimmed them. He was making a drag, a travois, and would take this elk whole back to the village. It probably weighed six hundred pounds, far too much to carry on the packhorse. Artfully, the Crow lashed crossbars to the poles, using thong, and then anchored the drag to the packsaddle. He positioned the drag downslope from the elk, to make things easier, and then he and Skye dragged the elk, bit by bit, onto the travois. It was exhausting work, and they could move the elk only a few inches at a time. But at last they loaded the elk. The saplings bowed under the weight.

"We will go back now," Walks Alone said. "The People will rejoice. We will have a feast."

"I would like to keep on hunting," Skye said. "You go on."

"But we have hunted this elk together. The People will honor you."

"It was your victory, Grandfather. The honor is yours, not mine."

Walks Alone studied Skye, something kind in his eye. "You

are a man of truth," he said. "This elk gave her life to me. That is what she told me. Be patient and ignore the bad words in the village. I have received wisdom from the seer, Red Turkey Head, and understand your ways. He says you are the kin of the great grizzly, the most terrible of all creatures, and someday you will show the People how a grizzly bear defends its nest. Your time will come and then the People will honor you."

Skye wondered whether it would. He stood quietly while Walks Alone started back. The packhorse slowly dragged the burdened travois, which threatened to snap under the weight. Skye watched his father-in-law go, feeling an unfamiliar affection for him. Soon there was nothing but two deep furrows in the soft earth, and Skye was alone.

eleven

Victoria's father, with the help of three others, hoisted the fat elk on a stout cottonwood limb. He sawed off the forelegs and fed them to the dogs. With a practiced hand, he gutted the animal and set the offal aside. Then he peeled the fine, thick hide in swift jerks, cutting gently where it adhered to the carcass, all the while enjoying the company of some of the village headmen, who had come to admire the elk.

Victoria watched somberly. This had been her father's kill, not Skye's. Her man was still out hunting. He wasn't good at it and didn't have the cunning that any good hunter possessed. She felt embarrassed that he was not present, sharing the moment. But she had been embarrassed a great deal by him recently.

When the hide finally pulled loose, her father folded it and gave it to her. It was so heavy she could barely hold it.

"Make a good elkhide coat for your man," he said. "The Cold Maker is coming and he has nothing to wear."

She nodded, knowing it would be good to do that. She could stake and flesh the hide that afternoon, and let it dry. Then she could hair it and brain-tan it and soften it. This was a prize elkhide, unblemished, soft, fine-grained. It would make a fine coat and some winter moccasins and maybe more than that.

But it should not be a gift from her father. Skye should be wearing the hide of an elk he killed. She watched her father a while more. He was cutting haunch meat and giving pieces to the friends who had helped him. Her brother, Arrow, was helping him. Walks Alone would give most of this elk away. He was a great man in the village of the Kicked-in-the-Bellies, and the more meat he gave away, the greater was the respect he would win. He cut pieces and sent them to his brother the chief, and to the seer, Red Turkey Head, and to the small lodge of Makes Sun, who was old and feeble but took care of three old women, his wife and her sisters. Boys hung about, eager to perform this service for the headman who had killed the elk, and he would give a little to them, too. But when he was done with the giving, there still would be meat in the lodge kettle for several days.

How adept her father and brother were with the knife, and how fast they butchered the elk. Soon it would be bones for soup and gristle for the dogs. Knives were miraculous tools, and so were axes that cut wood, and awls that punched leather, and iron kettles that cooked meat and didn't break apart over a fire. Her people could no longer get along without such marvels provided by the yellow eyes. She wondered what it had been like for her grandmothers, who cut meat with knives of flint or bone, poked leather with bone awls, and cooked meat by boiling it in leather containers over heated rocks or burying it in hot ashes lined with grass.

She toted the heavy hide to her father's lodge and reluctantly staked it to the ground and began fleshing it. She preferred flint fleshers to the metal ones made by white men. Slowly she scraped the bits of meat and white fat from the hide. She didn't really want to do that, not because it was hard work but because she didn't want to give the elkskin coat to Skye. She had another one in mind. Skye didn't deserve such a fine, flawless skin. Antelope would know better how to wear it. He had a way with clothing. He would see at once that the leather was perfect, soft, golden, and clean, and would wear the coat in a way that told the whole village it was the best coat of all. And all would know who made it for him.

But she worked on the coat for Skye anyway because her father had commanded it and because she cared about Skye. She toiled through the cold afternoon—the weather was changing—and ignored her friends. Across the way, young men smoked and lounged and sometimes turned her way with amused glances. She knew what they were thinking: she chose Skye when she could have picked a better one. Her brother, Arrow, had joined them, his smirk even larger and more obvious than those of the others. He had no use for Skye or any white man.

"Where did this fine hide come from, Many Quill Woman?" asked Turtle, one of her old beaux.

"It came from my father."

"Ah, and not your man. He has no medicine."

"He has been named Man Not Afraid of the Pawnees."

Turtle laughed. "No one is afraid of Pawnees. I am not afraid of Pawnees. I am not afraid of Siksika or Lakota, either. I will fight them anytime."

It was strange. Among his own kind, Skye was an honored man and a leader. He had done brave things, fought well, won the esteem of many. Beckwourth admired him. The headmen—Bridger, Fitzpatrick, Sublette—rewarded him. She had been proud of him then. But now, in her own village, she saw that he was without power. His name should be No Medicine, because that was what had happened. He had none; somehow, he had violated the grizzly medicine given to him, and now he was as powerless as a child. It saddened her. She could not say what had happened, only that he didn't belong in the village. Maybe she would set his belongings outside the lodge door. Then he would go away and she would be free to pick someone else. She needed to think about that.

Skye rode in empty-handed, just ahead of a swirl of snow. Wearily he dismounted, eyed her and the half-fleshed hide, and entered the lodge without a word. He put his Hawken within, along with his powder horn and the rest of his kit. Then he emerged into the sharp cold, rubbed the black horse with dried grass, and checked its hooves.

"I never saw an animal. Hunted north, in the foothills."

"You have bad medicine. The grizzly has turned his back on you."

He paused beside her, forming words, and then turned away. She had heard them all. He led the horse out to the herd. She watched him go. He walked wearily, and wore clothes that had been given to him, and led a horse that had been given to him by a war leader with much medicine.

She was cold, and tired of fleshing, so she rolled up the half-fleshed hide and took it into the lodge, where it would stay warm and she could unroll it again. Her heart was not good. Everything annoyed her this cold, blustery eve, and most of all Skye.

Tonight she would go listen to stories again in the lodge of Antelope. Maybe Stillwater would be there, maybe some of the other women. Antelope surrounded himself with women. He had invited her to arrive just after dark, which came early this Moon of Heavy Frosts. The lodge of her father was wearisome this evening. Skye and her mother avoided each other. Her father sat and smoked, tired out by all the butchering. She ate the boiled elk hastily, saying nothing at all to her man, and then wrapped her fine Hudson's Bay blanket about her and ducked into the night.

If Skye had power, he would give her a big lodge, with many robes, and have many fat Absaroka wives, much meat, and eagle feathers in his hair—war honors. And he would not have to deal with his mother-in-law. Jim Beckwourth had medicine. She liked that.

She scratched Antelope's lodge door politely and was invited in. He sat before a small bright flame, bare-chested, muscular, his tawny flesh much the color of an Absaroka's flesh. A necklace with a blue stone in it hung over his chest. He had loosened his wavy jet hair and it hung loose. He wore leggings and fine, beaded moccasins made for him by one of his many admirers.

"Ah, my fair Victoria—which do you prefer, Victoria or Many Quill Woman?"

"I am Victoria; so I was named."

"A beautiful name, the name of a princess. Your presence graces the lodge of Antelope this fine evening."

"Where is Stillwater?"

"I sent her away."

"That is strange, Antelope. What of the rest?"

"Pine Leaf will not come this evening. And Walks Beside the River is not going to be with us a few days. And the others—" He shrugged.

"You sent them away!"

He smiled. "I told them that this night I would take Victoria to my robes."

"Oh!" She didn't dislike that. He had made his intentions known long ago, and much had passed subtly between them for days. But she thought she would tease him some.

"What makes you think I would go to the robes with you?"

"You want a man, and I am a man."

"You are saying Skye isn't a man."

Beckwourth shrugged. "Skye is a great man and an old friend. But we are rivals now. He wants to take my business from me, and I want to take his wife from him."

"Is that the way of friendship?"

He grinned. "Of course it is. I will give Victoria what she lacks."

"I don't lack anything."

"You lack my attentions. I am a gallant man and famously successful with women. Every man in the village admires me. I have had more wives than anyone else, and they tell other wives to try me because they have such a good time."

"How you boast!"

"Now or later?"

All this amused her. How fine it was to receive the attentions of such a one. Who among the People hadn't tried this now and then? Even before she was old enough to bleed, she had learned all about these things from the grandmothers. They told funny stories that made everyone laugh, and they knew exactly what they were talking about because they had done these things themselves. That was what separated the Absaroka from other tribes. The Absaroka knew how to amuse themselves. She decided she wasn't in a hurry, and she would make him work for his reward.

"I have come to hear stories," she said. "This evening you promised more stories. You said you would tell about the fireboats that come up the river. I have never seen one."

"You don't want stories."

"Of course I do! And I would like some of your whiskey, too. If you are going to take me to your robes, I want stories and whiskey."

"No, whiskey will make you stupid. It is much better when you have all your senses. Then you will have such a good time you will tell the village that Antelope is a great man."

"How you boast! All you want is conquest. For you it is like war honors. Like counting coup. Like wearing another eagle feather in your hair."

"Ah, Victoria, it is so. But my hair is down and there is no feather in it."

He fed some small sticks to the blaze and pulled her to him. She pulled free and drew her red blanket around her.

"Maybe sometime," she said.

"So, Skye wins this night. But not for long. You will come to Antelope soon."

twelve

In the morning, just when Skye was debating whether to try hunting in a hunted-out land, the town crier, old Pretty Louse, made his decision for him.

"Now listen, Kicked-in-the-Belly people. With the next sun we will move to winter camp. The camp chief has decided. The council of old men has decided. The weather prophet has told us this is the time. We will winter on the Rotten Sundance River! Pay attention now, all of you. Buffalo have been seen there."

Pretty Louse wandered off to cry his news elsewhere. Skye knew that river by another name, Clark's Fork of the Yellowstone. He and Victoria had briefly followed it and crossed it en route to this camp. In some places, where the bluffs defanged the wind and the cottonwoods and willows grew thick along its banks, the river would make a fine wintering ground, especially if some buffalo were around.

The move was fine with Skye. He had grown weary of the big bend of the Yellowstone, weary of feckless hunts. That day he combed and groomed his horses and checked their hooves. Then he tried to help the women, but they shooed him away. What was women's work should not be done by men. He didn't know quite what the line between men's and women's occupations was, and counted it as another blunder they would hold against him. There had been many of those lately. The whole village lived by a web of traditions and laws he barely fathomed. He wandered over to the small lodge of Red Turkey Head, but the shaman politely declined Skye's assistance and said he owned nothing anyway.

Early the following morning the village formed into a caravan, somehow creating order out of bedlam. Skye brought his dun packhorse to Victoria, who squinted silently at him and then loaded it with their few possessions. Even its packsaddle was borrowed. He hoped he might travel with her this day, and perhaps the companionship would bridge the deepening gulf between them. But she busied herself, avoided him, helped drop the lodgecover and load it onto a travois, loaded the family parfleches upon packhorses, gathered lodgepoles into bundles and hung some from each side of two ponies—and ignored his efforts at conversation.

Walks Alone and Arrow had ridden forward, where a vanguard was forming. Skye saw at once that the great men of the village—the seers, Rotten Belly, war chiefs, subchiefs, war leaders like Beckwourth, were gathering. The procession would be led by Father of All Buffalo, the camp chief, with Rotten Belly close behind. Skye thought to ride picket duty out on a flank but was sharply turned away by a leader of the Kit Fox warrior society, whose duty and honor it was to protect the flanks as the caravan proceeded. That left the rear, so he rode back to where the horse herd milled—there weren't many because most animals were employed as transportation—and there he discovered youths, barely men, guarding the animals. They eyed him coldly. Behind them, forming a rear guard, were more of the Kit Fox warriors, who had the honor of guarding the village this day—or maybe this trip.

Within the forming column Skye saw all the rest: wives and daughters, children, old men and women, infants in cradle boards, little ones in baskets tied to travois, older ones sitting behind their mothers. There was no place for him, a man without status among these people. He scarcely knew where to turn.

To ride beside Victoria, and her mother, and her feeble grandfather, and her sisters, would shame her and him. To ride among those who didn't want him among them because he possessed few war honors would be to suffer rebuke.

Mysteriously, without any command, the village began its long journey amidst cries, the lashing of whips, the bellowing of horses, and the barking of a hundred curs. The great procession wound its way eastward along the Yellowstone River. Horsemen sat their ponies on almost every ridge and promontory within sight, guarding the People. Skye had seen villages in transit, but still he marveled. This was a festive occasion, and these people had gauded themselves in fine style, with bright tradecloth sashes, red headbands, jingle bells, beribboned manes, eagle feather bonnets. But all this didn't lift his spirits; he felt utterly out of place, not even welcome among his own lodgemates. He scarcely knew where to ride. He had a valuable weapon, a Hawken that could reach farther toward an enemy—or game—than anything else in the village, and yet the closed ranks of the Absarokas nullified its power.

So he rode his fine black horse in a sort of no-man's-land, well to the left of the column—the river flowed on the right—but far from the mounted vedettes who protected the vulnerable side of the column. And no one paid him the slightest attention, least of all the woman he called his wife.

They camped that night on a cottonwood flat beside the Yellowstone. In the morning they would begin a long detour around a gorge that boxed the river for several miles. The women broke out trail food—pemmican—because the vedettes, who doubled as hunters out on the flank, had made no meat that long dusty day. Everyone was in a festive spirit—they loved to travel, and every bend of the river brought its own excitement, even though they had seen all that country many times. Many of the women built wickiups of brush and covered them with robes for a shelter, electing not to raise a lodge.

Not until the early dusk was he certain he could even stay among Victoria's people. Some robes had been laid out for him, and he rolled himself up in one upon hard, cold ground. At least Victoria was beside him. Maybe there were other things to be thankful for, too. She had not whiled away time with Beckwourth all day.

"Victoria—"

"I am tired."

"You have a fine village. I have never seen such a great people."

She stared at him quietly, her eyes not cold this one moment, smiled, and then pulled her robes tight about her.

It was a long, chill night, but the weather prophet had been correct: no storm passed over them to make life on the trail miserable.

Skye awakened at the first hint of dawn, relieved himself in the river, splashed icy water over his face and beard, and stood quietly, watching the light thicken beyond the steep hills in the east. These dawn moments, when the whole world lay hushed, were holy to him, the time he saw into himself the best, and the time he understood and loved others the most.

He sensed the presence of another even before he turned to discover the seer, his friend, Red Turkey Head, beside him. The man reached to Skye's chest and touched the bear claw necklace.

"You have bear medicine," he said.

Skye nodded, unable to think of a thing to say.

"Today you will ride with me."

"I would enjoy your company, Grandfather."

The seer nodded. "Ride with me and they see."

Skye wasn't certain what the shaman meant. But it didn't matter. This day he would ride with the one in the village who accepted him wholly.

"I am the least of the prophets," the older man said. "So I ride where there is least honor."

"You are the greatest of the seers, Grandfather."

"I will not say it about myself. This sun we will ride behind the rest, and just ahead of the horse herd. That is the place I choose."

"Then I will join you there, Grandfather."

The seer nodded. "I will tell you the ways of the Absaroka, the people of the fork-tailed bird. It is good for you to learn the ways and beliefs of the People."

An hour later, after a breakfast of jerky, Skye found Red Turkey Head riding one horse while leading two packhorses that dragged his entire possessions, including his small lodge, perhaps fifty yards ahead of the boys herding the horses. They rode companionably through the morning, speaking little. Once in a while one of the Kit Fox Society warriors rode close, staring at the shaman and at Skye, and then returned to picket duty.

"They see you with me," Red Turkey Head said. "It is good. You are a blessing and a gift to the Absaroka people, Man Not Afraid of the Pawnees."

"I feel as if I'm not helping your people much."

"You follow your path, and the People do not understand it."

"Not just the People. My wife doesn't understand it."

"She is young, and her head is turned by others."

"I am losing her."

The seer remained silent a moment, and then spoke. "You will lose her if you let her go. You will not lose her if you don't let her go."

"Would you explain that, Grandfather?"

"If you want to keep Many Quill Woman, you will do what you have to do, and what your medicine tells you to do."

All that was a mystery to Skye. But the old man closed the subject by turning to another. "I will tell you the ways of the People, so that you may become one of us. You should know that many things are sacred to the People, gifts of the First Maker, the mystery of all Creation. This land is sacred to us. It is the center of the world. To the north it is too cold; to the south too hot and dry. But here, on the edge of the mountains there is water and wood and the sacred buffalo, our meat and warmth and lodges. Let me tell you, husband of Many Quill Woman, that he who walks with reverence upon the breast of the earth shall be rewarded. He who respects all that is, the four-foots, the winged creatures, the spirits of the rivers and hills, the grasses given us to feed our ponies and feed the buffalo—such a person will be welcomed on this earth by all the spirits and will have friends everywhere. The Absaroka people have friends in the sky and on the earth, in the forests and on the waters."

Skye listened for hours to the poetry of the old man, absorbing the wisdom of a people who did not feel that the world was a hostile wilderness but a warm, providing, friendly place where they were welcome. Skye marveled. For him, the wilds had been a place of struggle, desperation, bare survival, and vulnerability to the elements, animals, enemies . . .

Thus they rode, toiling over steep slopes until they came to a hot spring where the villagers paused to refresh and wash. The purling hot water, rising out of the base of a cliff, astonished Skye. Women crowded the banks, but long before everyone had washed or refreshed, the camp chief was urging the village on again, and the police society was prodding the procession forward.

That night they camped at a place where majestic cottonwoods lined the river and a tributary stream rushed out of the south and emptied itself into the Yellowstone. The Crows called it the Diving Water River, an appropriate name. Skye helped the shaman off his horse, and together they raised the lodgepoles and wrapped the lodgecover around them. Skye chopped an armload of firewood for the seer before heading to the lodge of Victoria's people. A cold wind followed by gray overcast had chilled the village. There would be no wikiups sheltering the village this harsh night.

"Thank you for your company, Grandfather," Skye said. "You have taught me much about the ways of the People."

He picketed his horses on good grass close to Walks Alone's lodge. There seemed no point in running the horses out to the common herd with so much grass underfoot.

"Tell the man who is Victoria's husband that we have a stew and he should eat," said Digs the Roots. That was as close as a mother-in-law could come to addressing her son-in-law, but even that represented a major change.

Victoria quietly repeated her mother's request, though there was no need for it.

After their meal, Walks Alone shared a pipe of red willow kinnikinnick and tobacco with Skye and Arrow.

Skye sensed that something had changed. A revered seer had taken the Englishman for a friend, and now his in-laws, as well as others, were treating him with courtesy.

He wondered how long it would last. A shaman's example had restored Skye to the Kicked-in-the-Bellies, but it had not won the Englishman any more honors or made him a man of parts in the village. Compared to the illustrious Beckwourth, he possessed nothing—except a treasured wife.

thirteen

The column halted. Beckwourth did not at first know why, but he pushed forward among the headmen and saw the rider. Far ahead, accompanied by two of the Kit Fox Society warriors in the vanguard, rode a stranger, a white man.

The camp chief, Father of All Buffalo, awaited him, along with the war chiefs, headmen, and Rotten Belly himself. They had made good time for several days, driven east by a sharp west wind that harried the horses and drove spikes of icy air down their backs. Beckwourth wished the seers and weather prophets had moved them to winter grounds much earlier.

The stranger wore a thick blanket coat and a hat made of glossy beaver fur, and protected his hands in crude gauntlets. Beckwourth couldn't quite place him. But as the man drew closer, Beckwourth guessed he was Creole, one of the Canadian or St. Louis French in the fur trade. The man reined up at last before Rotten Belly and presented the chief with a plug of tobacco.

"Beckwourth," the man said.

Rotten Belly turned, summoned Beckwourth to his side.

"Ah, there you are, *mon ami*. I am Bissette, American Fur. We haven't met. Would you translate for me?"

Beckwourth turned to the chief of the Kicked-in-the-Bellies.

"This man is Bissette, from American Fur Company, and he wants me to translate. I will tell you what he wants and tell him what you say."

Bissette plunged in. "We have start a post at the wedding of the Yellowstone and Big Horn, Monsieur Beckwourth. Kenneth McKenzie makes the trade with River Crows and he desire to serve the Mountain Crows, including your people. So he occupy old post of Manuel Lisa. Maybe he build good post someday. He say, plenty of blankets, powder, lead, rifles, knives, awls, good things. Buffalo are thick on the Big Horn, plenty of wood and grass a little to the south. Your people can winter there, one day's ride from ze post, make buffalo robes, trade for good things, have fat hiver, winter, ze Absaroka get rich, many guns, much meat, and happy times, *oui*?"

That suited Beckwourth just fine. He translated all of that, making sure that the camp chief, Father of All Buffalo, whose decision it would be, heard every word. Many of the village people were crowding in now, wondering about the halt and the visitor. He made sure that all of them heard the good news, too. He was employed by American Fur to steer these people to them and now he would do it—leaving poor old Skye helpless, to boot.

The camp chief listened sourly, his medicine and wisdom challenged by this proposition. "We will go where the spirits have told me to go," he said.

"Grandfather, your word binds us all," Beckwourth said. "But it would be good to send a few of our warriors back with this man Bissette, to see for themselves if the buffalo are thick on the Big Horn River." Bissette looked puzzled, so Beckwourth translated the exchange.

"Ah, monsieur, tell them zat McKenzie's trader, he make a gift to the headmen, one pair four-point blanket to each headman, more to Rotten Belly and Father of All Buffalo, much tobacco, *oui*? If they no like place, if no buffalo there, zen they go to Clark's Fork like you say."

Beckwourth explained all that. "Think on it," he added. All

this would result in deliberation. These people would not make a momentous decision without pondering it. "Many buffalo, a warm camp, plenty of wood and grass."

And so the column halted while the headmen debated. In either case, the camp on the Big Horn or the camp on Clark's Fork, they had a long way to go. They were passing through rough country now, where the claws of the mountains stretched down to the Yellowstone, forming steep pine-dotted canyons. They were close to the Buffalo-Jumps-Over-the-Bank River—or the Stillwater, as white trappers called it.

Beckwourth knew better than to intervene while the seers and headmen, whose office it was to decide such matters, discussed the issue, so he dismounted, stretched his legs, and turned his back to the vicious wind out of the west. Bissette's proposal was a good one. The village would winter fifteen or twenty miles from the new outpost, an easy ride, and bring in good peltries—beaver, robes, ermine, wolf, all winter.

Beckwourth spotted Skye out on the fringe of the crowd of spectators and strolled over to him.

"What's this about, mate?" Skye asked.

Beckwourth flashed his wry smile. "About trading. American Fur's set up shop on the Big Horn in an old cabin put up by Manuel Lisa, got it manned and provisioned. Bissette says there's plenty of buffalo and good wintering grounds south of there on the Big Horn, so he's inviting the village to winter there, get fat, arm themselves, and bring in pelts to American Fur Company. . . . Don't feel bad. Rocky Mountain Fur paid you to do your best. You did your best."

"It's not over."

That struck Beckwourth as pure blindness, but he simply smiled. Poor Skye would not persuade a single villager to hang on to his pelts and trade them at rendezvous next summer.

The villagers stood stoically as the headmen sat in a circle on the frozen ground, quietly debating. Beckwourth could only wait. He knew better than to push the issue.

Younger men looked over their horses or grazed them.

Women settled on the ground, wrapped in robes and blankets, and hugged their children. Beckwourth found a boulder that deflected the wind, and settled against it. He spotted Victoria, and she smiled at him. In a way, he hated to take her from Skye, but in another way he loved every moment of it. Victoria was the prize. Not only was she the prettiest of the Absaroka girls, she was the wisest, the most traveled and schooled. And she spoke English, more or less, after the years in the fur brigades with Skye.

The headmen and seers seemed to be taking forever. He wandered back to their circle and listened to the deliberations. Father of All Buffalo was resisting; the rest wanted to go to the place where buffalo were thick and they could turn every robe and pelt into something valuable.

Finally Rotten Belly intervened. "We are divided. I will say this. I will send four wise men to the Rotten Sundance River and they will look for buffalo and wood and grass. And I will send four wise men to the Big Horn, and they will look for buffalo, grass, and timber. We will decide at the place where the Rotten Sundance River flows into the Elk River."

Beckwourth translated for Bissette. "They'll send a party back with you to look over the Big Horn, and another party will work ahead and look over the Clark's Fork, and they'll decide at the junction of the Yellowstone and Clark's Fork in a week or so."

"Ah, it is less than we hope."

"No, we'll see them on the Big Horn—if the buffalo are there."

That was how it played out. Father of All Buffalo didn't look happy, but the council had not rejected his winter ground. Beckwourth watched four veteran war and police and camp leaders of the People ride east with Bissette, and watched four others, all appointed by Plenty Coups, ride ahead to the Clark's Fork area.

The village didn't get much farther that day. A worsening of the weather caught them. Temperatures dropped sharply until not even a hooded blanket capote turned the cold. They had made no meat this trip, and the stocks of trail food were declining. All the more reason to head for the buffalo, Beckwourth thought. Father of All Buffalo had waited much too long to move camp.

He and Stillwater set up their small lodge under a sandstone escarpment to escape the vicious wind that night, and then he rubbed down his fine brown horse. A temporary village of sorts had sprung up along the Yellowstone, the People huddling against the bitter weather. It would be a great night to have company, but he knew Victoria wouldn't enter his lodge until they were well settled in their winter camp. Travel was exhausting, especially for women, who bore the brunt of the work, raising and lowering lodges, packing up and unpacking, wrestling with sullen horses, caring for children, dealing with dogs, butchering any meat their men brought in, and trying to put food in the mouths of their families.

The next several days they struggled east in relentlessly cold weather. The only good about it was that it didn't snow or rain or mire man and beast. Beckwourth was ebullient. The more desperate their circumstances so late in the year, the more likely they would be to winter on the Big Horn, close to American Fur's outpost. The traders would ship many packs of beaver and robes downriver in the spring—and Beckwourth figured it would net him a raise.

On a gray day with flakes of ice in the air, they reached the confluence of the Yellowstone and Clark's Fork. There, the party sent up Clark's Fork awaited them, and their news delighted Beckwourth. No buffalo that direction, but plenty of deer. There was no reason to tarry there; the Big Horn awaited them, but Rotten Belly decreed that they would stay and hear the news from the other party when it returned. The village chafed at the delay, wanting to settle in for the winter. But grass was plenty, and the weary horses and mules could fatten on it while the village waited.

Then, one evening two days later, the Big Horn party rode

in—and drew a crowd. One, Man With Many Horses, had been seriously injured in the thigh, which was covered with blood-stained leather bandaging. His woman, Sweet Root, cried out and helped her man off his pony. They all soon had the story. The Crows had ridden to the Big Horn, found that Bissette had spoken truly: there were buffalo everywhere, wintering in small herds that occupied adjacent valleys. The old trading house was located on the flat just west of the confluence, and each man had received a twist of tobacco as a gift from the American Fur Company.

But the rest of the story was darker. Returning to the village, they had been set upon by Piegans, a dozen roaming horse thieves out of the north, and had barely escaped. Only because one of them, Big Moon, had a musket that reached beyond the Piegan arrows had the outnumbered Absaroka escaped. An arrow had lodged in the thigh of Man With Many Horses, and he had bled almost white.

What now? Beckwourth saw the chance and stepped forward, addressing Rotten Belly as well as Father of All Buffalo and other headmen. "Let us camp where there is ample meat, and we can trade robes for guns. Then I will personally lead a party against the Piegans to avenge this terrible thing. I will take many scalps."

No one disagreed. In the next gray dawn, they would start for the Big Horn.

fourteen

And so the Kicked-in-the-Belly people wintered on the Big Horn twenty miles south of the American Fur Company outpost, in a sheltered bend of the river where thick cottonwood forest supplied firewood, brown grasses stretched in every direction, and high bluffs baffled the wind. Buffalo were plentiful, even as the trader at the outpost, Samuel Tullock, had said.

But no sooner had the village erected its lodges than a storm howled in, dumping a foot of snow on the village. Father of All Buffalo, never reconciled to the change, nodded knowingly. Women fought drifts to cut firewood with their hatchets. Others cut brush and packed it around the lodges to subdue the relentless wind and protect man and animal. The herders checked the horses now and then and hastened to their lodgefires, knowing no thieving enemy would be out in such weather. Horses, huddled rump to wind, pawed through snow for brown grass or stood quietly and endured the caked snow on their backs and whatever else life brought them. The days grew short, and Father Sun hovered low in the south and vanished midafternoon.

Only at night, when the temperatures plummeted and the stars looked like chipped ice and the snow squeaked underfoot, did the weary, bone-cold People relax their constant labor to settle in. In those times, they gathered together to gamble with sticks, or tell stories, or smoke their special mixture of red willow bark and tobacco, or make clothing to subdue the icy breath of the Cold Maker. The new winter would be long and hard, but most of all boring, confining an outdoor people to tiny leather cones.

But as harsh as winter was in these days of endless darkness and twilight, the Absaroka people didn't much mind. The village seemed almost magical, especially in the evenings, when lavender light crept over the snow and vanished in the tree-blackened bluffs, and orange light from the lodgefires glowed luminescently through the tawny lodgecovers, turning every smoke-stained lodge into a street lamp. This was a land of plenty. Beside or within each lodge was a pile of dry firewood, dead cottonwood limbs. From the few trees within the village, frosty quarters of buffalo and mule deer hung, fresh and ready for the black cast-iron cookpots gotten from the traders.

A few hardy hunters supplied the village with ample buffalo meat. The lumbering animals didn't run well in snow and were easy to pick off in box canyons or narrow draws. Skye was among the hunters. From the moment the Kicked-in-the-Bellies arrived on the Big Horn River, he had saddled the weary black horse and ridden out for meat. He shot several buffalo, employing his Hawken at a distance to save his horse a risky chase over snow-covered, treacherous ground. He shot carefully, aiming for that vulnerable heart-lung spot just back of the forelegs, preserving his precious caps and powder as he had learned to do with the fur brigades. After each shot, Walks Alone and Arrow lifted their numb hands to the gloomy sky and prayed to the departing spirit, apologizing for taking its life to feed themselves. Their profound spirituality affected Skye. He liked a people who so respected all life that they would apologize to the killed animal. Then he and Walks Alone and Arrow butchered the bison and dragged bloody quarters back to camp on a groaning travois, one at a time.

Skinning a carcass was itself an ordeal that took time and

numbed the hands. Once they had skinned one side, they had the brutal task of turning the buffalo over to skin the other, no mean feat because the hump prevented it. Sometimes not even the three of them could turn over a carcass, and then they had to use a horse to help them.

Once, just as they approached a cow lying in a pool of reddened snow, the buffalo struggled to her feet, snorted, sprayed blood from her mouth, lowered her massive head until her horns were swords, and thundered toward Walks Alone. Skye was just then ramming a new charge home. Swiftly he extracted the hickory rod, fumbled a cap over the nipple, and shot into the chest of the pain-crazed animal. It dropped just before careening into Walks Alone, whose retreat was slowed by the snow. They stared, shaken. Skye reloaded with shaking hands, not bothering to clean out the fouled nipple, and then they set about gutting the lifeless animal, each of them working in wary silence. During those hard winter days, when they toiled from the late dawn to the early dusk, Skye sensed that he was being accepted, though no word was ever spoken. The hunting had bonded the men of the lodge.

The women soon had five prime winter-haired buffalo hides to flesh and tan, but the grim weather prevented them from making robes. The hides were stacked outside Walks Alone's lodge, stiff boards of hair and skin. Frozen meat hung from cottonwood limbs, enough to feed the lodge for two moons with juicy hump meat, delicious tongue, and spicy backfat that seasoned every pot. The big white guts were carefully washed and packed with shredded meat and fat for future use. And one by one, the buffalo's very bones were cracked open and the delicate marrow scraped from them for a sort of pudding that set their mouths watering. These were good times, despite the numbing cold. Walks Alone and Digs the Roots were happy. The hides were future wealth. Skye's position among his in-laws improved a little. His Hawken had ensured a fat and happy winter.

Around the wavering fire, the women toiled endlessly. Victoria completed the elkhide tunic for Skye, embellishing it with blue quillwork across the breast, the blue for sky. She presented him at last with a golden coat, while her father smoked and watched.

"Here, dammit," she said, holding up the shirt. "I make this for you."

It fit him well, and warmed a body too lightly clad.

"It is beautiful, Victoria," he said. "Now I am warm. You have chased away winter. You are good to me."

Then she surprised him by extracting a pair of elkhide moccasins, cut high to turn the snow and lined with the soft pelt of a rabbit.

"My mother make these for you," she said.

The moccasins were much needed, and wrapped his cold feet in instant warmth. "Tell the one who is your mother," he said, politely avoiding her name, "that I am pleased and honored and wish her the blessing of a happy lodge and plenty to eat and many grandchildren."

The last evoked a sharp look from Victoria as well as her parents. Their marriage had been barren, but in Arrow's lodge, three children had been added to the People. It had been something to hold against Skye.

In some ways, the camp on the Big Horn was the best of times. Other lodges were enjoying the same bounty. Wolves circled the camp, shy by day but bold at night, driven half mad by the smell of meat hanging well above their snapping jaws. Skye often listened to the wolves at night, aware of how thin the buffalohide wall of the lodge was against the full ferocity of nature.

The deep cold and darkness enforced intimacy, and at last he spent hours with Victoria. At first he tried to engage her in English, but her responses were always in Crow, and he realized it was impolite to address her in a private language in the midst of her family. Everything spoken between them would be for all to hear. That was still a nagging problem with him, and made him yearn all the more for his own lodge.

Each day he took generous cuts of buffalo to his friend Red

Turkey Head, and brought armloads of dry wood scavenged from the surrounding hills. And each day he paused to visit with the old man, often wondering why the seer stayed so much alone in his small cold lodge during the most social time of the year. The shaman had been steadfast in his friendship, and Skye wished he could do more for the man whose vision embraced things unseen by others.

"Your time will come, and then the People will know who you are," the shaman said one afternoon. "The bear sleeps in his den all winter, but when he awakes the world trembles," he said on another occasion.

All these things Skye filed away in his mind, wondering what they might mean. He had come to the Crow village because Victoria needed the company of her people, but this old sage was telling him that he would have a larger destiny among the Crows.

Whatever the future might bring, Skye was fairly certain it would not include future employment with Rocky Mountain Fur Company, except perhaps as a trapper or camp tender. Beckwourth had been quick to exploit his new advantage now that he was close to a source of trade goods and could easily deliver peltries to the trading house on the Yellowstone. His lodge had bloomed into a small store where a Crow could trade buffalo robes, beaver pelts, fox, otter, wolf pelts, weasel, ermine, and even deer hides for almost anything—lead and powder, rifles, awls, knives, bells, blankets, calico, flannel, salt, sugar—and whiskey. Alcohol was illegal in Indian territory, but that had never stopped American Fur Company from supplying it. Beckwourth was suddenly doing a lively trade in jugged Indian spirits—actually grain alcohol, river water, tobacco, and a dose of cayenne pepper for flavor. Whatever the elders thought of it, they averted their eyes. Beckwourth was a headman, an authentic hero among the people, and a gracious friend of most of the senior warriors in the village.

What was winter for, if not to gather in lodges through the long dark afternoons and evenings, laugh, tell tales, gossip, gamble—and now drink the water-that-makes-one-crazy. Skye registered the subtle change in the village and knew that some of those parties, most of all Beckwourth's own, had grown wild. And even as those parties drew crowds, so did his supply of robes and pelts grow. His periodic trips to the Yellowstone, laden with furs, told the tale.

Skye had lost the Crow trade and could never get it back. Worse, now that the camp had settled into its long winter's night, Victoria had started once again to frequent Beckwourth's lodge.

fifteen

These were good times for Jim Beckwourth, yet he was not content. What more could a man ask for? First there was the beauteous Stillwater, boon companion in his robes and devoted to making him happy and comfortable. She was a bright-eyed, honey-fleshed woman with blue-black hair she wore in a single braid, often with a yellow ribbon tied into it. She was also fun, and had a belly-shaking laugh that erupted through his lodge now and then.

Secondly, he had Pine Leaf—after a fashion. She was the slim young woman who had become famous as the woman warrior of the Crows, having vowed revenge upon the Blackfeet who had killed her brother. She was fast, lithe, adept with lance and bow and arrow, and had come to Beckwourth's aid several times in pitched battles, once saving his life. Pine Leaf had vowed never to marry, but that didn't prevent her from enjoying lovers, of whom Beckwourth was the most prominent. He had often asked her to marry him, and she had always replied, "When the pine leaves turn yellow."

Which they never would.

Of all the women he knew, he loved Pine Leaf the most. Stillwater was all for having more wife-sisters around to share the work and provide companionship all day. If Beckwourth did manage to acquire more wives, she would be the senior and most important one, the sits-beside-him wife, seated at the place of honor beside him in the lodge. And she could boss around the younger and lesser women to her heart's content, which she intended to do.

It came down to Victoria Skye. He wanted her as much as the others, and her refusals only spurred him to find the way to win her. He wondered why, in the midst of success, he could not be content. He pondered it, looking for answers. Was he trying to prove something? He couldn't say. He knew only that some worm kept eating at him, making each of his triumphs bitter because it didn't fulfill him. If he couldn't take Victoria from Skye, then nothing else mattered very much.

No woman among all the Absarokas had been more perfectly formed or walked the earth with more grace and poise. No other woman was more splendidly dressed or did finer quillwork. And only Pine Leaf outdid Victoria when it came to armed struggle, because Skye had taught Victoria all he knew of lance and knife and muzzle-loading rifle. Beckwourth envisioned a lodge filled with beauteous women, a veritable army of women, and maybe even a few children, too. Even now Stillwater bloomed with child.

It wasn't that he wanted to wound his friend Skye; he liked Skye, and liked talking English with Skye now and then. And he respected Skye's prowess as a mountaineer, for the Englishman had proved himself over and over to be resourceful during starving times, danger, war, and brutal weather.

He was halfway rich, thanks to all the trading he was doing. Some of the villagers chose to trade directly with Tullock up on the Yellowstone, which was fine; Beckwourth got the credit for steering the Mountain Crows to the little outpost that American Fur had set up there. But more often, the villagers bargained directly with Beckwourth, and he scrupled to deal fairly with them and charge slightly less than the company did, or at least offer more for a pelt or hide or robe. Whenever the hard winter permitted, he rode north, with packhorses bearing his furs, and exchanged them for more trade goods, always making a little in the process.

He profited especially from the illegal nectar of the fur trade, smuggled countless leagues up the Missouri, well hidden from the watchful eye of the army at Fort Leavenworth. American Fur contrived to have a few barrels of pure grain spirits on hand, carefully concealed in a bunker yards from the Yellowstone post in case some wandering official—or rival—should show up. At this priceless fountain, Beckwourth regularly replenished his jugs—and then added the water and plug tobacco and spices that turned spirits into Indian whiskey. And this he sold at his little soirees, usually after supplying a free sample just to prime the pump. It was amazing how the pelts accumulated in his lodge from just one little party.

But that wasn't what was on his mind one January afternoon when he decided to have another party. Victoria was. He mixed more of his trade whiskey and announced to Stillwater that he would have another party that evening and he would invite all the grandmothers to tell their bawdiest stories.

"Oh, I would like that," Stillwater said.

"I will invite Victoria Skye—Many Quill Woman. Maybe a little whiskey will warm her cold heart."

"You're not going to get her into the robes."

"I'm going to try."

"I'll tell her that Antelope is the greatest lover in the village. No man makes a woman happier."

"That should entice her."

"I would enjoy a time in the robes, too, but I am getting big."

"So I noticed."

"I will turn my back and listen. I will see whether you are the same with her as you are with me."

"Are there any better among all the Absarokas?"

"I wouldn't know," she said, and laughed happily. "Maybe I will find out sometime. The women say that Standing Otter is a great one."

"Ha! His otter wouldn't stand long."

"Maybe I'll find out. Then I will be able to tell you."

"Then you'll know why you married Antelope."

That evening he welcomed twelve guests, who entered his lodge, respectfully nodded toward the hearth and its sacred hearth spirits, proceeded by custom to seat themselves in a circle around the small, hot fire, and await the libations of Antelope.

Among them was Kills the Dog, the old woman, wife of Sees at Night, who was renowned for telling the bawdiest stories known to the People. No woman was her match, although some said that Pretty Eyes was close. But Kills the Dog was much older and more experienced, and knew just what sort of story to tell on a cold January night. What else was there to do in the deep darkness of winter but tell stories?

Thus Kills the Dog was escorted to the place of honor, next to Beckwourth himself. She had grown fat with age, and that made her wobble as she stooped around the circle of the lodge and settled herself. Beckwourth surveyed the rest cheerfully. Bad Medicine, a fine warrior and hunter with plenty of pelts to trade; Lame Dog, another one of Antelope's war companions, a famous drinker and womanizer; Two Horns, a gorgeous young virgin, half sister of Stillwater; Pine Leaf, of course, a seductive tigress; and Many Quill Woman, whose good humor contrasted so sharply with the dour Skye. There were many others, of course—those who loved a good cup of whiskey, various female candidates for Beckwourth's attention, and a couple of good storytellers, both old women.

"Ah, friends, let us bless the Cold Maker for making us come together on a bitter night. Now we will have a party. I will pass the jug around; take a good drink to warm your spirits. After that, we will tell stories. Kills the Dog promises to tell you the worst stories that ever assaulted your ears."

Kills the Dog smiled toothlessly.

Beckwourth uncorked his jug and passed it first to Kills the Dog, who took a mighty swill, coughed and sputtered, and passed it to the next. No one refused such a generous largess, a gift worth a pelt if one took a long guzzle. Beckwourth eyed Victoria with interest as she swallowed slowly.

"Sonofabitch!" she said in English.

The jug made the rounds and returned to Beckwourth, who corked it and set it next to a tin cup. When anyone wanted more, a pelt would come around the circle, and Beckwourth would fill the tin cup with his concoction and send it to the buyer. By the time it reached the buyer, it was usually much diminished by samplers along the way. Which was fine with everyone.

"Now, Grandmother," he said to Kills the Dog, "tell us a story."

Kills the Dog licked her lips, shook her head, and said that the cup needed to go around a few more times. Only then would her stories melt the wax in their ears.

So Beckwourth invited another grandmother, Elktooth, to begin.

"I will tell the story of two young people whose families did not want them to marry," she began. "But they lived long ago, and were among the first to come to this country where the Absaroka belong forever. One was Pretty Fox, a beautiful virgin, the younger daughter of Makes the Birds Fly. Pretty Fox had eyes only for her beloved Buffalo Hoof, but her parents told her she could not marry until her older sister was married, because her older sister had a bad temper and no man wanted her. So Pretty pined and waited, and Buffalo Hoof decided that the best way to have Pretty Fox was to marry both sisters at once."

This was a good story, and Beckwourth settled back to enjoy a fine evening. Soon the grandmother came to the crux of the story: both sisters were married to Buffalo Hoof but no sooner had they moved to the lodge given them by the village than they quarreled about who should be the first to enjoy Buffalo Hoof in the robes. The older sister said it was her right; the younger said she was the one Buffalo Hoof loved. So Buffalo

Hoof, who was a magician, put them both asleep, and when they awoke neither knew who had been first, and he wouldn't tell them when they asked.

"Ah, I would not put any woman asleep," said Beckwourth. "That is a bad story."

"You would put me to sleep, Antelope," the old woman retorted.

That was how the evening went. Once in a while the Cold Maker shot icy air down the smoke vent, pushing smoke into the lodge, and then Stillwater had to go out and adjust the smoke ears, because the wind was coming from all directions. But that was all that marred a splendid evening. The cup went around many times, and by the time it was time for grandmother Kills the Dog to tell her terrible stories, she could hardly speak.

Beckwourth watched Victoria enjoy herself. Skye's wife was laughing with all the rest, and her eyes glowed. She sipped every time a cup passed by, and then swore mighty oaths she had picked up from the trappers.

That was all fine with Beckwourth, and when at last his guests had their fill of wild stories and departed one by one through the oval door covered with a flap of buffalohide, he detained her.

"Tonight you enjoy the robes with me," he said in English. "Stillwater says she is too big now, and she says you should enjoy my attentions."

"You got too many attentions. Goddamn, maybe sometime, Antelope, but not now," she replied, not soberly. "I got to keep Skye warm."

And then she drew her blanket tight around her and plunged into the night.

sixteen

A harsh wind rattled the lodge of Walks Alone, and Skye knew the day would be mean. Victoria slept late into the morning, exuding the stale odor of spirits. Skye had studied her somberly as she lay curled in her buffalo robe. She was not the girl he had married. Not much was left of the bond they had forged during his years with the fur brigades. Spirits were his own demon, and they were becoming Victoria's as well.

She awakened as he gazed at her, stared crossly at him, and rolled over. Then at last she got up, straightened her doeskin skirt, tied her beaded buckskin leggings around her calves, pulled up her moccasins, and drew her red blanket about her. She vanished into the cold and returned minutes later, still silent and avoiding contact with him.

Her mother and sisters had gone somewhere, probably to collect wood, a relentless and demanding task through the winter. Her father had settled into his backrest and stared at the small fire, idled by winter.

Skye wanted to talk to her. He had things to say, things building up in him for a long time.

"Victoria, we'll go get some firewood," he said.

"It is cold."

"Then we will brave the cold."

"It is women's work."

"Then we will do women's work together."

"Dammit, leave me alone."

"We will walk along the river."

Irritably, she pulled a blanket about her, pulled a thick shawl over her head, and drew gloves over her hands. "It is too cold," she said. "I do not feel like a walk."

He drew a buffalo robe about him, and put on a thick beaver cap, and they exited the lodge, smacked hard by a brutal wind that pierced their clothing.

"You see? We go back now."

He took her elbow and steered her down toward the river, over glazed snow and treacherous drifts, until they hit a regular path near the bank—in fact, the trail north to the trading cabin.

She walked in stony silence, radiating rank hostility toward Skye. He couldn't help that. His marriage was in grave trouble and he was going to talk about it. The vicious wind would punctuate his every sentence, and maybe that would have more effect than long counsels around a cheery lodgefire. Also, he wanted to talk English, which was not possible when they were among her family.

"You are going to tell me not to go to Antelope's lodge."

"No, I'm going to ask you. I won't tell you."

"You should tell me. All men tell their women what to do."

"I prefer to ask you. Then, if you agree, I have your consent."

"Goddamn, I don't understand you, Skye."

"I said I'm going to ask you and I mean it. It has nothing to do with obedience. If you obey without wanting to, you will not think of me as a friend and husband."

"No, I think maybe you care about me if you tell me no. Maybe I keep wanting you to say, 'Goddamn it, Victoria, do not do this or you can find someone else.' "

"You are not my slave, Victoria."

She glanced at him sharply. A gust of wind lifted her blanket from her, and she cursed. "Let's go back," she said.

He shook his head. "I'm going to tell you what I believe. We've never talked about it. I know what you and your people believe, and what you think is right. But now I want to tell you about what I profess and honor, and what I was taught by my elders. Then maybe we can understand each other better and make a better marriage."

She didn't reply.

The pain of coldness was good. The whole bleak scene before them, the black river running between sheets of ice along the banks, the spidery web of naked gray limbs, the overcast sky, the occasional outcrop of tan rock, the dark junipers and pines, matched the spiritual winter of his soul.

"For years when I was trapped in the Royal Navy, the ones above me told me what to do, and I did it because I would be punished if I didn't. I especially hated that life because it wasn't my own. That is one way of life. A marriage can be like that. Some white men's marriages are like that. A man tells a woman what to do, and she does it. Your Absaroka marriages are mostly like that. Some women enjoy it. They want to be told what to do. If their man says, Don't go to Antelope's lodge, they obey. That may be the way of your people, but it is not my way."

"Maybe you don't know women. If you don't tell a woman what to do, she don't respect you."

"You will respect me more if I ask you. And it is a mark of my respect for you. You will always have the right to choose. Some white men give that respect to their women. Some don't."

"Where the hell are white women? The *mah-ish-ta-schee-da* have no women."

"The yellow eyes will bring their women someday. They live mostly in villages and cities."

That gave her pause.

Skye felt the cold begin to numb his cheeks and nose, and

wondered whether to turn back. He was more vulnerable to this sort of penetrating cold than she. He decided he would endure. On this morning he would endure anything, bear anything, suffer anything to save his marriage. He hastened the pace to stir his blood.

"Where are we going?" she demanded.

"I hope to a new place of the heart."

"You going to make me?"

He laughed, and she glowered at him.

"I am cold," she said.

"Yes, you are cold. The words are well chosen."

"Maybe I'll go back now."

"I want to talk more about our marriage."

"You not gonna make me walk?"

"Not if you don't want to. I want us to walk side by side through life because you want to walk with me."

She stared and drew her blanket tight about her. But she did not turn around. That was good.

"Your people and mine have different ideas about marriage. For us marriage is very sacred. We marry forever, all of our lives. Yes, we can escape a bad marriage, just as you can. We can get a divorce, but it is difficult, especially in England, where I come from. But we try to follow the laws of God, and he wants us to stay married. When white men and women marry they make sacred vows to love and honor each other all their days, through good times and bad; to be faithful and caring; to follow the Christian faith together. All this is done in a church, the House of God, so that those who make the vows do so in the presence of God—the First Maker, as you call God—so everyone knows that this is holy."

"Goddamn! No wonder all you come out here and escape the women. For us it is different. Sometimes it is no damn good and then we put everything outside of the lodge door to tell the other it's no damn good."

"Yes, that is it. Your ways and my ways are different. I am married for better or worse. I hope you will be, too, because that is how love works. If you love me when times are bad, and I do not provide for you, and I am not a great man in your village, then you truly love me. And if I keep on loving you when you drift away and will not be my friend and lover, then I truly love you."

She had no response to that at first, but he could see she was registering it, thinking about it.

"If marriage is sacred among the *mah-ish-ta-schee-da,* then why does Antelope collect women? Why do all the mountaineers buy Indian girls at the rendezvous?"

Skye didn't have a very good answer to that. But he tried. "What is sacred to the yellow eyes is not accepted by all of them," he said, choosing his words carefully. "Nothing requires them to believe anything. It is up to them. The very ones who come out here to the wilderness—"

"What do you mean, wilderness? This is my home."

"Well, if I could show you how people live in cities, you'd know what I mean. This all seems like a country where no one lives."

"But it is full of people."

Skye didn't argue that point. These people lived in portable towns and left little mark of passage. "Anyway, the ones who come here are usually the ones who reject all those things. They come here to escape. Most do, anyway. Jed Smith—you met him—he's a believer."

"That is a bad religion, then. It is too hard. It drives people away."

"Some would say so. I think the rules are mostly good. The rules about marriage are good. They are good for the children, good for the women and men."

"Do you think our ways are not sacred to us? Or bad?" She was angry. "You think you are better than us?"

"Your ways are sacred, Victoria."

"I am cold," she said.

He stopped. His face was stinging from the bite of the wind. Going back, with the wind, would be more comfortable. "All right. It is cold." They turned back. "Now you know that I will never tell you to do something. I am not your chief. I am asking you now not to go to Beckwourth's parties. I don't know what he has in mind, but I don't trust him."

"You are goddamn strange, Mister Skye. An Absaroka would not let his wife disobey him."

This walk had all been for nothing. But he had, at least, told her for the first time who he was and what he felt. "I want you and love you. But I also know I may not be wanted. I don't fit into your village very well. The future is up to you, not me."

He left the rest unsaid. If she didn't want him, she would put his gear outside the lodge someday, and he would suddenly find himself a single man again.

They walked in silence, the wind harrying them back, so that the return was shorter than the outbound walk. It had been a good walk. He didn't know whether she would accept what he said, or him. The more he dwelled upon the customs of the Absaroka people, and the customs of white Europeans, the more he believed that there was an unbridgeable chasm between the two people. He could not become an Indian. Maybe he wasn't much of a churchgoing Christian, but those were nonetheless his sacred beliefs, and if he let go of them he would be a man without a center. There were many customs of the Crows he could easily accept and enjoy, things that would trouble most white people. But he could not turn himself into an Absaroka, or any Indian.

They reached the lodge, and she turned to him, searching his face. He saw perplexity in hers, but not anger. She took his hand in hers and lifted it to her face.

"Goddamn, Skye," she said, and then ducked through the lodge door. He followed, not knowing how it ended.

seventeen

A chinook swept away the snow in hours, and the Kicked-in-the-Belly people emerged from their lodges, shed their blankets and robes and gloves, and stretched in the wan, welcome sun. The Cold Maker would soon return, more furious than ever, but for a few days the People would enjoy the blessings of mild weather. The strange warmth seemed heady to Skye; the winter had been long and bitter. He rejoiced as the snow melted into the thawed ground and he took long hikes along the Big Horn soaking up the sun.

No sooner had warmth come than warriors dreamed of horse raids and glory. Now, for a while, they could carry their lances, bows and arrows, tomahawks, and clubs out on the plains, extending the dominion of the Absaroka people over a fiercely contested land. Jim Beckwourth quickly seized upon the warmth to assemble his long-delayed foray against the Siksika. He progressed from lodge to lodge inviting the finest fighting men in the village to go with him; there would be ample powder and lead for anyone with a musket or rifle, thanks to the American Fur Company.

He found Skye sunning himself beside the river.

"Ah, friend Barnaby, the time's come to even the score. We'll catch the Blackfeet in their lodges and make them pay. I'm leading a large party on a raid, and I'd be most honored if you supplied us with your keen sharpshooting."

"Weather might not hold long enough."

"War honors mean a lot to these people, my friend. You've the makings of a headman."

"And if we lose? Men die?"

"It's unlikely. Are you coming? We need that Hawken."

"I think I might."

Various of the Crows were standing about, but they could only surmise the nature of the English-language exchange.

"Good. We're leaving at once while we have the weather. A couple of eagle feathers in your bonnet wouldn't hurt, you know. And a few coups. It's all a game, Skye."

"War's no game, mate. I've seen more killing and wounding than most men. And I rarely saw a need for it, except against pirates."

"We'll catch them in their lodges. They don't fight in winter."

Skye had a reply to that but kept his counsel. A raid would improve his lot in this village, especially if he returned with a few ponies and more coups.

Skye felt at odds with himself. He owed it to Bridger and Fitzpatrick and Sublette to go out and make war on the Blackfeet. Of all the tribes of the northern plains, the Blackfeet posed the greatest danger to the Rocky Mountain Fur Company. They had been armed and motivated by the British to attack Yank brigades, and now the American Fur Company had started trading with them, along with Hudson's Bay, supplying even more rifles and knifes and lance points. The Blackfeet were a proud and powerful league, brilliant in war, a terror to all the surrounding tribes. Anything Skye could do to subdue them would earn him praise and thanks at the rendezvous.

"When are you leaving?"

Beckwourth flashed one of those smiles that had made him a reputation. "Get your gear," he said, and headed over to the lodge of Pretty Weasel to invite the man to the party.

That very hour, the invited warriors, thirty-eight in all, including Pine Leaf, gathered their war ponies, put together their fighting gear, their leather bags of war paint, a little jerky or pemmican, flint and steel, hooded capotes, leggings, spare moccasins, war shields, braided lariats to deal with stolen horses, and a winter robe or a pair of blankets to sleep in. Then they assembled beside the river while the People watched silently. Skye joined them, mounted on his winter-gaunted black horse, with the dun for a spare.

Skye sensed something was amiss when he told his father-in-law what he would be doing. Walks Alone stared stonily at him. Beckwourth had not sought the blessing of the war leaders, or the consent of Rotten Belly, or a reading of the auguries by the shamans. It was rare not to dance, to supplicate the Above People, to make medicine, to consult the spirits, to read what lay beyond the sky and wind and earth.

But the interlude of the warm winds would be short; they must act at once or not at all. It wasn't that the warriors ignored their medicine. Many paused, arms upraised, to sing a war song, to open medicine bundles and examine what was within, to go off alone to talk with the Ones Above. Indeed, one of the invited men, Barking Wolf, turned away, saying his medicine had warned him of death and cold. He was no less a man among the People for following his medicine.

But the moment arrived that very noon when Beckwourth, Skye, and the proud warriors rode out of the village on their shaggy war ponies, first to supply themselves at the trading house on the Yellowstone, and then to strike north and west, across two hundred miles of rough prairie and intermountain basin, to the heartland of the Piegans.

The old men of the village, the women, the chiefs who stayed behind, the youths who weren't invited—and who would defend the village in the event of attack—studied the departing band. Beckwourth was leading nearly a fifth into battle on winter-weakened horses, going such a distance that they would surely risk death by freezing, storm, or starvation, when the chinook died. For what? Because a Crow had been injured in the thigh last November?

But there was honor in all this: the old men might disapprove—and yet, in some ambivalent way, the whole village exuded pride at these daring men, and would richly honor their success when they returned. If they did return. Skye wondered.

As the war party rode out, Skye discovered Walks Alone watching, and beside him Victoria, wrapped in her blue blanket, staring at him, her solemn expression ineffable. They had reached some sort of accommodation. She had neither gone to another of Beckwourth's drinking parties nor given Skye her boundless love, as she had when they were among the fur brigades. He hadn't lost her, here in this Absaroka village of hers—nor had he recovered her affections. Some fresh war honors might help, and he admitted to himself that that was the real reason he was going.

They rode north under a fitful and low sun that somehow belied the eerie warmth of the chinook and reminded him that this was January. Still, by day, at least, the weather remained pleasant, though cold crept back as soon as the sun plummeted in mid-afternoon. This group of Absaroka warriors was uncommonly silent, as if they were all wondering about the wisdom of a sortie fought without the blessing of the People. Maybe death would ride beside them this time.

Beckwourth followed the same route he had taken the last time, taking his Crows through the bleak gateway that divided the Belt Mountains on the west and the Snowies on the east, and into the snow-swept Judith country. The weather held, though some days a high overcast reminded them that Father Sun was powerless against the ferocity of the Cold Maker.

Beckwourth headed straight for the square-shaped butte that served as a landmark. A somber creek there would take them to the Missouri, which would have to be forded, no small matter in the middle of winter. They had no trouble finding game, which was herded up and easy to kill because the deer or antelope were weakened, slow, and faced decaying snowdrifts in every direction. Each dusk they roasted deer or antelope, picketed their horses on thin brown grass, and then lay in the icy dark, not wanting to give their presence away with a night fire.

By the end of the third day, Skye sensed that the chinook was about to end. He could not say why. Everything looked and felt the same. But the air had a different scent, the arctic smell he knew so well. They were traversing a desolate land of great bluffs and valleys, barren, brown, gray, and patched with dirty snow.

At midafternoon, with the light failing, Beckwourth began looking for a place to camp. They weren't far from the Missouri, and not far from the heartland of their enemies. Skye surmised that their leader would settle for a spot a mile or so ahead, where some cottonwood mottoes offered firewood and a respite from the raw wind. They lay on a creek between steep bluffs.

The Siksika struck without warning. One moment the Crows were riding quietly north lulled by the soft clopping of hooves; the next, swarms of bright-clad Blackfoot warriors were racing their little ponies down the tan bluffs, howling the Devil's music. Ambush. And a bad place. Beckwourth reacted instantly, motioning his band forward to the woods, where they could find shelter and erect a defense. But no sooner had they whipped their gaunt horses toward the woods than another swarm of Blackfeet burst from that cover, with wild howling punctuated by the dull bark of smoothbore musketry and the rumble of hooves.

Trapped. Attacked on three sides. The Crows started to mill, uncertain of direction. One swift glance told Skye they were facing eighty or ninety Blackfeet, who held the high ground and largely surrounded the Crows. Beckwourth saw the situation, too, and turned his pony east, where the creek flowed between cutbanks that would pose a barrier on one side.

So much for Beckwourth's optimism, Skye thought. Some Kicked-in-the-Bellies would die this day. Skye spotted a buffalo wallow and raced toward it, while around him swirled the melee of battle. It was time to put his Hawken to use. It reached farther than the Nor'wester rifles the Blackfeet had traded from Hudson's Bay. But it wasn't much of a weapon to use from the back of a galloping horse. He reached the wallow, dropped off the black, and sprawled on the half-thawed mud, feeling ice water soak his leggings. He paused a moment to slow his pulse and aim, then fired. A distant warrior was smashed off the back of his spotted pony. Swiftly, Skye loaded, a guessed-at charge of powder, a patch and ball, rammed down the muzzle. A cap over the nipple. He lowered his rifle, his elbows solidly supported by the frozen mud, saw a Blackfoot looming over his Crow friend Running Duck, squeezed a shot—and saw blood blossom in the warrior's shoulder. Running Duck dodged the war club and escaped.

The nipple was fouled. Skye stabbed at it, scraped away the stinking powder residue, reloaded, and shot again. But time was running out. He would be overrun in a few moments. He loaded, sprang for the black horse, which was trotting rapidly toward the retreating Crows, and saw it might be too late. A Blackfoot was cutting him off from his horse. Skye whirled, aimed the Hawken point-blank, fired, and hit the horse rather than the rider. The pony collapsed instantly, throwing the warrior. Skye barreled in, clubbed the man, and then raced for his horse. He had run out of time. Half a dozen Blackfeet were closing in. He reached the black, clambered slowly, much too slowly, aboard the frightened horse, and urged it south toward the retreating Crows. An arrow pierced Skye's buckskin tunic, tearing at him but otherwise doing no harm. The howling behind him served better than spurs or whips to drive the black forward, and then suddenly Skye found himself temporarily alone.

He tugged the black's rein, slowing him down, husbanding what little energy remained in the bony animal. Ahead of him, the Crows were retreating pell-mell toward home, a defense abandoned. He glanced behind him, discovering knots of

Blackfeet on the ground, scalping two Absarokas. In spite of their great advantage, they were not pursuing. Maybe the Hawken, a weapon they knew and dreaded, was staying them.

His rifle was empty. He tried desperately to reload while on the run, but his hands were numb, he was shaking, and he could barely sit his horse. Except for his belt knife, he was unarmed. But it didn't seem to matter just then. For whatever reason, the Blackfeet weren't giving chase. He peered about, not quite grasping what was happening, and then saw what he had missed in the fading winter light: a bank of ominous black clouds had massed across the western sky, blotting out the residue of sunlight. Within an hour, the warriors would be fighting an enemy far worse than the Siksika.

The retreating Crows were a sorry sight. They had lost horses, and some rode double. One badly wounded warrior, apparently unconscious, was held in the saddle by another less injured one. In the thickening darkness it was hard to see. Beckwourth was all right, and leading the pell-mell flight out of that valley of doom.

They found no shelter in the Judith country when the wind quickened, the air turned sharply cold, and then stinging crystals of snow drove into their necks, numbed their ears and hands and feet, and collected on their robes. There was nothing to do but keep on going, running down the wind, away from the Blackfeet and the howling storm, which began blowing murderous gusts of lacerating snow into them. The ground whitened; they lost all sense of direction, but walked grimly onward, the horses exhausted and sullen, the injured warriors near death.

Beckwourth finally hit a patch of woods on the Judith River and they found some small shelter in it. Building a fire was out of the question in the blizzard and darkness, but at least they could rest the horses, feed them cottonwood bark, and try to gather their strength while rolled in robes that did little to turn the bone-numbing cold. Skye's whole body ached. He needed fire, fast, instead of a howling wind, penetrating snow, and shocking cold. In utter darkness he wallowed about, trying to make camp with hands that wouldn't respond to his bidding. His colleagues were doing much the same, but he couldn't see them. He finally pulled his Hawken from its sheath, released the black to make whatever living it could, and crawled deep into a thicket of junipers, which brushed his face and stabbed at him. There, in a sheltered hollow, he pulled his thin robe over his head and tried to rest, lying on gnarled roots that tormented him, hoping he would survive until dawn.

It was the coldest and longest night in his memory. He wondered if his fingers and ears and toes and nose would survive the frostbite. He and the whole party were at death's door—and for what?

eighteen

Out of the howling snow late one gloomy day came Skye and the army of the fallen, each man and horse snow-caked, the living hunched in their saddles, the dead frozen over their mounts. They came softly, their passage muffled by the veils of snow, the sight of them curtained by layers of white gauze. No one perceived their arrival; no one was out in the midst of the Cold Maker's revenge for the stolen days of comfort.

But for a subtle shifting of the silences, no one within the Absaroka lodges knew of their arrival, so their entry went unremarked until the few with keenest senses wondered, poked their heads through the oval lodge doors, and beheld disaster. The news passed among the lodges, but slowly on a day that paralyzed life and held it hostage. A woman sawing buffalo meat from a hanging carcass saw them, wailed, but her soul song died among the sheets of snow. She stared, spellbound, as if she were seeing spirits, not mortals. She began to wail, her mewling sharp in the brittle air.

Bitter cottonwood smoke hung over the village, driven to the ground by the avalanche from the sky. She watched them make their way to the great lodge of Arapooish, for they must report in exact detail all that happened, even in the midst of misery. She beheld Antelope, Beckwourth, in the lead, followed by two snow-caked ponies bearing dead men, and then the rest, some of them humped against the jolting of their horses in a manner that told her they were wounded.

"Eee!" she cried, and this time other heads poked through lodge doors, and a somber, blanketed handful of people followed the fallen army to the lodge of their chief. Now at last the wailing of the women crescendoed beyond the censorship of snow, and the village came alive, erupting from the lodges as swiftly as they all could gather robes and capotes and blankets about them to stave off the Cold Maker's deadly attack. By the time Antelope's war party had gathered at the great lodge, half the village had gathered around.

But Arapooish took his time. He already knew, and the waiting was his statement of anger and sorrow. Even as the fallen army waited, the tallykeeping women somehow discovered the names of the dead, and the widows wailed.

Skye hunched deep in his saddle, wanting only to reach the warmth of a lodge. His hands were useless, his ears blackened with frost, and his toes little more than a memory. Beckwourth sat his fancy pony, the hood of his blanket capote off, his head bare to the snow, waiting for the stragglers. Some, maybe most, were suffering frostbite or fevers. None among them bore scalps on a lance, or wore the ensigns of victory, or had painted up. None drove captured ponies before him. Some rode double.

At last Arapooish emerged, gaunt and rawboned, wrapped in a thick black robe, his obsidian eyes alive with some emotion Skye couldn't fathom. His wives and children, swaddled in bright blankets, arrayed themselves around him. It was up to Beckwourth to talk, not an easy task for a defeated war leader. But Beckwourth, formidable in all ways, was up to it.

"My chief and friends, we found the Siksika as we had intended, on a fine day, near Square Butte near the Big River, on our way to the ford where we might cross to the land of the Piegans. There, actually, the Piegans found us, traveling through the valley where we had ambushed them not long ago. The good weather had enticed them from their lodges, just as it had drawn us out of ours, with dreams of victory.

"They came down upon us from both bluffs, howling their curses, catching us without cover. When we ran forward we met with yet another bunch blocking our passage. But we fought bravely, for these are the best men among us, and retreated, taking a toll of the enemy. But there were many of them, a hundred to our thirty-eight, all well armed by Hudson's Bay, and deadly. The husband of Head-and-Tails Robe and the husband of Little Horns received their mortal wounds at that time, and the two sons of Sings at Dawn died later and are here."

Now the women wailed, sorrow for the widows of the fallen, grief for the warriors, gouting from them.

"Plenty Wood, Light Robe, and Old Skull were wounded, but they are here with us, alive in spite of the efforts of the Cold Maker. Behold them. We lost five horses. Mister Skye, Man Not Afraid of the Pawnees, killed one Piegan, or so we believe, and fought bravely, slowing the attack. And so he has a coup.

"We retreated while a storm gathered and the enemy headed for shelter. We were caught in the storm, without any place to hide from it, and most of us have been frostbitten."

No one spoke. Snow whirled down.

Arapooish nodded. "So it is," he said, and returned to the warmth of his lodge. The abbreviated report was done. Skye observed the wives and parents of the fallen, all grief-stricken, some weeping. Most of the fallen had large families, brothers, sisters, children.

Skye wished he had resisted the temptation to enhance his status in the village. It was foolhardy. He had counted coup—the sole warrior to do so—but at what price? He wondered whether his frozen body would ever recover. He looked for Victoria but didn't see her. It was hard to know who was who, so wrapped in robes and blankets were the spectators.

Somberly, the village boys led the ponies away from the encampment. There, in the cottonwood groves, the youths would chop green limbs and let the ponies gnaw on them. The softer bark was good fodder. The families of the dead lifted their men off the ponies, finding that they had frozen into an elbow and could not be properly laid on a death scaffold without thawing. The cottonwood groves would soon hold upon their limbs the bodies of two warriors.

Beckwourth walked proudly back to his lodge, ignoring his frostbitten feet and the stares of the shamans, ignoring especially the calm assessing gaze of Red Turkey Head. Pine Leaf and Stillwater helped him.

The snowflakes drove needles of pain into Skye's face, and he retreated swiftly to Walks Alone's lodge, where he discovered gloom. Digs the Roots, Victoria, Rosebud, and Makes the Robe wept. Walks Alone had sunk into his backrest and stared numbly into the cold, wavering fire. Walks Alone's old father had burrowed into his buffalo robe and was staring at nothing, probably dreaming of warmth and sun.

Victoria silently pulled Skye's thick moccasins from his feet and began massaging the numb toes, which shot prickles of pain through him. He wondered what she thought of all this.

The storm abated in the night, and at dawn Skye beheld a frigid world, the sun glaring off white snow, the temperature so low it bit his face and numbed him even in the small time it took to relieve himself in the willow brush. But at least the village had come alive; it would endure whatever it was forced to endure. The cold was harder on women; it was up to them to gather wood, and they half froze for the sake of warmth. Paths began to appear from lodge to lodge, several to the river, which remained open in places; many to the brush where Skye had gone.

Within the lodge, his father-in-law greeted him pleasantly. "Your medicine was good. You counted coup. You are a good warrior."

Skye nodded.

Victoria said, "I am sorry you went with Antelope."

That surprised him.

"All this was seen," said Walks Alone. "The seers knew. Yet the young men did not open their eyes or ears. It was bad medicine. It was bad to leave in haste and return in sorrow. It was wrong."

Skye gradually realized that he had risen a few notches in their esteem, while Beckwourth had fallen. By insensible degrees, Beckwourth's leadership would wither. Warriors would decline to go out with him. The gossips would find fault. The women would shake their heads and warn their daughters that he was a man of bad medicine. It would take mighty deeds, many coups, many horses, for Antelope Jim to regain what he had lost among his people this winter.

Skye saw the change most visibly in Victoria, who tentatively began conversing with him, always in Absaroka, usually cheerfully. He had not experienced her cheerful chatter for a long time.

And, Skye thought, all this might just open the door for the Rocky Mountain Fur Company.

The next bitter-cold afternoon, the village bundled itself and followed the grieving families out to the burial scaffolds, which stood ready in the limbs of two majestic cottonwoods. The dead had been thawed and straightened out and bound with their possessions within a good buffalo robe. Their faces had been painted according to the ritual for the dead, the symbols representing their clan, their warrior society, their coups and honors.

Skye followed. He didn't really know the dead, except as names. Yet he felt constrained to pay honor to the fallen, and braved the brutal weather, Victoria beside him. Against all temptation to hasten this business, the families took their time, enduring what had to be endured. Most of the village attended, but he saw notable absences. Except for Skye, none of the frostbitten had come, including Beckwourth, who had frozen two toes. But Stillwater represented that lodge.

The elders sang, the notes brittle in the icy air. The bundles were lifted to the scaffolds, faces to the heavens, and left there to be reunited with the nature from which they had sprung.

No one spoke the names of the dead, for that would provoke the spirits of the departed. At last they trailed back to the village, Skye hobbling on aching feet.

He had fought and suffered for Victoria's people. And now he wondered what it meant.

nineteen

Beckwourth endured his frostbitten toes, which had turned dark and painful, and pondered his fate. He was one to learn from his mistakes, and he knew now that his rash exodus with a war party, without consent of the high chiefs and seers of the village, had damaged him and his enterprise. But not seriously. The Absarokas had a native affection for any of their number who would take war to their enemies. When the dust settled, more would remember him for his daring winter raid on the Siksika than for the losses to the village. The winter keeper might even call this one Winter of Antelope's War and record it on his buffalo robe.

He was not without resources. He had the might of the American Fur Company behind him. He had already led the Kicked-in-the-Bellies to a lively trade for pelts, leaving Skye and his employers in the dust. But fences needed mending. Throats needed lubricating. The winter had been long and hard. He would give some extravagant gifts to the chiefs and headmen, and he would entertain as never before. He liked being an important headman of the Crows. He even looked like one of them, no doubt because he was one-eighth black, the child of a white man and a quadroon woman, his delightful mother who lived quietly with his father outside St. Louis.

That bit of black blood served him ill back in that world but served him well here. If he had stayed in Missouri, he would have run into strange walls, sharp, questioning moments, swift rejections. Here it was quite the opposite. That slight tawny tint of flesh made him one of the Absaroka. Where else in the world could a man have several wives? Where else could a man lounge, hunt, make love and war, and be taken care of by adoring women? Ah, life was good in the mountains.

"Stillwater, we are going to have storytelling parties," he said to his ever-accommodating mate. "Prepare the lodge."

"I like parties. Will you serve spirits?"

"More than ever before, and without a tally."

"You will have many young men, then. Only the Old Bulls"—she named a society of traditionalist elders—"will be unhappy."

"I will give them tobacco. It is the peace offering."

"You will invite the women."

"I always invite the women. Soon you will be my sits-beside-him wife, and you will have less work. I am going to fetch Many Quill Woman to my side."

Stillwater smiled. "She is a good choice, but she has a sharp tongue."

She would be a fine choice, and he could talk English with her, which was more than he could do with Stillwater or Pine Leaf or the others. He would take her from Skye. What the Briton really needed was the company of white men again. He was buffalo-witted among these people, didn't know how to become one of them in spite of his war honors. Take his Victoria from him and he would drift away, and so would any threat from the Rocky Mountain Fur Company.

Beckwourth began his rehabilitation by hobbling to the lodges of the headmen and giving plugs of tobacco to them. These were accepted, and the ceremonial pipes that followed sealed his acceptance. The Crows were not going to abandon a valuable and well-armed war leader like Antelope. He visited Arapooish, offered tobacco as well as a good knife, and received much the same acceptance, plus a good buffalo tongue meal proffered by the chief's several wives and daughters.

He limped to the small, isolated lodge of Red Turkey Head, and there altered his routine. He was admitted into a chill dark lodge, the fire little more than embers. But that was how the seer, ever the ascetic, preferred to live.

"Grandfather, I bring thee tobacco, and more. I bring the sorrow in my heart that I did not seek your medicine, your vision, before I led the brave young men of this village to a winter war—and defeat. I seek your counsel now."

The old man closed his eyes a moment, accepted the plug, whittled some into the bowl of a long-stemmed red-bowled medicine pipe, found an ember, plucked it up barehanded, lit the tobacco, and puffed slowly, never saying a word. Antelope knew that things had not been settled.

But at last the shaman handed the pipe to his visitor, and Beckwourth drew the fragrant smoke. They had made peace.

"Tell me what is in your heart," the shaman said.

"I wish to restore myself to the graces of the elders, Grandfather."

"What else?"

"I am a trader. I wish to prosper in my trade and supply the Absaroka people with good things."

"And?"

"I was a notable war leader among the people, and I wish to be again. I am ambitious for honors."

"And?"

"That is all that is on my mind, Grandfather."

"I think there may be other things."

"I can think of none."

"Very well. It is as you say." He drew smoke and exhaled it and watched it drift out the smoke hole above. "Hurt no Absaroka, and be kind to guests of the People. Do no harm to rivals. Give the people nothing that would destroy their senses and honor our ways. Keep the peace of the village and put the People ahead of your own ambitions. This is all I have to say to you."

Beckwourth found himself dismissed, and retreated from the smoky lodge to the clean bright air of a February day. The old man had all but forbidden him to continue his parties.

That very evening he invited a dozen people to his lodge and greeted them joyously as they filed in. Victoria Skye was among them, and he rejoiced. She still was the most beauteous of the Crow women, the only one who could speak his tongue, and the one with the most vital inner life, thanks to her exposure to another world.

"This is a good night," he said when his guests had settled. "This night I will pass the cup around many times, and we will tell the best stories."

And that was how it went. He charged nothing for the spirits, and the stories evoked laughter and sometimes controversy. That evening flew by, and he knew he would soon have the people back in the palm of his hand.

As winter decayed and the timid sun cut holes in the snow around rocks and trees, Beckwourth's parties lubricated the life of the whole village. The Kicked-in-the-Bellies were having a grand time. Beckwourth's trade increased, and he frequently rode up to the outpost on the Yellowstone with packs of robes and pelts and returned with more of the goods and spirits he needed to foster trade. But these were running short. He could no longer get sugar, coffee, tobacco, or blankets at the post. And Tullock told him they were out of spirits.

Even so, Beckwourth had the Crow trade locked up. He eyed Skye almost with pity those days. Skye never came to the parties, and Beckwourth discerned that the man was embarrassed by the bawdiness of the Crows. But the Briton was hunting daily, often shooting buffalo at great distances from the village, but somehow managing, along with his in-laws, to bring meat and good winter-haired hides back to the village. These hides, tanned by his wife or mother-in-law, were starting to accumulate, and he soon would have enough for a lodge of his own. Each of those thick winter robes was worth two lodge skins, and as soon as his women had finished with their preparation, Skye would have his own lodge—and probably the renewed loyalty of the exquisite Victoria.

It was time to act. Beckwourth invited her one evening when spring lay tantalizingly close and all the teeth had been pulled from the Cold Maker's jaw. For this great occasion, Beckwourth accoutered himself in his gaudiest glory. His wife washed and oiled and braided his long black hair until it hung in two glowing cords, cleaned his best golden elkskin outfit, and quilled his new moccasins. He took a sweat to steam the winter out of his pores, and enjoyed the ferocity of the steam as well as the sacred rituals, the sagebrush and sweetgrass, the holy chants, that accompanied the ritual, for the Crows purged soul as well as body when they sweat. Then he dressed, added a red sash, tucked his two notched eagle feathers, won in mortal combat, within his blue headband, rubbed the astringent sage over his body as a perfume, and awaited her.

She arrived at sundown, as invited, and found only Stillwater and Beckwourth present.

"Ah, my dear lady, lovely woman, whose beauty rivals even Stillwater's—welcome. Would you care for spirits?"

Victoria surveyed the almost-empty lodge—usually it was packed for Antelope's parties—and smiled.

"And how is Skye?" he asked solicitously.

"He is much in favor. He brings the People much meat and shares it. We have many hides. The headmen invite him to smoke with them."

"Yes, he makes progress. Good for him. But all those hides must wear you out. Tanning a robe is hard."

"The women do it together."

"Are you happy?"

She smiled. "I do not hear Magpie, my spirit-helper, scolding me."

Stillwater ladled good buffalo tongue from a pot and handed the horn bowl to Victoria, and then another bowl to Beckwourth. His wife smiled again; Beckwourth always enjoyed Stillwater's smile, which spoke of merriment within her soul and a generous spirit. He had found a good wife in her.

They ate quietly and then settled back into the multiple robes that formed cushions across the floor of the lodge and held the cold at bay.

"Many Quill Woman, we have a proposal. My beloved Stillwater and I want you to join us as my second wife."

Victoria didn't startle. She had been expecting something like this. She simply nodded.

"Stillwater wants company; she would love to share the cooking and cleaning and sewing with one she cherishes. I would honor you as my woman, love you both equally, and keep you well clad and comfortable. I am a rich man. I am honored in the village. I am still learning the ways of your people, but with each day I am closer to being the Absaroka you would want as your man."

Victoria kept her counsel, and Beckwourth scarcely knew where he stood.

"Now, Skye is a good man. He toils each day. But he does not seem at home among your people. I am at home. Be my wife. Put Skye's things outside the lodge. He will go away, for he has no one else."

"I will think about it."

"Well, it is good to think, but I want an answer now. Tonight we will share the robes, and I will show you that Antelope is a man who makes a wife happy." He turned to Stillwater. "Isn't that so?"

"Ah, you are too much for me, almost. I need to share you with her so I can have some peace."

They laughed.

"Tonight," Beckwourth said. "Tonight in the robes. With the next sun, you can put Skye's things outside of your lodge."

Victoria sighed. He was sure he had never seen a fairer beauty, perfect at the age of twenty. She set him to burning with as little as a smile. Tonight they both would burn.

She examined him and Stillwater, who was beaming with joy. He could almost see her mind racing back and forth like a rabbit between coyotes. A cauldron of anticipation boiled within him.

"I will be your wife, Antelope," Victoria said.

twenty

She was not in the robes beside Skye that morning. He realized she hadn't come home. He stared sharply about the lodge. His mother-in-law looked away. His sisters-in-law were not about. His father-in-law was eating.

All this was normal enough. The Crows drifted endlessly from lodge to lodge. Their children were almost interchangeable, staying at one lodge and then another, foster and real parents almost indistinguishable. But Skye didn't like it. He arose dourly, pulled on his moccasins, drew a robe about him, and stepped into a wintry morning. An inch of fresh snow covered the older and dirtier layers. The gray sky spread gloom over a hushed landscape.

He didn't know what to do. Doubts crawled like maggots through his soul. She had gone too far with her parties. Probably had gotten drunk on Beckwourth's spirits. He walked to Beckwourth's lodge, on the other side of the encampment, making tracks in snow. Smoke curled lazily from the vent. Someone was up. Stillwater was probably fixing something to eat.

He scratched politely on the hide next to the doorflap, the Indian way of knocking. No one answered for a moment, and then Beckwourth replied, his voice muffled by the lodgecover and liner. His response, in the Crow tongue, asked who was present.

"Skye."

"Come back some other time."

"Is Victoria there?"

A long pause.

"Yes."

"I want to talk to her."

"No."

The response triggered a rage in Skye. He eyed the doorflap. It might be buffalohide but it was as sacrosanct as a locked door. It was unthinkable to violate it.

He yanked the flap aside, flooding the lodge with snowy light. Victoria was sitting in the robes, bare, her dress, leggings, and moccasins cast aside. Beckwourth wore nothing. Stillwater was at the fire, cooking.

Skye stared, pierced to his bones. "I'll kill you," he said to Beckwourth.

"Get out."

But Skye didn't. Victoria cried and dove under the robes, pulling them over her head. Stillwater screamed and backed away from the fire. Skye had invaded their lodge without invitation.

"Get up and I'll kill you," Skye said, his fists balled. He started for Beckwourth, who whirled away. Skye followed him around the fire. He was going to catch Beckwourth and fry his hide in that fire, hold him over it until the man hurt as much as Skye hurt. Victoria screamed. Stillwater fled into the snow.

Beckwourth reached his wife's cooking items and clamped his hand over a knife.

"We'll do this outside," he said.

Victoria cowered under the robes, weeping.

Skye glanced at her, grief running so deep and wide through him it was like a spring flood, sweeping all before it. "Get out," he said to her. She drew a robe around her honey-fleshed young body and fled barefoot into the cold, wailing.

Skye had no knife. He had not expected to use one this winter dawn when he had first stepped outside.

"Get out of my lodge, Skye. We'll settle this outside."

The blade sliced air between them.

"I'll kill you," Skye said.

Beckwourth stepped toward the center, where he could stand. "For what? She's divorcing you. She's going to be my second wife."

Those words stung like whiskey in a wound. "You took her. You destroyed my marriage. Step out and we'll see who's marrying and who's dead."

Beckwourth grinned. He ambled back to the robes, pulled on his breechclout, tied on his leggings, drew a soft flannel shirt over his lean frame, pulled on his moccasins, and motioned Skye out.

Skye stepped out first and didn't give Beckwourth a chance to right himself as he crawled out the oval lodge door. He bulled into the man, throwing him into the snow. Beckwourth rolled to his feet unscathed, knife in hand. Skye found a long piece of kindling to deal with the knife—he had fought knives with a belaying pin in the Royal Navy, and now he and Beckwourth circled round and round, thrusting and parrying. The dead limb wasn't much of a weapon, and Skye had to hold it with both hands. But he was mad, and backed Beckwourth into a crowd of silent Absarokas. Victoria wasn't in sight.

Beckwourth lunged; Skye cracked the wood over the man's arm. The shock sent the knife flying, and Skye thrashed into him, knocking him back. Beckwourth fought hard and easily. He was taller than Skye, longer-armed, but lighter. Skye knocked him into the snow again and landed on him, his rage flowing like a river, his thick fists hammering, even as Beckwourth hammered back, threw Skye off, and gouged at his eyes. Skye was scarcely aware of the bite of the snow, the gathering crowd, the moaning of the women, and sobbing of Stillwater. He saw only his tormentor, and he hammered at the man, at the same time taking whatever Beckwourth delivered, oblivious to his own pain or punishment. He didn't care how he hurt; he cared only to hurt. They rolled, one or another on top, one or another bucking the other into the slush.

The imperial voice of Arapooish cut through the mayhem. Skye ignored it. The voice repeated itself sharply. Skye didn't give a damn. He was giving more than he got from Beckwourth. His fists ached from hitting Beckwourth so hard, and Beckwourth was hurting.

Hard hands yanked him away. He fought maniacally to free himself, but more hard hands stayed him, and he found himself caught and being hog-tied by the Kit Fox warriors, the village police this season. Beckwourth had ceased resisting and stood, panting. Snow slathered off his soaked clothing.

Stillwater wept, great tears flooding her golden cheeks.

There had been no satisfaction in it. Victoria was gone; this man had slept with her and stolen her. He could pound Beckwourth to pulp and not put his life back together again. Skye sagged, suddenly hollow, his rage dripping away like the melted snow trickling down his bare back.

The chief said something. Skye was too upset to understand the tongue and stood, dazed, while rawhide thongs imprisoned him. He saw Red Turkey Head, wrapped in a gray blanket, watching him sharply. He saw the village chiefs, the headmen, the elders, the shamans, the powerful scarred face of Night Owl, chief of the Kit Fox police. They didn't need explanation. It was all clear.

They were waiting for Skye to clear his head, for Skye's wildness to ebb. Then at last the chief spoke, slowly so Skye could understand.

"You have violated the peace of the village. You have entered a lodge without being invited. You have stamped upon our customs and laws. You have fought with a war leader. You have shed blood—it is there upon the snow. Therefore, hear me now. You will leave our village. You may not return to the Kicked-in-the-Belly people. You will get your things—all that is yours. You will get your horses. You will prepare for your passage from us. The Kit Fox Society will see to it."

Skye felt bone cold. His elkskin clothing was soaked. He felt as cold within his breast and heart and mind as he did within his body. He walked wearily through the emerging dawn to the lodge of Walks Alone, followed by the police and by his erstwhile father-in-law. He saw his friend Red Turkey Head turn away. Vaguely, among the women, he spotted his in-laws. He reached the lodge, put together his kit, pulled on his belt with scabbarded knife, hung his powder horn, and carefully lowered his bear claw necklace over his cold, soaked shirt. Then he filled his bag with his possibles, the spare moccasins and mittens Victoria had made for him, a beaver hat, his battered top hat, and his flint and striker.

Then he rolled up two robes—a fair-enough exchange for all the buffalohides just outside the door—and stepped back into the cold world. Victoria had vanished. Just as well. He couldn't bear the sight of her now. Not after seeing her sitting naked in Beckwourth's robes, her golden bare shoulders, her bare breasts and legs and feet, her long black hair loose and tangled, beautiful, shocked by the intrusion. He would see those things in the nights ahead. He would see them as he rode down trails. He would see them writ upon the sky. He would see them on his deathbed and on his way to hell.

They had gotten his horses for him, and they had put one of Walks Alone's saddles on the good black, and on the dun a packframe, which held a large slab of frozen hump meat, enough to keep him fed for a week. Walks Alone was giving him that much, anyway. Walks Alone's face was inscrutable, but Skye felt sorrow lay behind the blankness. Walks Alone and Arrow had become his friends and workmates.

They would not look at him. He could not say good-bye. He mounted the black, studied the faces of these people he loved, and rode away, towing the packhorse behind. The Kit Fox warriors followed, two by two, saying nothing, leading him far beyond the village, north up the river a mile or two. Then they halted and wordlessly let him continue. They stayed there. He was soon out of sight.

He would ride a while and then build a fire and try to dry out his sopping leather tunic. He didn't much care if he lived or died. Everything inside of him had died in those moments of dark revelation that dawn. He didn't know what to do, or where to go, or why to live, or how. And it didn't matter. If he didn't survive this winter odyssey it wouldn't matter.

It would be a mild day once the sun got up on its haunches, but that didn't matter. He rode cold and alone the long silent miles to the Yellowstone. When he came to the fur company cabin, he paused, not wanting the company of anyone. He had lost Victoria, and no company could replace her. Maybe someday he would remember the good times, the days under the clean blue skies when she rode beside him, the times they gazed at each other, saying more with a glance than any string of words. He would remember the silky beauty of her flesh, the crush of her lips, the laughing banter she made with the other trappers, the swift clean butcheries that turned game into food.

Maybe someday he would heal, and remember his Indian wife of four years, a girl in her late teens, barely twenty at the last. Maybe that would be the best way to remember her, a girl not yet twenty, the image frozen within him as he grew old.

But maybe it would be best not to remember her at all, because it hurt too much to even speak her name, as he was doing as he led his horse along the river.

"Victoria," he said, and nothing answered.

twenty-one

In his short life, Skye had suffered all sorts of wounds. His nose had once been broken, swelling his face into an aching pulpy mass. He had been flogged thrice in the Royal Navy, ten lashes less one, and his back still bore the scars where his lacerated flesh had knitted itself into ridges. Each lash of the whip had shot raw red pain through him, spasming his young body, forcing howls from him. He had once suffered dysentery during the Kaffir wars, and lay dehydrated and feverish, wishing he could perish rather than endure the raging sickness and weakness of his flesh. On board the frigate he had fought brutal seamen, larger, meaner, crueler than he ever imagined, and they had pounded on him until his flesh ached and his bones hurt and his head rang. Here in the mountains he had frozen and boiled, starved until he was mad, been knocked senseless in a scrape with Cheyenne dog soldiers, and awakened sick and nauseous and seeing double images.

All these he had borne, and none of them had affected his will to live. In fact, many of these insults to his body had kindled the rage to live and triumph and be a free man. He had not surrendered.

But now he wrestled with a new kind of wound, one far more piercing than anything he had ever experienced in his young life. He could scarcely find words for this wound—betrayal, loss, anger, despair, desolation, rejection, breach of trust. Words didn't describe the plunge of his feelings, as if he had been thrown into the abyss. Physical pain was an old and known enemy that he dreaded but understood. But this pain of the soul he didn't understand. He was born under a curse, and whatever small handhold he had purchased on the cliffside of joy had crumbled, and he was falling, ever downward.

He paused at the small log structure at the confluence of the Big Horn and Yellowstone, resurrected for the season by American Fur. The present tenants had repaired the roof and covered it with a foot of sod. He saw small portals on the two sides visible to him, but these held no glass. Hides scraped thin enough to pass light filled each small frame. He had been in rude huts like this one, immersed in perpetual twilight even on a bright day.

He stared, not knowing what else to do. The cabin stared back solemnly. He had never been here. He tried to think but couldn't. His mind had numbed and narrowed down to blankness and instinct. He knew he should try to reach one of the Rocky Mountain Fur Company brigades, but that was really not an option. The largest brigade, led by Bridger and Fitzpatrick, was wintering in the Three Forks country, the headwaters of the Missouri, on the other side of a vast and snowy range of mountains that locked him out until spring. He might, if he could find snowshoes, negotiate the icebound pass that would now be choked with twenty or thirty feet of snow. He might with a backpack manage to ascend and descend, endure the icy blasts and treacherous fog on the ridge, and reach the Gallatin valley without his horses or kit. But he had no snowshoes or cash to buy some. The other RMF brigades were even farther. One was wintering down in South Park, actually in Mexican territory, and the other, in the Snake country, was equally out of reach until the spring melt.

None of that made any difference. He sat his black horse, staring at the blind-eyed cabin, watching blue smoke eddy from a fieldstone-and-mud chimney. The cabin gave him no answers.

"Well, come on in or be gone," came a voice from the dead cabin. "We don't take kindly to varmints aiming to do us harm." Skye saw the muzzle of a rifle in a slit.

Skye nudged his black forward and stopped at a hitch rail in front of the place. The massive hand-sawn plank door swung open and he beheld a potbellied red-maned giant with a pair of dragoon pistols in hand.

Skye stared inertly, neither dismounting nor talking.

"You ill?"

Skye didn't respond.

"Well, get down, dammit."

Skye shook his head. He had no business here, no business anywhere. He turned his horse and tugged his dun packhorse around. Nothing mattered.

But the red-haired giant sprang out the door, cursing, and yanked the black's head around. "Now get down and abide a wee."

Skye heard Scotland in the voice. And saw Scotland in the face: freckles, fierce blue eyes, crags and ridges running across brow and cheek.

Skye sat the black, paralyzed. "I'll go," he muttered.

The Scot glared into Skye's face. "You're a man staring into a grave," he said. "You're sick."

A second man, this one dark and cross-eyed, with a luxuriant black beard, appeared.

"Help me get this mountain of dead meat off his plug," the Scot said to the other.

They pulled the black's head around and took the reins from Skye, and waited for Skye to dismount. But Skye sat.

"We'll lift ye off," the Scot said.

Skye let himself be lifted off. He was confused. Why were they doing this?

"Take the plugs out to the pen and bring his kit in. We'll get some tea into the mon," said the Scot.

Skye had yet to say an intelligible word. They steered him into the place. It wasn't much; a small room with rough-hewn shelves on the far side, earthen floors, gummed by spit and sweat and grease, and scabrous gray logs. A few trade goods on the hand-hewn shelves; pots; knives; awls; powder and ball; jingle bells; blue, red, and green beads; bolts of chambray; iron lance points; steel arrowheads; hatchets. A rude counter of splintery cottonwood. A low opening to a rear room where a fire burned. A perpetual gloom about the whole outfit.

The Scot herded Skye into the rear room, half of it stacked with robes and hides and exotic pelts, the rest reserved for bunks and a cooking area around the rock fireplace. On each side was a plugged gun port. The hides and pelts and robes exuded dead animal smells, rancid and thick and choking.

"I'm Tullock, American Fur," said the Scot. "My partner's Pierre Bonfils. And who are you?"

Skye stood, dazed. He couldn't bring his name to his lips. He didn't want anyone to know his name.

"You sick? Get some heat into you thar," he said, gesturing. "Your leathers are soaking. You must be colder than a grave. Give us that shirt and we'll dry it."

The golden elkskin shirt with fringed sleeves, Victoria's fine quillwork on it in blue and red patterns. Skye stared.

"Your shirt, man. You're cold."

Skye shook his head and sat down before the fire.

"You have a name? You Skye, down with the Kicked-in-the-Bellies? You fit the description."

Skye nodded.

"Well, that's progress. You hungry? We got us more frozen buffler here than we can eat in a month."

Skye shook his head.

"You in some kind of trouble? Sick?"

Skye stared. A faint heat penetrated the clammy cold of his elkskin shirt.

"You know Beckwourth? Our man down there?"

Skye stared, rose, wrapped his robe about him, and headed for the door.

"Hey! You come back here. You're not fit to go out."

The burly dark man caught Skye at the door and forcibly steered him back.

"Let go of me," Skye said.

"Well, at least ye can talk," the Scot said. "Something's happened to ye."

"I have to go."

"Na, laddie, don't ye be going now. We'll pour us a bit of whiskey I've been hiding from Pierre. Something's happened and ye need a dose."

The Scot pulled a grass-filled tick from his plank bunk, revealing a jug wedged against the cottonwood log.

"Sacre bleu!"

"Real whiskey, not the other. Ye need a few droughts of medicine, that's what I'm thinking. Ye act like ye've seen the Devil, old Bug himself."

Tullock uncorked the jug, poured a generous slug into a tin cup, and handed it to his guest. Skye sipped, coughed, swallowed, and sipped again. The spirits, taken neat, scorched his innards. Silently he handed the cup back to his host, who sipped and passed the cup to his partner.

"It's getting dark and you had better stay here tonight, Skye."

Skye nodded. "It's Mister Skye," he said.

"Eh?"

Skye felt the spirits permeate his body, even as heat from the fire dried his buckskins. "Forget it," he said.

"Now, what's the trouble, mon? Are ye ill?"

"Thank you for the spirits," Skye said, and rose. "Time for me to go."

"No ye don't, laddie."

"I am a free man."

"You're a sick man. Ye'll stay, and we'll see what the morning brings."

It didn't matter. Right now, in the warm dark of Beckwourth's lodge, Victoria was probably coupling with her new mate. The images filtered through his mind. She would enjoy herself with Antelope. Maybe more than she had enjoyed herself with her husband of four years. She had abandoned him, just like that. He was like most people, struggling to make some small sweet life out of nothing, but surrendering what little they possessed piece by piece by piece.

He began to doze, the spirits working in him. He was conscious of someone pulling a robe over him, of his hosts boiling some buffalo tongue in a pot suspended over the fire. The heady smells of cookery filled his nostrils.

But it didn't matter. Nothing did, or ever would.

twenty-two

Skye did not know where he was. Dim light filtered into a log room. A banked fire exuded a residual heat from under the ash. Then he remembered and wished he hadn't awakened. Someone stirred out in the trading room. He threw off the robes and stood. His hosts were not in sight.

Stiffly—he felt ill—he drew a robe about himself and walked into the better-lit room, where Tullock was standing at a counter entering something in a ledger with a quill pen.

"Ye lived, did ye?" the trader asked, surveying Skye's face.

Skye nodded, and headed into an icy dawn. He found the Frenchman out there chopping wood. There would be a fire and breakfast soon.

Later, he poked at a slab of buffalo for breakfast. He wasn't hungry. The traders eyed him curiously but didn't probe.

"I'll be going now, mates. Thank you for quartering me."

"Nay, mon, ye'll be staying a while. A fever eats ye, and it's not a fit day."

"I'm going."

"And where, may I ask?"

Skye shrugged. He would go until he froze to death, and that was all he envisioned or wanted. He rolled up the robes, collected his kit, and headed for the rude door.

"If a mon's bound and determined to die, not much can

save his mortal soul," Tullock said. "But if a lad's a wee bit uncertain, he ought to stay put. Buffalo meat we have aplenty."

They were curious about him, but it didn't matter. Skye continued his preparations.

"Where are my horses?" he asked.

"Enjoying some cottonwood bark for breakfast. If I let ye at them, I'd be an accessory to murder, seeing as how you're bent on destroying yourself."

Skye set down his kit.

"That's better. Now have some meat and get close to the fire. I have a wee bit of good tea, and we'll brew it up and get it down ye."

Skye sipped tea—it tasted just fine—and slipped back into his buffalo robes. They left him alone that day. No one came to trade, and the traders whiled away their time chopping wood, playing monte, and observing the unchanging dull weather. Skye's body mended a little, but the pain of having to live deepened and cut like a knife wound. In a way, the pain was good. It prodded Skye, harried him, forced him to contemplate Victoria and come to grips with events. But it didn't change anything.

That afternoon he rose, washed his face, brushed his leathers, and ran a bone comb through his unruly hair, while his hosts watched silently.

"I'm better now, mates," he announced.

"Well, Skye, tell us your plans."

Up to that moment, Skye had none, but suddenly he did. "I'm heading east," he said.

"East? The States? Not without grass for your horses and a wee bit of sun on your back."

"Tell me the way."

"The way is to recover your mortal soul, recapture your mind, become master of whatever lies within ye. That is the way."

"I'll be all right once I'm on my horse. I go down the Yellowstone to Fort Union, eh?"

"Fort Union's not so easy as that. It's on the left bank of the Missouri. A lot of water between you and it. A mon goes east in a keelboat or maybe a pirogue or even a raft or bullboat—if he's willing to brave the Rees—the Arikara—who pump arrows into passing white men. If I were going east, I'd wait at Fort Union for the spring and go down with the crew on the keelboat that supplies the place each year. Hire on to take the peltries back to St. Louis. Ye could find employment and succor there. Kenneth McKenzie needs all the hands he can get."

"I'm obliged not to, mate. I'm bound by debt and contract to the Rocky Mountain Fur Company."

"A good outfit, with sterling men. I count Bridger and Fitzpatrick and Sublette among the best in the mountains. But these things can be dealt with, Skye."

"Mister Skye, sir."

"Yes, so I remember. Mister Skye. Fortunes change. These things are understood. We could buy out your debt and outfit you and you'd work for us. Your name precedes you."

"I don't want to stay in the mountains."

"What happened there with Arapooish, may I ask?"

"A private matter."

Skye said it with such finality that Tullock didn't probe further.

The next morning Skye thanked his hosts and left. They had described a ford just below the post that would take him to the north bank of the Yellowstone, and they described another ford on the Missouri that would take him to Fort Union—if he was lucky enough to locate the ford. This time of year, even the mighty Missouri offered crossings. If he couldn't find the ford, he was to proceed to the bank opposite the post and fire his rifle. They would come for him with a barge.

He plunged into a bright day under a brittle blue sky, the hint of spring enough to make travel bearable. He was glad to be alone again. He didn't want the company of anyone. The silence engulfed him. He was passing over an empty land. The river hurled its way to the Missouri, and ultimately the Gulf of

Mexico, usually running in a broad valley between sandstone bluffs. The country was anonymous and dull, without notable landmarks, without soul-lifting beauty, colorless, oppressive. It suited his mood. Usually he followed the river road, but on one occasion he had to detour widely around a vast ice jam that had dammed the river and sent it over its banks.

For food he sawed at the frozen buffalo meat, wrapped in duck cloth, he carried on his packhorse. He saw only ravens to remind him that life existed, and was glad. He didn't want to see life. This country was as empty as the seven seas, which would be his destiny. This river would take him to New Orleans, and New Orleans would take him to sea, either in a merchant vessel or in the United States Navy. That is how it would all play out: a lone man, walking the hard decks in an empty world until he died. For a living he would do what he knew how to do, live under sailcloth, be driven by the wind, and surrender his stunted will and ignore his fractured dreams.

Somehow he would pay back Rocky Mountain Fur. For a while, they would receive small deposits from him out of his seaman's wage, and when that had been settled, he would be a lone man, without obligation or tie or family or friend. And that is how he would remain until they put him ashore, or wrapped him in sailcloth, added some ballast lifted from the bilge, and slid him into the lapping waves. He knew the sea. All his life he would be at sea.

He rode quietly through March and then found himself one day at the confluence, a small sea of currents where two great rivers married. Tullock had told him to ride west, past Union, a stockaded fort with opposing bastions erected close to the river, to a place a mile upstream where the river widened and rilled over submerged rock, visible only this time of year. But he could not find the spot, and when he bullied his reluctant black horse into the river at likely points, he plummeted deep into a channel and could barely get himself out. The river and its banks had a relentless sameness that defied a newcomer to locate the place of passage.

So he retreated to the post, which brooded darkly across a ripple of sun-dotted water. He was pulling his Hawken from its leather sheath to alert them when he heard a faint shout on the wind. Someone on the far bank had noticed. Skye waved his rifle and waited. Presently Creole boatmen poled a scow across and boarded his horses and himself. No one said much; they eyed him curiously as they worked their poles. One's gaze halted at the bear claw necklace.

He debarked on a well-trampled levee and pierced Union through tall gates, finding a yard and buildings under construction within. The Creoles were not far behind. The place rivaled Fort Vancouver, and Skye had an uneasy stirring of fear. Would he be clapped in irons here and shipped away?

But no such thing happened. Two clerks, each in a black broadcloth suit, materialized. The attire astonished Skye. He had not seen a gentleman in a suit since his days in the navy. Not only that, but their boiled shirts were snowy, their hair and bodies were groomed, and even their boots bore fresh blacking. What sort of place was this?

They, in turn, surveyed a young man in worn buckskins, unkempt and haggard and grim. "Sir? Welcome to Fort Union. Do we know you?" asked one.

"No. Mister Skye," he said.

"Ah. We do know you. I'm Largent, chief clerk, and this is Bonhommais, second clerk. Please, sir, let me fetch Mr. McKenzie."

Skye permitted himself to be led back in. Engagés instantly led his weary horses to a hayrick and unburdened them, while Skye watched uneasily. The imperial designs of Americans were as plain here as the imperial designs of Britons out at Vancouver. And betwixt the millstones fell unlucky mortals like himself.

Still, he was not without weapons; his sheathed Hawken in hand, a hatchet and Green River knife at his waist, and the will to be free—or dead. They led him to some apartments, humble enough at first, but then into a dining hall with accouterments that stunned him. A long table, covered with a snowy linen cloth and thick linen napkins, had been set with Limoges china, crystal goblets, silverware, pewter platters, and bottles of French wine. And standing at the head of this astonishing wilderness apparition was a powerfully built man Skye thought might well be a duke but knew at once was the Scots-born lord of this wilderness empire, Kenneth McKenzie.

twenty-three

Skye had not seen such a man as Kenneth McKenzie since his youth in London, when he occasionally glimpsed the peers of England. But here, improbably, stood a man radiating power, with a pugilist's face, a body beefy and imperial, and a gaze that owned the entire universe within the man's vision. He wore a fawn-colored waistcoat under a green cutaway, and pinstriped trousers over gleaming boots. His hands were the size of sledgehammers, and Skye didn't doubt that the lord of this corner of the universe could employ them with martial intent. But all that was prelude to something larger, a palpable force of will that brooked no resistance. He was a dread and absolute sovereign of this wilderness empire.

"You arrived during our dinner hour, which was impudent," he said. "What is your name?"

"Mister Skye, sir."

"Oh, yes, the opposition. Well, Skye, be off now. We'll put you up if that's your intent."

"It's Mister Skye, sir."

"Oh, yes, I've heard about you. We'll humor you. But a gentleman's title is reserved for gentlemen, namely my senior men here." He waved at a raft of human penguins in black worsted even now gathering at their ornate chairs in military rank.

Skye had already had enough of this place. He would make his way down the river to New Orleans without the help of these popinjays. He turned to leave.

"Just a minute, Skye, I haven't dismissed you."

Skye ignored him and headed toward the double doors.

"Skye! Where are you going?"

Skye didn't stop. Two beefy clerks detained him, clasping hands upon his arms. Skye didn't wrestle free.

"When you address a man civilly, with ordinary courtesy, you will receive your answer."

McKenzie laughed. "*Mister* Skye, where are you going? Why did you come here? Why are you not plotting and scheming to steal our Crow trade from us?"

"Mr. McKenzie, if you will kindly let me go now, I'll be off. If you are a gentleman, then conduct yourself as one."

The rebuke astonished McKenzie. "Mister Skye," he said, "I'm going to eat now. I'll instruct my staff to feed you in the mess, and put you up. You may leave if you choose, but I would like an interview with you after dinner. I'll summon you in a while."

The tone had changed. Skye nodded. He was hungry. He departed as the clerks gathered about their dining chairs, waiting for the signal to be seated.

A servant took Skye across the yard and into a mess hall next to the kitchen. The fur company's employees—engagés, they were called—had long since eaten, not observing gentlemen's hours. But, upon direction from the old servant, the cook dished up leftovers, including a substantial buffalo stew—and bread. Skye had not had bread in his hands for many years, and the yeasty loaf was indescribably delicious.

He ate quietly, reflecting on recent events. McKenzie was a legend, and Skye had heard much about the man around the campfires of the brigades. He was a well-born Scot who had come to the New World as a youth and entered the fur trade, first with the old North West Company, and then in partnership with some Americans, and finally as the most important man in the Upper Missouri Outfit, mistakenly known as the American Fur Company. He was related to Alexander McKenzie, the first white man to cross the North American continent.

Kenneth McKenzie was ruthless, brutal to the opposition as well as his own men, and got things done without scrupling much about how he did them. He operated his satrapy with absolute authority, down to fining, imprisoning, flogging, or banishing anyone he chose without the slightest pretense of a trial. He had justified this on the ground that he operated in a dangerous and lawless wilderness far from the reach of courts and sheriffs and prisons. His stated goal was to rub out the opposition and reign supreme on the upper Missouri.

Skye wondered whether the man would even let him out of Fort Union. Skye had been a prisoner before, incarcerated by men who had designs on his labor, or who simply loathed him, or who enjoyed the power to toy with the liberty of another mortal. He suspected that all three motivations threaded through the skull of his host, especially because Skye alone had questioned McKenzie's manners, if not his civility. Skye sighed.

After his bountiful dinner, the ubiquitous servants took Skye to a small guest room—not the barracks, as Skye had expected. That pleased him. He was in no mood to be sociable. He found himself in a room with a bunk, washstand, and wooden chair brought a thousand miles up the river. Even this crude quarter offered more civilization than he had seen in North America.

Deep in the evening McKenzie summoned him, and he followed a servant who threaded across a corner of the yard and deposited Skye in an apartment under the stockaded wall of Fort Union. Another lackey steered Skye into a large private room heated by a cheerful fire. Here, too, luxury abounded. A blue Brussels carpet decorated the plank floor; oil portraits graced whitewashed walls. A desk, stuffed chairs, footstools, sconces for oil lamps, a shelf with gilt-stamped leather books upon it, all contributed to a certain patrician aura. The man in the center of this wildly incongruent life stood quietly, awaiting his guest. He offered a hand and Skye shook it.

"Mister Skye, have a seat there. I am about to have a snifter of brandy, as is my wont. May I pour you the same libation?"

"Yes, sir."

McKenzie handed a snifter to Skye, who sipped and marveled.

"Now, then, why are you here?"

"I am leaving the mountains. I intend to go to sea, which is my trade. I came to ask whether I could go down the river with your keelboat this summer, working my way for passage. Until then I propose to work here for nothing but room and board. That's why I wanted to see you."

"Abandoning your post, are you?"

"No, sir. Chief Arapooish forbade me the village."

"He did, did he? Did you do murder?"

"It's a private matter, sir."

McKenzie stared. "Well, I'll get the story from Beckwourth. But you've let down your masters."

"I've disappointed them, yes."

"And you'll not repay them."

Skye rose, irritated. "I'll leave in the morning."

"Sit down, blast you. What sort of crime did you do? I could put you in prison, you know. We've a gaol here, or I could send you down under indictment."

"You could imprison my body, sir—for a short while."

"That's a strange reply. If you go down the river by yourself this time of year, you'll die."

"That may be the better of my options, sir."

"Death? You're a desperate man."

Skye turned. "I'll be out of here as soon as you swing open the gates."

"Oh no you don't. You don't escape the clutches of Kenneth McKenzie so easily, Skye."

"I have nothing more to say."

"Stubborn cuss. Very well. You failed Sublette and Fitzpatrick. You were sent to the Crows to worm business away from us. Why should I employ such a man?"

"I'm withdrawing my offer of service. I'll go alone."

McKenzie guzzled a long, fiery bolt of brandy, and wheezed. He set down the snifter and glared. "I don't know what to do with you."

"Then don't do anything. I shouldn't have come here."

"You intrigue me. What's all the story I don't know and you're not telling, eh? All right. I know who you are. I know the name of every man in the mountains, or nearly all. You were offered the chance to be a brigade leader last summer. Ah, don't look so startled. Kenneth McKenzie has ears everywhere. Do you suppose Beckwourth has never talked of you? You chose to come to the village of your wife. Where's she?"

"She's not my wife, sir."

"Well, squaw. Harlot."

"She is neither of those."

"Marital discord. That's it. Woman trouble."

Skye stood, poised to leave, mute. A few minutes with McKenzie had persuaded him that he would be better off taking his chances with the Indians and winter on his own.

"How much do you owe your masters?"

"I was indebted nearly three hundred, employed at two hundred for the winter with the Crows. I intended to pay the rest with robes tanned by my wife. Also, five hundred in trade goods were stolen by the Pawnee. I am liable for it."

"That's a lot." He surveyed his guest thoughtfully. "Men are scarce here, and you made a name for yourself out in the field. I could put you in Vanderburgh's brigade."

"Thank you, but that would not be honorable. I am obligated by debt and contract and my own word."

McKenzie laughed.

Skye began to boil. If this didn't stop, he would land on McKenzie and give better than he took, even if he ultimately went down the river in irons. He stepped forward, bristling.

"I'm as good as my word. And I'll back my word with these." He lifted his fists and edged toward the man. They were of a height, both blocky, both hardened by mountain life. McKenzie was a little older, but showing a paunch that suggested too many brandies and too much time at table.

Stunned, McKenzie set down his snifter but didn't lift his fists to defend himself. Instead, he lifted a silver bell and rang it.

An engagé, a big Frenchman, ambled in.

"Escort this man to his quarters."

Skye wheeled away, leaving both men behind him, stepped into a sharp night, found his way to his quarters, rebuilt the dying fire with a cottonwood stick, and settled in his robes, wondering how a man in the mountains could become a seaman.

twenty-four

In the morning they took him to the mess, where he encountered about twenty men, mostly Creoles, and served him a steaming bowl of gruel and tea. The oats tasted just fine, and the tea was a treasure. The others sitting on the bench seemed to know all about him and greeted him amiably. Word obviously flew around a fur post. These men bore the wounds of a hard life. One lacked two fingers. Another had been scalped and wore a skullcap. Yet another had a peg leg strapped to the stump of his right leg, while another wore a black eye patch. They were served by an Assiniboine woman—wife of one or another of the men—who lacked an ear and an eye and bore a slash across her brown face. Despite all that, she was pretty, and she smiled at him, her face bright with curiosity.

Some of these laborers would tend horses and cattle, others would hunt buffalo, still others would continue to build the post—two buildings were being constructed in the yard. One or two others would salt or season the pelts and press them into packs for transport down the river, while one or two others would cut firewood and distribute it to the various stoves or fireplaces within.

Skye thought he could do some of those things—if he stayed. He would prefer to risk his life traveling to St. Louis in late winter than to face the hauteur and contempt of McKenzie. After the hearty but simple breakfast, they took him to McKenzie's lair. This time the man wore a black cutaway instead of the festive green one, but otherwise looked much the same, beefy, florid, and Scots to the bone.

"I can use a man," McKenzie said without preamble. "I'll hire you."

"Maybe, maybe not, sir."

"I set the terms; you don't."

"My terms are these: twenty dollars a month until I go down the river with the keelboat. After that, crewing on the keelboat in exchange for passage. The accrued wage will be sent to General Ashley, agent for my employers, as payment on my debt. I will not compete with my employers. That is, I will not deal with the Crows or trap in Vanderburgh's brigade."

McKenzie stared so long at him he thought the man hadn't heard.

"Berger needs a man," the factor said. "Would you trade with the Blackfeet?"

"Yes, sir. Fitzpatrick and Sublette have no dealings with the Blackfeet." But he had misgivings. He would be befriending Victoria's enemies. But what difference did it make?

"We have an outpost on the Marias. Berger and a man or two are trading with Bug's Boys. If they succeed, I'll send Kipp to build a post next fall. They've built a cabin—that's all it is—and it's vulnerable. But the Blackfeet want to trade, and Berger's fluent in the tongue, so I think you'll be safe enough. We opened up trade just this fall. Berger brought forty of them here, and we did a good business. I'll send you there. He needs help. You're too valuable to put to work here laying up cottonwood logs or cutting firewood. Three months on the Marias, then bring the returns here by pirogue, and then join the keelboat crew in July. Twenty a month, the funds to be credited to Rocky Mountain Fur through Ashley. Subsistence for you and your horses, and an outfit as needed. What you lose you pay for. You will use your horses on company business. I am sending some resupply to Berger on your packhorse. Tell him we don't have much left here, but there's powder, lead, knives, blankets, awls, beads, molasses, and a bolt of flannel. I am entrusting you with supplies. Live up to my confidence in you."

That faint praise came as a surprise to Skye. "All right, sir."

"Maybe by July I can persuade you to stay."

"No offer would do that."

"I'm going to find out what happened, Skye—ah, Mister Skye."

"Mr. Beckwourth will tell you."

McKenzie looked irritable. "Go to the trading room and get what you need. Sign for it. You can read and cipher, I take it?"

"I was preparing to enter Cambridge—Magdalene—when the Royal Navy press gang took me."

"Likely story."

McKenzie dismissed him with a wave. "Be off now. It'll take you a week by land. You'll be driven far from the Missouri. You'll ford the Milk and several lesser tributaries. Berger's post is on a flat close to the confluence of the Marias. Take this letter with you. It will tell him about you."

Skye took the letter and headed for the cheerful trading room, staffed by cynical black-clad clerks who looked to be more prosperous than their fur company salaries would permit. He selected a pair of four-point blankets, a small brass kettle, half a dozen beaver traps, a ball mold and bar of galena, and some DuPont powder.

The post seemed to anticipate his every move, such was McKenzie's genius. In the yard his saddled horses waited, the packhorse laden with his robes and the resupply. He added the gear he had drawn from stores and rode into the morning light, once again a man alone. No one saw him off, but he didn't doubt that many eyes watched.

What had he done? He couldn't say for sure. He was only trying to survive, far apart and two or three snowy barriers from his former employers. Someday, the ledgers kept in St. Louis would record payment in full by the Briton who left the mountains.

Bug's Boys. He had met them only in battle, and all too often at that. Now he would trade—take in their beaver and pass through the trading window muskets and powder and arrow points and knives and lance points—with which to slaughter his friends and wage merciless war upon Victoria's people. Oh, what had he done? Had he just sold his soul to the Devil?

He had learned a little about the Blackfoot Federation—the Piegans, or Pikuni, as they called themselves, the Bloods or Kainah, and the Siksika, or Blackfeet proper, all speaking the same tongue, all proud, warlike, powerful, and brilliant. Every neighboring tribe feared them. But most of all the Yank trappers feared them; any encounter would become a fight to the death, war waged with the most relentless, cunning, gifted soldiers in the mountains.

He traversed an empty land, a solitary figure riding across snow-patched plains. Far distant, the Missouri oxbowed eastward in a broad, low valley, almost featureless. Skye scarcely knew where he was going, but he couldn't miss if he stayed with the great river. He saw no signs of passage, no hoofprints in the frozen mud, no tracks of deer or antelope, no startled ravens breaking for the skies. He felt dwarfed by the surrounding emptiness, as small as he had felt at sea. Wind bit at him, found every pinhole in his clothing, but he ignored it. He had come to live in nature by enduring it. When you knew you couldn't stop the wind or warm the air or abolish the rain, you endured. By the end of that March day he wondered whether he had made any progress at all. Nothing had changed. He steered his weary black and packhorse down a long, shallow coulee toward the river bottoms, where he would probably find wood and a place to escape the wind. But he was not lucky that night. The flats were as barren as the country above, and he knew he would roll into his blankets and robes with little more in his belly than some gnawed jerky.

All the more reason to leave the mountains. His thoughts turned to Victoria and then shied away from that topic. He wanted to draw a curtain across all of that, but couldn't. An ancient love persisted. In the weeks since he had found her with Beckwourth, he had slowly recovered a will to live. He still told himself he didn't care whether he lived or died—without her life wouldn't be worth living. But it was in him to keep on, no matter how bad things were, just as he had kept on as a seaman.

He did better the next night, warming himself in the reflected heat of a sandstone cliff, boiling Darjeeling tea in his new brass kettle, drinking it while it still scalded. He had plentiful cottonwood beside him, and the horses were staked close at hand on abundant brown grass. But such was the land that he swore he had made no progress at all from sunup to sundown. Nothing had changed. The mute river ran distantly, often out of sight, mysterious in its trench in the plains. No one was abroad.

He forded the Milk, a shallow opaque river dividing stands of naked trees. He kept his gaze sharp and expectant; predators gathered at such places, but he saw none, and knew that he probably would not survive an encounter with a roving band of warriors, no matter that the American Fur Company had opened trade with the Blackfeet. He eyed his back trail nervously. Behind him was a telltale wake of hoofprints pressed in the midday mud and frozen to stone each evening. Anyone could find him, and no doubt would.

The country turned rougher, and he often camped beside a half-iced creek instead of finding his way down to the river. The hills crowded in, the empty flats vanished, and he could no longer see his fate hours before it engulfed him. Now, amid slopes and wooded groves and rock, he faced ambush and surprise.

Then one day he struck a large stream flowing southeast and followed it toward the great river. It was either the Marias or a good imitation of it, according to what he had been told. He found the cabin just north of the Missouri, and beside it a whole village of Blackfeet, their smoke-stained lodges emitting lazy coils of sour cottonwood smoke. Bug's Boys! He rode uneasily through them, even as they stared silently at him. They were a gorgeous people, proud, tall, honey-fleshed, slender, and attired in blankets and bonnets that featured shades of blue. These people plainly loved blue, or else it had some sort of religious significance to them. He had seen many an Indian in his mountain years, but these were far and away the most handsome he had ever encountered.

An old mountain man lounged in the doorway, watching him. This one had been baked the color of an ancient saddle by the sun and wind, and his face was framed by a mop of snowy hair that hung loose to his shoulders. But he was more or less clean shaven; the man probably scraped himself once a month.

"Mr. Berger?"

"I don't know the first word, but the second's me."

"I'm Barnaby Skye, sir. Mr. McKenzie sent me to help out."

"Well, ain't you the politest devil in the hills. You talk like an Englishman. A greenhorn for sure. Don't know that I need help. Got these Piegans hyar, peaceable and trading plews. But they'd as soon slit my throat, the way they think about us. You bring any trade goods? I'm scraping bottom."

"Mr. McKenzie sent some, all he could spare. He told me to help you this spring and then help bring the returns down the river."

"You know the tongue?"

"No, but I'll learn it."

Berger spat. "I need a whole pack train of goods and they send me a greenhorn with one packload of trinkets. Well, git down. That horse'll come in handy until it's stolen. What do you do?"

"I have trapped and hunted mostly. Been a camp tender."

Berger spat again. "You bring any spirits?"

"No, sir."

The next wad of spit landed closer.

"I guess you can cut firewood."

"I can do that and make myself useful, if that's what you want. I cooked plenty as camp tender."

"Camp tender for who?"

"Jackson, Sublette, Fitzpatrick."

"You desert them?"

"No, sir. I can't reach them until the snow melts."

"Likely story. I'll hear the rest of it later. I guess I'm stuck with you. You just keep your mouth shut, don't rub them Piegans wrong, and mind your manners with their women. They ain't loose like the Crows."

twenty-five

Victoria boldly moved into the lodge of Jim Beckwourth, determined to have a happy time. She relished her new life as Antelope's woman. Stillwater was big with child, so Antelope devoted all his amorous attentions to Skye's former wife, giving her little gifts almost daily. A yellow ribbon one day, a string of beads the next, a jingle bell another day; needles and thread, a new awl, a sharp knife. Stillwater delighted in having a younger wife with her to share the work, especially now that she was so heavy and everything was harder to do. And Stillwater cherished being Antelope's sits-beside-him wife, with seniority over the new one.

Of course, Antelope did not abandon his long-standing romance with Pine Leaf, the woman warrior, and sometimes he left both of his women in the lodge and went visiting for a night. Those were the only times Victoria was unhappy. Lithe, beautiful Pine Leaf, the sister warrior who fought beside Beckwourth and had saved his life, was a rival that Victoria couldn't hope to equal in his heart.

He continued to call her Victoria—Skye's name for her—and she knew why. Every time he pronounced that name, it was with a sense of victory. He had not only vanquished his rival in the trading business but had taken Skye's wife from him as well. The thought made Antelope very happy and it amused Victoria, too. Sometimes he joked about it and they both laughed. Odd how it had all worked out. Skye had stolen her heart long ago, but when she brought him here to her people, he proved to be nothing, and wouldn't even go out and steal horses or make war. She put him out of mind. Antelope filled her thoughts.

She was very rich. Antelope had more of everything than anyone else in the village. She had everything an Absaroka woman could ever dream of: her new man was a war leader with many coups to his credit, and he could wear the notched feathers of an eagle. He sat in the old men's councils and his voice was heard. He had many women, which proved his greatness. He was the best host and party-giver among the Kicked-in-the-Bellies, and people rejoiced when word came to them to come to his lodge for a merry evening. He always had spirits, and quietly took in robes and pelts as he filled the cups.

Mostly the village nodded and winked and laughed at what happened to Skye. Everyone but the Old Bulls, the society of grandfathers who devoted themselves to the religion and traditions of the People and disapproved of change. But there weren't many of those because they were always making life so painful for everyone else. The Old Bulls would stare at her when she passed, but that was nothing. She loved being young and Antelope's lover and full of life and the woman of a great leader.

She had eyes for Antelope, but she had eyes for others—Young Horse, for instance. They had been eyeing each other at the parties, and maybe someday she would see what he had to offer. She had lost her virtue, but what Absaroka woman hadn't? That was the big joke. And what had the loss cost her? Nothing but Skye, who was gone now. Antelope was a true Absaroka even if he had been raised as a yellow eyes, but Skye never was anything but a yellow eyes. She should have known better than to marry him, but she was just a girl back at that rendezvous, and full of romantic ideas. Now she was a knowing woman; she knew all there was to know about a man, and yet she was only twenty winters.

There was one other who stared at her, and he wasn't an Old Bull. The shaman, Red Turkey Head, kept his counsel, but she knew he disapproved—and that the old man influenced her father. But she did not need her father or the shaman anymore now that she had Antelope. She remembered the long months with Skye in her parents' lodge and how frustrating it had been. He did not fit. She wondered what she had ever seen in him. She was glad she was in Antelope's lodge now. She avoided her father and brothers and sisters and grandparents, and especially avoided the old shaman, often walking in a different direction when she saw him. It made her angry, all this silent disapproval. She would live her time on earth as she chose.

At least she hadn't lost her mother. Often, Digs the Roots and Many Quill Woman slipped away together to chop firewood, and then they talked.

"You are better off. The one you were married to," she said, properly avoiding Skye's name, "had no understanding. Now you have a good one, this one who has another wife. The one who is your present man, he will give you all you could ever want. He is good with a woman, which is why he has many. Half the girls in the village would like to be that one's woman."

Victoria giggled. "Skye's feet smelled like skunks."

"The yellow eyes are dirty," her mother said as she hacked at a dry limb a long way from the village. Firewood was growing scarce in this last decaying gasp of coldness.

With the budding of leaves came the budding of war dreams among the men of the village. There were scores to settle, especially with the Siksika. Antelope sensed the time had come, even though many days were still chill and horses mired themselves in the muck.

"I'm going to go looking for Piegans," he announced to her

one day in the Moon of Budding Leaves. "I'm taking Pine Leaf with me, and a few others I trust."

"Why Pine Leaf? You should fight with men."

"Because Pine Leaf is a great warrior woman, and because we are happy together on the warpath."

A stab of jealousy cut her. "Then take me. Skye taught me how to make war."

"You're ninety pounds soaking wet."

"What does that mean?"

"You're too small."

"I can hold the horses. Skye taught me to shoot."

"War isn't for women. What chance would you have against a big, tough Siksika twice your size and weight?"

She fell into silence. She hated it when Pine Leaf intruded on her new life. She had taken a dislike to Pine Leaf, even though Stillwater liked the warrior woman.

"I'll bring you back a scalp," he said. "Count coup just for you."

"Ha! The only coup you count is on Pine Leaf."

Antelope laughed. "That's a good way to put it," he said.

"I'm going, even if I have to follow along behind the rest of you."

He turned serious. "No, I will make sure you don't."

But when the dawn came she threw her blankets over a pinto that Beckwourth had given her, gathered her bow and quiver, strapped her knife to her belt beside her flint and steel, found some jerked buffalo, and defiantly joined the rest, some thirty hard, watchful warriors who eyed her coldly. But she didn't care. Antelope sighed, relented, and let her come. She would give a good account of herself, and as long as she was along, Beckwourth would be forced to divide his time between her and Pine Leaf.

The warrior woman immediately joined her as they rode north in a brisk wind. "What does Magpie tell you?" she asked.

"Magpie does not tell me anything."

"You have come to war without knowing?"

"Yes!" She had not sought medicine wisdom, nor had her spirit-helper come to her. She had cast aside the powers that had been given to her. "Don't criticize me," she snapped.

"You may die. Or they may capture you and use you and then torture you to death slowly."

"I will show you who's the better warrior woman," Victoria said.

"I go to war against the Siksika because of a sacred vow. I will avenge the death of my brother, and many Siksika will die at my hand. It is not for myself. It is for the People. A sacred calling. I will never marry. My life is not given to any one man. It does not matter to me who I am, only that the People be safe and strong. I do not live for me. This came to me in a medicine vision when I was not yet a woman. What is yours?"

"I will not tell you."

"Let me be a sister to you, then. You can help. Sometimes women come along not to fight but to tend the wounded, find food, hold horses. I will show you how it is on the warpath. You are young and need a grandmother—a teacher."

"I am going to fight. I will show Antelope who is the best between us."

Pine Leaf gazed at the rebellious girl and rode away silently. There would be no friendship on the warpath between these two. Victoria was delighted. She didn't want to live in Pine Leaf's shadow.

That evening, deep in the Yellowstone country north and west of the winter village, they camped in a ravine where they could strike a spark into tinder without suffering the wind to extinguish the tiny glow before they could breathe it into flame. Brown grass, flattened by snow, matted the slopes, enough fodder for the ponies. Victoria had neglected to bring a picket line and knew she was in trouble.

"I need a picket line," she said to Antelope.

"Lots in the village," he said.

She didn't dare ask the other warriors and certainly not Pine

Leaf. She ended up turning her pinto loose. It wouldn't drift away from the rest but would be hard to catch at dawn. That evening she would begin to braid a line out of something—maybe the antelope skin she used as a saddle pad, or the edge of one of her robes. But she had gotten off to a bad start, and raged silently. She didn't like this, but the worse things got, the more stubborn she became.

She sensed the warriors were expecting her to feed them, but she scorned them. She chewed on the tough jerky and made do with that. She would be a warrior, not a camp follower.

The men had changed. These were the same men who lounged in the village, smoking, gambling, hunting, laughing, enjoying their children, eyeing all the wives and single girls, giving gifts. But now they were all strangers. She had never been on the warpath before, and the change in them excited her. They were moody and silent. Above all, they communed with their spirit-helpers, with the One Above, with those things around them that would influence their fate. Some fasted. Some observed strange rituals, walking in a circle, or lifting a hand to the sliver of new moon, or chanting to the setting sun, or removing their medicine bundles, opening them, minutely examining the totemic items within before retying the bundles and hanging them at their breast. Most of them sang their own medicine songs, devised to inform the spirits, or plead, or boast, or recite honors, or repeat a vow.

She watched, amazed at the transformation in these men. One thing she now knew: war was serious and these warriors took it seriously. Somehow all the war fever of the village had little to do with this, out upon the breast of the earth, where a warrior might fight and die.

twenty-six

Jim Beckwourth had ambitions, but not the ordinary kind. He didn't mind money or comfort or power, but these were not what his soul yearned for. He could take or leave wealth, didn't need to be a chief, and was as much at home out on the trail as in a comfortable warm lodge. Assorted wives and sweethearts were always welcome in his life, but he could manage without them if he had to.

What James Pierson Beckwourth lusted for was legend. Somewhere along the way, he had discovered that a reputation was exactly what satisfied his yearnings. So he began creating one. He did not wish merely to have a great reputation as a mountain man or a Crow warrior. No, he wanted his reputation to transcend all those lesser things. It would not do merely to be known among the Crows as a fine warrior. He needed to impress his mountaineer friends that he was the best of the best at everything. The best hunter, best warrior, best womanizer, best child-begetter, best shot, best knife fighter, best scalper, best scholar, best tracker, best leader, best guide, best horseman, best dresser, best looker, and best storyteller and friend the West had ever seen. He modestly supposed he was not quite all of these things, but if he nurtured the legend a little, people would think he might be.

Fame was, after all, a heady delight for a young man who

had technically been born a slave, even though his father had raised him as a free man. Back east, such a person, even though he was only an eighth a man of color and looked entirely white, had little hope of winning any sort of reputation at all, except perhaps as some sort of rascal. But here in the free and wild wilderness, reputation was the narcotic that filled his veins with joy.

A reputation took nurturing, pruning, and planning. It was not, after all, some weed that might grow and bloom all by itself. And so he had begun, way back in his fur brigade days, to let his colleagues know of his prowess at virtually everything, from reading and writing to shooting his Hawken. It required only a little embroidery, and he was always careful to stick closely to what everyone knew was true. He was not alone at this, either. Most of his campfire colleagues were past masters at the art of inflating their derring-do, especially when whiskey lubricated their tongues.

James Beckwourth knew well enough that fame had to be accompanied by deeds, that while he could embroider, he could not defraud or he would lose the whole game. And so, among the Crows, he was always ready to lead horse-stealing parties, acts of war that won acclaim with minimal risk. It wasn't hard to slip into a sleeping camp and make off with horses, or fire a few shots at awakening enemies, or even count coup. And that was what he was about on this adventure.

It did not hurt to have not one but two women along vying for his attentions, the famous fighting woman Pine Leaf and beautiful Victoria, Many Quill Woman, who had learned plenty about war from Skye. Some of his Crow colleagues no doubt disapproved, but so what? The women only added to his luster.

His objective this time was not to steal horses from the Piegans but to continue north to the Sweet Grass Hills and beyond to steal horses from the Bloods, the most formidable of all the enemies of the Absarokas. The Crows scarcely even respected the Piegans, especially the Little Robe band, which usually lived in a sort of unwritten truce with the Crows. But the Bloods, the Kainah, were a different matter. They were powerful, ruthless, daring, proud, colorful, and masters of mayhem. Counting coup against the Bloods was a dream that burned and smouldered in the soul of every Crow warrior. Let a Crow defeat a Blood and he would be great among his people, storied and feted, adored by the women, admired by every youth yearning to go to war.

The Bloods, then. They roamed country a little north of the Piegans, but forayed south now and then to torment the Crows. Beckwourth intended to catch them at their spring hunting grounds around the Sweet Grass Hills, and if not there, then across the medicine line into British territory, which was home to them. This would be a long trip, with the possibility of a long retreat and a long pursuit if the angry Bloods came after them. But that only made the prospects more enticing and ensured the glory of all the Crows. They were strong enough to thwart the Bloods, especially with Beckwourth's big Hawken that could deal death at a thousand yards, many flights of arrows distant.

Day by day they rode north through an early May chill, ever watchful for the enemy. They cut the trail of war and hunting parties on two occasions, the hoofprints embedded in the moist soil of springtime. Later in the year, when the sun had hardened the earth, it would be far more difficult to read as much from the passage of horses. But with cunning and care they made their way north unmolested except by a two-day cold rain that caught them on grasslands far from firewood and shelter and numbed them into misery. They were traveling for war and had not brought their heavy robes. Little Tail, one of the finest men among them, soon took sick, fevered by disease, and discovered that his medicine had failed him. They left Little Tail in a hidden swale, where he would endure until the sickness passed. It was a bad omen, and many of the Crows ascribed it to the presence of women.

Their passage took them across a vast and lonely prairie broken by occasional buttes and oddly formed hills. They reached the Missouri and tried two well-known fords before they found one that permitted passage. Even then they had to swim their horses through twenty yards of swift cold current, early spring runoff, and lost a horse in the process. Another bad omen. The shivering party gathered on the north bank, stripped off sopping leather clothing, built a miserable fire that threw no heat because of the wind, and tried to dry itself out. Some of Beckwourth's warriors eyed the women sullenly but said nothing. If either of the women belonged in the hut of the time of the moon, then the whole party was in danger from evil medicine. Pine Leaf never fought during those times, so the warriors eyed Victoria with dark suspicion and avoided her.

Beckwourth laughed. He believed in nothing, or almost nothing other than the explosive force of powder and the lethal effect of a lead ball. Victoria was an asset. She would hold the horses when the warriors crept on foot toward a Blood herd, and she could fight if she had to, using her own lighter bow and arrows. She had soldiered without complaint, making the brief camps comfortable.

One day, from an observation point halfway up the side of a butte, they spotted a whole Blackfoot village on the move, the motion almost invisible against the shadows of puffball clouds plowing across the land. Closer inspection revealed vedettes far out from the main body, two of them passing under the butte. Beckwourth, as war leader, opted for concealment, though some among them would have liked to swarm down on the vedettes and take scalps. No one among them could say whether these were Piegans or Bloods, or less probably Gros Ventres, Crees, or Assiniboines.

They pierced deeper into hostile country, their senses alert and nerves ajangle with the sudden flight of any bird or the slightest shift of the silences. Far to the west the white spine of the Rocky Mountains formed a rampart. For all the members of the Blackfoot Federation, those mountains meant home.

The next day they discovered a large herd of buffalo grazing in a shallow basin, and were just contemplating a feast of tongue and hump meat when the herd stirred. Something at its farther periphery agitated the black creatures, and the stirring spread into a sinuous movement, and then a slow trot, and finally a rush, as the huge animals began stampeding, their speed astonishing and improbable for such lumbering creatures. The source of all this soon became apparent. Blackfoot hunters were running the herd southward, darting among the great beasts on their swift buffalo ponies, drawing close enough to punch a lethal arrow into the heart-lung spot just behind the forelegs. Only the excitement of their hunt, and the mile distance, choked with buffalo, kept them from seeing the Crows.

Beckwourth watched, delighted even though they would not make meat just then, knowing they had escaped detection. He drew his men into a shallow gulch just out of sight, prepared to fend off the warriors who would want to catch and kill the buffalo hunters, steal their ponies, count coup, and go home triumphant. It would be an easy victory—but not against the Bloods, if Beckwourth's instincts were true. These hunters were Piegans, and they were probably tied to the passing village.

"These dogs, these Piegans, are too easy," he said, preempting the discussion. "They aren't worth chasing. We will go for the Bloods, and we will return with more honors. What is a coup against a Piegan? Nothing. We will show the People how to make real coups."

"I will count coups against these," said Sitting Man.

"No, that would betray us to them."

"I will count coup. It is the way given me. I will take some scalps and their buffalo runners. I want a fast horse. This is my way."

Beckwourth didn't like it. As war leader, he could forbid it—and face the consequences. Or permit it—and face the consequences. To prevent a warrior from acting upon his medicine was a grave matter, one that could sour the rest of the foray. But to give in might lead to discovery and defeat by overwhelming hordes of Blackfeet.

"Go, then, Sitting Man," Beckwourth said unhappily. "But they will follow your trail back to us."

Sitting Man didn't wait. He climbed onto his pinto pony, made medicine a moment, singing his war songs, and rode south, a lone knight.

Beckwourth had no choice other than to put distance between the war party and Sitting Man. The buffalo were long gone, and nothing but a swath of trampled, muddy grass told of their passage. He eyed the distant cloud-shadowed hills uneasily, saw nothing, and rode north as hard as the horses would move across soft and treacherous earth. He headed into the middle of the trampled area, hoping to conceal his party's passage, and rode north, ever north, to the land of the Bloods.

Far ahead, across a featureless plain, lay the Sweet Grass Hills, three great buttes rising over three thousand feet above the plains, the center butte much smaller than the massive ones east and west. Somewhere northwest of the hills, in the shadow of the Rockies, they would probably find Bloods—or Bloods would find them. But to get there they would cross a land without stories. Nothing ever happened there, nothing that could be told and retold. Nothing on that hollow plain spoke of time, or habitation, or events. So they would ride through a place without time.

An eerie isolation surrounded the hills, which perhaps was why the Blackfeet thought they were the habitation of spirits. One could gaze upon the dark buttes and see the spirits congregated there, unhappy, fearsome, isolated, and maybe vengeful, too. Beckwourth didn't like the looks of the hills, and neither did his warriors. The quest for glory had turned dark.

twenty-seven

Death wove a red thread through Skye's every hour. Berger's little post was subject to every whim of the Blackfeet. The Piegans suffered it simply because it was a convenient source of white men's goods, much closer than the Hudson's Bay posts far to the north.

Not that the Piegans liked or trusted the Americans, with whom they had been at war ever since they had skirmished with Lewis and Clark. Many a warrior entered the cabin not so much to trade as to measure the heads of those within for the scalping knife. If the traders survived, it would be only because of Berger's formidable presence. He refused to be intimidated. But as the scanty supply of trade goods dwindled, and the pile of robes, prime beaver pelts, and other skins mounted, the Blackfeet took more and more liberties, wandering behind the crude counter, daring Berger to cause trouble, pilfering whatever they could.

Skye knew that he and Berger and the Creole, Arquette, wouldn't last ten minutes in a fight. Not with scores of warriors lounging about ready to burn the rough cottonwood log cabin and fry its occupants. But peace held, perhaps because Berger assured the Blackfeet that the American Fur Company would build a larger post there and sell more goods for better prices than Hudson's Bay. That slender thread was all that kept their topknots on their skulls. That and Berger's fearless diplomacy.

The little outpost did not deal in whiskey even though spirits were the most lucrative—if illegal—business of all. Berger knew full well what a jug of Indian whiskey—raw alcohol, river water, and a plug of tobacco or pepper for taste—would do to these tribesmen who weren't accustomed to spirits. They were explosive enough sober; with drink in them they would pay no heed to tomorrow and butcher the hated Yanks just for the joy of it.

At Fort Union an Indian could show up at a small window after dark, any night, and trade a pelt for a cup. But Fort Union could defend itself even from a mob of whiskey-crazed warriors on a drunk. Its stockade was all but impenetrable. So the only risk in the illegal liquor trade was discovery by the United States Indian commissioners.

Skye yearned for a jug, but Berger kept not even a drop for his own use. Skye woke up each morning wondering if he would survive the day. His task was to cut firewood, which took him far from the post and subjected him to the whim of any Blackfoot who decided to kill him. Another of his tasks was to feed the horses any way he could, putting them out on the tender spring grasses and watching over them while they grazed, or cutting grass and bringing it to his animals, which were penned behind the cabin. He expected them to disappear at any moment, with the itch of any Blackfoot, but the theft didn't happen. Still another was to hunt, because the post's provisions had long since been exhausted. Berger traded goods for meat now and then, but the food supply had become precarious and monotonous.

Blackfeet came and went. Some days a whole village would erect its lodges around the cabin; other days there wasn't an Indian in sight and Skye could do his chores without the underlying terror that usually accompanied them. Skye was assigned the meanest and most dangerous tasks because he was junior, while Arquette sorted and pressed beaver and other furs into packs, and cooked as well. Berger lounged, traded, meandered among the Blackfeet making friends as much as possible. He did not neglect to hand out small gifts—a plug of tobacco here, a few beads there, a knife to a chief or headman.

Skye tried to learn the tongue, but confused it with the Crow, and had trouble. Still, he figured every word he mastered was a word that might help him in a pinch. "Arrow" was *aps'se.* "Water" was *oh kiu'.* "Wind" was *su po'.* "Fire" was *is'tsi.* The Marias River, close at hand, was called *Kaiyi Isisakta,* which really meant "Bear River." He mastered fifty, then a hundred words, but Berger never let him trade. That business was too delicate and the Blackfeet too unpredictable.

So Skye headed out each morning with his packhorse, walking past the handsome lodges of these people while enduring their curious silences, chopped cottonwood limbs, bundled them on his pack saddle, and returned, amazed to be alive. He took his Hawken, but Berger instructed him not to use it except as a last resort. He was to stand firm, prevent theft of his horse if he could, show no sign of dread or fear if he could, and hasten back to the post.

Then, for a while, the Blackfeet vanished. They were off on raids, hunting, visiting relatives in other bands, marrying, making ready for the Sun Dance, which they held at the time of the summer solstice, going on vision quests, opening sacred medicine bundles—the beaver bundle was opened about this time each spring, Berger explained. That was fine with Skye. His sojourn at this vulnerable little outpost was coming to a close and he was still alive, to his astonishment.

He debated whether to pull out, head across the opened passes, find Bridger and Fitzpatrick, report for work, confess his failure with the Crows. It was tempting, but the thought of Victoria stopped him cold. He was done with the mountains. Any hope of healing the hole in his heart lay in some Yank place like St. Louis or the mysterious cities to the east. No, he wouldn't do that, nor would he betray McKenzie. He would not add that black mark to all the rest.

More Piegans arrived, thirty lodges led by a burly old chief with five or six wives. Skye had never seen such tall, handsome Indians. They exuded pride, beauty, power, arrogance, assurance, and lordship over all this country. They drifted south during the brief summers, making trouble for their neighbors. Their lodges had been gaily decorated with moons and fallen stars painted around their bases, bright insignias suggesting clan and medicine painted on the sides. These people favored blues of all shades in their dress, beadwork, and even on the parfleches.

Swiftly they traded prime beaver plews for Berger's powder and lead, lance points, kettles, arrowheads, knives, and awls. By the middle of May they had reduced Berger's stock of trade goods to a few items, mostly awls, flints, fire steels, knives, and beads, which made Berger uneasy. Empty shelves only tempted the Indians with visions of blood and fire. It was time to get out of there, build some bullboats and float the pelts down the Missouri to Fort Union on the crest of the spring runoff. Skye, with his horses, would take a load overland, a dangerous business for a sole white man during the high summer days when every warrior of the northern plains was out roving, looking for adventure and plunder and coups.

Berger talked at length to Little Crow, the chief of this band. He seemed more amiable than many of his younger warriors, who apparently considered the traders disposable now that the post had been largely emptied of the miraculous goods white men traded. Little Crow genially announced that his people would summer west of the Sweet Grass Hills where the buffalo were thick, and maybe raid the cowardly Crows on Elk River—their name for the Yellowstone—for horses, or join the Bloods on a joint venture southward for plunder. The medicine was good; the seers were brimming with fierce optimism; the weather was fine, the land full of grass to fatten ponies; and all the young men were itching for honors. Who could resist? The fierce Blackfeet were the best of the best on the plains and would take many scalps, capture many children and women, and torture hundreds of Crows to death, the sound of their howling proof of their cowardly natures.

They left after three days, and Berger decided it was time to head down the river. He elected to build two large bullboats to carry his packs of fur to the fort, one man in each boat. Some additional furs would go back upon Skye's packhorse with Skye. Berger set Skye to cutting willow saplings for the bullboats, while he and Arquette prepared a stack of raw buffalohides by trimming the edges. All this required brutal toil. Skye buried the ends of the saplings in the earth, forming an elongated circle, and then bent them over and lashed them together into a framework that looked like an inverted bowl. The hides, properly dressed with fat, sewn tight, and sealed with pitch and tallow, would form the skin of the bullboats and would last long enough in the water to get the furs and traders to Fort Union. Maybe. The light boats were treacherous, hard to maneuver, and likely to capsize in white water.

Rain stopped the work. It came in cold gusts, sheets of icy water that drenched a man and set him to shivering. They swiftly ran out of firewood, and Skye was elected to cut some, which he did between spring showers, often getting soaked in the process. Arquette nursed catarrh, while Berger coughed and cursed, and Skye wrestled with bilious fever between his cold bouts of woodcutting. But he persisted. His three months as an engagé for American Fur Company were drawing to a close, and soon sixty dollars would be applied to his debt to Rocky Mountain Fur.

The only good thing about living among the dangerous Blackfeet was that time flew. Danger honed a keen edge on every minute, and he scarcely thought about Victoria, or loss, or the emptiness of his future. It was enough to survive among tribesmen who were itching to take his scalp and leave him soaking in his blood until wild creatures ate his meat and plucked out his eyes. But when he did think about her, he knew that his pain had not lessened, love had not dwindled, and his anger at her and at Beckwourth had not abated. Time had healed nothing.

By early June they were able to work on the bullboats again. Time was growing short. They needed to reach Fort Union with the season's returns by July 1, when the keelboat was due from St. Louis and scheduled to load and turn around as fast as possible. They finished the sturdy, flexible frame of one boat and began lashing the hides together with thong and fitting them over the frame. This too was hard work. The seams, including every hole made by an awl, needed to be caulked with pitch drawn from a pine, and the hides soaked in tallow to waterproof them. They finished one boat, and it looked so fragile and makeshift that Skye, the seaman, wondered whether it would survive a mile of water. They began the second, only to discover they lacked hides and would have to find and skin some buffalo. That or build a log raft, which was itself a risky way to carry the hides. Rafts tipped over in rough water, soaked the hides, and resulted in even more disaster than bullboats.

So Arquette and Skye hunted buffalo while Berger guarded the post through the high sweet days of June. The hunt was fruitless. Buffalo had long since gathered into great migratory herds and drifted off to prime grasslands to calve, fatten, rub off ticks and fleas on any useful tree, wallow in mud puddles to clean their hides of varmints, and fight off the wolves that silently shadowed the herds, looking for the injured, the old, the isolated calf.

Berger cursed his subordinates for their barren efforts and decided on another expedient: he would trade for packhorses and send the furs back overland, two men with horses, while he navigated with the sole bullboat. There wasn't much left to trade, but he figured he could get some horses out of what was left. One rifle—his own—would get him half a dozen horses with packsaddles thrown in. All he had to do was find some Blackfeet.

twenty-eight

Many Quill Woman—the name Victoria was fading fast—looked for a sign as the Absarokas rode past the Sweet Grass Hills. She sensed that those gloomy forested slopes were the habitation of the dead, the place where the spirits of the Siksika came to live as shades in the other world. The peoples of the plains knew each others' stories. In her village were two captive Blackfeet women who had become wives, and several captured children who would be raised as Absarokas. In the villages of the Siksika, the Lakota, the Cheyenne, and other tribes there were Crow women, sometimes wives, more often slaves. And so the stories were shared, and each tribe well knew the sacred rites of the others.

She looked for the spirits but saw none. Maybe she was wrong. The Siksika believed the spirits of their dead went to the Sand Hills to wander forever—but maybe these weren't the Sand Hills. These hills rose in utter isolation, surrounded by emptiness, and spread night out upon the sunny plains. A place like that deserved respect. She spoke gently to the grandfathers and grandmothers whose shades surely resided there. So many of them; others walking the spirit trail, arriving each day. She felt the coldness of death pass through her, and hurried her pony westward, eager to put the hills behind her. This was not a good land, like that of the Absarokas.

The others in her war party eyed the hills somberly. If these hills weren't the abode of the Siksika dead, they certainly should be. Maybe some of the spirits who resided there had been sent to this place by Absaroka arrows and lances and war clubs. This was not a good place for an Absaroka to be, with the eyes of the spirits upon them, ever watchful.

She was having misgivings about coming with Beckwourth. She wasn't afraid of death, like the yellow eyes. Life was short. One could die for the People and be remembered. But she wasn't a warrior and knew little of the ways of death—except for what the one who had been her man had taught her. In this kind of land, where there was no place to hide, even a horse holder was as vulnerable as a warrior who crept into a Siksika camp.

This was not a good land—it lay open and barren and without history, and the white wall of the mountains in the hazy west rose like the end of the world. Her Absaroka world had no end, but this Siksika world stopped in the west. This was a cold land, too, and there was no place to hide from the cold. Even now, well into spring, cold gusts whirled down off the distant mountains and sliced heat out of her lithe body.

The others rode quietly, saying nothing, their thoughts upon war, their silences profound. Pine Leaf rode apart, isolated, small, odd, like a doll. Many Quill Woman had never seen the woman warrior like this, and now she understood the sacredness of Pine Leaf's vows to kill Siksika. Something flat and hard emanated from the woman warrior here in the land of her enemies.

Many Quill Woman summoned her courage. She had seen no magpies this entire trip. Usually they flocked about, raucously following the passage of horses and men. She knew her spirit-helper had turned her face away. Bad medicine. But Many Quill Woman knew she would continue. She would ride with Beckwourth even with bad medicine. That was how much she enjoyed her new man.

That's what she told herself, anyway. But in softer moments, doubt flooded her, fear and a cold dread. Even now, they might be observed. Or Sitting Man might have given away their passage. She thought Beckwourth should have commanded Sitting Man to come along and not chase after the hunters. But now it was too late. She doubted that any of them would see Sitting Man again.

Black-bottomed clouds spun off the distant mountains and rolled over the prairie like dark stones, bringing with them the little death of the sun. She did not like the clouds or this land, and wondered whether the Absaroka warriors did. Even Beckwourth had grown quiet, the loquacious storyteller and party-giver oddly solemn. How could they steal horses when there was no place to hide? Well, it worked both ways. If there was no place for Absaroka to hide, then there was no place for the Siksika to hide either.

But nothing disturbed their passage. They rode through a quietness that began to grate on her. Would not even the west wind make a noise? Was this the land of the dead? Twilight settled over them, veiling their passage, shrouding them in the funeral clothing of night. They would halt at some creek, water and graze the ponies, and sleep without a fire, huddle under their horses if it rained, and then arise to hunt their prey before dawn.

Beckwourth led them into a shallow draw running a trickle of water. The draw put them well under the surface of the plain and protected them from the all-seeing eyes of the Siksika. Maybe with the next sun they would find the Bloods, the Kainah, and then they would wait quietly for the cloak of another night to hide them when they filtered into the herds and stole fine fat ponies. They were well concealed; there would be no need for guards this night, hidden in a crease of the prairie.

They picketed their ponies on stakes. Victoria employed the line she had braided out of much of her robe. Her brothers the warriors seemed uncommonly quiet this night. She lay in the chill of the draw, wishing she could escape the flow of cold air down it, staring at the many stars in the heavens, each star the spirit of one who was gone forever. Like Skye. She tried to abolish his name from mind, but his name was there. He was like the dead now; she should put him out of mind, if she could.

Few of them slept. One could hear sleep, hear the sigh and fall of breath, but not now. The ponies were nervous, wheeling on their pickets, snorting softly, their nostrils catching the scent of something—wolf or man or bear. Who could know? It would be a long night.

She tossed the whole night. The hard cold earth bit her. She could not find a level place in the draw. She swore owls drifted past her. Owls were sacred, and their presence portended death. Shapes in the night changed, loomed over her, retreated. Surely these were the Siksika spirits from those brooding hills. Her bones ached. Why had she come on a warrior's mission? What a foolish young woman she had been. Why had not Red Turkey Head said anything? Where was Magpie?

The wolf cry in the predawn light wasn't a wolf, and all the Absaroka knew it. She bolted upright in the murk. An arrow struck her buffalo robe. They had hunted for the Bloods but the Bloods had found them first. She saw, or thought she saw, Blackfoot warriors on either side, loosing arrows into the Absarokas below. One brother grunted, cried something, and then groaned. The groaning stopped. She froze, unable to decide what to do. Around her the Absarokas were struggling out of their robes, reaching for their bows and quivers, stringing bows. She heard another thump of arrow on flesh, and someone toppled with a terrible cough and a sigh.

Fear paralyzed her. Near her, Pine Leaf was yanking her pony's picket pin from the ground and easing over the back of her fear-crazed pony. Pine Leaf steered the pony straight upslope at the warriors who were loosing arrows from above, recklessly steering toward the enemy. Other Absarokas followed her, and Many Quill Woman heard the sounds of desperate struggle from that quarter. She stared, astonished. Most of the Absarokas were fleeing down the draw on foot or horseback. She saw a horse stagger, whinny, grunt, and roll over slowly. That was her salvation. She raced to it, fell behind the still-heaving body, strung her bow, pulled an arrow from her quiver and nocked it, and tried to discern the enemy, who were gliding downslope on foot, barely visible in the curtains of darkness. She rose, loosed an arrow at a crouching warrior on the slope. It missed. She ducked behind the carcass and nocked another.

Goddammit, where was Skye?

She heard Antelope howling like a wolf, his voice unmistakable. He was rallying his men against this unseen enemy. A dozen Absarokas raced in his direction. But the arrows came thick and fast, finding their marks. Many Quill Woman saw another Absaroka stagger and fall and writhe on the bloody grasses. She knew that one, Diving Hawk, husband of her friend Little Weasel, and a new father.

Someone fired a rifle, the crack shocking in the silent cusp of day. She saw forms darting downslope, crouching, looking for targets, loosing arrows. They spoke the tongue of the enemy. One stopped, threw up his arms, and tumbled. So one Siksika dog died, anyway. She would kill another. She would kill before they killed her. Where had her people gone? She could see none, but she heard the low thud of hooves across the throat of the earth. Where were her warriors? Where had Antelope gone?

She heard the sounds of struggle up above, on the plains, grunts and cries, howls of rage, horses coughing and collapsing. For the moment the war departed from her. Those who had crept down the slopes had run back up again. The light thickened into a soft gray, enough to make things out. A half dozen Absarokas lay dead or groaning. They would lose their scalps soon enough—and so would she. But she saw several Bloods—if that's what they were—on the slope, some looking dead; another was sitting with his leg cocked sideways, useless. She suddenly realized she had to find her people, find Beckwourth, get a good horse and flee. Wherever the fighting was, it wasn't in the draw. Black lumps sprawled on the slopes told her of death. Weeping, choking, gasping, groaning, singing, told her of dying. Suddenly war took on a new perspective for her. This was real; the victory parades through the village had never been real. How would she feel with an arrow in her chest, unable to breathe, her world turning over?

Beckwourth had raced up the draw, the one direction that offered salvation. She would follow. She abandoned the carcass, felt an arrow pierce her skirt, tumbled to earth, and tried to find the arrow's source. The injured Blood on the slope was still fighting his battle, and his arrows were lethal. Another smacked the grass inches from her nose. She bolted forward while he armed himself. She turned, loosed an arrow at him, and it struck his bow, spoiling his aim. His arrow vanished somewhere. She raced up the draw, heart pounding. Where were they?

She splashed through the rivulet at the head of the draw and felt the icy water soak her moccasins. She climbed a short steep embankment that took her to the undulating plains, and freedom, and beheld bloody light across the eastern horizon. She saw no one for a moment; the running battle had taken both sides far away. Her heart slowed. She wished she had run when Antelope called, jumped on any pony instead of lying behind a dying horse.

A warrior loomed out of nowhere. He was leading a lame horse. She saw in a flash this one was a Blood, and he would kill her with the knife in his hand. She drew her bow, but he lunged, knocking her flat with his shoulder; a club just missed her face. She tumbled to earth and scrambled aside to avoid the blade.

But the thrust didn't come.

twenty-nine

They stared at each other. Her heart raced. The Blood was mature and powerful, and he bore the marks of war. A scar cut across his cheek, from the corner of an eye to his mouth. But for it he would be handsome. He stood over her, enjoying his triumph.

She would die. The knife in his hand was poised to cut her throat. She ached to kill him, but his moccasin rested heavily on her chest, crushing her into the earth.

She didn't want to die. Not after only twenty winters. But helplessness stole through her, the helplessness of a baby bird caught in the hand. She did not rebuke herself for coming on this ill-fated venture. There wasn't time. She needed to summon her wits and begin to sing a death song, but words deserted her.

Something shifted in his eyes, and he lowered his hand to his side. It wasn't mercy she saw, but something else. And then she knew. He would enjoy torturing her later. The Siksika were good at it. She would die slowly, her flesh roasted and peeled from her living body, her screams involuntary no matter how hard she sought stoic death. She ached for the blade and its swift sure mercy.

He took his foot off her and said something she didn't understand. The pain where his foot had crushed her chest throbbed. He smiled darkly, picked up her bow and snapped it in two, pulled the knife from her waist sheath and left her there. She knew if she moved, or fled, he would be back in an instant. He studied the distant prairies, listening for the sound of strife. His lamed horse had ended the battle for him. He studied his horse, lifted a foreleg; the horse screamed its agony, and he let go. In one blurred motion he slit the throat of the horse. Red gouted from its neck. It shivered, sagged, and dropped heavily to the ground, its limbs flailing, its body convulsing.

The Blood warrior walked downslope toward the wounded or dead Absarokas. She watched him, filled with knowing. The man was powerfully built, with flesh the color of honey, jet hair worn in a single braid, and wearing leggings and moccasins and breechclout, but nothing save a medicine bundle above the waist. A second scar puckered his left arm. He was older than she, and he had seen many battles and won many honors.

He approached Little Otter from behind. The Absaroka lived, but soon wouldn't. An arrow pierced clear through his chest. The Blood grasped Little Otter's two braids, lifted them high, and ran his scalping knife clear around Little Otter's head, across his brow, over the ears, around the back, and to the brow again. Little Otter groaned. The Blood yanked mightily on the braids, and the scalp popped free with a sucking sound. The Blood watched the Absaroka sag into the ground and left him to die slowly, his spirit homeless evermore. The Blood lifted his fresh scalp and offered it to the heavens, seeking the blessings of the rising sun upon his victory.

One by one, the Blood scalped the rest of the dead and injured. Six scalps in all, a great victory for the Blood; probably his greatest ever. He would tell the story of many coups to his people soon. Many Quill Woman watched her friends die. Without scalps their spirits would wander through eternity and never walk the trail to the stars. Now this empty plain, without history, had a new story.

The sun crimsoned the new grass and then lifted off the breast of the earth. All this had happened between first light and sunrise. Off to the east, the Sweet Grass Hills brooded and mocked. The hills had seen the Absarokas all along and had told the Siksika where to find enemies.

So this was how her young life would end. In unspeakable pain and torment. They would soon return, probably bearing more scalps, and then she would know the fate of her people. She would count the scalps and know. Then they would turn to her, the survivor. Her fate would be decided entirely by the one who captured her. He held the power of life and death over her now, and none of the others would intervene. They might all use her, one by one, and then cut her throat. They might beat her until she couldn't endure the pain, and they would beat her the more. They might take her with them for a while, and torture her this evening, sport around a campfire, her shrieks blotted up by this empty silent land until she died. And the death would be a mercy.

She knew their tortures. A favorite was to jab splinters of pine into the victim's flesh and then ignite them and watch living flesh roast. They might cut off her fingers, joint by joint, slowly, so she didn't die quickly. They might suspend her by her feet from a limb, the blood rushing to her head, and then cook her head over a fire. Or they might simply beat her to death, each of them counting coup, kicking, hitting, cutting, until she passed out of this world and into the spirit land. If only she had her knife she could plunge it into her breast. But she didn't. She lay aching, dreading, aware of a fate that she had brought upon herself.

Magpie. The bird settled near her, pecked at something in the grass, and flew away in a burst of black and white and iridescent feather. Why had Magpie come now, when all was over? To watch her die. Many Quill Woman had ignored her own medicine-helper, and would pay. And Magpie would remind her as she died in pain what it was to ignore what had been given to her.

She discerned a knot of horsemen in the distance, returning slowly, and she knew the rest of the Bloods were gathering at this scene of triumph. There were about twenty. So her Absaroka party had been the stronger, but the courageous Bloods had attacked and won on this day, taking advantage of the land they knew so well, and the night, and maybe Beckwourth's recklessness. She had heard only one shot during the entire affray; it had been Beckwourth's. These Bloods lacked firearms and fought with arrow and club, war ax and lance. A rifle cost many robes, many beaver pelts, and few could own one. Only a few chiefs, with many wives tanning robes, had rifles.

Sorrow swept her. Foolishness! She had been swept along by giddy girlish dreams, Beckwourth's seductions, bad company. She might yet live, but she was doomed. She lay quietly on the grass while the Bloods rode in, stared at her, talked with her captor, and gazed at the six scalps. They lifted a lance that bore three more. She feared she would find Beckwourth's beribboned braids, or Pine Leaf's lighter colored braid, but did not see them. Nine dead, no doubt more wounded. This was the worst tragedy her village had known for many winters. Horses, too. The victors drove a dozen Absaroka ponies before them, including hers. She knew them. Some still bore medicine paintings on them. The Bloods had triumphed in many ways this day: horses, scalps, and a captive to torture.

They wrapped their dead one in a robe and lifted the body onto a horse, which sidestepped nervously, smelling blood and death. Her captor kicked her hard in the ribs, shooting pain through her, and motioned her to stand. Now they all stared at her. She was lithe and pretty, and she knew that they were seeing a woman to use, a woman of the hated Absarokas to use and torment and kill. They brought her a horse and she mounted, her body aching. Some came and punched her, counting coup. She was cold, but they gave her no robes. It would be a long time before the sun was high enough to warm her, and she would still be cold. She would never be warm again, and when her time came, she would die cold, even if they killed her with fire.

They rode west, she knew not where, her captor leading her

horse with a braided lead rope. They stopped only to water the horses at a creek and drink some themselves, and then were off again. They gave her none, and her body cried with thirst. All that morning they rode toward the western mountains, each step taking her farther from her people.

They began talking to each other at last, their talk almost cheerful in spite of the dead man among them. It had been a good fight this day, and the Bloods were the lords of the plains. Many coups had they counted. They shared pemmican but fed her nothing. She grew faint and didn't know what was worst: utter hopelessness, dread of the torture to come, or thirst. The day warmed, and blossoms bobbed in the zephyrs. The sun stroked her doeskin skirts but did not warm her.

They stopped early on a sizable river she did not know, one lined with cottonwoods and willows—firewood for what was to come. She watched Magpie flit from limb to limb, dodging behind leaves, swooping just in front of her horse. Magpie had come to watch her die. Her captor motioned her to step down, and she did, collapsing in the dirt beside the river. He said something, kicked her, and she rose. He pushed her toward a stately willow and lashed her to its trunk. This would be the place of her torment.

They ignored her, built a fire, staked the ponies on tender spring grasses, washed themselves, went into the bushes, devoted themselves to their prayers, their medicine, each in his own way. They trod this land with a lordly step, knowing themselves to be invincible. These people were much taller than hers, with hawkish faces, not the moon faces of her people. They had thinner noses and some of their eyes were gray instead of black or brown. She loathed them all the more for their proud manner, their handsomeness, their arrogance.

She grew dizzy, bound to the rough bark by tight thongs, and wished she would slip away into the spirit world. It grew dark, and she sensed anticipation among them. They eyed her now and then. They looked to their horses, examined the ones they had won at battle, made their medicine. Night came, and this night would be the night of all nights.

She watched their war leader, their headman, who issued quiet commands that were instantly obeyed. This night the horses would be well guarded. He sent three of his warriors into the deepening darkness. They would wander among the ponies this night, and none would fall to the Absarokas. They were warriors first, and whatever entertainments they had planned for her came second.

Her captor came at last, freed her, and led her away from the tree. So they would not torture her there. The warriors gathered about her now, and she understood what would happen this night. It was written upon their faces.

thirty

Her captor took her broken body to his village, but she was elsewhere. He had granted the Absaroka woman a reprieve—for the moment. Her fate would be whatever his whim might be. He could, even after she spent months of faithful service as a slave, choose to kill her and no one would interfere. She had become property.

She sat upon a pony, oblivious of the world. Her mind drifted away from its moorings and her thoughts turned to sacred things. She hurt, but not even that mattered. Her dress had rents in it that let in air and male gazes, but that didn't matter either. What would they see that they hadn't seen?

She rode through a fine spring day but it didn't lift her out of her long drift into a spirit land. She had had nothing to eat for two suns, and it dizzied her. If she fell off her pony and they brained her with a war club, that would be a mercy. She was parched as well; they had not given her water. Her heart raced because of her thirst.

Then, at noon, they reached a creek that ran between barren banks, not a tree or bush in sight. Her captor untied her hands and pulled her to the ground, commanding something. She crawled to water and they let her drink. She sipped a little, and it tasted good. She cupped her hands and drank more, and more. Water was the ultimate blessing. A person could endure hunger, but thirst raked a body. The effect was immediate. With water came the will to live if she could. Around her warriors drank and left her alone. She took care of her needs, always in plain sight, and then went back to the creek to drink some more, soak her lithe body in water. Then she washed, not caring what they thought: her face and hands, her neck and limbs, her violated torso. Then she drank again.

The water even assuaged her hunger a little. They did not feed her because they were almost out of trail food and had shot no game. A warrior expected to go without if he had to, and she shared the warrior's fate. The water restored her body to her, with its pain and shame. Now, at last, in the brightness of a summery day, she studied them. They were very like her own people, most of them dressed only in breechclouts, some with leggings and moccasins. They had started to paint themselves, each daubing color according to his medicine, drawn from small kits they carried with them. The colors had been found in nature, mostly from vegetation and blooms, but sometimes from the clays and rock of the earth. They were painting for victory this occasion. They could not be far from the Kainah village.

These were seasoned veterans of the warpath. Her captor was one of the youngest, she thought, but still a veteran warrior. These were tall people, muscular, their color ranging from amber to copper, their skills at war evident in their every gesture, in their elaborate war shields made of the thick neck hide of a buffalo bull and capable of deflecting arrows and even a musket ball that quartered into them. Their medicine was powerful: otters, lightning, falling stars, bears, geometric designs, crimson, blue, white, tan.

Her captor motioned for her to mount, and after she did he tied her hands with thong so tightly it slowed the blood to her fingers. This time he tied a braided rope around her neck, and mounted his own horse holding the other end. The device would symbolize her captivity when they rode through the village.

How often she had stood in her own village while the warriors rode in, their paint, their war emblems, and the burdens on the horses telling their tales without words. How often she had watched the arrival of a captive being brought to the Kicked-in-the-Bellies, and had spat at the victim, heaped insults upon whoever it was, woman or man, and enjoyed the thought of the beatings the enemy would justifiably receive. The Absaroka didn't torture, not the way some people did, but the captive would suffer abuse—kicks, pummeling, starvation, exhausting work, cold, lack of clothing, discomfort. It was all the just reward of making war against the Absaroka.

Now all this would be her lot. She should be angry but she was beyond that. Anger required energy, and she had none left. But she might still be proud. Let a noose dangle from her neck; she would show the Siksika dogs that no noose and no abuse had broken a Kicked-in-the-Belly woman. She would sit so imperiously that they would know what she was, know that nothing they could do to her would break her pride or shame her. They would see her pride and wonder whether torture would shatter it. They would see her pride and envy her. The women in particular would torment her, cut her hair, jab at her, prick her flesh with knives, disfigure her, whip her, leave her naked to the cold. But they would not break her pride.

The war party paused at the edge of the village, which lay in a half-moon along a river they would ford to reach it. There they were greeted by the village wolves, the sentries always on guard against surprise. The villagers began to gather across the sparkling river, women, children, old men, and boys itching to be warriors. The boys would do her harm as she rode by, pelting her, jeering, running close with a stick to count coup, maybe even driving blunted arrows from their small bows into her. She had seen boys in her own village put out the eye of one captive and open the wounds of another until she bled over her skirts. She braced for that.

Then the war party descended the gravelly banks of the river and they forded the low, glittering stream, which rose only to the pasterns of the horses. Her captor jerked his line, yanking her by the neck until she nearly fell, but she clung to the mane of her pony. To fall was to die, because he would not stop dragging her. What better entertainment than for the village to witness the death of an enemy? She clung, absorbed each yank of the cord, kicked her pony forward to gain some slack in the braided cord. Now they were walking through an aisle between crowds of people. This was a large village; the Bloods were many.

The women began to keen; she knew that sound. Their eyes weren't upon those fresh Absaroka scalps dangling from lances but upon the burdened pony at the rear of the procession, upon the paint that told all who had eyes that this great victory was not without a price. The Bloods eyed her coldly, and she eyed them back, gaze for gaze, glare for glare, the stares locking. She did not surrender to their gaze. A rage to live rose in her; she was among the enemy and that became reason enough to survive. She would show these hated people what it meant to be Absaroka.

The boys she dreaded soon began walking beside her, shouting at her from both sides. She gripped the mane and held on. A rock stung her ribs, knocking breath from her. Then a youth darted close, a war club in hand, and swung it. The club landed on her shoulder, knocking her clear off her pony. She tumbled to the grass, felt the yank of line on her neck, flailed dizzily as the club found her skull, and then felt her head snapping under the tug of that cord. She crawled forward, not fast enough. Boys kicked at her, screaming their taunts. She grabbed hold of the line, let herself be dragged by it until she could put her bare feet under her. The line never stopped; her captor never slowed. She bounded up and forward, found her footing, and careened ahead. Her captor had speeded up, enjoying her desperation. The boy's war club found her back, knocking her to the ground, where she writhed. This time the line slackened. She heard a sharp male command, and the boy retreated. She was too spent to continue; hurting, tired, starved, so faint she couldn't even get to her knees. The Bloods swarmed about her, some taunting, others silent. She had to get up or die. She pulled herself to her hands and knees, staggered to her feet, felt blood welling from her head, pushed back tears and rage, and found herself glaring at the tormenting boy, a lean laughing youth on the brink of becoming a warrior. She slapped him. He was so astonished he didn't respond.

Then the village women swarmed in, pummeling her, knocking her to the ground. She felt pain welling up in her until it burst in her skull, and she fought and clawed at the swinging feet and hands. Then something hit her on the head, and she saw whiteness. She did not lose her senses, but she lost time and place in a wash of bewilderment. Everything hurt. She heard a sharp command, and the pounding slowed and then stopped. She lay bleeding on the grass. Someone carried her somewhere, darkness, a lodge, silence. No one tended her. She lay in gloom, wanting oblivion, her last strength gone. She had not known a mortal body could yield such pain to its possessor.

No one was about. She lay there, the ache not diminishing, the Bloods celebrating. Some were drumming and singing or dancing. She heard the steady heartbeat of the drummers. This night they would be celebrating a great victory, each of them telling of his role, boasting of his prowess, calling down his medicine. Those rich in captured ponies would give them away, one for a youth, another for a widow, one for a woman with many children, and the best buffalo runners and war ponies for their friends, their colleagues at arms. She heard the beat; the throb of the drums matched her pulse, and when the drums quickened, so did her pulse. She was grateful for the darkness, and wanted night, blackness to enfold her.

She did not know how long she lay there, only that it had

been long. Then she grew aware of some stirring. Her eyelids were so swollen she could barely open them to see. Her captor sat in the place of honor, opposite the doorflap, leaning into a reed backrest. A woman handed him a bowl and a bone ladle. He quietly ate stew. They noticed Victoria staring but offered nothing.

She drifted into darkness again. She was allowed to lie in the place of least honor, next to the lodge door. No one gave her a robe. Ants crawled over her. She grew aware that this lodge sheltered others, mostly women, and two or three children, who whispered, pointed, poked her, and laughed. If she lay very still, almost not breathing, the pain lifted a little. To breathe was to hurt. She thought a rib might be broken; her shoulder was numb, and she could not move her left arm. Her head throbbed. A lump had formed on the side of her head, another just above the back of the neck. She could barely swallow, and she could not turn her head.

She lay adrift, the night passing through her brain like dark clouds, the stars glittering and then vanishing, the moon racing. She thought of Skye, long lost, and loved him as she had when she first set eyes on him at a white man's rendezvous long ago. He had talked about strange things, his God, his long imprisonment, his desperate escape, the sacredness of marriage, his quest for peace, his hatred of slavery, his loathing of war. He would fight if he had to, she had seen that often during the years with the fur brigades; fight with the bear medicine he had received if war came to him. But he found no joy in it, sought no honor, and fought only for survival—or his liberty. She had left him, found his world not enough, played dangerous games with Beckwourth, and had come to this.

thirty-one

Victoria drifted into something like sleep that wasn't sleep, and when she returned to consciousness light leaked through the smoke hole and the women of the lodge were arguing about her. She didn't understand a word, but she knew. They were gesticulating, pointing, examining her. She lay inert, enduring pain, barely able to move. Her throat and neck were so swollen she had trouble swallowing.

She could imagine what was agitating these women: whether to feed her, kill her, torture her, nurse her, or throw her out. She was an enemy of the people, brought to these women by the master of this lodge—a trophy of war. She lay on the dirt, barely caring, feeling ants crawl over her body, find their way through the rents in her dress, and march across lacerated and abused flesh.

The warrior was not present. She was at the mercy of these Blood women, and knew them to be masterful in all the arts of torture and abuse. Better at it than the men. But then an old woman halted the chatter, dipped a trader's tin cup in a kettle of water, and brought it to her. She tried to sit up to drink it, but couldn't. The woman helped her and pressed the cup to Victoria's lips. She drank slowly, barely able to swallow. The raging thirst didn't leave her, and she drank more. The old woman brought her buffalo meat that had been boiled into a sopping softness and fed her a little. Victoria couldn't swallow it but managed to down some broth, which miraculously poured strength into her. So, for the moment, they were succoring her. But for what reason she didn't know.

There were five women in the lodge: the old one, no doubt someone's mother; what appeared to be three wives, perhaps sisters; and a girl of perhaps twelve winters. Victoria suspected there had been more men present once, but they had either died in battle or of diseases. Maybe they had died in fights against her own people.

The village did not move that day, and she lay in the shade of the lodge, grateful to be left alone. Her hurts dominated her consciousness. It wasn't really possible to think of anything else except all the ways she ached. The warmth built; she could see blue sky above, a golden summer day. But she scarcely moved, barely aware of the traffic in and out, brushing past her as they entered and left the lodge. Thinking took too much effort, so she drifted through the day without dreams of freedom, escape, revenge, reconciliation, or anything else except a profound hatred of these Blackfeet.

That evening, as twilight purpled the village, she heard the sounds of drumming, singing, and dancing. So the celebration of their great victory was continuing. She knew she would be a part of it. They had kept her alive for their celebration, and not out of mercy, though she thought she felt some small tenderness in the old one's touch. They had fed her again late in the day, giving her the strength to know her fate this night.

Outside the lodge, the drumming throbbed through the village, lifting to climactic moments when the war singers cried out their victory chants, their medicine, their prayers. This celebration had its own mesmerizing effect on all of them, and even on her.

Two warriors pushed through the doorflap into the darkness of the lodge. One was her captor; the other she did not know. They found her too weak to stand or walk, so they dragged her out and carried her to a meadow lit by a small fire, purely for illumination on a warm night. Here the entire village had gathered in a loose circle; the drummers around two large drums, the chiefs and elders in bright ceremonial dress, the dancers in breechclouts, women holding small children, and restless packs of older children.

They carried her to the center, near the fire, and she supposed they would throw her on the fire and she would die shrieking from pain beyond imagining. Instead, the dancers circled, approached, and counted coup, each warrior striking her hard, the blow stinging, with foot or fist or a coup stick. The blows rained down one after another, each convulsing her, shooting red pain through her. She had no refuge. If she covered her head, the next blow might crack her knee or land on her arm. She felt her body spasm, felt her flesh howl. And yet they had taken no blood and didn't even consider this torture. This was a matter of war honors.

The drumming ceased, and for a few moments the blows stopped, although the pain didn't. Then the drumming began anew, and this time the chiefs and elders counted coup, their blows as rough as those of the warriors. And when she could no longer endure these, the rest of the village began to count coup, the women first, yanking her hair, kicking her, pounding her arm. And after that the children, some of them more cruel than the rest, jabbing her with sharp sticks that did pierce her and bleed her. And then the very old, some of them gentle, ritually touching her and doing no harm.

She lay in a stupor, confused, her body a monstrous alien thing she didn't know and couldn't bear. Now they would toss her on the fire and listen to her death throes. But they didn't, for some reason. Perhaps they thought she was too far gone to know her own end. The drumming ceased; quietness came, and she sensed they were leaving her there to her fate. To die or not, the Absaroka dog among them. She could barely breathe; her lungs were almost paralyzed by the pain in her ribs and breasts. She could not swallow at all.

Then she was alone, and the coolness of the night took some of her fever out of her and lessened the pain a little. She felt the hard earth under her, unyielding, relentless, destroying exactly as much life as it nurtured, her few moments of life momentarily defying the rock and clay and water.

They had not tortured her, but the result was worse. They had feasted upon her, each coup an act of war, each blow rising from their primeval lust to destroy enemies. It had been worse than torture. Now, after sustaining two or three hundred coups, more than she could count, she bore the venom of a whole village in her bosom. Each blow had taken something from her.

She drifted again, her mind awhirl as the night cooled and her body complained. She wished she could have a drink, but she could not manage to walk, or even crawl, to the stream. Was this war? Was this what Skye hated so much? She wished she had listened to him, instead of mocking him with a girl's foolish fancies. Tears formed in her eyes, but her face was too swollen to release them, and they clung to her lids, blurring her vision of the night, even as this night had blurred her vision of the world.

She sensed someone stirring near her, wondered whether she would now die of a knife wound. But someone—a woman—lifted her head, let her drink from a gourd dipper, and again. Cool water, yes, and more. Some distilled herb gave it a bitter flavor. Her benefactor pulled an ancient buffalo robe around her, rolling her onto it so that she was encased in it. The hands were young and soft. Now tears came, sliding down her cheeks, welling hotly in eyes that could not see. This one bade her to sip again, and she did greedily, slowly swallowing one sip after another. Who was this one, this Siksika woman? What sweetness—or pity, or mercy—inspired her to comfort her enemy? The woman cradled Victoria's head in her lap, crooning softly, wiping away Victoria's tears and washing her face gently, speaking in her unknown tongue, words miraculously understood.

"I am Magpie," said the woman. "Magpie, of the Kainah

people, and I am here to comfort you. You are very brave and very beautiful, and you will grow strong again."

Victoria wept softly. Magpie, Magpie, her spirit-helper, the One she had defied, ignored, pushed away.

"You love your people as I love mine," the woman said, and Victoria couldn't fathom how she understood, but she did. "Your husband will find you," she said.

"He is gone," Victoria mumbled.

The woman didn't reply, but lifted the gourd dipper, and Victoria drank again. The herb was slowly and sweetly erasing her pain and making her sleepy.

The woman slid aside and arranged the robe. "When Sun comes, we will go from here. If you are well enough, you will go as a slave; if you cannot rise, you will die with one blow of the war ax, and your scalp will dangle from your captor's lance."

"Magpie," Victoria said.

The woman stood, and Victoria saw her staring down. Then the woman slipped into the blackness and Victoria lay alone, and yet not entirely alone. The herbal tea gave her rest and respite from pain, and she dozed in a cocoon of warmth. Somewhere in this village was a woman whose love reached even to the enemies of her people. Victoria wondered whether, among the Kicked-in-the-Bellies, there was any woman with such love. She wished there were. Maybe, if she ever returned, she would be such a woman. She was no longer the person she had been just a few hours earlier, accepting everything her people had taught her, laughing at Skye, never questioning whether other ways of life might be better. Now she questioned. A Siksika woman named Magpie had opened the door to a new life.

When she awakened in the gray before dawn, she found herself on the bare earth again, the robe gone. Perhaps she had imagined the succor she had received. She hurt. And yet she knew that she had been restored to life and that some merciful woman among the Siksika had given her precious gifts. She made herself sit up, knowing she would soon be put to a test that could lead to her doom if she failed. She stood, blessed Father Sun, walked shakily to the burbling creek, washed, avoided looking at her reflection in the water for fear of what she would see, and stood again. She scrubbed her body, dipped her long jet hair in the chill creek and felt the water play with it, washed away the filth upon her even as she washed away the darkness in her heart. Skye had talked about something like this once. He had called it baptism, a washing and a dedication. Those were his ways, not hers, but now she remembered.

She could walk, but only in a sea of shocking pain. Her groin hurt. The muscles in her limbs howled. Her head throbbed, her throat barely permitted passage of air and water and food. And yet she walked. She walked a step, two, five, fifty. She paused, addressing Sun and Morning Star and the morning breeze, lifting her aching arms to them, her back arched, her fingertips reaching toward the heavens.

They were watching, but she didn't care. They were watching a new woman. She would give herself a new name, or maybe wait for one to come to her. If ever she saw the old seer, Red Turkey Head, she would tell him her story, leaving out nothing, and ask him for a name. Many of them had gathered beside the meadow, along the stream, and now they all watched her. She stood in prayer, the sweetest and most urgent prayer of all her twenty winters.

She saw the black-and-white bird, its iridescent feathers glowing in the dawn sun, and apologized to her spirit-helper, and thanked the wise bird. Then she walked slowly, but like the woman of a great chief, slowly toward the lodge of her captor. She could barely remember the way, but she would find him and present herself to him, a woman of the enemy made new.

thirty-two

Victoria found the lodge of her captor and entered. He was gone, probably collecting the horses that would transport his Blood family. The several women stared at her purpled and blackened flesh. One of them, a squinty, hard-faced woman, gestured for her to help. They were rolling up robes, stuffing things into the parfleches, dismantling her captor's backrest.

No one offered her food. She saw some pemmican, shredded meat, fat and berries stuffed into buffalo gut, and she reached for it only to have the meal dashed from her hand. The woman shouted something at her, gesturing imperiously. Victoria expected to be beaten, but she hadn't the strength to work, especially without food. So she lay down in the place of least honor beside the oval door and waited for the blows to rain down.

She was not disappointed. The mistress of the lodge loomed over her with a whip and lashed it across Victoria's shoulder. But two younger women intervened, and a heated debate ensued. Victoria did not understand a word but hoped it would last long enough so that the new pain would fade a little. She curled on the bare earth, awaiting her fate.

One of the younger women gave her some pemmican. Victoria nibbled slowly, having trouble swallowing. She wasn't hungry after all. The other women ignored her, hauling parfleches out the door and then unpinning the lodgecover. It slid down the lodgepoles, filling interior shadow with sun. Victoria lay inertly, watching, grateful for the small mercy of lying there. Her captor returned, leading four horses, surveyed his women, studied her, and went off for more horses. It took many to move a lodge. The women talked with him about her but nothing came of it.

The women began bundling the lodgepoles and anchoring the bundles on either side of a swaybacked old horse. The household parfleches they hung on the packsaddles of the other horses. The heavy lodgecover they folded and laid on a travois. Around them, their neighbors were loading up in similar fashion, everyone working, even small children. The village was being swiftly dismantled, and very soon they would all be heading for the next place—wherever the seers, the village chief, the war chief, and the elders decided.

Her captor returned with four more ponies, better ones, all of them saddled. The women tied smaller burdens to these riding horses while her captor vanished one more time. The town crier drifted through the village, announcing something—probably the imminent departure of this Kainah village. Her captor returned, this time with his own mounts, five of them in all, some still painted with his war medicine.

Then the village began to form a column. The women of the lodge clambered into their saddles, hiking their skirts to ride. The youngest girl and the old man rode her captor's war and buffalo ponies. There were two horses left over, and Victoria wondered whether one would carry her. The man who had captured her barked words at her, and she understood them all right. Walk or die. She was the enemy.

This day she would die. She could not walk for long, not in her condition. She gazed at the instrument of her death dangling from her captor's waist. It was a war club, a shaped stone bound by rawhide into a forked haft. Sometime this day it would bash in her skull and they would leave her to the crows and coyotes.

Still, she would try. She would never surrender. She would walk until she dropped, and then get up and walk again. She would walk on her bare feet until they bled and every step tortured her, but she would walk. She would show these, her enemies, that she was worthy of their respect. She would show them what an Absaroka woman could be. So when the procession began, she forced one foot ahead of the other, step upon step, ignoring the pain that lanced through her with each movement. They watched her, curious, and that was good. She wanted them to watch.

They were heading east and south on a fine day in the month Skye called May, no doubt looking for buffalo and good prairie grasses to fatten their ponies, or maybe opportunities to torment their enemies. Victoria walked carefully, not wishing to wound her feet. Like all the People, she had walked barefoot much of her life and her soles had hardened. But now that her life hung by a thread, she took care where she stepped.

The pace was slow, accommodating the grandmothers and grandfathers, all the children, and the harried mothers who had to beat on slow horses, kick the dogs away, and see to it that nothing came undone or was lost. The pace blessed Victoria. She could endure that but no more. Her captor rode a spirited white horse and disappeared for long stretches, mostly to ride in the vanguard with other leading men of the village. When he did return, Victoria took the opportunity to scrutinize this man whose whim governed her life—and death. He spoke little to the women, eyed her noncommittally, and showed every sign of being a powerful warrior, or a subchief. He lived for war, and maybe for the hunt, and wore the honors of battle, two notched eagle feathers, inserted in a bun of hair at the nape of his neck. Who was this hard man, and what did he think of her?

The village settled into its travel routine, and now women visited with one another, children knotted together and raced up and down the procession making mischief and alarming horses until someone rebuked them. A few little ones rode in reed baskets attached to travois or in their mothers' arms. An old woman fell in beside Victoria and began talking in the Absaroka tongue, which astonished the captive.

"You are the one they talk about," she said. "I can speak the Absaroka tongue. When I was young, ten winters, your people took me away from my lodge and I grew up in one of your villages. I missed my people. One day I was married to one of your warriors and bore him two sons and a daughter. Then he died, fighting the Lakota. I went home; no one stopped me. Now I am a Kainah again."

Victoria knew that this simple story concealed much of a lifetime within it, but it was not the way of most people to dwell long upon such things. Maybe this was the one who came in the night with the herbal tea and the robe.

"Who are you?"

"I will not give my name to a dog. My name is for the People, not for you."

"They talk about me?"

"They say that for an Absaroka dog, you are brave."

"Who is my captor?"

"He is Grandfather of Wolves. That is his new name. Before, he was Cut Face. And before that, Little Fawn. Our chief, Crow Dog, gave him the name, which is sacred to us. Grandfather of Wolves is a name that makes people quiet when they hear it."

"Why was he given this name?"

"No Kainah is more like a wolf, and he is the grandfather of them all."

"Will he kill me?"

"You are an Absaroka dog."

"Did the Absaroka people treat you badly?"

"I was the enemy."

"Do you think your people should make war on my people?"

"The Absaroka are dogs."

"Did you feel that way when you lived with us?"

"Always."

"Were my people so different?"

The woman reflected a moment before replying. "They are not the People. We are the People."

"Then why do you talk to me?"

The woman laughed. "Just to find out."

"Will they put me to death?"

"They should. I myself would cut slices of flesh from you or burn you with embers. It would be good. But Grandfather of Wolves has not said it is to be done. Maybe he will soon. It is said you will bring misfortune on the People, and maybe the chiefs will say it. Then you will die."

Victoria felt a new wave of weariness crawl through her. Only the slow pace of this procession kept her from stumbling to the earth. But they had not paused all morning, and she knew she wouldn't last no matter how strong her spirit was.

"I was married to a yellow eyes who hates war."

"That is the way of them. We will drive them away. He is a coward, then."

"No, he is the best warrior I have ever seen. He has the medicine of the bear."

The old woman grew agitated. "Then he is the fiercest warrior of all and will hurt my people. I will not talk to an Absaroka dog anymore," she said, and hurried away.

Victoria was glad to be left alone. She was desperate now, and needed to concentrate on walking, because to fall would be to die. She edged over to the side of a travois and leaned on it, letting her body rest against it and letting it drag her along. But the old woman of the lodge spotted her and shouted curses at her and threatened to club her until she withdrew her hand and stumbled ahead.

She reeled forward, stumbled, found her footing, and

walked a while more, her flesh defying her spirit and her muscles like wax. They were traversing open plains, far from water or shelter, the long line of villagers protected by vedettes out to the sides, along with a rear guard and scouts ahead. There would be no escaping, no disappearing here upon an ocean of young green grass. She tried again to find support, this time behind a horse whose tail she caught and held. This time the fierce old woman caught her instantly and bounded toward her, a thick stick in hand, and arced it menacingly. Victoria let go.

She was all used up, scarcely half a day into this passage. She could walk no more. She glanced about, seeing the sunlit meadows rife with yellow wildflowers, bold blue sky, the brooding Sweet Grass Hills to the northeast, the circling hawks high above. Tears came unbidden, not because she was about to die but because of the aching beauty of this land, which stirred her heart. She had lost.

She reeled to the warm earth, which received her gently, the soil still soft from winter's snow. She pulled herself up so she might sit cross-legged and wait for the blow. And she began to sing her death song.

I am Many Quill Woman.
I am Victoria, named by yellow eyes Skye.
I have seen the good world, and the flowers.
I am one of the People.
Now I will walk upon the long trail to the stars.

This she sang, once, twice, and again, scarcely aware of the Siksika gathering around. But then she found herself in shadow and looked to see what blocked the sun.

thirty-three

It was not her day to die. Her captor lifted her onto his buffalo-running pony, and that was that. She clung to the mane, barely able to stay on the lively horse, but this was the gift of life so she gripped the thick mane in small fists and hung on.

The Bloods stopped early that day beside a lively creek dotted with willows and brush. Grandfather of Wolves lifted her off the pony and took the pony away. His women ignored her, for which she was grateful. She wondered what he had in mind. Whatever her fate, she lay in warm grass now as the villagers set up camp for the night. Few raised lodges, because the sky was cloudless. They would cook and sleep in the open, even though the predawn chill might put frost on their robes. She hoped they would give her a robe against the night cold.

They seemed to be drifting out upon the plains, almost aimlessly but actually heading toward buffalo grounds. Or perhaps to make war on the Assiniboine, who lived in this easterly direction. Since she could not speak with these people, she really didn't know. She had not seen the old woman again, so she had no one to talk to.

Her body still hurt from the coup counting. She dragged herself to the creek, drank and washed, and then lay down. Her captor's women paid little heed. They would tax her with hard work later, when her body was ready. That they didn't demand anything of her now was clue enough: she would be a slave, a dumb animal put to their use.

Was that better than death? She faced loneliness until she could master their tongue, and she faced drudgery. But most of life was drudgery. Hard work absorbed the energies of any woman of the People. There was always too much to do: firewood, cooking, fleshing and tanning hides, making moccasins, preparing pemmican, berry gathering, root digging, beading, quilling, making lodges, making clothing, packing and unpacking lodges, dealing with horses, children, dogs, and guests. These things she would be doing for this Blood lodge. But it would be different because she would be under command and have not the slightest freedom of her own. Her life no longer belonged to her.

That is how the next suns spun out. As soon as her broken body mended they put her to work, always at the meanest and hardest tasks. They did give her a robe to sleep in; she would be of no value to them sickened by cold. Was this her life? She remembered the laughing girl in the village; the harder, lonelier life with Skye and all the trappers whose tongue she didn't know. But at least she had Skye then, and the trappers were friendly, not enemies forcing her into slavery. Those were idyllic times compared to what she was experiencing now.

The Moon of New Leaves passed, and the Moon of Buffalo Calves, and she toiled ceaselessly for the Bloods, who continued to drift south and east, enjoying the spring and anticipating the high, sweet days of summer. Each day, as the village drifted, riders rode out to find the buffalo, but they rarely found any except a few old bulls that had abandoned the herd or had been driven out. That meat wasn't good but it sustained them. No one ever went hungry, including their new Absaroka slave.

They reached the Big River, the river Skye called the Missouri, one afternoon. It ran high and swift, bank to bank, carrying the mountain snows far away. Skye said the water went to the seas, many suns away. The Blood seers and elders paused there, watching the swift cold waters, and elected not to cross. There was no need, and it would endanger the old ones, and the children, and maybe some horses, too. They would wait to make war on the Absaroka, and meanwhile look for buffalo and perform the spring ceremonies. Soon all the Siksika would gather for the opening of the beaver bundle. Then, in a while, would come the Sun Dance, the high, sacred time of the year. Skye had compared it to the Easter of the white men.

Maybe they would ritually torture and sacrifice her for that dance. But she doubted it. She was learning a little of their tongue—when the women of the lodge told her to cut wood or scrape hide, she understood. When they told her to leave or come or cook or not to think too highly of herself, she understood. Sometimes they were almost friendly—not that they spoke to her or attempted to befriend her. But a small smile or a little touch of a hand spoke worlds to her.

They camped on the Missouri a while, watching the Big River deliver its water to the lands far to the east. That was when Grandfather of Wolves came to her in the night. Two of his women were in the menstrual hut, so he came to her robes beside the doorflap and pulled the robes open and pierced her swiftly and forcefully. He had captured her; that was his right. She did not respond. Grandfather of Wolves would never be her beloved, and by lying quietly she let him know that. But he didn't seem to mind. In a moment he was gone, but those in the lodge, the grandfather and grandmother and the daughters, all knew, and so something had changed. Victoria did not hear the sounds of sleep for a while. She wondered if she would have the child that she and Skye never had. If so, it would be taken from her and raised a Blood. As a slave she could not even possess the child of her womb.

One day some Piegans visited the camp: fifty-six warriors, no women, and en route to the south, where they would kill Absarokas and capture many horses. Victoria watched them bitterly. These were powerful warriors, seasoned, mostly older men, ready to destroy her people if they could. They conferred with their Blood relatives, smoked in the lodge of the chief, a great circle of elders, war chiefs, leaders, and seers, and then the Piegans stripped, swam their ponies across the flooded river, having great trouble doing it, and collected on the other side, dripping cold water. Within a day or two they would make widows and capture slaves and kill many. She hoped the Kicked-in-the-Bellies—if that was the village to be assaulted—would be ready for a fight and that Beckwourth would defeat the invaders. But somehow she doubted it. Beckwourth loved to raid; he loved spoils, but would he defend a village?

The Bloods drifted along the river, finding deer and an occasional elk to feed them. The great river ran between steep bluffs, having cut a channel deep into the surrounding plains. Now the western mountains were no longer in sight. She wondered when the Bloods would settle down for a long encampment. Every day or two, they packed up and wandered once again, restlessly whiling away the sweet days. Soon after the summer solstice, when Father Sun reached highest in the heaven and had almost vanquished night, they and all the Siksika would gather at some prearranged place for the sacred dance of summer.

Then one day, out on a neck of land between the Big River and the one the Blackfeet called *Kaiyi Isisakta,* Bear River, they came to a small log cabin hastily thrown together from cottonwoods and chinked with mud. A pen for horses was attached. A narrow flat separated the post from the Big River. Some yellow eyes were building bullboats there and were nearly done. They had stretched hides over one willow frame and sewn them tight, and now were sealing them. So they would soon be leaving. She learned that this was a new trading post. The Piegans had told them about it. Not many goods left, but maybe some powder and lead and arrow points; maybe a war ax or lance point or two. Good things to have when killing the Absaroka. They would trade here.

So the lodges went up. They would stay a while. Victoria helped put up the lodge of Grandfather of Wolves and move the household items into it. But she was curious about the yellow eyes, as her people called them, and soon she would slip away to peek at them. There were only three, two lighter, one dark, almost like one of the People. But maybe there were more inside the cabin. The three stopped building and went into the cabin to trade. She hoped they had nothing to trade. The Bloods wanted guns and knives and hatchets and lance points to kill her people.

The women of her lodge did not let her leave it; indeed, they told her not to go to the white men or she would die. They were only three. If she tried to escape, they would kill her—and the white men. Victoria registered that and knew she must obey. So it was that the village traded and she stayed close to the lodge of Grandfather of Wolves. The Bloods grumbled because these traders didn't have much left and were about to go down the river, taking their pelts with them. Some of the younger Bloods wanted to kill the white men, take the pelts, and trade them at Hudson's Bay for lots of fusils and powder and balls.

All this she heard with her quickening understanding of the Siksika tongue. She learned there was an older one who was chief of traders, another who was dark and had warm brown eyes, and another who had blue eyes, a stocky build, and a big nose, the grandfather of noses. The description made her think of Skye, but he would not be here. This was not even the same white men's company. This was another company, not Fitzpatrick, or Bridger, or Sublette. Skye was far away, going to the place where he learned things. These traders were very cautious and did not much show themselves. They obviously feared the powerful Bloods, who could destroy them in a moment.

So the Bloods traded for the last of the goods, grumbled about the place, debated whether to destroy it so these traders could not trade with the Cree or Assiniboine or Lakota, and decided to let it alone. The traders had told them they had built the post to trade with the Siksika and would be back in a while with many more goods and would pay a good price for beaver.

The women of the lodge were disappointed. The traders had no ribbons or beads left, and only a little cloth, which the chief's wives took. Night fell, and word came from the crier that the Blood people would leave in the morning. She dreamed restlessly that night, her thoughts on Skye, her love for him building day by day as her captivity continued. She scarcely thought of Beckwourth. He had appealed to the girl; Skye had evoked the woman.

The next dawn the village dismantled itself, poorer in pelts and richer in the tools of war and implements of cooking. They had cleaned out the traders of every last pot and flint and fire steel and knife and arrow point. The traders rose early to watch the Bloods leave, and now they even wandered among them.

That was when she saw Skye. There was no doubt. That build, that rolling seaman's gait, that nose, those eyes. She stared unbelieving, speechless, as he and the dark one wandered past the busy Bloods.

"Skye!" she cried.

He whirled, saw her, mouth agape.

"Help me, Skye!"

The women of the lodge swarmed over her, shouting and pulling her hair and dragging her away from the white man.

"Victoria!" he yelled. He hastened toward the lodge, but Blood warriors casually blocked the way.

That was the last she saw of him.

thirty-four

Skye stood, paralyzed. Victoria was a captive. He started toward the lodge where he had glimpsed her, but Blood warriors swiftly blocked the way. One, a large man with a scarred face, threatened to kill him—the gesture was unmistakable—if he proceeded.

That was the last he saw of her, but her cry to him seared his soul. Somehow she had been taken a prisoner. That was rare enough; the usual fate of an Absaroka prisoner was death. Skye watched the Bloods pack and saddle and depart, heading who knows where, with Victoria among them. There were a hundred adult women in the village, and he could not tell her from the others. And none of them looked back.

He knew he should forget it. She had abandoned him for another. She had been unfaithful. She had laughed at him and scorned his ways. He could not think of one good reason to try to rescue her. He had other plans now. He had debts to pay to two fur companies, a trip east in mind, and dreams of a life back in civilization. What's more, he couldn't just leave his two colleagues here; he was needed to take the peltries down to Fort Union.

That's what his mind told him. His heart spoke otherwise. Her cry for help tore him to bits. If she needed him, he would help her. Somehow, some way, he would free her. But how?

Walk into a Blood village and—steal her? Buy her? Trade for her? No white man walked into a Blackfoot village alone, not even Berger, who had befriended a few of them. Skye knew what would happen if he pursued: the village guards would catch him, torture him to death as slowly as possible, making the torment extralong for a white man. He knew only a smattering of words and couldn't make himself understood. He knew the hand language, or some of it, but he doubted it would help him.

"What be ye staring at, Skye?"

"My wife, Victoria. She's a prisoner."

"A Crow. Forget it. Ye walk into that village askin' for her, and they'd slit her throat and hand her to ye. The Cree named 'em Bloods for good reason. They got bloody hands. Some say it's because they paint up with red earth, but that's not it. You're talking about *bloody Bloods*."

"I have to get her out."

"Skye, damn me, do ye like being hung by your feet from a limb and having your living brains roasted over a fire?"

"You could go after her—she's not a mile away. Here—trade my rifle for her."

"You're crazy, Skye. Forget her. Find another mountain wife if that's what devils ye."

"She cried out for help."

Berger contemplated Skye for a moment. "Come on now, Skye. I've traded for a few bufflerhides, enough to build the second bullboat. Them Bloods don't have any too many horses, and they wouldn't trade. But they had hides aplenty. Now, I'm tellin' ye, get to work. We've got to get on down the river."

Berger was right. Skye knew he had to let go of the past. Victoria had been a happy interlude in his young life. It had come to a bad end, but he wouldn't remember that. When he was old and comfortable as a merchant, he might quietly invoke the memory of her glowing beauty, and the wild free days lived close to campfire smoke, and the sweetness of her kiss, and he would know he had been blessed.

He walked listlessly to the frame of the second bullboat. Arquette was already at work, shaping a green buffalohide to the frame.

"What be de trouble?" the Creole said, surveying Skye.

"My wife. I saw her in that village. She's a captive. She cried out to me but they hustled her off."

"Ah, one squaw's good as another. You wan' a good life, try variety, *oui*? We get you three, four nice Cree ladies and you forget this wan, I think."

"I love her."

"But she don't love you, eh? Not from what you tell us."

She loved him. He knew that. She loved him in spite of all that had happened with Beckwourth. He felt a weight on him so heavy he could barely lift his hands.

"Skye, we build dis boat now."

But the more Skye tried to work again, the more his mind wandered. He mostly just stared at the horizon where the Bloods had vanished, until Arquette roundly cursed him in two tongues.

"*Merde*, Skye! You not worth a sou this day."

Listlessly, Skye did work after that, his mind elsewhere. But one by one the hides were shaped, laced to each other, and the seams caulked. They could leave for Fort Union in the morning, Skye with his horses, Berger and Arquette each in a loaded bullboat.

The afternoon ebbed as the pair pulled the upside-down bullboat frame out of the earth and bound the hides to the gunnels.

"You no say ten word this afternoon," Arquette grumbled. "You deciding you go get yourself kill for a little Crow lady."

Skye had been deciding exactly that. He didn't respond. They finished the boat, tethered it with a line, and tested it on the swift current. They found half a dozen leaks, and set to work with tallow and pitch once again. Skye distrusted the miserable, light, leather-lined boats, and was glad he wasn't being required to steer one clear to Fort Union.

That evening he sank into a deep melancholy, saying not a word to either of his partners. Berger's sharp glances and head-shaking told Skye what the others thought, but they left him alone and didn't try to dissuade him. If he was mad enough to get himself killed for a faithless little squaw, then there was nothing they could do about it. Skye didn't sleep that night. The image of Victoria, her cry for help, and the swift harsh response from the Bloods, returned to his mind over and over, keeping him up and deviling him. He rose in the morning in a black mood, weary and despairing.

They loaded packs of beaver into the bullboats and then added heavy packs of buffalo robes and assorted other peltries, including luxurious ermine, mink, weasel, otter, elk, and deer. The amazing little craft could haul enormous loads. Then Berger loaded Skye's packhorse with still more beaver plews, as well as Skye's kit.

"All right, Skye. We'll see you at the fort. Don't waste a minute. You'll beat us because of all the oxbows in the river." He squinted at Skye. "Don't let me down."

Skye nodded. So Berger had even discerned Skye's temptation and was warning him. Skye ached simply to ride away, forget the debts, forget his sixty-dollar income—which he would receive only if he completed his tour at this post—forget it all and go get her—somehow.

"I'll go straight to the post," he said.

"If you don't . . ." Berger didn't complete his thought.

He helped Berger and Arquette clamber into their wobbly craft and shove off. Each had a pole and crude paddle for steering and dodging rocks and rapids.

Then he was alone. Now Victoria was ten, fifteen, twenty miles gone. He climbed onto his black horse, untied the dun, and led it along a trail that soon took him far from the Missouri. He would rarely be close to the river all the way back. He rode listlessly, as if his whole life had bled away from him. If the world was a paradise in June, he didn't notice it. He had turned inward, seeing nothing but the images stamped upon his soul.

He missed the last of the spring wildflowers, the red-winged blackbirds and meadowlarks, the emerald grasses swiftly growing their seedheads, the turtles and frogs in the sloughs, the antelope that watched him from the crown of a hill, and the constant signs of passage—the hoofprints of large Indian migrations. He had not eyes to see, and didn't know that a few ticks of the clock earlier—or later—he might have stumbled into the clutches of Lakota, Assiniboine, Cree, and any of several bands of Blackfeet.

Thus he progressed to Fort Union like a blind man, having lost all his wilderness caution. And yet Fate—or was it the magpies he kept seeing—spared him a fool's death. He had become the ultimate tenderfoot. He saw nothing in that sea of grass that could hurt him, though a thousand perils lurked in every league. Even the weather seemed to respect his madness: the looming thundershowers that built up each afternoon veered away, as if determined not to soak or chill a man out of his head. The winds, which normally howled through the empty grasslands, quieted themselves and politely eddied past him, having mercy upon an innocent.

His journey took him on a wide loop around the breaks of the Missouri, around the oxbows that doubled the water miles to the post, but he didn't notice. The hours slipped by in quiet march, and he knew that he would not go down the river to St. Louis, and he knew he would outfit again at Fort Union, using his sixty dollars, and go get her and take her home, wherever his home would be. He would find that band of Bloods and her, and nothing would come between him and Victoria ever again.

He rode into Fort Union unmolested. A long keelboat bobbed at anchor on the levee beside the post. It had brought forty tons of trade goods and resupply to Fort Union from the village of Independence, a thousand water miles distant, all of it hauled upriver by pole and sail and cordelle, employing wind and the muscle of the Creole voyageurs. He eyed the long low craft and knew he would not go down the river aboard it.

From McKenzie, who received him in his suite, he learned he had arrived ahead of Berger and Arquette. The iron-willed factor questioned Skye closely about how the trading had gone, and Skye answered. Yes, a good season. Sold out all trade items, garnered fifteen packs of beaver, plenty of other pelts, all very successful. And yes, AFC should build a permanent post at that site and trade with the Blackfeet. They had plenty of well-cured pelts. And yes, last Skye knew, Berger and Arquette were on the river in two large bullboats and due soon.

"Good. You've proved that our strategy works. The company owns the river. And now we'll own the Blackfoot trade clear to the shining mountains. Now, let's talk about you. What's the matter with you, Skye?" McKenzie asked. "Something sure as hell is wrong."

"The matter? Nothing, mate."

"I've talked with you for an hour. Where are you? You aren't here, that I know."

Skye shrugged.

"Did you see any Indians?"

"No, sir."

"Odd. We've had half a dozen bands stop here. And every day we pick up rumors of big fights, bloody wars, horse thievery, massacres . . . outrages. You must have seen a dozen war parties. We feared all three of you would perish."

"No, sir."

"It's a miracle you still have your hair."

"I've changed my plans, sir. I wish to draw my sixty dollars, pay you something, and reoutfit myself. I'll be staying in the mountains."

"Something happened. Tell me what."

"Nothing, sir."

McKenzie's piercing gaze missed nothing, but his keen mind missed everything. "You are mad," he said.

thirty-five

It was madness. And it was love. In one piercing moment, as fleeting as a heartbeat, everything had changed. Victoria needed him.

In the post store, Skye replenished sparingly, but bought ample powder and precast lead balls for his rifle. The rest he agonized over: he needed something to trade for Victoria if it came to that. And peace offerings. He purchased ten plugs of tobacco for that. For trading he purchased a pair of blankets, which the Indians coveted, a kettle and knife, some awls, hanks of beads, and a bolt of red flannel. That was all he could afford, and it probably would not buy Victoria's freedom. He allowed himself some tea and sugar, paid fifty-nine dollars for the lot, and pocketed a dollar.

Kenneth McKenzie hovered about, wild with curiosity but shamming disinterest. "Where are you going, Mister Skye?" he demanded, abruptly.

"I'm going to the Blackfeet."

"The Blackfeet, are you? The Blackfeet! Then I've seen the last of you. I ought to prevent it, but I know better. Why are you going to the Blackfeet?"

Skye could not answer that one. There were things one had to do, however mad they seemed. "Just say I'm out of my head, sir."

"That you are. Well, I'll get the story from Berger. He ought to arrive today or tomorrow. Is there something about the Blackfeet I don't know?"

"No, sir."

"Which Blackfeet?"

"The Bloods."

"Ah, the Bloods, mostly living in British possessions. The Bloods, eh? Nice friendly people, the Bloods."

Skye laughed, loaded his new goods onto his packsaddle, and tipped his hat. He lifted himself into the saddle and steered the horses through the massive double gate.

"Skye, dammit, I'll never see you again."

"That's right," Skye replied.

"Well, you're mad, but I wish you success, whatever you're up to. If anyone can succeed, you can." McKenzie offered Skye his hand, which Skye took. "Good-bye, Barnaby Skye," the factor said softly.

Skye rode west, feeling the stares on his back. He followed a trail that would take him past the little post on the Marias. It wound far away from the Missouri, across empty flats where there would be no place to hide.

Alone at last, he began to calculate the ways he might free Victoria, and the more he contemplated that task, the more daunting and hopeless it seemed. He knew a few words he had picked up trading, but these weren't enough to help him. How would he ask other Blackfeet where the Bloods had gone, and especially this band of Bloods? How would he say he wanted to trade for an Absaroka woman held captive by one of those bands? Who would translate, pave the way, help him? How could he make his peaceful intentions clear, keep himself from dying a lonely death on the prairies, find allies, enter a camp of people who relished the scalps of any white men they could find?

Did he have the courage?

He didn't. He was deathly afraid.

Why was he doing this?

For Victoria. It was utterly simple. It defied the sort of calculation of prudent men, weighing risk against reward. It came down to Victoria. He would do what he had to do. And probably die soon. Or worse, see her death as a result of his efforts.

Unlike his passage to Fort Union, he was alive to menace now. He scanned the rolling prairies for signs of trouble, studied the morning heavens for columns of smoke, kept below skylines wherever he could, examined each slough for fresh hoofprints. He saw more signs of travel than he wanted to see this far from the Blackfeet. He was still in lands dominated by Assiniboine and Cree.

He camped in hollows, built fires out of sight, studied the whole country before risking a shot at game. He watched his back trail, climbed hills where he could see for miles behind him. So far, at least, he had dodged war and hunting parties. But when would his luck run out?

One fine morning he reached the trading post on the Marias—or what was left of it. The Blackfeet had promptly burned it, and all that remained were some charred foundation logs. He shuddered. So little did they want traders in their land that they had destroyed the little cabin hours after it had been abandoned. The surrounding meadow glowed serenely in the blinding sun, as if nothing sinister had ever happened there. He was in Blackfoot country now, with no more plan than when he started. But one thing had been building in him: he needed a guide and translator, someone who could take him to the various bands of Bloods and help him negotiate. And keep him alive.

He knew of only one band of the Bloods, the Fish-Eaters, so named because they alone among the Blackfeet ate fish. Hardly any Plains Indians ate fish. Victoria loathed them, and stared appalled whenever the trappers filleted and cooked trout for dinner.

Where would he find a guide, and how would he pay for one? He did not know. But maybe if he rode a while, he would find one, or one would find him. He ransacked his skimpy knowledge of these people, seeking a way. Eventually he thought he might have one. He needed to find the Little Robes. They were nominally Piegans, but so independent of them that, in a way, they were almost a fourth nation in the Blackfoot Federation. Berger had said they were more hospitable to their neighbors—to some small degree. There were occasions when Absaroka and Little Robe hunting parties had feasted together, proclaiming a truce during a good buffalo hunt. Maybe a Little Robe would take Skye to the Bloods.

Then there were the Gros Ventres, mooching "cousins" of the Piegans, whose lengthy visits were not entirely welcome among the Blackfeet. Maybe Skye could engage one of those people to help him. But it wasn't an option he relished. He needed a bona fide Blackfoot Indian to take him into the heart of their country—and get him out alive, with Victoria.

For five more days he rode into Blackfoot country. The Stony Mountains formed a wall ahead, still tipped with white. The Piegans called it the Backbone of the World, a good description of a feature that sliced off the Great Plains from everything to the west. He startled with every flight of a crow, broke out in sweat every time an antelope ran, fought fear whenever he saw signs of horse passage. Yet he saw no one, and the imagined terrors loomed larger than any real ones.

He camped one evening on the Marias, which he had followed northwest for days. He chose a well-concealed gulch with cottonwoods that would diffuse his woodsmoke and a seep for himself and his horses. The darkness seemed slow to come that time of year—probably July, though he had lost track—and light lingered across the northwestern heavens. He had been struggling to find food and had not used his rifle for fear of drawing Bug's Boys down upon him. But he thought he might fish the Marias for some trout. He slipped through dense cottonwoods to reach the river—and smelled woodsmoke. He ducked back into the twilight of the cottonwoods and studied the river flats. To the west was an encampment of some sort. His pulse leapt. He edged toward the camp, peering through a screen of alder and willow brush, and discovered twenty or thirty male Indians, either a war party or a hunting party, or both. They weren't painted. Most wore low summer moccasins, and he could not tell their color. He had learned anyway that most tribes made moccasins from the smoke-blackened upper hides of a lodge. The smoke and grease cured the hide, turned water, and added toughness to the leather.

His every instinct was to flee for his life. These men were tall, powerfully built, athletic, and looked entirely capable of murdering him on the spot. He crept away, his back itching with the anticipation of an arrow. Back in his own camp, he faced the dilemma: the Blackfeet terrified him, and yet he needed to make contact if he wanted to find Victoria.

There was only one thing to do: ride in. He would do it on horseback, because if he needed to escape, he would have his possessions with him and he could swiftly plunge into the safety of darkness just beyond the fire. He dreaded what he had to do. But the image of Victoria filled his mind, that searing moment when she cried out and was swiftly hustled away from his vision.

What was there but to go in? To live or die, he didn't know. Back in his own side gulch, he collected his horses, saddled up, loaded his kit, looked to the powder and priming on his flintlock, and then mounted, carrying his rifle loosely across his lap. But in his leathers he had a plug of tobacco, and in his kit some trade items—if he ever got that far.

It seemed like the longest ride he had ever undertaken, though the distance was less than a mile. The twilight had surrendered to blackness, though a band of blue still lingered above the Backbone to the west. Where were their guards? Would he stumble into the horse herders and be taken for a raider? He steered toward the trail along the river, scarcely knowing where he was going, the stars dancing pricks of light on the flowing stream.

Then, suddenly, the trees ahead reflected light, and he could make out moving forms.

"Hello the camp," he yelled, and kicked his black horse forward.

For a moment nothing happened, and he rued the folly of this quest.

"Hello the camp," he yelled again, giving notice, and this time he saw men stirring, racing for weapons, preparing for an intruder.

Then he rode in. In the light of the half-extinguished fire, he faced a phalanx of armed warriors, their faces terrible in the flickering light.

Skye's pulse raced so fast he wondered if his heart would burst. "Peace," he said, lifting a hand upward. "Peace." He remembered the plains hand sign for peace, but it was too late for that anyway. They could kill him in a trice. He saw nocked arrows pointing at him, a lance in the hand of a warrior. Several more stood with war clubs or tomahawks in hand. They were waiting for something, perhaps word from their headman. Skye looked for that one and thought he spotted the right one, a man with an imperious gaze, gaunt, hollow-chested, ugly and cruel, missing several teeth and an ear.

Skye lifted a plug of tobacco until it was plainly in sight of them all, and then walked his horse to the one he supposed led this party and handed it to the man.

But the unaccepted tobacco plunged to the ground.

thirty-six

Skye stared at the plug of tobacco in the grass and swung the rifle in his lap around to point at the headman. That would give him a few seconds while the leader thought it over.

The headman's eyes focused on the bore of the rifle, and Skye saw some subtle change in his face.

"Who speaks English? Anyone?"

No one replied.

Skye didn't know how to proceed. He could not remove his hand from the trigger, yet he needed both hands to make some hand signs. During his four years in the mountains he had acquired a good hand sign vocabulary, but now it was useless. He ransacked his mind for a few Blackfoot words he had learned during the trading.

"Kainah," he said.

These warriors stared impassively.

Much to Skye's surprise, the headman resolved the dilemma. Slowly, his gaze on the bore of the rifle, he stooped over and picked up the tobacco plug and held it high, thrusting it first at Skye and then at the Blackfoot warriors.

Skye peered sharply into the faces surrounding him. No one lowered a bow or lance. It had come down to trust. Slowly he pointed the rifle downward and uncocked it. Then he slipped it into its fringed leather sheath on his saddle. He glanced around him. None of the Blackfeet had lowered their bows.

Slowly, using a combination of Blackfoot words and hand-signs, he made his intentions known. He was a trader. He was looking for a band of the Bloods that had traded at the post on the Marias, *Kaiyi Isisakta,* recently. He wished to hire a guide to take him there safely. He wished to buy an Absaroka slave who was his wife. He would pay the guide well—a long knife and an awl and ten iron arrow points.

He wasn't at all sure he was understood, but at least they listened and watched his hands. Uneasily, he surveyed the bows and arrows in the hands of these warriors. No bow was drawn, but that offered him little comfort. In the space of two seconds he could be pierced by twenty arrows.

The Siksika are a great and powerful people, he signaled to them. One by one his hands formed words and ideas: He was glad they had accepted his tobacco. They would help a man who wished to buy his wife back. The Pikuni, Kainah, and Siksika were the most generous of all the Peoples.

They watched his hands, and listened to his occasional words, and stood in the flickering firelight without showing the slightest sign of acceptance or rejection, of friendship or murder.

His hands made new signs: If you will not help, I will go in peace.

The headman's hands made words: We do not know where Kainah are. Maybe we will see them at Sun Dance.

Skye responded: Where will the Sun Dance be?

"Mokwamski," the headman said.

The Belly River, Skye translated. Well up in British lands, a long, dangerous journey from here. The traditional home of the Bloods.

"Good. I am Skye," he said, making the sign for the sky and pointing at himself.

"Skye. Ah. I am *Istowun-eh 'pata,* Packs a Knife. We are *Nitsitapi,* Real People, Siksika."

These were Blackfeet proper, then. A little more inclined to let a white man live than the Piegans, or Pikuni, as they called themselves.

The headman pointed at Skye's bear claw necklace and said something Skye could not translate. But he understood suddenly that the bear claws might have saved his life.

"Take me to the Kainah," Skye said, finding a few words.

But Packs a Knife shook his head, and with a flurry of words Skye couldn't follow made it clear that this party had other plans. He intuited that they were looking for some Cree scalps.

Very well, then. Time to escape into the darkness before things took an unexpected turn. He dug into his saddle kit, found an awl, and handed it to Packs a Knife, who nodded. Then Skye made the sign for going. He pointed to himself, then held his right hand before him, palm upward, and gestured outward three times. The headman nodded.

Skye turned his black away from camp, tugged on the line of his packhorse, and rode away, his back prickling. But no arrow stopped him. Swiftly the night cradled him in its safety. Not that the Siksika couldn't follow and kill him; they could go wherever he could go. But Skye sensed that he was safe. He had found the courage to walk straight into a Blackfoot war camp and ask questions. Suddenly, as the merciful blackness engulfed him, he felt the terror depart. His body sagged, his muscles released, and an incredible weariness stole through him. He wanted to dismount and lie in the grass until he recovered his strength. But he rode on, not really knowing where he was going except that his horse took him alongside the river. He wanted to put distance between himself and the warriors, so he rode onward in the deeps of the night. He didn't know where his passage took him, only that each step of the horses was a step toward safety.

He hadn't found out much. Sun Dance on the Belly. There was a lot of Belly River, and he could miss the whole affair. And what would the Bloods think of a white man showing up for their most sacred ceremony of the year? And in British

Canada, where he was still a wanted man, as far as he knew? The Sun Dance would be held in the midst of that great fiefdom possessed by Hudson's Bay Company—which had a price on his head.

He had found out something this night. He could walk into the very camp of the Blackfeet and come out alive. If they had caught him running from them, he would be dead. But if he boldly walked into their company, he might live.

He rode into dawn, amazed to see another day. The heavens grayed, forms began to emerge, and soon a hot sweet July day embraced him. He beheld a grand and open land, prairies laced with rushing rivers tumbling out of the great Backbone to the west. The Blackfeet claimed a mighty country, and it blessed them. He was too tired to continue, and the horses were dragging, so he turned up a side gulch, found a copse of box elder under a sharp low bluff, and made it home for the nonce. The shade would shelter him and the horses in the July midday heat; the innocuous grove of trees would conceal him from passing river traffic. He picketed the horses out of sight of the river, checked the warm slope for prairie rattlers, and curled up on a mattress of grass.

That whole day spent itself without the presence of Skye, who slept the sleep of the dead after his ordeal. When he finally did awaken, twilight was not an hour away. He studied the country, looking for signs of passage, and finally decided it was safe to water the horses. He led them to the river and watched them lap up water, pause, and lap up some more.

He felt lonely. For days he had traveled in solitude, enduring whatever fate was in store for him. He missed his old friends and knew they were gathering on the Powder River for the rendezvous of 1831. Maybe, if he raced south at breakneck speed, he might catch the tail end of it and enjoy one last hooraw with Jim Bridger, William Sublette, Davey Jackson, Joe Meek, and Jed Smith. The thought of that headlong plunge tempted him, but he knew he was already too late. He wouldn't show up, and they would wonder about him. Beckwourth would show up and brag about his triumph over Skye, and boast that he had even made off with Victoria. And the free trappers would figure Skye either went under or had fled the mountains, a whipped dog. Maybe it was just as well that he didn't go back this year. He scarcely knew where the Powder was, except that this rendezvous would be far to the east of the previous ones, out on buffalo plains, and closer to St. Louis.

Missing the rendezvous made him feel bad. Those were his only friends. He was still the lonely Englishman with no roots anywhere, adrift in an alien world. He had come to love the mountain life, and had endured four years of it, enough to make him a veteran of the fur trade. And yet, without Victoria, it had all turned to ashes.

He gathered his kit together, saddled his horses, and continued on alone, a solitary man who had never chosen to live out his life all alone. With the thought of rendezvous came the realization that real friends were more valuable than gold. Not all the wild beauty around him could assuage the hungers of his soul. No sweet wilderness or utterly free life in the midst of nature could equal the worth of a wife and friends.

He rode ever northwest along the river, through a sea of purple and lavender and blue, as the twilight tinted the Great Plains and painted the distant buttes and steppes with shadow and darkness. The scene was a good imitation of his soul, he thought. There wasn't much light within him.

He rode into the deeps of the night, guided by a thin moon and an inertia that carried him into the jaws of death almost against his will. But when the hour approached midnight, as best as he could judge, he called it quits and made camp. He was out of meat, and feared that he would have to subsist in the morning on his old emergency food, the ever-present and foul-tasting cattail root.

That night he sank into desolation. He couldn't help it. The entire year since the previous rendezvous had been a disaster. From the time the Pawnees had stolen everything he possessed, to the time in the Crow village when he watched Victoria slip away from him and Beckwourth defeat him and frustrate his mission, to the bitter discovery of betrayal, to the long, hollow days and hours toiling eastward, to his miserable, lonely life as a trader in a remote cabin—all these things had crushed his hopes and dreams and had thwarted the life he had so bravely pursued ever since escaping the Royal Navy.

He had a good kit, was armed, had horses, had all the means of surviving in a wild land—and yet lacked the most important of all things. The will to continue. The thought of the rendezvous had sent him into a downward spiral that made him wonder whether Barnaby Skye had been God's mistake, an accident of Fate.

The thought of the presence of God in all the corners of the universe, even here, a thousand miles from the nearest settlement, didn't really comfort him. Where was God now, when he camped in the midst of the midst of the most dangerous tribesmen known to the trappers? And yet, in the soft silence and the midnight mists, he discovered the eternal stars, and with eternity came a vision of love. God loved him, and there was purpose in Skye's life, if only he could find it.

He could not remember the lucid and sweet supplications he once had read in the Book of Common Prayer long ago in London, so he recited the one he remembered, the one called the Lord's, and asked for the courage to pick up his cross and carry it when dawn came.

thirty-seven

Skye awakened to a benign world. The terrors and loneliness of the night had vanished, and now he gazed upon a glowing land. He felt refreshed and ready to travel to the ends of the earth to free Victoria.

Somehow, in the dawn of a sweet summer's day, the Blackfeet seemed different and approachable. Did they not have their own honor, love their children, defend themselves against enemies, just like all mortals? Surely all that he had heard around the brigade campfires had been exaggerated. How the trappers loved to tell a tale and embellish it until it barely resembled reality. Something within him this golden morning told him that with courage, love, and faith, he would find his straying wife and win her liberty—and her heart.

The trappers called them Bug's Boys, the Devil's boys, but there was a reason for that. Long ago, the Yank explorers Lewis and Clark had tangled with them, sowing the seeds of later trouble. But Skye wasn't a Yank. He considered himself a man without a country.

He packed his gear, paused at the riverbank to listen to whatever might be told on the breeze, and then he mounted and rode off, filled with a prescient belief that this very day he would make friendly contact with the Devil's boys. His path took him ever westward toward the Backbone of the World, which now loomed as a mighty rampart, layer upon layer of blue mountains that pierced the sky. He continued to follow the Marias, the stream that would lead him to the heart of the Blackfoot Federation.

At noon he topped a grassy knoll and beheld a village in the distance, forty or fifty brown lodges camped on a river flat near abundant woodlands. He paused, soberly assessing his chances and his fate, and then touched the ribs of his black and rode straight down the long grassy slope. A while later the village wolves, the guardians, spotted him and raced out to confront him. He knew that fear or flight would kill him, so he made a show of waving at them and proceeding straight toward the village.

They surrounded him, first two, then five, and eventually nine, the imperial warriors of the Blackfeet, all of them in leggings and little else. None threatened him; no one needed to. His rifle was sheathed, and they grossly outnumbered him. He held up a plug of tobacco, the universal peace sign. In spite of his renewed belief in the goodness of life and the comforts he had discovered in the past hours, fear crept through him. These warriors studied him, and none looked friendly. One of them, a leader no doubt, motioned him toward the village, so Skye spurred his horse and headed toward the lodges, surrounded by an imperial guard.

He in turn studied them, vaguely puzzled by something. They seemed familiar. He reached the outskirts of the village, and now the villagers crowded about, and once again he admired the people for their dignity and handsomeness. No Plains Indians he had encountered matched the Blackfeet in physical beauty, pride, grace, and carriage. They seemed familiar, and then he remembered: these people had traded at Berger's log cabin. Skye had met many of them across the trading counter. They knew him for a trader. A flood of relief ran through him. They would honor him within their village as a protected guest.

Piegans, then. And they would listen to his request.

He passed well-made lodges, remarkable for their decorations. Many had what appeared to be a row of stars around the base, and all of them displayed beautifully dyed totem figures and colored geometric designs that spoke of the owner's personal medicine. Their clothing showed the same care and elegance. They had fashioned it from a mixture of hides and furs and trade items, such as flannel, buttons, conchos, and jingle bells.

By the time he reached a sort of plaza, or open space in the center of the village, the elders and headmen had already gathered there. He handed his plug of tobacco to the chief, who stood ahead of the others, and it was swiftly accepted. He now had the safety and courtesy of the village. There followed the usual Indian smoking ritual, and Skye puffed the pipe as it passed by, deepening the peace. They took their time, and it struck Skye there was wisdom in it. They could assess each other, compose their thoughts, rest, and prepare for whatever would come.

Skye began with hand signs, plus the bit of their tongue he knew, and also a few English words. At Berger's post the Piegans employed a bit of English, probably picked up from the clerks at Rocky Mountain House, the Hudson's Bay post far to the north where many Blackfeet traded. These would suffice if Skye chose his signs and words carefully.

He told them he wished to be taken to the Kainah, the Bloods, in peace. A band of them, which had traded at Berger's cabin, had captured his wife, an Absaroka woman, and he wished to free her if he could by trading some things he had brought. He simply wanted his wife. He didn't even know the name of her captor.

"Grandfather of Wolves," the chief signaled. "He has the Absaroka woman."

Finally, a name. That was his first real progress.

"What band?" he asked.

"*I-sis-o-kas-im-iks.*" Hair Shirts.

"What are you?"

"We are *Sik-ut-si-pum-aiks,* Black Patched Moccasins, of the Pikuni. I am Bull Turns Around."

"I am Skye."

"Why would a man want an Absaroka wife? We have better."

"I love her."

"Let her go."

"I will give a good knife to one who takes me safely to the Hair Shirts and Grandfather of Wolves. And a hatchet if I succeed."

Bull Turns Around pondered that. The elders sat quietly, observing Skye with questioning faces. One of them leaned toward the chief and spoke at length in the Blackfoot tongue. The chief nodded.

"Every man should have a woman. But not an Absaroka woman. She must be a slave. We would like a trader in our band. We will give you a fine, works-hard Blackfoot woman, young and comely."

"I want only my Absaroka woman."

The chief pondered that. "We have among us Running Crane, *nisah,* elder brother, of Grandfather of Wolves. It is for brothers to decide." He turned to one of those sitting just outside the circle of elders and addressed the younger man at length. Running Crane stood, responded slowly, and sat.

"He will not go with the white man. It would cause trouble, asking for the slave. Grandfather of Wolves would be offended. Running Crane says for the pale man to turn around and go back now. This is not good."

Skye saw how this was going to end and lamented the defeat. But he would continue north, regardless.

"Tell Running Crane his counsel is wise. But I must try. I would like to learn the language of your people for a few suns. Will Bull Turns Around give me teachers?"

"That is a good request. We will teach you many words, but we cannot go with you to the Hair Shirts or help you. You will be a guest in my lodge."

So, miraculously, Skye found himself safe among the fearsome Piegans, in the very lodge of the chief of the Black Patched Moccasins. He intended to put every moment to use, mastering the tongue, absorbing the customs, picking up any bits of information that might help.

The visit turned out to be fruitful for both sides. The Piegans were starved for information about white men, especially the Yanks they hated so much. They knew many of the trappers by name or reputation, which surprised Skye. Somehow word filtered through the tribes. Ashley, Jed Smith, Jim Bridger were all familiar to them, and their young men dreamed of killing them all. They wanted to know where white women were hidden and why the men came alone. They wanted to know why the trappers armed the Crows and Shoshones and all the rest of the enemies of the Blackfeet.

Skye couldn't answer adequately, especially with his sketchy knowledge of their tongue and the hand signs. But the elders, who came to smoke with Skye each day, were patient, and whenever there was confusion or misunderstanding, they paused until Skye or they made themselves clear. Skye, in turn, learned much about the fierce Blackfeet; how they loved their children, how the husbands lorded over their wives, whose duty was to obey without question anything that their men demanded. Skye saw several terribly scarred women whose noses had been cut off. He learned that these women had been unfaithful, and cutting off their noses—making them forever ugly—was the penalty. Skye wondered how feisty Victoria could long endure under such a Blackfoot regimen. She would either be killed as a rebel or die of despair. He had to reach her, and soon.

But the delay helped. He began to understand the daily rhythms of life in a Blackfoot village; the habits of the horse herders, the war games played by young men, the equestrian skills of the warriors as well as the powerful religion and spirituality that guided these war-bent people. Each warrior had cried for a vision had a spirit-helper. But they worshiped Napi,

Old Man, lord of the universe, but also something of a jokester who could foil their dreams and plans.

He learned words, but knew there would be too little time to become fluent enough to converse. He focused especially on family words, for these would be the ones he would need the most. The word he wanted the most was "wife": *nit-o-ke-man.* Just as helpful would be "husband": *no-ma.* "Father" was *ni-nah;* "mother," *ni-kis-ta,* while "son" was *no-ko-i,* and "daughter" was *ni-tun.* All that was good. He could now tell the Hair Shirts he was looking for his *nit-o-ke-man.*

Skye stayed until the village prepared to leave for a buffalo hunt. The Piegans were less committed to the Sun Dance than the Bloods, and often ignored the ritual. He learned that the dance was new to the Blackfeet, though well established among the Plains tribes to the south, including the Crows.

Skye didn't want to go on a hunt; he wanted to find Victoria, so he departed, giving gifts of awls to the chief's women, who had waited on him as if he were a duke. He rode north, while the Black Patched Moccasins rode south, toward the Judith Basin, where they knew the buffalo were thick.

It had been a good visit. He began to doubt all the terrible stories about the Blackfeet he had heard from the Yank trappers. These northern Indians were as amiable as any other, he thought. He would find the Blood bands gathered at Belly Buttes, near the Belly River, observing the sacred ceremony that involved purification, self-torture, an ordeal of endurance, and petitions to Sun for everything from healing to victory over enemies. Skye thought that would be a good time to deal with them, and so he rode north, refusing to worry about what fate might have in store.

thirty-eight

The Bloods found buffalo on Big Sandy Creek, west of the Bear Paw Mountains, and raised their lodges there for a hunt. These hides would not make good robes now, with the winter hair clinging in patches and the summer hair not yet grown, but the hides would make fine lodgecovers, clothing, saddles, and moccasins, while the meat would provide a feast. Some of it would be jerked into trail food for warriors on the warpath.

Victoria's young body healed, but her spirit languished. Day by day she drudged, doing whatever the women of the lodge demanded. Mostly they gave her the most miserable of tasks, scraping hair off a hide staked to the earth until it was naked leather, and then brain-tanning it. She was used to such toil. That was the lot of women among the Peoples. So she scraped with a metal-edged fleshing tool the Bloods had gotten from the traders, slowly peeling away hair and flesh, working on her knees in hot sun, enduring the smell and grease and clouds of green-bellied flies.

They gave her no respite. She was a slave, and if she sought a moment of rest they beat her with sticks or threatened her with knives. Only the old one, the grandmother, eyed her with any sympathy and offered the gift of an occasional fleet smile or a gentle touch of the hand. Once, when Victoria's ragged doeskin dress fell apart, the old one brought an awl and patiently repaired it, lacing a seam at the side with new thong.

But the other women, all wives of Grandfather of Wolves, vied with each other to make her miserable. His sits-beside-him wife, Sisoyaki, or Cutting Woman, was hardest of all to cope with, and was determined to set an example of meanness for the other wives to follow. The youngest wife, Going Out to Meet the Victors, Pi-ot-skini, looked as if she wished to befriend Victoria, learn Crow words, and help lift her burden, but the older woman ruthlessly crushed the slightest tendency toward warmth. And so Victoria toiled alone.

At least she didn't lack food. Even slaves needed food, and they didn't begrudge the tongue or hump meat or backfat she ate, though in hard times, which afflicted all the Peoples now and then, she would be fed last and least. But there was food for the body and food for the spirit, and of the latter she was starved. She was never so aware of her hungers as when twilight came and handsome youths played the love flute sweetly outside the lodges of their beloveds. She knew those melodies; they were the same for all the tribes of the young and tender. These Blood people were much more fastidious than the Absarokas, and watched their daughters strictly. The girls were virgins when they were given away by their parents. She found herself wishing she had been raised in such fashion, with none of the bawdiness and wanton conduct of her own people. She had been too knowing too young, and maybe that was one of the things that had led her life to this fate, this brokenness.

So she dressed and tanned the skins and saw some of them replace worn hides in lodges or turn into good moccasins. When darkness stopped her hide dressing, they gave her other tasks. One was to stuff buffalo beard hair into cushions and pad saddles. Another was to pound meat and mix in fat to make a trail food rather like pemmican, though it was too early in the year for the other ingredient, berries. Not until the master retired, often late at night, was she permitted to collapse on an old robe in the place of least honor. In a few scant hours she would begin the same routine over again.

Each day the younger women harnessed travois to ponies and went out to the killing fields, there to butcher the buffalo the hunters had killed. The Bloods wallowed in buffalo, eventually cutting only the tongues from them, and sometimes hump meat. They loved cow, which was tender, and sometimes brought back an unborn calf, whose soft hide was prized. Even the camp dogs had their fill and slept lazily instead of gorging on the carrion. Plentiful meat, the true food of these people, made them happy, and they began to slacken their efforts. All except the slave, who toiled on because she faced the lash or a stick if she paused. The village had more meat and hide than it could possibly use. The buffalo were so plentiful that a foray into the midst of them hardly disturbed the giant herd, which slowly grazed its way south.

Then the chief—she had found out that his name was Crow Dog—decreed that the Hair Shirts would go to the Sun Dance, and soon she found herself packing the lodge's wealth into parfleches, large rawhide containers, and loading them onto the ponies. The horses would be overburdened this trip, carrying all the jerky and pemmican that had been salvaged from the buffalo brothers and sisters, as well as fresh hides and tanned robes. It meant she would walk, but now that she was stronger she preferred to. Some of the bruises remained, yellow-and-purple reminders of her ordeal, which she wore like prisoner garb.

The walking gave her a chance to reflect on her life. As long as she didn't stray from the other women, they left her alone. She could not converse, even though she was mastering all the words she could. It was one thing to recognize words and commands, quite another to string words together and talk to these Siksika. So she walked through golden June days when the world ached with pleasure, her thoughts on the new reality she faced. She had lost dominion over her life; every minute of it belonged to her master and mistresses. She had lost the hope of many things, including husband, reputation, friends, esteem, and her freedom to organize her days as she chose.

The causes for all that lay in the past, in her folly, in her girlish worship of warriors and war, but those things could not be undone, so they were best forgotten. She still faced a future, however limited, and she would have to find some sort of bearable life among these enemies of the People, or else roll over and die. Skye was long gone. Why would he try to find her and save her from her own foolishness? Why would he come, after she had betrayed him? No, he was on his way to the east and the many-houses villages he had told her about.

She probably would have to make a life with the Kainah and then die. She had learned that *Kainah* meant "Many Chiefs" and that Bloods was a name bestowed upon these people by their enemies the Cree. On her war trip with Beckwourth she had departed a girl; now she was a woman. She had changed forever, a passage as real as her passage from freedom to slavery. As she walked, she came to understand herself as a woman who would not surrender. She would look for a chance to escape. Someday the Absaroka would show up in force and free her. Or someday when things were just right—an impending snowstorm, or chaos, or a desperate fight—she would walk away. Someday, sometime. And meanwhile, she could make life bearable by learning the tongue, avoiding abuse as much as she could, pleasing those who really didn't wish to be pleased, and perhaps even winning friends among those who wanted mainly to despise her.

She had never again heard from her benefactor, the woman who had saved her life the night of the coup counting, but she knew that somewhere among these people was a woman whose name was Magpie, and someday she would find and befriend that woman. Her other source of strength and courage was her spirit-helper. She found time for the traditional crying, and grew certain that her counselor was leading her through this ordeal for a purpose—maybe to make a beautiful woman of her. Magpie was wise; magpie did not flee south like other birds, but endured, even as she, Many Quill Woman, must endure this winter of the soul.

She learned to work without being asked or bullied. By the time the village was settling down for the night, she had found firewood, unloaded parfleches, and spread the robes. The elder wife didn't really like this; she wanted to yell, and itched to beat the slave. So she found fault no matter what Victoria did, but the torrent of abuse slid by Victoria like leaves floating on a stream.

They traveled farther north than she had ever been, and now the Backbone of the World shown whitely to the west again. The Bloods possessed a good and bountiful land, though not half as sweet as the land of the Absarokas.

They came to a great grassy flat lying at the foot of mysterious and strange buttes, and there the Kainah were gathering. Several bands had preceded the Hair Shirts. Victoria beheld a great encampment, rather like the white men's rendezvous. The days had grown hot, even scorching, and the sun was driving the last of the green from the grasses. This had been a dry summer, for which she was grateful. She had almost no clothing; a tattered dress that was rotting away from her lithe body, and no more. With the coming of cold, they would either clothe her or let her freeze to death. She could not know her fate.

Her master, Grandfather of Wolves, had not come to her for many suns, preferring his own women, and that pleased her. Perhaps that was because she had been too still and submissive, giving him nothing. Whatever the reason, he left her alone, and she was able to sleep entire nights, rest her weary body, and awaken refreshed, even if desolation stole through her as she faced another hollow, brutal day.

They kept her far away from the sacred lodge they were erecting to worship Sun. This, the most arduous and sacred of ceremonies, was only for the People. She didn't wish to see any of it. They had stolen it from the Absarokas, who had honored Sun long before the Bloods. And before that, it had come from

the Arapaho. She di
that. These Bloods were
nation in the Blackfoot Fede
luctantly, that perhaps they were
and perhaps raised its greatest chi
suggested.

The great blessing of the Sun Dance for
the Siksika ignored her. Sacred ritual absorbe
woman of impeccable virtue was chosen to lead
worship of Sun; there were prescribed dances, often
night. They had built a sun lodge, a circular arbor with t
ditional sacred pole in its center, to which the dancers would
tethered in the final act of ritual sacrifice.

Now the drumming never ceased, and along with it the eagle bone whistles and flutes. This mesmerizing throb filled the whole plateau with heartbeat, life's pulse. Had this been the ritual of her own people, her spirit would have overflowed with pride and joy. But these were not her Absarokas, and the ceremony had a reverse impact on her. With every beat of the drum, with each prayer and song lifted on eagle feathers to the Above Ones and Four-Foots, she was flooded with an ineffable sadness.

Skye rode north, a solitary horseman passing through the land of the Blackfeet. The mountains, the Backbone of the World, rose ever present on his left, severing these featureless plains from whatever lay beyond. This was a brooding land, with perspectives so distant that it set the mind to thinking about eternity. Nothing but a few scattered buttes supplied features to a featureless land. From any slight hill he could see his fate in the day to come. This country made him feel small, as the sea had sometimes made him feel helpless.

He saw no Blackfeet, nor did he even discover signs of passage. Yet he was now in the heart of their country—and not far from British possessions. He had no way of knowing when he might cross that line, the 49th parallel, but it didn't matter. The Crown had no power here, and his escape from the Royal Navy frigate would be long forgotten. Trouble, such as it was in such country, would more likely be the crossing of a treacherous river or a sudden storm. He had crossed two northeast-flowing streams, and suspected they were the south and middle branches of the Milk, a river that rose in the western mountains, hurried north into the British possessions, and then curved south again to empty into the Missouri.

The long country evinced long thoughts, and the one that

preyed on his serenity had to do with Victoria's heart. In that brief encounter at Berger's post, she had cried to him for help. And in his own fantasies, he had expanded that heart-cry into something it wasn't: a wish to return to him. She wanted help, escape, freedom. Not a word or gesture in that fiery moment had suggested love or caring. As he rode, he came to grips with that painful truth.

At first he believed it would have to be an act of faith; he would rescue her, drawing courage from his certitude that she loved him and would return to his arms, his hearth fires, forever. But then he knew even that was delusion. He simply did not know. She might be very grateful, quite distant, and once returned to her people, quietly shut the door to him again. So he wondered anew whether he was on a fool's mission. He could turn back, unscathed, probably find one of the Rocky Mountain Fur Company brigades and sign on—with his scalp on his skull.

The thought tempted him. Around his campfires, each skillfully hidden in a brushy coulee, he let the temptation run, wanting to see it whole. He owed her nothing. He loved her—nothing would ever change that—but faced rejection once again. Why had he set out on this fool's errand?

In the stillness of that sweeping land, when even the breeze seemed hushed and scarcely a bird sang, there came to him another reason: no mortal should live in captivity. Victoria's life was not her own. Why had *she* been set upon the earth? To be a slave? She was experiencing much the same ordeal as his own. He had not been in possession of himself. All he had, during his long burial in the crowded fo'c'sle of the H.M.S. *Jaguar,* was his dreams and his prayers. Nothing else. He owned not even the clothing on his body, and received a meal only when his masters felt like giving him one. What had sustained him then was hope. He had never stopped dreaming of the time when he would be a free man.

So it was with her. She probably was as much a slave as he had been. Perhaps her life would be better than his. At least she had land under her feet, and with it the chance of escape. And probably she did just about the same things she had done in her own village. She might even be given in marriage. And yet in some respects her lot would be worse than his. She didn't know their tongue; he and his shipmates and masters shared the English tongue, which had assuaged his loneliness.

Skye realized, then, that his purposes were larger and more generous than simply the recovery of a woman he loved and had once possessed. He would free her if he could—and then offer her freedom from him. He would free her because of every bitter memory of being at the mercy of others, of the lash and whip that had befallen him whenever he resisted or failed to do what was required of him. He would free her because no mortal on earth should be forced into servitude. No one deserved that fate.

He studied the country as he passed through, uncertain whether he would know the Belly River even if he stood on its bank. The scant direction he had received from the Piegans scarcely prepared him to find his way in a land without landmarks. He forded another modest stream flowing northeast, and believed it to be the north fork of the Milk River. He topped a low divide and found himself in a different drainage, this one with scattered lakes lying ahead. Somewhere beyond the lakes would be the medicine line, the beginning of Grandfather's Land, as the Piegans had described it. From there it would not be far to the Belly River . . . and the Bloods.

They weren't pretty lakes, nor were they set in green forests. But they harbored thousands of ducks, geese, cranes, and white swans. One somber evening Skye made a meal of a Canada goose he shot as it lifted from the shimmering water. Skye didn't much like this silent country. It lacked the graces of beauty and surprise. Neither did he much like dining on goose. It took too long to gut it, pluck the pinfeathers, clean it, roast it, and saw it into edible portions.

He arrived at the northernmost of these lakes the next evening and beheld a campfire across the water. So, at last, he would make contact again, for better or worse. He waited for the darkness to settle, which was a long time coming in that latitude in summer. But at last he walked his horses around the grassy shore, edging closer. He wanted a good look before he made any decisions. He tied his horses to a juniper and negotiated the last quarter mile on foot. If trouble came, he would be shielded by darkness.

He saw that there were five or six standing around the fire, which burned brightly and too large for concealment. He spotted several horses picketed close by and what appeared to be packs on the ground. On closer examination, he discovered still more men sitting on logs near the fire.

"You out there, do you come in peaceably or do we hunt you down?" came the voice, startling and harsh in the velvet silence.

Skye sprang backward, fearing the firelight had revealed him.

"I know you're there. Every one of our beasts faces toward ye, ears pointed. You're not a catamount or a wolf. The beasts don't act like that except around mortals. Now, are you friend or foe?"

Skye watched the others casually lift weapons and settle behind the packs, which made fine barricades. He thought he detected some familiar ring to the voice, and what he heard did not remind him of Yanks.

"All right," he said. "I'm alone."

"Ah, I knew you jolly well weren't a red man," said the voice. "Ye speak the tongue known to us. Come then, and warm yourself at our fire, if that's your purpose. I will tell you straight off, we are Hudson's Bay men."

Skye paused. HBC once offered money for his capture. But that was four years ago, and the episode had long been forgotten, even by the HBC men he had encountered at the rendezvous since then.

"I'll come in," he said. "It'll be a few minutes."

He retreated to his horses, wondering all the while whether

to leave them as a means of escape, and finally decided to bring them in. He wanted to talk to these men.

He collected the horses and led them toward the distant glow, and finally walked into camp. There he encountered others dressed rather like himself, in a mixture of flannels and buckskins, a wedding of native and European manufacture. Sitting on a log were several Creoles, dressed identically in red flannel shirts and blue trousers. They appeared to be voyageurs, and Skye spotted two large canoes nearby. They and the gents in buckskins all wore beards; some wore their hair shoulder length, like the Yank trappers. All but one. That fellow, amazingly, had outfitted himself in a heavy black swallowtail suit. That one looked for all the world like a duke. He had a ducal presence as well, examining the world about him as if he owned it. Now that penetrating gaze focused on Skye with obvious curiosity. Skye gaped at the apparition, this powerfully built gentleman in business attire in the middle of a wilderness.

"I'm George Simpson, governor of HBC. And who are you, sir?"

The name shot fear through Skye. Simpson was the most powerful Briton in the New World. Hudson's Bay had a charter that permitted it sovereign rule over a large portion of North America, and the governor of that fiefdom, who ruled not merely a business but operated a private government as well, stood before him. Here was the man appointed in London by the board of directors, a quasi-official of the Crown, the superior of Dr. John McLoughlin out in Fort Vancouver. Here was the man who oversaw an empire from his lair at York Factory on Hudson's Bay, as well as from Fort Vancouver itself.

And a man who might remember Skye's name, even after four years. But Skye doubted the man would remember the name of an ordinary sailor.

"Governor Simpson, I'm honored to meet you, sir," Skye replied. "I've heard much about you."

"And you, sir? Have I heard much about you?"

"No, you haven't. I am Barnaby Skye."

Simpson looked puzzled. "I know that name, yes. Somewhere, blast it. Well, come in and have tea. Yes, and the men'll put the horses up, and you'll tell us how a man like you rises like some wraith out of the wilderness and approaches a fire."

"I'm on my way north, sir, to the Belly River, where I wish to do business with the Bloods."

"What sort of business?"

"My wife is a captive. I wish to free her."

"Your wife? A white woman?"

"No, she is a woman of the Crows, the Absaroka. And I intend to get her back."

"You are an Englishman; quite plain in your speech. Yes, London. But not Billingsgate, not Cockney. What is it, then?"

"My father was a merchant, sir, import-export."

"Well, that's it, then. But you're not one of our men."

"No, sir. I'm not associated with any company at present, though I've trapped with a Yank brigade."

"Damned near treason, Skye."

"It's Mister Skye, sir."

"Mister Skye, is it? Now I remember. The Royal Navy. A damned deserter." He thrust a finger at Skye. "Seize him!"

forty

So it wasn't over.

Skye sprang toward Governor Simpson, wrestled the man around, and pressed his knife to the man's throat. The Hudson's Bay governor writhed until the keen edge of Skye's knife drew blood.

"They'll kill me, but you'll die first," Skye whispered.

"Don't move, don't move," Simpson bellowed.

Skye hated this. He had no quarrel with valid authority, only with injustice. He might die in the next moments. That couldn't be helped. He would not—ever—go back to England or spend his days in a dungeon. When he had finally escaped the Royal Navy, he vowed that no bars would ever come between his eyes and the heavens.

Around him, burly Hudson's Bay men stood frozen, ready to spring at him. Skye was one against twelve or fifteen. More than that. Simpson didn't beg, but stood composed, aware of the deadly blade pressing against his jugular.

"I will never be taken alive," Skye announced to the men, who even now were edging around behind him, preparing to spring. "And if you attempt to kill me now, Simpson dies."

They believed him. He could see their wariness in the flickering light. Yet he didn't know how to escape. With one arm around the governor, and the other holding the knife to the man's throat, he could not lead his horses away.

"For God's sake, be careful," Simpson said. It was a command to his men. The governor wasn't pleading and hadn't lost his composure. Skye admired him.

"I will make something clear," said Skye. "I prefer death to capture. Remember that. Mr. Simpson is a good and honorable Englishman. Don't cost him his life. He will have it if you heed me."

He wrestled Simpson toward the edge of camp, where the firelight dimmed. Simpson walked readily. The bores of several Hudson's Bay rifles followed. When he reached a place where some brush blocked the view, he steered the governor behind it.

"One man, bring me my horses," he yelled.

They debated a moment in the light of the fire.

"Tell them, sir," Skye said softly.

"Damned if I will."

Skye pressed his keen blade into the flesh of the man's neck. Simpson wilted.

"Bring his horses—you, McGill. Do it."

A man led Skye's black horse and the packhorse out of the firelight and brought them near.

"All right, go back," said Skye. "If you value the governor's life, don't follow. Sit down at the fire. Everyone."

Skye watched them reluctantly sit. He knew one or more lurked in the darkness, maybe even now circling around to pounce on him. He listened closely, hearing nothing.

Skye steered Simpson toward the horses. "Take the reins," he told the governor.

Slowly, Skye steered the governor into the deeps of the night, following the lakeshore northward. Water glinted on his right. A quarter moon spread pale white light over the darkened landscape. Skye paused frequently, listened for sounds of pursuit. He heard none.

"Are we in British territory?" Skye asked the governor.

"Where Hudson's Bay is, Britannia rules."

"Where were you coming from and where are you going?"

"I am returning from Vancouver and stopped to see Fort Spokane."

"And?"

"Up to the Saskatchewan River."

"And then to York Factory?"

"How far are you taking me?"

"You won't get lost. Not with that lakeshore guiding you back."

"You're an abomination before man and God."

"Think what you will."

"They should have thrown you into the sea."

"Quiet now. You're talking to give me away."

"I'll talk all I choose."

"You don't much care for your life, then."

Skye released him, took the reins, and prodded the governor forward at knifepoint. They traversed another mile or so of lakefront. Then, as the shore curved east, Skye turned north. A grassy slope took them out of the lake basin and onto prairie. The whole bowl of heaven lay over them.

"I'll let you go now," Skye said. "Go down the slope to the lake and follow the shore. And don't start yelling. As long as you are in my sight, you are not safe."

"I'll see you hanged, Skye."

"Be gone now. Do not yell. I am armed and watching. Remember that."

Sir George Simpson glared, whirled away, and marched off the ridge. Skye swiftly moved to his left and then swung north again. When he reached some brush he paused, mounted the black, and rode swiftly. He could scarcely imagine how he escaped. And he knew that at least some within Hudson's Bay had not given up their effort to ship him back to London.

He cut westward, putting the North Star on his right. The maneuver wouldn't long slow down an experienced mountain man, but Skye intended to do all he could to elude his followers. He rode swiftly through the night, intending to put distance and more distance between himself and Simpson.

He wondered what the Hudson's Bay governor was doing so far south of the usual voyageur's passage from Fort Vancouver to York Factory. But he didn't have to wonder long. Simpson was probably offering weapons and ammunition to any who would make relentless war on the Yanks. Hudson's Bay had been doing that ever since Ashley's free trappers penetrated the mountains. The British didn't want an American presence in the Oregon country, which ran from the Rockies to the Pacific and was under joint rule until a boundary could be established. Thus did Hudson's Bay further the imperial designs of the Crown.

Skye sensed he wasn't done with Simpson. The man might well show up at the Sun Dance. Where else could he stir up so many Blackfeet? If that was the case, Skye would be in even more jeopardy if he were to walk in to the great Blood tribal ceremony. If he intended to free Victoria, he would have to get in and get out before Simpson's large party showed up. Skye wished he had kept quiet about his plans back in those amiable moments when he first encountered Simpson. But it was too late to repair the damage.

He swung north again and continued until he felt the horses tire. Not long before dawn he made a dry camp in a coulee, picketed the horses well below the skyline, and rolled into his robe. He made no fire and went hungry. After four years in the mountains, he was inured to starving. He didn't sleep.

At first light, when the world was gray, he studied the surrounding country, which was open and grassy, and then collected his half-rested horses. He rode ever north, a solitary figure on a mission that seemed crazy. At every rise he paused to study his back trail, but saw nothing. The country began to change. Forest stretched along slopes, and the land seemed better watered. He supposed he was in British territory, but didn't know. A boundary had never been surveyed.

That afternoon he struck a goodly river that ran in a shallow canyon. Its clear cold water had the lingering taste of snowmelt. It ran northeast. Skye believed it was the Belly and he was close to the Bloods, but he couldn't be sure. From now on it would be guesswork. Very little the Piegans told him helped now, when one river seemed like another.

From a hilltop he studied the half-forested, half-grassed country. What he hoped to find was some distant buttes, the Belly Buttes—at whose feet the great Sun ceremony was even now proceeding. He saw nothing he could define as a butte or tableland, but maybe that was because he was too far west.

He sat his horse, examining a land so vast that a man could spend months mastering it. Somewhere, in some direction of the compass, was Victoria. He felt a helplessness once again. There were so many times, throughout his life, when he barely knew where to turn or what to do. He clambered off his horse and settled in the wind-rippled grass, letting himself absorb the country before him. He didn't much believe in intuition, but he did believe that if he opened all his senses to the world around him, he might get information, see or hear or smell the things he would otherwise miss.

One of these was buffalo. Below him, in the boxed valley of this river, he spotted a dozen of the great black animals peacefully grazing. They reminded him that he was hungry and out of food. These looked larger and darker than any he had seen before, and he wondered whether they were the woods buffalo the trappers had spoken of, a shaggy northern version of the plains buffalo to the south. From his vantage point he watched the shadows of puffball clouds plow the earth, roll over forests, climb slopes and disappear. He felt, as he sometimes did, that he was not alone, that the strangeness of his life had some hidden purpose he might yet fathom when he was an old man.

Below, a small barren cow grazed. He would eat her tongue and regret leaving so much more. It had been a long time since he had tasted the splendid, firm meat of the bison. He let his horses graze a while more, suddenly in no hurry, and then rode down a game trail into the narrow canyon. The herd saw him descend the canyon wall and trotted downstream, tails lifted, wide-eyed. Skye slid his mountain rifle out of its fringed sheath, checked the priming, which was dry, and rode easily down-river, driving the herd before him.

Then the cow he had his eyes on stumbled and fell, and he beheld an arrow in her side and a swarm of Indians boiling out of the bankside willow brush.

forty-one

They saw him just as he saw them. They barely paused at the fallen buffalo cow, and rode instead toward Skye, fifteen, twenty of them, all armed, some with rifles, most with deadly bows and arrows.

Suddenly Skye became the hunted, along with the buffalo. The howl of the hunters told him that. Swiftly, Skye kicked his horses straight up the slope. He intended to top the rim of the river valley, which was his sole hope of escape. But his burdened horse and packhorse lost ground to the buffalo ponies of these warriors. He saw an arrow hiss by and knew he was within range. He huddled low over the saddle to make a smaller target and urged his black up the steep slope, which it devoured with great leaps that almost unseated him.

The Indians had the advantage of the angle, and drew closer as he scaled the grassy slope. Another arrow reached him, this one smacking into the kit behind his cantle. An arrow struck the black, and it screeched. Sky saw a line of blood where the arrow had plowed a trench along the croup. Not a fatal wound, but the black horse kicked and screeched and bucked itself over the rim of the valley, and for a few seconds Skye enjoyed a respite.

His nearest succor was a patch of pines half a mile distant. But the lumbering packhorse was slowing him. He let go. His life was worth more than his kit. The horse thundered along behind Skye anyway, not wanting to separate itself from its companion.

The hunters spilled onto the grassy plain and fired volleys of arrows. Skye heard the packhorse wheeze. It grunted and stumbled to the ground, three arrows in it, one through the neck, one in the ribs, and the third into the rump. Another volley of arrows hit his black, and one arrow pierced his leather shirt. He felt the black buckle under him, shudder, and cave in. Skye pulled loose just before it collapsed, and found himself flat on the grass, the wind knocked out of him. He tried to unsheath his rifle, but it lay under the weight of the flailing, dying horse.

So this was it.

Moments later they swarmed over him, a dozen—more, twenty—powerful, tall, golden-fleshed Blackfeet, Bloods probably. They studied him, saw he was alive, and crowded around, each counting coup. Blows rained down on him. They kicked and pummeled, jabbed with coup sticks, knocked him about. The blows came so fast and hard he had no place to escape, no way even to fight.

Then the blows stopped. They had all counted coup. He supposed they would kill him now; a coup against a live enemy was worth much more than a coup against a dead one. He tried to sit up, but a foot smashed him to the ground again. He rolled over, beheld a circle of them over him, lances poised for the kill. But a sharp command of a headman forestalled that—for the moment. Skye wished they would finish the job. From the ground he saw them pillage his kit. They ripped open the panniers on the packhorse and pulled out all the trading items he had planned to use to win Victoria: knives, awls, beads, pairs of blankets, powder, bars of lead, flints and steels, a bolt of tradecloth. These they examined, sometimes glancing at him. He lay still, awaiting his fate. The leader of this band of hunters signaled two of them to roll the dead black over. He wanted to free the rifle. Moments later he possessed the prize, a fine, octagon-barreled percussion lock and a fringed and beaded sheath. He held it high, sighted down it, aimed it at Skye, and laughed.

"Shoot, Bug's Boy," Skye said.

But the warrior didn't. Instead he hefted the rifle, ripped Skye's powder horns from his chest, and took Skye's knife for good measure. The bear claw necklace caught his eye, and he examined it closely, plainly fascinated by the length of the dark claws. Now at last he examined Skye as a person, not just a white enemy. Then he said something Skye couldn't translate. The headman yanked at the necklace, trying to pull it loose. Skye resisted.

"That's mine; leave it alone, you devil," he roared.

The headman yanked harder, so Skye smacked him with his fist.

Surprised, the headman reeled back, sprang to his feet, and pulled out his war club, a mean weapon composed of a shaped piece of rock bound by rawhide in the fork of a haft. The warrior slashed down sharply; Skye rolled, and the club grazed his ear. Skye kept on rolling, got to his feet, and rammed toward the warrior, who brought the club back and down, smashing hard into Skye's shoulder. Skye went numb with shock. His shoulder felt as if it had been severed from his body. He pushed, and the warrior staggered back. Skye landed on him, but the tribesmen pulled him off, a dozen hands lifting him off the fallen chief by main force. They cast Skye into the dirt, where he lay panting, waiting . . .

When they turned to the chief to help him up Skye sprang again, his heart wild in him, his fists hammering at any flesh he could see—and he did not lack a target. Something berserk had loosed in him; his senses had become unmoored, and now he fought one and all, crazily, too powerful for any or several to grip him or topple him, though they tried. Then a sharp command stopped them, but not Skye. He was beyond stopping, and launched murderously after one, then another.

A blow to his head shot white through his brain, and then blackness. He knew nothing. . . .

He awakened now and then to the throb of a mighty

headache, and knew from the pain that he lived. But he couldn't think and didn't understand what had happened. When he finally did come around, he felt only thirst and pain. He lay in a darkened place but couldn't focus his eyes enough to know where he was. His body gave him no comfort, but in spite of raw hurt he drifted into oblivion again. The next time he came to, he realized he was in a lodge. The poles at the smoke hole formed an apex. Blue sky lay beyond. The Bloods—if that was who they were—had taken him to this place. And spared him for reasons of their own. He knew their reasons, and wished they had killed him outright instead of the slow style they had in mind.

He heard a drumming and wasn't sure whether it was his angry pulse or the beat of a ceremony. He decided it was a ceremony and that the Sun Dance was under way, or about to begin, or in a preliminary phase. He closed his eyes again; to see was to hurt. He discovered that he still possessed his bear claw necklace, powerful medicine to these people and any other tribe. It lay across his chest, hurting him. The brush of a feather would have hurt him just then.

This night they would hurt him more.

He dozed. He was conscious of people entering the lodge, poking him, talking over him. One lifted his bear claw necklace and then dropped it. Some woman lifted his head and gave him water. He drank greedily and slumped back to oblivion. Let them examine him all they would; his life was no longer his own, and he had surrendered it. Maybe, when he could form words better, he would pray for a good death. No one much thought of the importance of a good death, but any mountaineer did, and a plea for a good death lay in the heart of every man he had met in these wilds. There were so many deaths of the other kind.

He lay awake in the quiet of the empty lodge, studying what had been stored within. He needed the means of self-immolation, a way to a swift sure death, without the pain of what was in store for him. He saw nothing. His captors had been careful. He was not bound in any way, but his moccasins had been taken from him. Nothing more was needed to keep him there.

No one bothered to feed him, but he hurt too much to care. All the long day he heard in the distance the dancing of the Bloods. For four days they would honor the Sun, perform ritual acts of repentance and sacrifice and cleansing. They would dance on a bed of fragrant sagebrush, around a Sun pole with buffalo skulls at its base. They would whistle with bone flutes, compose prayers to the powerful Sun, pleading for peace, for fruitfulness, for increase, for victory at war, for blessings. And some would beg Sun for darker things: vengeance, fulfillment of a bloody vow, death upon enemies. These were the most sacred hours in the liturgy of the Blackfeet, more sacred even than the opening of the beaver bundle in the spring. During all this, his captors would ignore him and fulfill their obligations to Sun and to the tribe.

Skye mended swiftly. His young body had been bruised and battered but not stricken by disease. Nor had any of his internal organs been damaged, or bones broken. He lay on his bed of grass, alert now, growing curious about his captors. He probably was in the lodge of that headman, the one who had led the buffalo hunt that supplied precious meat to this great tribal gathering. So many mouths to feed required relentless hunting for anything edible, and the buffalo Skye had hazed straight into the waiting Bloods must have seemed to them a gift from Sun himself.

On the third day of his captivity he wondered where Victoria might be and what her fate was. She probably was there, maybe within yards of him. No longer did he have the slightest chance of rescuing her. All his carefully hoarded stock of trade items intended to purchase her release had been taken from him. He lacked so much as a horse or a saddle—or covering for his feet. She would survive, tough and resilient and strong in her own way. Maybe she could fashion a life among these mortal enemies of the Crows. He knew it was commonplace for captive women to come to love their captors, marry them, become members of the once-hated tribe.

He was grateful she didn't know he was in the village, helpless. She didn't know he had tried, had plunged all this distance, taken all these risks, all because of a single plea to him before she was silenced. He didn't want her to bear that knowledge. But if she did find out—and she might during the torture—she would know that he had come. That was all. He had come for her. Let that tell her about his love.

They left him alone another night and slept outside the lodge because of the summer's heat. So he rarely saw the Blackfeet who held him. A woman fed him broth now, enough to sustain life—for the sport to come.

That day the sound of the drumming changed, the beat darker and more tormented, interrupted by intense singing. It was the time of sacrifice, when those making the sacred vow fulfilled it. The flesh of their chests or backs had been pierced, a cord run through the incision and strung to the Sun pole in the sacred medicine lodge. And there the young men who were making their sacrifice to Sun danced and would keep on dancing until they ripped free of the Sun pole and lay half dead in a pool of their own blood. Maybe his captor had been one of those.

The drumming continued deep into the night, and then slowed, and finally stopped. A great and terrible silence fell upon the camp of the Bloods, and Skye knew the dance had passed and the next day might be his last.

forty-two

The yellow eyes had come to the great encampment of the Bloods, and Victoria caught glimpses of them as they presented themselves to the chiefs and headmen. The women of the lodge had told her not to go to the place of the gathering, so Victoria had to be careful. The white men had gathered before the lodge of the greatest of Blood chiefs, Sees Afar, over among the *Ah-kai-po-kaks*, the Many Children band. All the other chiefs and headmen had gathered there, including Crow Dog, chief of the Hair Shirts.

Still, Victoria found ways to glimpse all this. She drifted that way, lost among the crowds of Siksika women and children, and saw some of it. She risked a beating but what did it matter? She could live like a whipped dog or she could try to make some sort of life for herself.

These were the other white men, from Grandfather's Land across the great waters. Hudson's Bay Company, the very ones who had chased Skye and tried to capture him years before. Most of them looked like the trappers she had seen in Skye's brigade, hairy men in buckskins. But she saw some darker ones, the Creoles who spoke another tongue, and these were dressed alike in blue pants and red flannel shirts, as if they were all eggs from one nest. They interested her, but not so much as the other one, the great chief of the Hudson's Bay men. This one wore black, except for a white shirt. Black from head to foot; a coat of black that dipped like the tail of a bird in back but was shorter in front. He had a meaty, cruel face, with bold eyes that missed nothing. He looked and acted like a great chief, too, a lord whose power and word won instant obedience.

She didn't like these men. These were the ones who had supplied guns, axes, arrow points, tomahawks, and all the rest to the Siksika so that they might war upon the Absaroka and kill off rival yellow eyes men in the fur brigades. She studied them closely; they were from Mister Skye's land and shared his blood.

She could see what all this was about: the black-clad man was seeking trade and giving gifts. He asked each chief to come forward, and gave each one a shining rifle. Those were mighty gifts, and they would assure that this company would have the Blackfoot trade for many winters to come. He was making a great speech all the while, and two translators were making his words into Siksika words so all could understand. All this was done with ceremony. One of the yellow eyes stood with a flag made of red with a certain sort of cross upon it. Skye had told her once that this company had a flag with the Cross of St. George upon it, but she didn't know what that was. Another man held up a pole with another flag, this one red and blue and white. Skye had called that one a Union Jack, and it was the medicine of these Beyond the Water men.

After that there were many speeches, as each of the Blood chiefs stood, had his say about friendship and peace and trade and the alliance of Hudson's Bay with the Siksika. She couldn't follow all of that. But she knew the gist of it: between them, the Hudson's Bay Company and the Siksika would drive out the other pale men from this land forever, and the Siksika would drive the Lakota and Cree and Assiniboine and Absaroka away, too, and be lords of the earth. She didn't like this gathering. The many-gifts white men were plotting and scheming, and the Bloods were dreaming of power.

The Blood chiefs rose. The gathering was dissolving and the

pale men would soon be gone. But the grandfather in the black clothing was talking to Sees Afar about something. And the great chief talked to someone else, who talked to someone else. Then a Blood warrior came forth, a powerfully built man wearing war honors. He had counted many coups. The grandfather summoned his Hudson's Bay men to him, and soon they brought him another shining rifle and a pair of red blankets and other things. The warrior accepted these and vanished. Everyone stood there, waiting for something. Victoria wondered what it might be.

Then she saw what they were waiting for, and the sight sucked her breath from her lungs. They brought Skye to the grandfather man of Hudson's Bay. Skye! He looked weary and bruised. She wormed her way closer, desperate, wanting to cry out to him but knowing she couldn't. He had come for her. They had caught him. They had hurt him. He looked worn and wounded, but he stood alert and strong, something indomitable about him. His keen blue eyes surveyed the grandfather and the Hudson's Bay men. The warrior who had captured Skye pushed Skye the last few feet and sent him sprawling at the feet of the grandfather man. Hudson's Bay had bought Skye. They would take him back across the waters.

Victoria's heart ached and she felt a flood of anguish. She had to help him, somehow, some way. But how?

"Well, Barnaby Skye, we have you now," the grandfather man said.

Her man did not reply, but kept looking at the blue skies and the wild lands, as if not even seeing the grandfather man.

"It'll be the dungeon for a deserter, Skye."

"It's Mister Skye, sir."

The grandfather man laughed derisively. "Tie him up. We'll be off for York Factory," he said.

With that, some of the Hudson's Bay men bound Skye's arms behind his back.

Frantically, she maneuvered through the spellbound Bloods,

who watched all this with intense interest. Only Skye's captor wasn't watching. He was cocking and uncocking his new rifle and sighting down its steel barrel.

She wormed forward, past the proper place for women and toward the warriors who crowded around Skye and the Hudson's Bay men. She had to let him know! A Blood warrior noticed her and barred the way. The council was not a proper place for a woman. He growled at her, and she stepped back, slipped away, and tried again at a different point, only to be rebuffed by more warriors who eyed her coldly for violating the custom.

She was on the brink of a whipping or death or torture, and yet she had to let Skye know she was there. Just one glance, one meeting of the eyes, that's all she could ask. She found a way, this time through a crowd of the Hudson's Bay men, trappers, and vogageurs, who stood amid their piles of gear and canoes. This time she darted through, stood not ten yards from her man, and waited, hoping that her spirit-helper, Magpie, would reveal her to Skye and conceal her from the eyes of the Siksika.

He did turn, did see her, and in one eternal moment they faced each other. In one moment that lasted forever and was written upon the stars, she and he saw each other, and it was like lightning from a cloud struck the earth so great was the force of their gaze. And then, after the briefest of smiles, he turned away—to protect her, to conceal the great event from these Siksika and Hudson's Bay. No one had noticed. She fled backward, her heart racing. She had to free him. She had to escape these people. She might never see him again. She knew his vow: they would not take him alive. If he had no way to escape before they put him in the big canoe and took him across the water, he would find a way to go to the land of the spirits.

Somehow in the confusion she retreated without rebuke or trouble, and soon stood among the women, once again looking through a wall of Blood warriors at the pale men as they prepared to leave. She choked back a flood of emotion. He had come for her. Alone, through the land of the dangerous Siksika, he had come. He had seen her at Berger's post, heard her cry, and had come. Tears welled. No man had ever given her as much. Skye's love had endured, survived even the cuts and wounds she had inflicted on it—and on him. Skye's love had triumphed over her own folly and unfaithfulness. Skye, not Beckwourth, had come to rescue her if he could. She could not stop weeping now, as she slipped quietly back from the gathering and watched from under the boughs of an aspen.

The grandfather's men were dividing into two parties. The trappers in buckskins formed one horseback party and headed west, while the burly voyageurs in the red and blue lowered their canoes into the Belly River and began loading them with mounds of peltries and supplies. Others lifted great packs they were going to carry. She marveled at how much one of these men could carry. They attached a pack to Skye's back and made him carry it barefooted. Soon his feet would bleed. And then a man with a strange device of metal and wood and cloth and leather, a sort of bag connected with a flute, made this device wail mournfully, its melancholic howl piercing the quiet. She knew about this thing that Skye called a bagpipe, and knew how that mournful noise spoke of war and blood and honor—and greatness. Only the white grandfathers had a piper who piped for them.

And so they departed after the piping of the man who squeezed the bag and made the beast howl. So terrible was the noise that all the camp dogs lifted their throats and howled, as if this was a great gathering of wolves. The black-clad grandfather got into a canoe with some of the voyageurs. Other voyageurs shouldered their packs and walked. She watched Skye walk away with them along the riverbank. He was stooped under the weight on his back and unbalanced because his hands were tied together. And yet he walked. He did not glance back to her. Perhaps he was saying, Good-bye, my beloved; good-bye now forever, until we meet again on a distant shore.

She watched until the Hudson's Bay men and Skye vanished behind a wall of trees. Her heart walked beside him. The Bloods watched, too, and then the crowd dissolved. She hastened back to the lodge of Grandfather of Wolves, her mind awhirl with hopes. She had somehow escaped punishment—so far. But surely she had been seen. She hurried past the lodges where the Sun Dancers lay on their robes, recuperating. So great had been their ordeal that the various bands would not travel for a day or two. Grudgingly, Victoria admired the young men who had spilled their blood to honor Father Sun and thus win great blessings. The Siksika women were tenderly nursing all the dancers now, and honoring them for their courage.

No one was in the lodge of Grandfather of Wolves. She peered about, looking for any of her captors. How could it be? Were they all off visiting relatives in other bands, or collecting firewood, or doing one chore or another? A wild impulse struck her: go now, go swiftly, flee while she could. She forced herself to stop thinking such mad thoughts. They would find her and kill her. How could a small lone woman hide from warriors such as these? Surely they would know exactly where she went—along the Belly River behind the Hudson's Bay men.

But why would they think that? They didn't know that Skye was her man. They would think she'd fled south toward her Absaroka people, not north or east. But how might she survive? And how might she free her man? What would she eat?

Swiftly she surveyed the lodge. Everything she needed would be here—if she could only escape the village unseen. She knew she would try. Skye had given up his life to save her; she would give up her life to save him. There, hanging from a lodgepole, was the bow and quiver of her captor. She had never touched it. If a woman touched a warrior's weapons she rendered them powerless, polluted. Skye had never felt that way, and enjoyed showing her how to hold his rifle or his knife.

Heart racing, she examined what else she might take. Skye would need moccasins, and there were several pairs that would fit him. She needed a knife, flint and steel, anything she could carry that would help her and Skye escape. Swiftly she ransacked the parfleches, scooping up jerky and a fat tube of pemmican. She found a sheathed skinning knife and a flint and striker. She dug out two pairs of moccasins, big ones for Skye, a spare pair for her, plus some patching leather. She found an awl. Gingerly—fear lacing her—she lowered the bow and quiver full of arrows. She rolled all this into a light summer robe, one she could carry, and tied it tight with thong. She peered out of the lodge door, seeing only a sleepy encampment, slowly recovering after the excitement and exhaustion of the high summer gathering. The sun rolled lazily toward the northwest. The day would fade in a while, and that was good. Darkness might hide a small, lithe Absaroka woman bent on fleeing the whole nation of Bloods. Sharply she studied the People. Plenty of them were about, tending their affairs, sunning, talking. She gathered her breath and her courage and walked west, bearing the rolled robe over her shoulder and carrying a woodcutting hatchet. She did not look directly at any of the Bloods, for fear they would register her passage, but instead penetrated the woods that grew back from the river, passing two or three women who were industriously hacking at branches. Then at last she was alone. She swung north, walking through pine forest laced with open parks, and emerged well north of the camp and almost around Belly Buttes. She knew she was on the river road the Hudson's Bay men had taken.

As she walked, she wept.

forty-three

Skye staggered under the pack they had loaded on his back. His bare feet bled and smarted, and each step shot pain up his legs. He bore the bruises of the beating the Bloods had given him while counting coup. His shoulders ached almost beyond endurance, and his legs threatened to collapse under him.

Sir George Simpson eyed him now and then when his canoe drew alongside or they portaged around rapids. There was smugness in his face but he said nothing. He had his man at last, and the Crown would be pleased—and so would the honorable directors of Hudson's Bay, back in London. The governor bore no burden, but had to walk like everyone else whenever walking was required.

Skye marveled at the voyageurs, burly Frenchmen who had carried two canoes on their backs across the Rockies for the forthcoming voyage down the Belly, Oldman, and South Saskatchewan Rivers, while others wrestled awesome loads. The party now consisted of Governor Simpson, two other Englishmen, and the French-speaking voyageurs. Skye supposed that the mountaineers and their horses were headed back to Fort Vancouver.

Skye contemplated his options. He would be swiftly tossed into a dungeon as a deserter from the Royal Navy, there to rot to an early death on the swill they would feed him. Or else they would simply return him to a man-of-war, there to slave away the rest of his days 'tween decks, the surly sea his prison. The navy was always shorthanded, and would make do with almost any sort of live body.

The overland contingent tramped along the rough banks of the Belly, which had incised itself deep into the undulating prairie above. They circled occasional sloughs that were choked with ducks, climbed steep bluffs where the river crowded passage, maneuvered through wooded hills to shortcut a bend in the river, but were never far from the Belly and the canoes of the rest of the party.

No one spoke to him until they halted for the night next to a glade of box elders back from the riverbank. Skye had somehow managed to endure, to make his battered body move, step by step, mile upon mile, to this place. He doubted he could do the same in the morning with his feet so badly lacerated.

"Well, Skye," said Simpson, "you had the good sense to come along and not fight your fate. You may live or die as you choose; it's of no consequence to me. Your feet are bleeding, and we'll fit you up with moccasins in the morning. You're a beast of burden, and that's your entire value to us."

"It's Mister Skye, sir."

Simpson chortled. "Caught by the Bloods. We knew we'd find you lurking about, just as you said you would. You haven't the brains of an ant. You could be safe in St. Louis or the States by now."

"Yes, I could have been safe long ago, sir. But I have chosen to pay my debts, and I have chosen to help one I love."

Simpson looked faintly surprised, but only for a fleeting moment. "It's all nonsense, trying to butter me up so I'll feel some sympathy. Forget it, Skye. We'll feed you well—that's how one cares for a beast of burden—and then truss you up. Don't try to escape or it will go harder for you tomorrow. You see, Skye, the arm of the Crown reaches everywhere, even here."

Skye said nothing. Around him, the Hudson's Bay men made camp. They did a good job of it, settling down in a defensible place with shelter and firewood. He didn't doubt that these engagés were fully the match of the Yank mountain men when it came to survival. He settled into the grass, grateful to have the burden lifted from him. He hurt as much as he had ever hurt. No one spoke to him, but the whole company eyed him from time to time, their thoughts private. He suspected that very few spoke English.

In time he smelled roasting meat, and in a while they brought him some sizzling buffalo on a platter of bark. He would have to eat it with his fingers when it cooled enough. The scent of good meat made him dizzy. When at last he could handle the meat, he thought that it tasted better than anything he had ever eaten. He chewed mouthful after mouthful of the succulent steak, feeling the meat energize his wounded body and comfort him. They brought him more when he had downed the first helping, and he ate that, too, until he could not swallow another bite. The Indians had always said that buffalo meat gave them strength; they were right.

After he had his fill, they trussed his ankles with thong, and then his wrists behind his back. He would sleep miserably, but they were taking no chances. They did toss a robe over him, and the warmth comforted him. Full darkness settled over the camp, until he could see nothing but the twinkling stars in the vast heaven above. He had vowed once that there would never be iron bars between him and the stars, and now that vow lingered in his mind as the camp lay quiet.

He fought sleep because he needed to think. He might be a prisoner, but he had decisions to make, and his choice would be fateful.

Victoria.

She had seen him. She knew he had come. All that had passed between them had vanished in that terrible, beautiful moment. She knew what faithful love must be. He knew what it meant for her to renew her love. All of this lay beyond repentance and forgiveness, and in the realm where two souls meet and are inseparable to the end of time. Surely, surely, there must be a separate bower in heaven for true lovers. Maybe someday, beyond the beyond, he and Victoria would share that bower in the City of God.

He had no regrets. She had cried out to him, and he had come. If it meant tossing aside his life, then that was his destiny. It had all been worth it, this sweet interlude, an unasked-for wilderness idyll so far from everything he had known as a child.

He had a few options at that. He could refuse to take another step, refuse to participate in his imprisonment. If he chose not to walk, not to carry a burden, they could execute him, which he doubted they would do; flog him, which seemed quite possible, except that it would render him unfit to walk; bind and carry him on a packhorse, which was quite possible; or let him go, for want of means to take him to his destiny—which he deemed wildly improbable.

He had another option: cooperate, walk, gain strength on the plentiful food, heal his body, and look out for a chance to escape. He had jumped ship with almost nothing; he could do it again during this high summer warmth and the forthcoming time of berries, fruit, and roots. The engagés were skilled wilderness men, but so was he after four years in these wilds. He might outsmart them.

He pondered both options as he lay there, trussed and uncomfortable. Walk or not walk. The decision was portentous. He was so young, yet he had always known he would give up that most precious of gifts, life itself, rather than submit to iron bars again.

The rest came in a flood of understanding. He had managed his escape from the Royal Navy only when he stopped resisting and seemed outwardly to cooperate. It had meant that he no longer was thrown into the ship's brig whenever they came within sight of land. They let him stay in his own bunk because they had seen the change in him. The implication was clear: for the moment, he would cooperate with them, give them no reason to think he might be plotting his escape. He would be cheerful, humble, accepting of whatever they imposed on him. And when at last their vigilance lessened, then he would escape—or die.

That was a somber thought, and he pushed it out of mind. He possessed the optimism of youth. He would find a way, and escape, just as he had done in the past. He felt sleep overwhelm him at last, but paused to ask his Maker for mercy and a way. Comforted, he drifted into a dreamless sleep.

The next morning they fitted him with moccasins, fed him gruel swiftly boiled over a campfire, and loaded him with an impossible burden again. The moment it sagged from his shoulders, he hurt anew.

"I can carry it, mates," he said.

No one replied. They had obviously been commanded not to traffic with the prisoner.

Simpson inspected him minutely. "Well, Mister Skye, you're going to walk another fifteen miles today. If you give us any cause, you may be certain blows will land on your head."

Skye nodded.

"I'll tell you something for your own profit. Behave yourself. Maybe you'll have a future, eh?"

Skye wondered what that meant. He remembered encountering the great Hudson's Bay man Peter Skene Ogden years before, and how Ogden had tried to recruit him. Hudson's Bay was as short of seasoned wilderness men as were the Yank fur companies. Skye suspected that Simpson's desire to make pence and pound for his lords in London exceeded even his loyalty to the Crown. And that Skye's cooperation might be the test.

It was going to be a bloody hot day, judging from the way the heat built within an hour after they had started out. Skye's back ached with the burden—he guessed sixty pounds—he bore. So heavy was his load that he stooped forward to balance it. He marveled that the voyageurs carried even more.

He fell in beside the two English-speaking mountaineers, each of whom shouldered a load. Was this how HBC got its furs out of the American Northwest? No wonder they didn't much bother with buffalo robes, preferring the more valuable beaver instead. They had to carry and portage and canoe everything from the Rocky Mountains clear to York Factory on Hudson's Bay.

He observed Simpson's heavily loaded canoe far ahead, and began talking quietly to the silent men around him. He supposed that the better they knew him, simply as a fellow mortal, the less likely they would be to hurt him. So he began simply to tell his story, keeping his voice low and quiet. He swiftly described his youth in London, the press gang that changed his life, his years in the Royal Navy, and his desperate escape. He didn't say much about his subsequent life with the Yank rivals of Hudson's Bay. They would know it anyway, and he didn't want to bring up a sore point. They listened silently, no one objecting, but no one giving any hint of sympathy either. And thus did a broiling day pass, and at the end Skye was never so glad to collapse into the grass and let his aching body find a moment of peace.

The voyageurs beached their canoes in a deep canyon of the Belly that hid the river from the surrounding plains, and were eventually joined by the men on foot. They fed him well and bound him again that night, and he dozed fitfully until he was awakened by something, he knew not what. And then he knew: he smelled the foul exudations of a bear, and then felt the snout of the animal nudge his robe and sniff his head. His spirit-brother had come.

forty-four

Victoria fled deep into pine forest. The day was still young, and this thin arm of woods that followed a gulch was all that concealed her. She padded far beyond the woodcutters and continued up a forested slope far from a trail. There she found a viewpoint and waited. She could not move far until darkness cloaked her.

For a while she saw no activity. Then four warriors rode casually north along the bank of the Belly River, on the trail taken by the Hudson's Bay men. They acted as if they didn't expect to find her going this way: why would an Absaroka woman go to the men from the grandfather's land who were allied with the Siksika? No, they would look for her to the south, supposing she fled toward her people. Still, they were taking no chances, and these young warriors had been sent to guard the trail in this direction.

They paused now and then, their senses keen, but they could not see her in her grassy bower, surrounded by pine, sitting so still that not even the birds gave alarm. But now these four stood between her and the Hudson's Bay men—and Skye. She settled into the thin grass, rubbing pine needles over her to subdue her own scent, and peering alertly in all directions, lest foot searchers came upon her.

She eyed the powerful bow she had taken. It was fashioned

from yew, a wood that grew far to the west, which meant her captor had traded for it. There were few good bow woods in the land of the Siksika or Crow. The Sioux got Osage orange from someplace far east and south, but the People of the northern plains and mountains were hard-put for good bows. She did not feel she had done anything wrong by taking it. Her captor had taken everything she possessed when he caught her, including her horse. Still, it was wrong for a woman to touch an instrument of war. A weapon had to be purified by a warrior, bathed in the smoke of sweetgrass and offered to the Ones Above before it would recover its power. But now she had touched it—and the arrows, too. She wondered if the bow's power now belonged to her. She tried stringing it and found that her strength was barely enough. This was a bow for a strong warrior, not a woman. The long sinew, taken from the backbone of a buffalo, stretched taut and ready. She nocked an arrow and waited, well armed against an enemy.

But no one came. She thirsted but was far from the river. It didn't matter. She could endure, and she wouldn't move until night enfolded her.

She had no plan, utterly no knowledge of how she might free Skye and how they might escape an intensive search by skilled men who could read sign as well as the People. But she would find a way and employ the night to conceal them. All doubt had vanished. She knew what she must do, and she would do it if she could. Her every thought was focused on freeing Skye and escaping. He might not want her, yet she would do it anyway. She would free him even if it meant that he would go east and never see her again.

When dusk finally came, she edged down to the riverbank trail that the Hudson's Bay men had taken, but stayed off it even though this caution slowed her passage. She was rewarded a while later by the dim sight of a warrior on horseback, sitting quietly, listening. He had heard her, and now moved slowly in her direction. She nocked an arrow, but settled silently into gloom beside some brush. He passed by without seeing her, never knowing that an arrow had pointed straight at his chest for a moment. She padded onward as the last light faded, and then stepped onto the trail, now lit only by starlight. She paced ahead, scarcely knowing where the trail took her, except that the North Star was on her left and as long as she followed the river, it would take her to Skye.

Then, suddenly, she found herself in the midst of horsemen, Siksika who had been waiting for her. They sensed her just as she sensed them, and rode her down. She whirled, loosed the arrow at one, heard a muffled cry, and dodged off the trail through grass and then brush, making too much noise. She pulled another arrow from her quiver, nocked it, and waited, feeling her heart race. She heard male voices, the clop of unshod hooves, groaning, and then nothing. She squinted into the murk, trying to discern what lay out there. They had probably left one behind to catch her. She edged closer, this time taking care not to make noise, and did finally make out what she thought might be a Siksika standing near something that was probably his horse. He was as alert as she, and no doubt as well armed, but she couldn't really tell. She chose to wait, and settled down right where she stood. Sometime he would leave, and then she would be free—perhaps.

He guarded that place a long time, and she knew he was waiting for Mother Moon to come and shed her milky light so he could see again. Indeed, she saw a glow on the horizon where the moon would soon appear from behind the edge of the earth. She had little time. If there was one, there probably was another she didn't know about. She dared not move, and simply sat quietly, not knowing what would come. When the three-quarter moon did appear, she saw the gray horse better than she saw the Siksika. The horse was staring at her, ears forward. That should tell a good warrior what he needed to know, but he was facing the other way.

Time passed, and the warrior mounted his pony and rode toward the east, toward the Hudson's Bay men. And another warrior joined him. She heard them talking, the two horses walking side by side. So the Siksika still lurked between her and Skye. They were following the trail, which lay clear now in the silver light. She watched them walk into the milkiness of the night, knowing what little chance a small lone woman had against them, even if she had a bow she could barely draw. They knew she was here and where she was going; they knew she had a bow and had hurt one of them. They would find her and kill her.

Slowly she stood, peering sharply into the duskiest places. She was in a hilly country with grassed valleys and wooded slopes, and gulches choked with brush. The trail ran through open meadows. In the white light, she could not approach the horsemen without being seen.

And yet . . . she would. She knew, suddenly, that she wanted those horses. One for her, one for Skye. And she would have to kill the Siksika to take them. And what chance had she? She flexed the bow, feeling its power, feeling it tug at her. She would try this thing, a frail woman against two powerful men. She pulled arrows from her quiver, wanting to touch them, invest her power in them also. She touched each arrow, making it hers, not her captor's. Somehow this was important. She slid her hand along the thin shafts, one by one, feeling the deadly iron points, the feathers that had been bound with sinew to the shaft, and the little slots that took the sinew of the bowstring.

She would do this thing! Her spirits soared. Some primeval power coursed through her, savage and wanton, hot and deadly. She had rarely felt this before; now she bathed herself in it. She might scalp these Siksika, a scalp from each, and let their spirits wander forever, without a spirit-home. She trotted after them, swiftly, deadly, silently, her moccasins somehow making no sound. She was a wolf trailing buffalo, a lioness gathering herself to outrun a deer and sink her teeth into its throat.

She saw them ahead, leisurely walking their ponies, a gray and a darker one whose color she couldn't make out. She would have to get close because she had little skill with this weapon. Close enough to drive an arrow into their backs. If she missed . . . what did it matter! It was a good night to die.

She walked boldly, no cover concealing her, onward toward these friends of Grandfather of Wolves who sought her blood and her scalp. She was close enough to put an arrow into them, but not close enough to be sure. So she walked swiftly, gliding like a magpie, spirit-driven. She gained ground, and now she could make out that one was thin, one stocky. They wore leggings, but their backs were bare.

Then one turned and saw her. He whirled, lifted his bow, loosed an arrow that seared her hair. He shouted as he turned his horse and pulled another arrow from his quiver. She pulled, feeling the terrible power of the bow, feeling her small hands wobble under such pressure, and loosed her arrow. It sailed home, burying itself in the warrior's side. He cried, coughed, drew his war club, and came on, kicking his horse. Now at last the other Siksika bore down on her, tomahawk in hand. She yanked an arrow, fumbled with it, finally found the bowstring, nocked and shot, all in one desperate moment. It missed. They both were riding her down. She ran sideways, leftward, but the tomahawk warrior easily steered his horse at her. She reversed herself, darting to the right as the horse came upon her. It hit her, bowled her over—and the Siksika rode by, without a target. She hit the ground hard, her breath knocked from her.

And then the other one rode her down, war club poised. But even as he approached, life fled him, and he tumbled to the ground almost at her side. He stared at her and then at nothing.

The other turned his pony with a violent yank of the hackamore, and the horse skittered and danced a moment. Victoria found her bow, stood, reached to her quiver, and met his furious charge with a well-aimed arrow that struck him in his thigh. He howled, spasmed, whirled past her, and clutched his gouting wound. She stood, shaken, trembling. It wasn't over. Blood boiled down his leg, dripped from his moccasin. His war club, its thong looped over his wrist, dangled. He turned his horse again. She saw a knife glint in his hand. She stood her ground, armed herself again, and stepped behind the body of the Siksika, knowing the horse would not step over it. The warrior yanked his horse toward her, but it dodged the fallen warrior, and he never came within knife range. She let him pass and released another arrow, which hit him in the shoulder and spun him off the horse. He landed hard, with a sob, and scrambled to his feet, soaked in his own blood. His arm was paralyzed and he couldn't hold his knife. He couldn't walk on his ruined leg. He writhed, settled into the grass, and stared at her.

She kept her distance, knowing how well he could lunge at her. Instead, she gathered the two frightened horses, quietly walking them down. She found the bloody knife glowing in the moonlight, and took it. She gathered the war club and bow and arrow of the dead Siksika, and found his sheathed knife as well.

She eyed the dead one. He was not her captor. She pricked the knife into his skull and took a ritual scalp, just a little piece. Her war honor. She did not dare approach the live one, and no longer felt like killing him, so she ignored him. He would probably bleed to death. Swiftly she tied her kit onto the back of the smaller pony, noting that she had acquired various things that had been tied to their saddles. She would find out what she possessed later, when she had put a night and more between these warriors and herself.

forty-five

Skye had rarely felt so helpless. He lay within a buffalo robe, hands and feet trussed, unable to flee the huge animal that was blocking his sight of the stars. A snout pushed and probed, exuding foul odors, sniffing at him, at his ear, his beard. He felt a tongue rasp his forehead, felt teeth clamp his shoulder. He lay too frightened and paralyzed to move or shout.

He did not know what sort of bear probed at him, black or grizzly. And then an odd thing happened: the bear licked his face, and Skye felt something had changed. For all his time in the mountains, he had sensed that he shared a brotherhood with bears, and this bear was being a brother to him. The bear whoofed softly and retreated, leaving Skye shaken and grateful to have survived such an encounter with Old Ephraim, as the men of the mountains called him. The stars returned and the night breezes calmed him. He could not say what mysterious thing had happened that moment but he knew that things would soon go better for him. It was as if that bear was a messenger of hope, sent only to him in that sleeping camp.

His fear and desperation left him, and he knew they would not return. All these things that had afflicted him in his short life had purpose, and had happened to him to strengthen him and prepare him for a life he could not yet discern. He fell into a sweet sleep, resting body and soul even on the hard ground, better than he had rested for a long time.

And he woke refreshed.

His captors came and rolled him over and untied his hands, which were lashed behind his back, and then his ankles. He rubbed his hands, restoring circulation.

"Well, mates, did a bear visit you in the night?" he asked them. But they didn't reply. Governor Simpson was sitting on a log nearby, watching closely.

"A bear poked his nose into my robes."

"No bear that I know of," said an HBC man. "But they's tracks, yes?"

Skye studied the grassy flat and found no sign of an animal's presence. The print of a bear looked oddly like the print of a stubby human foot, but the few barren places revealed nothing. And none of the packs lying about had been disturbed.

"Skye, you are not to talk with these men. You will not fill them full of stories or win their sympathies."

"A bear visited me."

"Dreams. Nightmares. Your past is catching up to you."

Maybe a dream. But Skye knew it wasn't. Maybe it was his spirit-bear. He thought back to what Red Turkey Head had once told him: he and the bears had an affinity. All he knew was that something had changed, and he had somehow won a bit of leeway, or tolerance, from these men.

"If I can't talk to your men, I'll talk to you. I feel like talking this fine morning," Skye said. "If you were at all interested in who I am, you might start with my upbringing. My father was a London merchant . . ."

Oddly, Simpson didn't stop him. He sat sipping tea, eyeing Skye with those penetrating eyes of his while his men boiled some gruel for breakfast and packed gear. Skye told his entire story—within earshot of the rest—and the governor let him do it. It was as if Simpson was seeing Skye for the first time.

"Very interesting, Skye, but not a word of truth in it. You're a clever one. You've read a few books in the ship's brig and learned to mimic your betters. I can't place your dialect, but Billingsgate comes to mind. London for certain. Born there, eh?"

"Yes, sir, Westminster, Kensington High Street."

"Rubbish, rubbish, Skye. You were born in the East End."

All that day Skye toiled under his heavy pack, saying little, his spirits actually buoyant. His body did not complain as much. His traveling companions seemed friendlier now, though none of them could converse with the prisoner. Something had changed.

They passed into country that was more level than not, and less forested than before. The Belly still took them northeast, toward its confluence with the Bow, and then the Oldman, and the South Saskatchewan River and ultimately Hudson's Bay. From one upland ridge, Skye discerned a valley choked with trees and suspected they were reaching the Bow, or perhaps the Oldman. He wasn't sure of anything now. Maybe they would load the canoes there, in much deeper water, and all crowd into the two vessels. But they would not reach the place until that night. Once the whole party was entirely waterborne, passage eastward would be swift and he would leave the mountains behind. The paddles would dip into the northern waters, and the canoes would race away from the country where he had spent several joyous years. Everything was coming to an end. Maybe his spirit-bear was telling him that.

That afternoon Simpson abandoned his canoe and fell in beside Skye, and Skye sensed that something was afoot.

"Skye, you tell an interesting yarn," the governor began.

"It's not a story, sir."

"I fathom that. Nonetheless, you're a deserter. In war you could be executed on the spot. The Crown wants you, and it's my patriotic duty to send you to your well-earned reward. However, Skye, there might be a different sort of future for you. I suspect a dungeon or another warship or maybe an Australian penal colony isn't quite what you had in mind for a life."

"No, sir."

"Maybe all that can be avoided."

"What is it you're proposing?"

"Perhaps nothing. It depends on you. HBC needs good men with wilderness experience. We never have enough."

"You're proposing that I join the company, is that it?"

"Maybe. Let's say that Barnaby Skye doesn't exist, but a man named Billy Blue does, and only I know the secret. Let's say that Billy Blue chooses to indenture to Hudson's Bay. Billy Blue gets all his needs provided for by the company; he agrees to ten years of service, after which he is free. He behaves himself, contributes labor and skill to the enterprise. He brings in the beaver. Billy's a young fellow. At thirty-five or so, he'd be a free man. Free to go live among the Yanks."

"And what's to keep me at my post, sir?"

"Your honor. I fathom you're a man of your word. Once given, it's kept. That's my gamble, not yours."

"And what would my wage be?"

"Your eventual freedom. We'd provide for your needs, outfit you. It would be quite costly, actually."

"And if I did well, would I advance?"

"Unfortunately, given the circumstances, we couldn't do much for a while. But maybe after six or eight years, we might offer some inducements. You could make a life career of it."

"And how do you feel about betraying the Crown?"

"Tut, tut. Life is expedience. If you wish, I will gladly return Skye to the Crown and consider it my patriotic duty."

"And what if there were—say—infractions? Billy Blue didn't measure up?"

"There would be no infractions. Billy Blue would measure up or face his fate, the fate that every step is now carrying him toward."

"And what sort of labor would this require?"

"Camp tender with a brigade. Or, since you're literate, clerk and supply depot work. Bookkeeping. Maybe other things.

You're an Englishman. Your presence would help keep the Yanks out of the Oregon country. It's a matter of some concern."

"Ten years is a long time."

"Well, if you're especially valuable, we might parole you after seven. I could hold that out to you. Incentive, you know."

"I spent seven years in slavery to the Crown, sir. Isn't that enough?"

"Moot point. Accept or go to London and face the Admiralty."

"On the one hand, Governor, you seem to accept my story. On the other hand, you hold me for the Crown. Why don't you just let me go if you believe me?"

"Impossible. You're a common seaman and a blackguard."

"Whose word is his bond."

"You are toying with semantics."

"You don't see me as a person, but just as one of a class of commoners whose labor you wish to exploit."

"Of course I see you as a person, and I've given you a most generous opportunity, if I say so myself." He paused, pregnantly. "Maybe on good behavior I'd let you go after five. Give the company five good years and I'll review your case."

Simpson's offer sorely troubled Skye.

An HBC mountaineer named Belfast Berkeley halted the sweating voyageurs, and Skye gladly unloaded his burdens and stretched. The governor was clearly awaiting an answer, and Skye was ready to give it.

"The answer is no, sir."

"Then be damned, Skye."

"It's Mister Skye, sir."

George Simpson whirled away in a rage.

Skye watched him go. Simpson had tempted him. But he would not submit to seven years of slavery to Hudson's Bay, or even five, toiling for no wage and kept in line by fear of exposure to the Crown. It might even be a pleasant and robust slavery, out in trapping brigades. But it would be servitude, and he had had enough of that for several lifetimes. The decision should have saddened him, but it didn't. He felt elated. He would not give his word of honor or commit himself to a prospect he despised. Let them call him Skye; they would find out soon enough—somehow, some way—that he was *Mister* Skye.

forty-six

Victoria raced down the Belly River, driven by some urgency she couldn't entirely fathom. She abandoned caution, and no longer scouted the bankside path ahead or slipped into cover where she could. She had the feeling that time was running out, that she must find and free Skye at once—or lose him forever. She pushed her ponies hard, sitting light and lithe in the saddle, speeding them along as much as she dared. The ponies had not been well cared for, and they lacked the energy for sustained speed.

With every slight rise she peered ahead, hoping to glimpse the Hudson's Bay men—but she saw nothing. She had come across their campsites, saw where they had beached the canoes, and noticed that some men among them—Skye included—had carried heavy packs. She saw only moccasin prints, and knew they had given Skye some footwear.

Then she rode across a neck where the river oxbowed, and she did spot them, miles ahead, a tiny moving party, like so many ants, crawling along the Belly, while two canoes, black dots, rode the river well ahead of the ones on foot. There was Skye, if she could catch him. Now caution flooded her. She had to get close, but this was open country with few trees except in pockets along the river. Far ahead in the summer haze lay a green-clad valley of another river. She was approaching a confluence. Now she knew why she hastened: there would be deeper water after that, enough to float heavily laden canoes. She paused a moment, gauging the land and distances with an eye that understood space. The Hudson's Bay men would probably camp at the confluence. Even now Father Sun was setting. And in the morning, they would all crowd into the canoes and shoot downriver, propelled by currents and the mighty arms of the voyageurs.

She returned to the river bottoms, hoping she could stay close and yet avoid being seen by those sharp-eyed men. She hadn't the slightest plan, and didn't even know how to find Skye among them, free him if he was bound. She didn't know whether they posted guards through the night.

This was the land of the Crees, and she didn't much like it. The mountain vistas had given way to undulating prairies, with one or two buttes on the horizons. It seemed gloomy even in the hot summer sun. No wonder the Crees were such terrible people. They lived in a bad land. The Belly had cut deep chasms into the plains here, and the banks had eroded into fantastical shapes that chilled her and reminded her of spirit-places. Yet she would brave even these habitations of souls if it meant finding and releasing Skye.

She scared up pronghorns and coyotes and white-tailed deer that found their home in the bottoms. She saw countless meadowlarks, and the wild rose bloomed everywhere. Ducks filled every slough. The Belly flowed mysteriously eastward, carrying the waters from the Backbone of the World far away. Back in the land of the Bloods the water had been cold and clear; now it was murky and slow-moving, working through gravelly bars and shallow channels.

At dusk she knew she was close, and she walked her horses cautiously, lest she stumble upon the camp of the yellow eyes. She found a turnoff where she could ascend the bluff and took it, wishing to survey the terrain. She rode one horse upslope and tugged the other until she topped the bluff and beheld the vast, lonely plains. She let her eyes adjust to the gloom so she could see how the country lay. Just beyond was a wooded river valley, and she knew she was very close to the place where the Belly joined the Bow. She thought she smelled smoke on the night breeze. On foot, she led her horses along the bluff, and a while later was rewarded. Below, just beyond the confluence of the rivers, was the camp. A fire burned, and she could see the yellow eyes working around it. Two long canoes had been beached and turned over beside the large river.

Where was Skye? How would this camp be guarded—if at all? She saw no horses, and was grateful. Her own would not betray her with a sudden whinny, answered by whinnying from the camp. She stood now in the open, trusting in the dusk to conceal her small form from their eyes. She ached to spot Skye but couldn't at such a distance. She wanted to know where the black-suit grandfather was, too. He would give the commands. She eyed the canoes, thinking that if she couldn't find Skye, she could still delay these Hudson's Bay men by cutting great holes in the birchbark walls of the canoes.

Her horse nudged her, rubbing its forehead against her back, almost unbalancing her. She liked this horse, even if it was a Siksika horse and ill trained. What did they know about horses? Not half as much as any Absaroka! She realized she had to adjust the packs so that Skye could mount immediately. There would be no time once she freed him to rearrange the load. So she quietly divided the packload between the two horses, tying half behind the cantle of each saddle. She needed to give Skye reins, too, and not just a lead line she had used to pull the packhorse along. So she made a loop of the braided line. Now he could sit the horse and steer it, and that was as much as she could do.

Full dark lowered, and the stars emerged one by one until all the spirit-people twinkled in the bowl of heaven. A night breeze lifted, already chill in these northern plains, and she felt a premonition of autumn although it was still the Moon of Ripening Berries.

If only she could find Skye, and if only they could reach

these horses, they would have a good chance. The river men had no horses to give chase. She heard coyotes barking along the hill tops, and welcomed them. Coyotes were brothers, and tricksters, and they liked to laugh. At long last the men below settled down. She no longer saw movement, and the fire gave off less light. It was time. She brought the horses with her, knowing she would need them fast, especially if Skye were hurt or ill after being a prisoner so long. She saw no tents. These were good travelers, even the grandfather, and she knew they could get along with much less than many yellow eyes. She found a way down the bluff and penetrated into the bottoms again, which seemed darker and more foreboding. If they had posted a guard, she might be caught. So she walked gently, not even breaking a twig, as her people had always learned to do. And then, suddenly, as she rounded a bend, she spotted the fire dead ahead. She halted. Now she needed to conceal the horses and then wait for sleep to overtake the yellow eyes, because not much time had passed since the camp quieted. She strained to spot Skye, but couldn't.

She thought of all the things that could go wrong: wakening the wrong one, tripping over something, being caught by a guard, trapped by someone who had gone to the bushes. But it did no good to rehearse all these things, and she concentrated instead on what was right and what would go well. She decided on a clump of tall trees next to the river, no doubt cottonwoods, as a place of concealment where she would keep the horses. She walked that way slowly, her every sense alert, and wrapped the reins around a low limb. She knelt beside some brush and watched, aware that the constant gurgle of the river concealed her passage. The yellow eyes were careless. None of the People would camp so close to the water that they couldn't hear other things.

The camp slumbered peacefully. But as she crept out of the trees, she realized it had become much too dark. She could not tell one man from another, and they all looked alike to her anyway. In the blackness of the night she could not tell a bearded

Frenchman from Skye. So she returned to the forest, waiting uneasily for the moon. She hadn't paid much attention to Mother Moon, and didn't know when she would visit. The horses behind her stirred uneasily, and she sensed that they were smelling something on the wind. Wolves maybe. They tugged back on their lines, making the leather groan and the branches creak. She didn't like that.

Whatever was troubling the animals didn't go away; her horses grew more and more restless until she feared they would awaken the whole camp or yank loose and stampede off. She stood, found the neck of one, and ran a hand under its thick mane, calming it as much as she could. Then she found the other, head back, line taut, ready to yank loose at the slightest provocation. She could not quiet that one. It stamped and jerked until she was sure the whole camp had heard.

Her vision was good; her eyes had accustomed themselves to the blackness, and she could make out the trees where they blotted the stars, and the meadow, a vaguely open area that hinted of space, and the orange eyes of the fire's last coals, which told her where these Hudson's Bay men were. But there was nothing she could do for the time being. So deep was the blackness that she could easily trip over one of the sleeping men.

There was Skye, so close, and yet so unreachable now, when she desperately needed to reach him. She sensed that someone stirred, but the night shrouded movement. Maybe that was good. What shrouded that one from her eyes would also shroud her from his.

A horse shrieked, pulled loose, and bolted. The other followed. She shrank into the ground with horror. The camp stirred. She could see nothing, but she heard voices, men grabbing their rifles. The glow of embers was blotted from time to time as men passed in front of it. She crouched, feeling helpless against such bad fortune. Had her wits deserted her, her spirit-helper misled her? Mostly these men shouted in the tongue she didn't know, that of the Creoles, so she understood nothing. But the whole camp was awake now. No one threw wood on the coals for fear of making a target of them all, but men were up and about, walking.

"Where's Skye?" asked the voice of the grandfather.

"Here, mate."

Joy and anguish flooded through Victoria. He was so close! She thought he was to the left of the embers, but she didn't know for sure.

"C'est un ours!" someone bellowed.

"It's a bear!"

"Sacre bleu!"

Now she smelled it. A bear. She thrilled to it. A bear, for Skye.

"Chase it away before it gets into the packs."

"I thought I heard horses."

"I thought I did too. But bears sound like anything."

"Formidable!"

Men scurried about. Someone threw some wood on the embers, but it didn't catch. One man loomed close, a shadow blotting out stars, and then she realized it wasn't a man, it was Grandfather Bear. She huddled still and quiet. The great hulk paused, sniffed, grunted, and went on.

She desperately wanted to run to Skye, but held herself in check. The wood on the embers smoked, the smell eddying her way, but didn't ignite. She waited until the camp quieted, aching to do something, anything. She needed to find the horses. They held everything she possessed except the quiver on her back and her bow, and the knife in her hand.

The night settled again, and she judged that the time had come. There was no sign of a moon, but for the moment she could walk among them and no one would imagine that the small figure looming above their robes was the woman of Mister Skye. She stood, padded resolutely into a camp that was fully awake, and hoped for the best.

forty-seven

Victoria edged toward the camp of the Hudson's Bay men, wondering how she was going to do what she had to do. The night had cloaked Mother Earth, and she could not even see her own moccasins, much less the sleeping men who lay under stars, without a fire now. Should she simply yell for Skye? But what if he was tied up and could not get free?

She didn't know, and that made her faint at heart. Even the starlight had vanished, and she realized the sky was now overcast. How could she find him, find the horses, escape? Many of these men were awake. They had just dealt with a bear. How easy it would be for any of them to reach up and catch her as she passed.

She ached to find the fire, find an ember to orient herself, but not even that small comfort was afforded her. She compelled herself to walk forward, until she tripped over one of the men, who grumbled, muttered something, and fell silent. She could not go farther without stumbling over many more. There were twice ten men here, one of them Skye.

She backed away, knowing she had no recourse except to wait for moonlight or dawn—any sort of light that would permit her to drift through the camp without stumbling over the voyageurs. She would need light as well to find the horses.

The gloom persisted through the long night. She could see neither stars nor moon. She heard the gentle gurgle of water to her right and knew she was close to the river. When at last the day began to quicken, she realized she was too late. Some of the voyageurs were already stirring, standing, stretching, heading for the bushes. She retreated into brush and hid there, her heart heavy. On this day the canoes would take Skye away forever.

Then she realized this need not be. She stood, a figure as vague to the Hudson's Bay men as they were to her, and stumbled through the gauze of night to the river, with only her ears to guide her. There nearby were two long canoes made of the white men's fabric over the ribs and sealed with some sort of shiny paint. They rested side by side, upside down, not far from the riverbank.

She slipped her knife from its sheath and approached the vessels. The next task was easy, but noisy. She slashed the skin of the canoe, long stripes, the work of bear claws, one after another, on each side of the ribs, many slices. No one loomed out of the murk to stop her. She performed the same mutilation upon the other canoe, gouging great holes in both of them. Every stroke of the knife sounded like thunder to her, and yet she knew most of the noise was camouflaged by the omnipresent gurgle of the river. She could not yet see her handiwork and worried that it might not be enough. But she knew it would take the voyageurs a while to repair the damage and load the canoes.

But did it help? She could not say. Now she had to find her horses. Maybe, with horses, she could follow the river as fast as the voyageurs could paddle—though she doubted it. The voyageurs, going downriver, would speed Skye to his destiny. The day bloomed into a drab gray, and she retreated from the stirring camp and up a grassy slope to find her horses and hide. From the height she could see the general shape of the country—the thick band of woods along the river, the plains rising on either side, some rocky escarpments, insolated patches of pine.

And no horses. What would the Hudson's Bay grandfather do if they found the horses, each horse laden with Blackfoot gear? She hardly dared imagine. She felt hungry but put aside her needs, as she had long ago taught herself to do. Some things were more important than the howling of the body.

She settled into a small hollow in a slope, well concealed by tall grasses, and peered down upon the camp. She could not yet make out Skye, though most of the men were up and stirring about. And then she knew. The last one lying on the ground was Skye, because he had been trussed up and could not move. The light thickened a little, but it was still so dark she could barely make out forms. She examined the grassy ridges around her and spotted her horses a long way away, grazing together. They would be small dark dots to the Hudson's Bay men, but she feared the sharp-eyed white men would see them anyway. There was little she could do.

Then she heard the rasp of excited voices and saw the men head for the riverbank, plunging into a wooded area. She could not make out words but knew they had found the damaged canoes. The grandfather was visible now, a black spot in the vague light. Anger and suspicion floated on the quickening breezes. Several went to examine Skye—she could see him lying there now—and looked at the bound wrists and ankles. Maybe they thought he had done it. Maybe not. Maybe they thought Grandfather Bear had done it. She had cut the fabric in strips, as if bear claws had ripped it.

Two of the voyageurs lifted the canoes and carried them into the open meadows, to where the fire had been in the evening. So they were going to patch the holes, and she suspected it would not take them as long as she hoped. She wanted the repairs to take all day, but white men had many tricks and did things that amazed the People. If they made guns of metal, they could repair canoes. As the day whitened—it would be gloomy at best, with thick gray clouds hiding Grandfather Sun—she saw the men at work on the canoes, cutting away the shredded fabric. Others stood about, examining the grassy hills, looking for signs of those who had done this thing. She froze, didn't move a muscle then, as she peered through the grasses. She prayed that they would not see the ponies. They didn't seem to look in that direction, back from the river, and she realized a swell of benchland hid the animals.

With the horses, she would follow them and keep up. Without them, she would fall farther and farther behind. They untied Skye's arms and legs, and she ached to signal him. He stood stiffly, barely able to use his freed body. He paid no attention to the canoes or the feverish work being done on them. Instead, he stood facing the hills away from the river, facing her almost. Then he slowly lifted both arms upward, toward her, toward one he did not see but whose presence he sensed. Ah, how much a torment that was, seeing him there, lifting his arms to her, letting her know. She dared not stand and could not reply. But then her friend the magpie flew close, alighted near her, and flew powerfully away. Then Skye was staring straight at her hiding place. She half stood one tiny moment and then folded back into the safety of the grassy hollow. Perhaps he had seen; perhaps not.

Thank thee, Magpie.

She could do nothing but hide. He could do nothing but perform his morning ablutions and eat the gruel the HBC men had boiled over a fire. A gray day ticked by while the voyageurs worked on the canoes. Some were shaping pieces of cloth and sewing them to the canoes. Others were collecting pitch from pines, heating it, and caulking the repairs. Soon they would have the canoes done and would be off. So her efforts hadn't amounted to more than a half-day delay. She squinted upslope, toward the horses, and found that they had vanished. She didn't know where they were.

Rain began, a mist at first, and then a cold pelting drizzle, and she huddled miserably in her unsheltered hollow. Below, the voyageurs ignored the wetness and continued their repairs. She watched the grandfather pace restlessly, a lion on a leash, wanting to be off. Her gaze was forever on Skye. He obviously possessed nothing but the clothing he wore, but he wrapped a robe around him to ward off the icy rain. The campfire began to smoke, and she knew the rain was extinguishing it little by little.

All that morning she debated what she might do. She had her bow and quiver of arrows, and contemplated ways she might use it: an arrow into each of the repaired canoes, for instance. But that would expose her to them. Now, with the rain wetting and weakening the sinew of the bowstring, she knew that she had no weapon at all save for her knife. Skye paused now and then and stared directly at her, or at least at the place where she crouched in wet, cold grass. She ached to know what he wanted her to do, ached to receive some sort of signal or instruction from him.

But maybe she had it wrong. Maybe he needed instruction from her. She needed a plan, and she needed to tell him. Escape would not be up to him: he could do nothing. It was entirely up to her. He knew one thing: who had damaged the canoes and why. She wondered if maybe he *was* signaling her. He walked about almost randomly, then lowered himself to the ground on the periphery of the camp and lay down, imitating sleep. Yes, there was a message in that. He would try to lie on the edge of the next camp. She watched him repeat the whole thing and lie down in the same place. In the next camp he would sleep on the periphery, and on the upriver side. She swiftly lifted her bow and quiver and lowered it, acknowledging she had understood.

He lifted his bear claw necklace and pawed the air with it. She didn't know what that meant. Could it be that the voyageurs thought a bear had clawed the fabric of the canoes? Did he merely mean that a bear had come last night? Before she could grasp what that was about, the grandfather came to Skye and ordered him to the canoes. The voyageurs were testing one in the river and loading the other. Soon they would be off, paddling easily down the Bow and then the Oldman River, many suns, many nights.

All but Skye were now employed with packing and loading the canoes, and none was remotely interested in what might lie in the grassy bluffs above the river. That was fine. She stood boldly. Skye saw her at once even though the grandfather had made him carry things to the canoes. She did not tarry, but trotted upslope and over the crest, out of sight. The two horses grazed just a little way away. She hiked through the cold drizzle, feeling hunger and chill. Swiftly she caught her Blackfoot warhorse, wiped the pad saddle dry, and climbed on, arranging her wide skirts. Then she collected the lead line of the packhorse. Nothing had been lost. They had simply been panicked by the bear, broken their tethers, and had drifted to this place after that. She repaired the reins with a knot and rode downriver. If she hurried and kept well back from the wooded bottoms, she might keep pace—almost—with the swift canoes. That sustained her more than food or warmth ever could. Somehow, some way, she would rescue Skye.

All that day she drove her horses through rain and cold, barely noticing the protests of her body. She lost track of the canoes, and when she sometimes turned toward a bluff or promontory, she could not see the canoes on the whirling river. Now she feared she was very far ahead or far behind, and would lose Skye after all. She had to rest the horses, but the river never rested, and the canoes required little more than steering.

But it would not be like that. The Hudson's Bay men would stop now and then to stretch. They would cook a meal, maybe, or use the bushes, or just walk a little. No one was chasing them; they didn't know of her presence.

She saw that the river made an arc ahead, and cut across the neck of land late in the day, hoping to get ahead. But when she reached the river again, she found they were ahead of her after all. They were setting up camp straight down the bluff from where she sat her horse.

She heard a shout. In that one fleeting moment, they had seen her.

forty-eight

Victoria knew she could escape if she chose; the voyageurs were on foot and she was horsed. She chose not to. Instead, she steered her two Blackfoot ponies straight down the slope toward the Hudson's Bay men. Skye watched alertly, his face a mask.

She didn't quite know what she would do. Nothing about her betrayed her Absaroka origins to the casual eye, and nothing about her horse furniture betrayed anything but Blackfoot manufacture. Nor would these men know that she was in any way connected to Skye.

They had unloaded the two big canoes and beached them. Piles of gear lay about, and a few bedrolls had been tossed into the bankside grass. There were many of them, and now they all stared at her, not overly concerned by the appearance of a lone Indian woman. She decided she would not speak but use the hand signs. Maybe she could stay the night. That was what she would ask.

The grandfather in black stared at her, his gaze relentless. He was a formidable man with the eyes of an eagle, his instincts keen. She would have to be wary of him. The others, the voyageurs, were big, muscular, dark men who spoke that other tongue, French. There were two additional ones from the grandfather's land who spoke Skye's tongue.

She peered at last toward her beloved, giving not the slightest sign of recognition. She saw Skye survey the spare horse, approving of the saddle and the goods tied behind its cantle. But none of what passed subtly between them was evident to the Hudson's Bay men. It was good to see Skye, even if he was so helpless. Soon he would be free!

One of the Englishmen made the hand signs, and she responded. She was cold and wet and hungry. The rain had made her bow useless. Could she share their food and stay the night?

Who was she?

She was a woman of the People, returning to her village after a visit.

Where were her people?

Far to the south.

What band of Siksika did she belong to?

She had lived with the Kainah, the Bloods. She would ride through the land of the Piegans soon.

The man translated his signs to the black-clad grandfather, who nodded. Skye had watched all this, reading the fingers and hands.

The signs continued. The man told her that this was a Hudson's Bay Company camp, very friendly with the Siksika, much trading, good to the People, and she was welcome. This was the camp of the greatest chief of the white men, and he was welcoming her for the night. She would be safe among his men. She was welcome to feast on a doe they had shot during the day. Soon they would have it hung and butchered. In the morning she could go her way and they would go downriver in their big canoes.

She nodded and dismounted. She untied her own bed robe, led her horses to grass a little distant, and picketed them. She hoped they would not notice that she did not unsaddle them. But Skye noticed. He also noticed the sheathed knife at her waist. That night he and she would escape—if all went well. Even now he was unrolling his robes as close to the horses as he dared. And laying his old robe in a way that would make his feet point straight at the ponies. Aiee!

The men had tied the doe to a box elder limb and some were gutting it, while others fed a hot fire. She and Skye exchanged glances, and she ached to know what stirred his soul just then. What did he feel for her? Was anything left? She would weep when she could, and tell him of her grief, her mistakes, her yearnings. Maybe he would reject her. But at least she would free him if she could. That would repay him a little for the sorrows she had given to him.

The grandfather in black told Skye to help with the butchering, so he did, paying her no heed at all. They were both going to great lengths to hide their relationship.

"Don't get any notions about escaping, Skye," the man said. "We'll be watching. I'm posting guards tonight. The squaw's horses may tempt you, but you're on your way to the Crown."

The grandfather stared thoughtfully at the prisoner. Perhaps he suspected something. She felt a chill run through her.

She feigned no knowledge of what she had heard in Skye's tongue, but was glad to learn about the guards. It was good to know of trouble.

The voyageurs eyed her now and then, not missing her lithe, young beauty. She grew aware of the darting gazes and ignored them. But they made her cautious. She decided she would ultimately bed close to her ponies that night, but would unroll her robe close to the camp at first.

The drizzle had dwindled to cold mist, and then, as the yellow eyes prepared a meal, quit altogether. It would be a wet, cold, miserable night warmed only by their cheerful fire. She doubted the heavens would clear, and this night would be as black as the last one. She did not know how she would deal with that. She ached to give Skye a knife, but doubted it would help if they tied his wrists behind his back. He had signaled that they did, holding his arms behind him, wrists pressed together. She would have to do it, in plain sight of the guards—somehow.

The voyageurs boiled the deer meat in a kettle, adding wild roots and herbs to season their stew, and soon they handed her a bowl. She ate with relish, utterly starved for want of food the entire day. She held out her tin bowl for more, and they laughed.

"Injuns got hollow legs," said one. "Feast or starve, that's the way of 'em."

She didn't let on that she understood, and knew it was a criticism. This was not a moment to reveal anything or show any displeasure. Instead, she smiled.

One filled her bowl again. They fed Skye well enough and then trussed him up. He never glanced at her, but stood with his back to her so she could see exactly how the thong wrapped his wrists. Then they let him sit down beside his robe, removed his moccasins, and trussed his ankles. One of them settled against a tree, rifle in hand, the guard she knew would watch that night.

It had grown dark. These men were weary, and so was she. In the last light she checked her ponies, making sure the saddles were tight and all was ready. Then she rolled up in her robe, oblivious of the stares and the almost palpable yearning for her that she felt around her. These were men without a woman. They weren't on the warpath, and they wanted her.

She waited for them to sleep, and almost succumbed to it herself. She could barely keep her eyes open and her mind clear after downing such a meal as that one. The embers died, and the night shrouded her, pressing down, the darkness suffocating her, a terrible weight.

It *was* weight. One of the voyageurs had come to her robes. She cried out, rolled, stopped herself from cursing in his tongue, and fought as hands clapped her wrists and a massive weight pinioned her to the grass.

"Aiee!" she cried.

No one helped her. She heard no uproar in camp. She fought hard, bucking and writhing, biting and kicking, and won a momentary reprieve when she threw him off and he rolled. Swiftly she plucked her robe and vanished toward the horses—toward Skye. She could no longer tell exactly where she was because the blackness offered no clue.

"Victoria."

The quiet voice lifted from almost underfoot, so soft it barely reached her ears.

"Here."

She found him and dropped beside him, her heart hammering. She waited there for the sounds of pursuit but heard nothing. The utter blackness would foil her pursuer—if she kept quiet.

Slowly, softly, her hands found Skye's arms and followed them to the thong binding his wrists behind him. She choked back her terror, pulled out her keen knife, and gently sawed, working in blackness, afraid she might slice into him. But a thong gave, and she unwound the binding. She found his ankles and released them. He paused, found her hands, and pressed them between his. There would be more, much more, but the feel of his hands over hers, warm and tight, was overwhelming in its sweetness, and tears welled up in her.

Then came the hardest part, slipping away, making no noise, finding the ponies on an overcast and moonless night in which she could not even tell sky from ground. She gathered her robe and took the thong as well—it would have its uses—and tried hard to fathom what direction to go. Little by little she came to an understanding. The night remained as black as ever, but an interior vision formed within, some mysterious understanding of where she was and where the ponies would be. She knew Skye would not have this gift given to the People, and so she quietly helped him to his feet—better to walk than shuffle on hands and knees through grass, making noise. She led him confidently away from camp, her inward vision sure.

She smelled the horses before she came to them, their acrid odor familiar and joyous. They tugged back on their picket lines. She guided Skye to the one she had prepared for him and lifted one bare foot to the wooden stirrup. He climbed on, and the horse grunted and sidestepped. She feared the whole camp heard. She pulled the pony's picket while Skye found a rein.

Then the camp did erupt into shouts. They had heard. Someone put wood on the fire, but she ignored that. She freed her own pony, climbed on, and kicked it straight toward the bluffs. Skye followed, depending on the soft sound of hooves to guide him.

She heard talk, anger, and shouting behind her, but never paused to look back.

forty-nine

Skye rode through darkness so thick he had no notion of where he was going. Victoria rode nearby but he could not see her. He thought they were going uphill, away from the Oldman River, but he couldn't be sure.

He rode through a tunnel without light, without direction, and it occurred to him that portions of life were like that, and that one penetrated various tunnels of life. He had spent much of his life in such darkness. He knew Victoria was near, but only the soft rustle of her horse confirmed it. That, too, was familiar. For too much of their union she had been beside him but invisible to him.

And yet she was there. She had come, brought horses, found a way to free herself from the Bloods. He had come for her, and she had come for him. She had left him, only to return, and in the act of returning and finding and freeing she had said everything that needed saying. He felt himself rejoicing that she was near. Neither of them spoke, and he knew he was afraid to speak. Maybe she was, too. He almost dreaded the moment when they would speak, for fear he would use the wrong words—or hear the wrong ones.

Maybe she didn't really love him. Maybe she just wanted to help him. He realized he was simply tormenting himself, and stopped it. She was there beside him and what more needed to be said?

After a while he stopped. It would not do to ride too far, because they would probably trace a circle that would bring them perilously close to Governor Simpson and his men. Better to wait until the distant dawn, get their bearings, and ride away. Her horse stopped when his did. He strained to see something, anything, but the overcast hid even the heavens, and the night lay so thick that there seemed to be no other world. Only himself and Victoria. Maybe that was how it should be just now: no other world at all.

She touched his leg, startling him. He had not heard her dismount. He could not see her even that close. She said nothing, as afraid to talk as he was. He sensed she was standing right there, touching him, holding the rein of her horse, waiting for him to respond. Perhaps she was afraid. He found her hand with his and held it. He wished he could see her face, read it, understand what lay upon it.

The darkness held. His wife, his lover, his mate was there—yet not there to his eyes. Everything about this trip through the tunnel of darkness was an act of faith. Slowly he dismounted and stepped into cold grass, which poked between his toes and chilled his feet even more than they had been. The horse had been his salvation, his mobility when they had removed his moccasins from him to keep him within their wilderness cage.

He knew she was close, and hesitant to come closer, so he drew the small hand to him, and found all that it was attached to, and drew her to him in the blackness and held her. She held him, and in the sacred holding they renewed themselves. He kissed her, and discovered her face wet with tears, the tears he could not see. The wetness flooded down her cheeks and now filtered through his beard and wet his own cheeks, until the wetness from his eyes mingled with the wetness pouring from hers.

Thus they held each other for a long time, coming to the

end of the darkness. She bid him to sit down, and a moment later he felt a robe enclose his cold feet and she joined him on the wet grasses, the warmth of the robe and love greater than all the coldness on earth. It was a good time to sit and hold her, an arm about her shoulder, and a time to say nothing in words because no words would do. She held the rein of one horse and he held the rein of another, and they heard the horses eat grass and wait to go somewhere else.

Life is like that, he thought. We walk through blackness, wanting to go where we will go. But in the blackness we cannot find our way, and we walk in another direction. Sometimes we find, when we come out of blackness, that it was a better direction after all, and it would have gone better for us to surrender to the unknowing, the uncertainty, than to insist upon the direction we had chosen. Maybe God permitted the blacknesses in all lives that we might let go, surrender, learn to trust in the guiding hand—or in no hand at all. Skye sat, content, knowing that the blackness had already passed. This Victoria, the chastened tear-stained woman in his arms, was not the Victoria who had followed her will into her blackness. He was not the same man, either.

Some time later the darkness began to soften, and with it their blindness. In time they found themselves on a lonely plain, without landmark, a vague place between heaven and hell, a place to choose a direction—any direction—and start on a long ride. They would have a long way to go through a dangerous country that was disputed by Blackfeet and Cree and Assiniboine. Chance, bad luck, a wrong turn could kill them. Daylight could kill them. But he wasn't really thinking about that. It was better to believe that they had already chosen a new direction. He would not go east and leave the mountains. She would not leave his side.

She pulled free, found some jerky in her kit, and handed him two pieces. They didn't assuage his hunger. Yet he didn't mind. She dug farther and extracted two pairs of Blackfoot moccasins. One set was too tight, the other too loose. He wore the tight ones, knowing they would stretch. She had thought of everything and found the means to bring it.

They had not yet spoken, and he was glad. All of this reunion was freighted with more than words would bear. But now she smiled, tentatively, half afraid. He drew her to him and held her again, and she held him very tight until their heartbeats were one. Then it was time to go.

The overcast denied him direction, but he wasn't really lost now. They had ridden from the right bank of the Bow, or maybe the Oldman, which trended northeast. So they were not traveling in a northerly direction and could not without crossing the river. When the sun came, they would get their bearings. He wasn't sure where they would go. Maybe she would choose a path.

She was as afraid to speak as he, so they didn't. He helped her mount her horse, and he swung up on his, and they rode, two solitary figures over a sea of dewy grass, silvery in the softest gray light of dawn. The Hudson's Bay men might follow their hoofprints, so he did not tarry, but rode with Victoria into an unclear future. All that morning they rode without design, toward nothing they could discern. But then the overcast lifted piecemeal, a wan sun gave them shadow, and they turned pale shadow into compass and drifted southward under a patched sky.

Thus they continued through the quiet day, ever southward as best as they could tell. They watered themselves and their weary horses at an alkaline seep and continued until late in the afternoon, when they descended a grassy slope and discovered a slender stream of sweetwater at their feet, bordered with chokecherry and box elder and willow brush. They scared up a mule deer there, a doe, and regretfully Victoria pierced it with an arrow and paused solemnly beside it, saying some Crow prayer to the departed as it spasmed and died. A spotted fawn lingered there and then drifted away, frightened and alone.

They filled their starving bodies that evening, but the image of the fawn kept coming to him. It probably would fall victim of a coyote or wolf or lion, its small life truncated. He took the episode as an image of life, which was not fair, which upset one's hopes and dreams, which killed randomly. They spent much of the twilight butchering the doe, which was hard and slow work. They roasted the meat to preserve it, and stowed it in their kits. They kept the hide, which might be useful to two refugees with little between them but a few things swiftly gathered when she had fled the Bloods.

All that day, too, they barely spoke to one another. It didn't seem right to talk, and words seemed shallow. They were each participating in a sacred ceremony of reunion, and words would spoil it. For once, Skye didn't trust words. He trusted her smile, her tenderness, and the touch of her hands. She searched him constantly for signs of his acceptance and forgiveness, and he gave them to her in his touch, his hugs, and once by wiping away one of her tears. They needed understanding, and she gave him hers, and he was giving her his. But often they gazed upon each other, reading souls, peering into the wells of the eyes and drinking the cool water that lay there.

They did not make love that night beside the prairie creek because it wasn't what was needed. That would come sometime when they found their bearings. But they held each other through the darkness, under the sparkle of a heaven full of diamonds, listening to the coyotes, and he was glad when she fell asleep with her head burrowed into the hollow of his shoulder.

That night he spoke. "I love you," he said.

She cried and drew him tight.

The next day caution returned. They saw a distant movement, specks of humanity on a distant ridge, and hid in a slough, which upset the ducks. But nothing happened, and they rode onward toward a new life together. This day they talked now and then, and she told him everything that had happened, from the time she had been captured by the Bloods to that moment. And he told her all that had passed in his life. She faltered only when she mentioned Beckwourth. It did not matter. Someday he would see Beckwourth again, maybe at some rendezvous, and it would all pass by. She had chosen Skye, not the flamboyant Crow chieftain.

He estimated that some time that day they had crossed the 49th parallel and were back in United States territory, far east of the Rocky Mountains. He knew little of this land, except that it could be the home of Crees or Assiniboines, who probably were friendly. But they had to be alert for invading Blackfeet, who whirled out of the horizons and dealt death.

"Where do you want to go?" he asked.

"Wherever you go, that is where I want to go, Mister Skye," she said. "My home is where you are."

That reminded him of the biblical Ruth.

"Maybe Bridger and Fitzpatrick and Sublette will take me back."

"Then we will go there."

"If we can find any of them," he added.

"Our home is wherever we are," she said.

He liked that. Home was here, with Victoria.

"Then we are home," he said.